SON
OF MY
FATHER
A FAMILY
DYNASTY

PEGGY HATTENDORF

Son of My Father – A Family Dynasty
Copyright © 2013 by Montrachet Publishing

For information about this title or to order other books and/or electronic
media, contact the publisher:
Montrachet Publishing
3267 Bee Caves Road, Suite 107-310
Austin, TX 78746
310-526-3380

Library of Congress Control Number: 2012917174

978-0-9853913-0-0 (print)
978-0-9853913-1-7 (e-book)

Printed in the United States of America

Cover and Interior design by: 1106 Design

PRAISE FOR
SON OF MY FATHER – A FAMILY DYNASTY

"*Son of My Father – A Family Dynasty* packs all the conflict of families, business, relationships, legacies and intrigue into one riveting story. Peggy Hattendorf, in what I expect will be the first of many books, has a style that holds on to the reader, making them become part of the story and wanting more when they are done. This American family is as complex as any other and while their tale is not average, their battles and intricacies can be seen in almost any family today. Our own battles in life are clearly mirrored in *Son of My Father – A Family Dynasty* and I think we have a new American author in our midst."

— BARRY KLUGER
Columnist, *The Arizona Republic*
Author, *A Life Undone: A Father's Journey Through Loss*

"*Son of My Father – A Family Dynasty* offers a panoramic tale of a family dynasty, corporate intrigue, greed and lust that will take the reader on an unforgettable international journey. Peggy Hattendorf's maiden novel hints of the generational writing of Tolstoy and the corporate executive grit of an Ayn Rand epic. Her personal experience as an executive in the travel industry and knowledge of the cosmetics field give a verisimilitude to the unfolding events in the narrative. This one is a page-turner."

— GABRIEL PHILLIPS, retired travel industry executive,
Former Chief Executive of the Major Airlines Trade Association,
Past National Chairman of US Travel Association

"Destined from birth to become the CEO of Barrington Holdings International, Christiana accepts the role her father gave her to become the son her father never had. Her journey to fulfill this destiny is beset with numerous obstacles and challenges, some arising from her personal life and some from the unpredictable manipulations of the corporate world. The author does a magnificent job of telling Christiana's story, gradually introducing and developing new characters, slowly unfolding the personal relationships between the characters, unveiling their pleasant qualities as well as their foibles. Everything is interwoven around a plot that is both intriguing and interesting; with an ending that is sure to surprise and amaze the reader. *Son of My Father – A Family Dynasty* is a well-written and entertaining novel, an enjoyable and satisfying read for both men and woman."

— JOHN R. CONNOLLY, PH.D. is Professor Emeritus of Theological Studies at Loyola Marymount University in Los Angeles, CA. He has published numerous articles in professional journals and is the author of a couple of books. His most notable work is the book, *John Henry Newman: A View of Catholic Faith for the New Millennium* (Rowman and Littlefield, 2005)

DEDICATION

Son of My Father – A Family Dynasty is dedicated first to my wonderful husband Mark—my soul mate, partner and love of my life. His unheeding enthusiasm, praise and nurturing remained a font of reassurance throughout my writing process.

Second, with love and thanks, to my children Rebecca and Charlie, their spouses and my darling grandchildren, they remain a source of pride and affection. In addition, I give warm appreciation to my brother Joe and sister-in-law Monica for their love and encouragement over the years.

Finally, I credit a number of dear friends who remain a basis of inspiration and validation. I am grateful for their love and friendship.

PROLOGUE

IT WAS ALWAYS "FATHER," never "Dad." Although the love and respect was manifest, so was the distance—the distance not as apparent. Having been introduced to the dynasty when quite young, Christiana's first words could have been Barrington Holdings International (BHI). The Company was the core of the Barrington family. "Groomed from the womb," she would quip.

Understanding and absorbing all things Barrington created enormous expectations. Constant self-examination plagued Christiana, as she tried to measure up, to meet, and to exceed *all* his expectations. She lived in the shadow of, yet in the likeness of, her father.

Proper education and preparation provided the foundation for Christiana to eventually run the worldwide behemoth BHI.

Life was a carefully constructed world built, presented, and controlled by her father, Jonathan Robert Barrington.

As a young woman, she'd achieved a success few ever realize. Yet, while at the pinnacle of her professional accomplishment, she had sacrificed her personal existence for the sake of BHI, or more accurately, her father.

Frequently she wondered if he'd wished to have a son instead of a daughter but she never dared pose the question. Maybe she was afraid of the answer.

CHAPTER 1

THE GLEAMING AIRCRAFT WING glistened in the late morning sunshine as she gazed out the window.

Father will be the last to arrive, making his usual theatrical entrance, thought Christiana Lynn Barrington, seated inside the plane.

"Can't wait to get home," announced Marshall Weston, the Chief Financial Officer, undoing his tie and removing his Brioni suit jacket. "It's been one hell of a week," he added, laying his briefcase on the table and stretching his arms across the width of the airplane.

"At least you're heading home," groaned the Chief Operations Officer, James Langston. "I've got a meeting in Toronto tomorrow. This job is going to kill me." *But you can't beat the money and the lifestyle it has afforded you,* Christiana mused.

Again glancing out the window, she caught a glimpse of Jonathan with his unquestionable aura of perfection, engaged in a telephone conversation and obviously in no hurry to finish and join the others onboard the plane. Jonathan Robert Barrington was one of the wealthiest and most egocentric men in the world. He began proceeding up the ramp to the aircraft.

Jonathan mumbled greetings to James and Marshall. "Thank you for coming back with us to New York. It's not customary for senior management to be traveling together, but this G550 has just been serviced and she is in fine form, just like BHI," boasted Jonathan. Patting Marshall on the back, Jonathan added, "We did it. Got the company we've been after; let me savor this victory."

Loosening his Hermes tie, Jonathan poured a scotch and invited the men to join him. Ensconced on a sofa in the corner, Jonathan's daughter, Christiana, sipped sparkling water. Every bit the elegant lady, she sat, legs crossed, as her gray-green eyes met her father's steely blues when he moved down the aisle.

As the plane lifted off from Los Angeles heading for the clouds, the celebration began. This team had completed a stunning but challenging major acquisition. Praise and triumph centered on Christiana, who had orchestrated the entire transaction. No easy feat in an industry dominated by men.

"Brilliant," crowed Jonathan of his daughter's performance. Barrington Holdings International now owned the largest diamond, gold, iron ore and phosphate mining companies, distribution entities and retail jewelry stores in the world.

I should be ecstatic, thought Christiana. However, she was reflecting on another event of the day— the end of her marriage to Michael Trent. Her divorce was final. The accomplished businesswoman and overachiever had failed miserably in her personal life and her empty heart told the story.

As her memories drifted back to Michael, she reviewed her "underachievement" as both a wife and mother. *Will I ever have it all again?* she wondered. *If I had a second chance, could I successfully balance every aspect of my life?*

She didn't know the answer.

Wishing not to place a damper on the festivities, she went to the back of the plane. It was time for introspection, not celebration.

Easing into the soft leather, she swiveled the seat toward the window and the recollections flooded her mind.

Christiana and Michael had a long, involved, complicated, and seismic relationship during their ten-year marriage. Michael's interests focused exclusively on the entertainment industry. Maybe she should have realized their relationship was doomed from the start since she never felt comfortable with the Hollywood glitz; but *that* was really not the issue.

With pervasive sadness, she knew the issue was and always would be her father and the prepackaged life he had created. One she had accepted, or at least resigned herself to lead.

While attending Harvard she met Michael, who was ruggedly handsome with brown wavy hair and a devilish chuckle. He attended Boston University and was taken with Christiana at first sight. She was "take your breath away" gorgeous, he'd told his college friends. Michael grew up with considerable comforts; was well traveled and viewed life from a well-heeled existence.

While Jonathan and his wife Elizabeth liked Michael, they were hesitant to give him their approval for they believed the entertainment business would mean either a move to Los Angeles or major fluctuations in income. They envisioned a "would-be" actor who might end up waiting tables in an LA restaurant.

Michael's brief acting career soon morphed into his true passion of theatrical and movie production. His entree was a small off-Broadway production that received good reviews, but did not generate the requisite ticket sales and closed prematurely. Nonetheless, he made some lasting impressions and invaluable contacts. The contacts and a dip into his trust fund helped launch him into theatrical production.

During their senior year at college, Michael proposed to Christiana and she spent the next twelve months planning the wedding. The wedding and reception elicited the social buzz of Greenwich and New York with a guest list that read like a "Who's Who" of the social, financial, and cultural elite throughout the world. All the trappings of aristocracy, nobility and royalty were the substance of this American dynasty.

Christiana became Christiana Lynn Barrington-Trent. Jonathan demanded she retain the Barrington name for business purposes even if she used it in a hyphenated manner. And the dutiful daughter acquiesced.

"I love you more than anything. You are my whole world, Michael," she remembered saying to him. *"I trust you won't let your father ever come between us,"* Michael would add. Those words would haunt her forever as well as her automatic response, *"I promise."*

Degrees in international business and finance and a clearly focused career path brought Christiana to the Manhattan corporate offices of BHI where she was propelled into the spotlight and center stage, as all things Barrington were noteworthy. Her father reminded her often, "Barringtons will always be in control of this company."

Meanwhile, Michael's career was skyrocketing and they both became immersed in their professional lives. Eagerly she continued to prove to her father how involved, smart, diligent and dedicated she was, to him and to BHI.

Shortly after the first year of marriage, Christiana discovered she was pregnant. Michael was thrilled—Jonathan was not. Now striving harder to fulfill her commitments to her father and Barrington, she did that and more.

Christiana continued her fast-paced lifestyle through her pregnancy. Fortunately, she gave birth to a beautiful healthy gray-green-eyed baby girl whom they named Jennifer Nicole Barrington-Trent. Christiana spent several months at home with Jennifer and had to tear herself away when she resumed work. Even while on maternity leave, she was never totally extracted from the day-to-day business of Barrington. Jonathan saw to that.

Michael's reputation along with his income climbed substantially. He begged Christiana to stop working and stay home with the baby but he knew she never would. Guilt and separation from Jennifer coupled with obligations to uphold lifelong commitments to her father presented a constant struggle between the young couple.

A number of theatrical triumphs for Michael sparked in him an interest to venture into other mediums. He saw his future in film and gained notice and support from prominent Hollywood players. She encouraged him to test the waters in LA, figuring he would soon become disillusioned and find his way back to New York.

That was not to happen.

Michael found Hollywood intoxicating, with contacts, promise and allure. Christiana was never a fan of Los Angeles as she was East Coast born and bred and her roots, her thoughts, as well as her style bespoke New York and Connecticut.

Michael's big break came with the film, *The Complete Idiot*. He took up residence in Los Angeles to start this new project and Christiana, while not pleased with the prospect, vowed not to tarnish his dreams. Soon, it was evident Michael would permanently move to Los Angeles and he persuaded Christiana to join him as often as possible. It would prove impossible.

With careers moving at Mach speed, so was the unraveling of their relationship.

Christiana prayed Michael would return to New York. Michael, however, embraced his new life and all LA had to offer. He was now in his element and she was so far out of hers, it frightened her. Michael's witty and fun-loving personality Christiana had fallen in love with evolved into a hard-charging, edgy, sharp-tongued, name-dropping, attention-seeking, flirtatious, narcissistic, and looks-obsessed Hollywood type. When they hit the tabloids and were endlessly pursued by the paparazzi, she reacted—first with tears, then by mandates. There would be no compromise to family life and no sacrificing of the Barrington name and reputation.

Michael told her he needed this attention to be successful in Hollywood and believed it was once again her father who was of prime importance in their lives.

Circumstances made her draw closer to her parents and she purchased an estate next to them in Greenwich. Michael bought a stunning home in Malibu with a theatre room the size of a small house and ample entertainment areas capturing sweeping views of the Pacific Ocean, making it the ultimate Hollywood party house.

Michael's compelling arguments urging her to come and live with him fell on deaf ears and he finally realized she was married to Barrington and ultimately her father called the shots. Persistent fighting forced Michael to ask her to decide between her marriage and BHI.

Sadly, as if writing the final act to one of his plays, he had told her he knew the ending.

Marriage and family were overshadowed by Christiana's career. She had to succeed. Failure was not an option. "Barringtons never fail. Barringtons think only of success." Jonathan's quote frequently appeared in her thoughts.

Staring out the cabin window into the blackness of the night, she was haunted by the departing shot Michael made when he left, *"No man will ever be able to compete with your father."* Sadly, she knew it might be true.

His input was easy to recognize and she felt his presence even before he spoke.

"Come, this is your victory, you can rest later. You have just added to the Barrington fortunes," said her father in an appreciative manner. He took her by the arm and escorted her back to the festivities.

Life took a hard landing.

CHAPTER 2

ONCE THEY LANDED at the Teterboro airport in New Jersey and were seated comfortably in the limousine for their ride to Greenwich, Jonathan pulled a gift from his briefcase and presented it to Christiana.

"What is this?"

"Open it and you'll see," answered Jonathan.

Untying the ribbon and lifting the top of the small elegant box, she gasped as she removed the beautiful emerald and diamond bracelet. "Father, this is gorgeous, but what's the occasion?"

"Your precise execution on this acquisition has brought BHI into a new arena. You need to wear the assets," he replied with a sly grin.

"I cannot possibly accept this expensive gift." Noticing a larger red jewelry box lying open in Jonathan's attaché, she stared at the stunning blond diamond necklace. "Mother will be thrilled; she adores yellow diamonds," beamed Christiana.

Rattled and irritated, Jonathan reacted, "That's for another occasion." Sliding his hand back into his briefcase, he retrieved an additional red box. "Here," he added, "is what I plan to give your mother this evening."

Christiana held the lovely diamond bracelet and responded, "Father, I am so sorry, I didn't mean to spoil your surprise. The diamond bracelet is exquisite."

"Now not a word about the necklace," admonished Jonathan. "I promise."

The car dropped Christiana off at Montrachet, her Greenwich home, before depositing Jonathan at his estate, Sur La Mer.

"See you in the morning." Leaning out the window, he exclaimed, "Christiana, brilliant job—you are a true Barrington!"

With her thoughts still focused on her divorce, all she could muster was, "Thank you, Father."

As she walked through the attractive courtyard and opened the door to her stunning home, everything seemed suddenly cold. All the trappings of success were brilliantly displayed, but she knew the best things in life weren't material.

Henri, the major domo, met her in the foyer to inform her Jennifer was finishing dinner in the family dining room with Marcia the nanny. "Would you like dinner now, Mrs. Trent, oh … ah … Ms. Barrington? I'm sorry; please let me know how you wish the staff to address you?" Henri asked apologetically.

I haven't thought that far ahead, lamented Christiana. *It would be easier to go back to Barrington.* "Ms. Barrington will be fine, Henri," she replied. "Henri, I would like to dine with Jennifer and Marcia, thank you."

"Right away, Ms. Barrington, and I shall inform the staff of the new protocol." He hesitated then added, "Ms. Barrington, I was very sorry to hear about your divorce. If there is anything I can do, please don't hesitate to ask." Henri George Deparde had worked for the Barrington family since Christiana was a small child. The attachment between Christiana and Henri was so strong that when Christiana bought the Greenwich estate, she persuaded her parents to allow her to employ Henri. Henri liked Elizabeth, tolerated Jonathan, but adored Christiana.

"You're home! Come, sit next to me," squeaked Jennifer. With her gray-green eyes and gorgeous thick hair worn loosely in pigtails, Jennifer bore a striking resemblance to Christiana. She could infuse a room with joy by her smile and sunny personality. The funny giggle and wicked laugh were the "Trent" magic that added up to make a delightful youngster.

But the full ramifications of the divorce were taking a toll on her as she missed her father. Ironically, she called him Daddy, never Father. Michael didn't respond well to the term Father and Christiana surmised it was because the term reflected best on and seemed most appropriate to Jonathan.

Marcia Peterson, Jennifer's nanny, smiled as Christiana entered the room and acknowledged, "I'll leave you and Jennifer to have a quiet dinner together."

"Marcia, I want to spend some time with Jennifer so I'll prepare her for bedtime," Christiana replied, stroking Jennifer's hair. Looking intently at her daughter, Christiana said, "I know you miss your father."

"When can I see Daddy?" Jennifer asked soulfully.

"Honey, I will arrange a visit very soon. I promise," said Christiana, struggling with this new dimension to her life.

"All right," said Jennifer, momentarily satisfied. The evening proved a particularly wonderful bonding experience for both mother and daughter but once Jennifer was asleep, Christiana's mind was racing. Long-term childcare was an issue since Marcia was studying nursing and would be moving out of state, but Jennifer's visits with her father were more paramount at the moment.

Walking into her bedroom, she glanced at the alarm clock. *Good*, she thought, *it's only eight in Los Angeles*. Reaching for the phone, she punched in Michael's number, surprised when he answered on the third ring.

"Hi, Christiana, how unexpected to hear from you today, *the official day of the termination of our marriage*," he said sarcastically. Suddenly she wished she had not called.

"Michael, I just had a conversation with Jennifer and she wants to see you. You are a wonderful father and must remain a major part of her life."

"It is also my desire to be a part of her life. What are you proposing?" he answered, his tone changing.

"I'm not really sure. I'm new at this; I don't know the rules."

"Honey," Michael said, "relax, there are no rules. We decide what is best for our daughter and our particular circumstance. We don't have to make any binding absolutes right now." Michael continued as she fell silent, "With the financial wherewithal and flexibility of travel, we can make things happen."

"True, however, I'm at a critical juncture with child care since Marcia will be completing school and embarking on her nursing career."

"I guess I forgot about her temporary status."

She cleared her throat and said, "Michael, I have one more subject to discuss tonight." She faltered. "I … I'm going back," and stopped in mid sentence. "What I mean to say is I am changing my name back to Barrington."

"Christiana, as much as I still love you and never wished for our marriage to end, you were, you are, and will always be a Barrington. Your father has seen to that," he bristled with the terseness he reserved for any mention of Jonathan.

"I won't contribute to a character assassination of my father," she retorted.

He had more to say. "Christiana, our marriage could have worked. Hell, I think our marriage was good, could have been great if it wasn't for your father and BHI. Do me one favor. In fact, it's really a favor to you. Get a life independent of your father before it's too late."

"Do you blame my father for the breakup of our marriage?" Christiana was angry and, as Jonathan's staunchest ally, immediately rose to his defense.

"Blame is the wrong word, but instrumental, yes. My criticism is anchored in your, or rather our inability to place top priority on our relationship. We became secondary and our marriage lost its strength," said Michael. Pausing, he then added, "There will be plenty of time to analyze us over the next few years, let's not try to dissect everything in one night. We have both been through enough. I want us to remain friends and with our daughter we have a good shot at doing just that." With an upbeat mode, he ended by saying, "I'll call you in the next few days."

"Goodnight. Oh, Michael, if it works, when you come to the East Coast, you might consider staying at Montrachet," Christiana suggested.

"Let me figure out my schedule and the logistics first. I appreciate the offer. Goodnight, Christiana."

CHAPTER 3

SHE HAD A RESTLESS NIGHT after her conversation with Michael but rose before dawn to get ready for her fitness instructor. Waiting when Joseph pulled up precisely at eight, she headed to Manhattan with her father. Jonathan, in his custom-tailored pin-striped Savile Row suit, was smart and stylish and could manage to look fresh and impeccably dressed even at the end of a laborious day. He was never flamboyant in dress or style, only occasionally in his language.

They faced an arduous week with the latest acquisition compounded by Jonathan's impending departure for Europe. He pressed forward to apprise Christiana of several business developments, including another potential acquisition. With Jonathan, it was never what you've done, but what you were going to do.

Slipping documents over to her, his eyes fell on her left hand, sans the wedding ring. Although he was elated the marriage was over, he hid his smugness. However, he did inquire, "I noticed you have removed your wedding ring?"

"Yes, Father, and I intend to retake the Barrington name and will contact my attorney later today," she returned, bracing for his caustic remarks.

But there were none. Instead, Jonathan leaned over and kissed her forehead, easing into his comment, "This has been a trying time for both you and Jennifer and please know your mother and I are here for whatever you need. We love you very much." With Jonathan you never knew what to expect but chances were you didn't expect what you got. Here again she was thrown off course.

The acquisition was front page news and the week was filled with interviews from prominent business periodicals and television news media. Much of the media interaction with BHI was governed by Christiana. She was a stunning beauty who possessed confidence, charm and charisma, all of which ignited the press.

With a whirlwind day of legal and financial meetings and prepping for a news conference, it was seven-thirty before Christiana called for her driver. She would miss having dinner with Jennifer by the time she returned to Montrachet.

In her efforts to keep her promise to Jennifer, she may have complicated issues ahead with Michael. Reoccurring thoughts had haunted her since their telephone conversation. *Why did I invite him to stay at Montrachet? What was I thinking? I've already extended the invitation, I can't retract it. He probably won't stay there anyway.*

The following morning she had barely touched breakfast when both the business and cell phones rang in unison. The easy decision as to which phone to answer came as she read Jonathan's number. "Good morning, Father."

Not one for idle chitchat during a business day, Jonathan reported, "Hello, Christiana, I'm on the way to an appointment in midtown. The meeting has been changed with the bankers until this afternoon at one."

"That's fine, Father. Where should I meet you?"

"In my conference room," he answered. "Christiana, I'm getting a phone call from London, I'll see you this afternoon."

Purposely arriving early for the meeting, she seized the opportunity to ask, "What is the urgency that's driving you back to London so quickly, Father? I recall it was your idea to celebrate the new acquisition with staff this weekend at my Palm Beach estate."

"Yes, dear, I remember. I plan on leaving Friday in time to arrive at Bellagio early evening."

A more definitive accounting of Jonathan's reasons to return to London this week was not forthcoming as the bankers entered the conference room. Jonathan lived by his own rules. One never questioned his reasons or decisions in either his personal or professional life. Christiana knew this only too well.

Concluding the meeting, Jonathan strode confidently from the office heading to the airport, having successfully restructured the debt of the new entity while using some of the equity for the necessary capital expenditures.

Returning from another meeting later that day, Christiana stopped to check for messages. Amanda Worth, petite in stature, but not small in poise, charm, beauty or intelligence, "a Halle Berry look-alike," was her primary assistant. Amanda graced the company with a pleasant personality along with respect, courtesy and maturity well beyond her years.

Michael Trent was buzzed through as Christiana closed the door to her office. Although she was happy to hear from him, she was still bothered by the terse and pointed telephone conversation they'd had the other evening.

"Christiana, I'm sorry to bother you at the office but my schedule allows me to be in New York a week from Wednesday. Will that work for you and Jennifer?"

"Yes, Michael, that's fine. I've planned a brief overnight trip that should give you some alone time with Jennifer. Will you stay with us at Montrachet?"

"Are you sure that doesn't pose a problem for either you or Jennifer?" Montrachet encompassed over seven acres with its own private beach as well as numerous gardens, indoor and outdoor pools, a pool house, tennis court, riding stables, two carriage houses for the household staff and two guest villas.

"We would welcome it. I will have one of the guest villas ready for your arrival." Just like Jonathan, Christiana ran on precision and order. This arrangement might bring some much-needed order to her hectic existence. *If he makes frequent trips, he could leave some clothes and other belongings, but I won't mention it at this point,* she thought.

"Great, I'll set up the rest of my meetings and purchase my airline ticket."

Due to the magnitude of this latest acquisition, a jubilant, but tired, Christiana found herself hounded by the press all week. By Friday, she was ecstatic to be heading to Florida for a welcome change of scenery and the staff thank you party.

Elizabeth had accompanied Jennifer and Marcia on a flight the previous day. Although living in the sophisticated world that was Elizabeth Matthews Barrington, she personified genuine warmth and kindness, apparent in her special relationship with her granddaughter.

Working through most of her flight, Christiana questioned a figure from one of the subsidiaries and rose from her seat to locate her CFO. Marshall's wife excused herself to allow them a private conversation. Marshall looked over at Christiana as she was fetching papers from her briefcase and asked, "How are you holding up?"

Never one for small talk or venturing into the personal world of the Barringtons, Christiana sat upright, surprised by his question. Presuming it was a reference to the acquisition and the media blitz, she responded, "It has been a tumultuous week, although things will settle down once we get the media campaign off the ground."

"You have the media eating out of your hands. Barrington is good story and *you* are great story."

She smiled at his comment.

"Actually, I wasn't referring to the acquisition; I was asking how you are doing personally. How's Jennifer coping?"

"I have my all-consuming work to keep me occupied, so I'm faring better than Jennifer. She's very close with her father and misses him immensely. Fortunately, Michael has a new project in New York that will bring more frequent visits," Christiana said, and added, "thank you for asking, Marshall."

After landing, they were met not only by chauffeurs and security teams, but also by the warmth of the Florida sun, which was a welcome relief after the rain of New York. Christiana owned an Italianate villa named Bellagio after one of her favorite spots in Italy. The twenty-five thousand square-foot, gated estate was defined by fine architectural accents and European understatement, with free-flowing large expanses of windows and terraces, majestic ceilings and marble floors, overlooking the splendors of the waterways, complete with two boat docks. The weekend would be spent partying onboard the yachts with a lavish reception and al fresco dinner.

Meanwhile, winging his way westbound from London to Palm Beach, Jonathan found time for contemplation, self indulgence and self accolades. Stirring his Belvedere martini, he savored a long sip and leaned back in the plush leather seat of his private plane. Loosening his seatbelt, he drank in the pleasures of his fine aircraft and the alcohol.

A self-made man, he had brought BHI up to become one of the elite top ten companies of *Fortune's* top five-hundred companies worldwide, making Jonathan one of the wealthiest men in the world. If the United States had a monarchy, surely he would be king.

All this and not so long ago …

His father's small investment firm paid handsomely for his college education. Kicking the laziness that plagued him as a child, Jonathan sailed through Harvard where he developed the need to excel and compete. Maturing in looks, refinement and temperament with his six-foot-one sculptured body, razor-sharp steel-blue eyes, and an almost too-perfect head of sandy brown hair, he did not lack for the attention of the ladies. But then he met the future Mrs. Jonathan Robert Barrington. Elizabeth was a challenge with her cool sophistication and European aloofness, and was not easily taken in by his boyish charms. Raised in France and Belgium, she ventured to the United States to attend Princeton. Gorgeous with porcelain skin, high cheek bones, and shoulder-length blond hair, Elizabeth radiated a sense of well being that was coupled with a tremendous strength for discipline of mind and body.

Upon their graduation, the two married.

Armed with his advanced degree from Wharton and all the accolades of a man on the fast track, he set off to make his mark in his father's company. The father-son relationship was turbulent at times as Jonathan Senior was not ready to be sidelined. But like a caged lion, Jonathan Junior remained restless and wanted to embark on building his own empire. Angling for a way to do so, he prepared to give his father an ultimatum—either he become president or he would seriously consider the offers he'd been batting away. That conversation never took place as his father suffered a massive coronary and was dead before Jonathan reached the hospital.

At the age of twenty-six, he now had the company under his direction and control. It was his turn to perform and the best way to predict his future was to invent it. And that was what he set out to do.

At the birth of their daughter, Christiana Lynn Barrington, in May 1965, the baby graced the Barrington family with an heir and became the center of Elizabeth's world. This allowed Jonathan to stay focused on the building of the company. Although he was bruised by several rough starts, miscalculated risks and acquisitions, soon he saw the business start to grow. More of a gambler than his father, he discovered that action cured all fear.

He then experienced the turning point of his career. A former top end hotel had faded from glory and was in the process of being shuttered as the owners could neither afford the repairs nor the taxes. One year later, the building reopened with a fashionable reception, retaining her former name, the Regal Plaza, followed with, *by Barrington International.* From that point forward, he was determined to have his name attached to everything he owned. Purchasing several hotels in Europe, Jonathan set up operations in Germany and Great Britain. He started to spin his business dynasty with a bounty of acquisitions, seeking sound companies to keep the brand and the management. The corporate name was changed to Barrington Holdings International (BHI) to better represent his goal of divergent holdings worldwide.

My father should be so grateful to have had a son like me, he thought as he took a long gulp of his martini. Yet as he sat staring out the cabin window, in a private and vulnerable moment, he still wondered if his father would have been proud. The emptiness of the unanswered question would remain as deep as the Atlantic Ocean that stretched below him.

That thought was pushed from Jonathan's mind as he was interrupted by his lead pilot Richard Dennison. A former commercial pilot, Richard jumped years ago from his airline job to work at Barrington. BHI paid handsomely and although Richard missed the flight benefits afforded by the commercial airline industry, Jonathan more than compensated for that loss with his total benefits package.

All positions at Barrington were highly coveted and if one could bear the brutal demands, you rarely left its employ. BHI was known to make or break careers.

As the pilot approached Jonathan, he said, "Are you having a comfortable flight, Mr. Barrington?"

"Yes, Richard, just allowing myself a little self-indulgence," he laughed as he held up his martini glass.

Richard continued, "Even with the delay getting out of London, we should be arriving on schedule in West Palm Beach this afternoon. The weather has been cooperating and the head winds are not as strong as first indicated."

"Ah, that's good news. Thanks for the update."

"You're welcome, sir." Noticing Jonathan fidgeting with his empty glass he added, "I'll send Christy back to freshen up your drink. I'll see you once we're on the ground." A marathon runner in his prime, Richard Dennison still had the physique. Graying only at the temples, he rode his age with the same élan and surefootedness he employed to pilot his aircraft.

The effects of the alcohol coupled with the rich canapés made Jonathan feel sleepy and he opted for a nap. Closing his eyes was the last thing he remembered, until the flight attendant gently nudged him in preparation for landing. Checking his watch, he was pleased to see he had slept two hours, and headed for the lavatory to freshen up.

CHAPTER 4

WITH THE BLAST OF FLORIDA SUN, London was a distant memory. After he finished checking voice and emails on his ride to Bellagio, he placed his phone into the pouch of his briefcase and touched the gift for Elizabeth.

Feeling guilty for his sustained absences, he'd splurged on another expensive piece of jewelry. It eased the guilt somewhat, although he knew all Elizabeth ever wanted or needed from him, was him. Still the true love of his life, she deserved better.

As he entered the foyer, he saw a number of people engrossed in conversation out on the patio overlooking the intracoastal waterway. Taking a glass of champagne from the butler, he chatted with Marshall and James along with their wives.

Anxious to find Elizabeth, he excused himself and went in search of his wife. As he stepped out on the upstairs terrace, he spotted Elizabeth and Jennifer poolside.

Jennifer noticed Jonathan's arrival and yelled, "Grandfather! Look at me. I'm swimming." He proceeded down to greet his family.

"Wow, look at you. You swim like a little fish."

Elizabeth rose from the chaise and warmly greeted her husband. "You look tired, Jonathan. How was your trip?"

"Do I really look tired? I thought I looked refreshed as I slept a couple of hours on the plane."

Stepping out of the pool dripping wet, Jennifer nuzzled up to her grandparents.

"Jennifer, I have a present for you." Glancing around and not finding Christiana, who would reprimand him for giving sweets, he handed her a box of Belgium chocolates.

As Jennifer stood shivering and shoved two small candies in her mouth, Elizabeth bent over to put her arms around her granddaughter. "Sweetheart, let's get you out of your wet bathing suit."

Jonathan patted her on the head and watched them walk through the gardens back to the house. He accepted another glass of champagne from a passing wait staff and started to rejoin the guests when the ringing of his cell phone momentarily suspended his movement.

This will have to be a short conversation, he thought as he caught sight of several people mingling poolside. The opening comment from the caller elicited an exasperated response from Jonathan. "I *did* leave you a message. I'm in Palm Beach, at Christiana's home for a Barrington party. Honestly, it slipped my mind until I spoke with Christiana earlier this week. Yes, I should be back in Europe within a week. Now I must get back to the party. *Ciao.*" Miffed by the interruption, he placed his phone on vibrate, gulped down the remainder of the champagne, and retrieved another glass.

As the sun retreated in its westerly crawl, the temperature cooled and the party heated up. Rewards for successful accomplishments at BHI were legendary and the party purveyors were anticipating lavish bonuses and luxury gifts, which Jonathan would convey over the weekend.

Breaking away to say goodnight to Jennifer, Christiana lingered at the edge of the terrace before returning to her guests. She smelled the signature scent before her mother uttered a word. Placing an arm around her daughter, Elizabeth said, "Your father is so proud of you. This is a major triumph for Barrington Holdings International. But how are you holding up, sweetheart, with the stresses, both personally and professionally?"

"Honestly, Mother, work has been a Godsend as it hasn't given me much time to focus on my personal life."

Elizabeth grasped her daughter's hands and Christiana knew her mother shared her profound sadness. "Mother, please tell me your secret to a successful marriage?"

Without hesitation she answered, "I entered his world and never looked back."

Questions leaped to Christiana's mind but by the look on her mother's face, she knew to trespass no further. Before Christiana could respond, Elizabeth added, "You could not have been a Barrington if you had allowed yourself to be absorbed by Michael's world."

Putting on a smile, Elizabeth broke the mood by saying, "Come, let's join the party. It looks like dinner is being served."

Once dinner was completed, Christiana presented the opening remarks. "I welcome you to Bellagio and our thank you party for all the hard work and dedication you've given to this acquisition. I extend special appreciation to the families who have endured these last grueling months." When she was finished she introduced Jonathan.

"Isn't this place magnificent?" proclaimed Jonathan to the appreciative applause. "I am gratified to see each of you here this evening. You have played a vital role in bringing this bright star to the Barrington portfolio of companies. Here's to Jewels *by Barrington*. Now you are probably wondering if I'm going to give out bonuses tonight. But I'm holding that special acknowledgment until Grant Pemberton arrives tomorrow." At this, the audience groaned. "There is one surprise, however, for this evening, reserved for the ladies." Reaching for a bag at the side of his chair, he personally handed each lady a small jewelry box. Returning to the head table he said, "Please open the boxes." With gasps and gratitude, the ladies held up the diamond bracelets.

"And in conclusion, to my beautiful wife Elizabeth, you are my pillar of strength and to you I will always be grateful. My wonderful daughter Christiana, you are the prize that makes this all worthwhile. I love you both." He raised his glass in their honor. "Now let us continue with our celebration," Jonathan ended his speech.

James, the COO, stood up as Jonathan resumed his seat. "Not without special thanks to Jonathan and Christiana. I believe I speak for the management team when I say it is, and continues to be, a pleasure and a privilege to work at Barrington. *Now* let's celebrate!"

The light from a brilliant sunrise Saturday morning streamed into the gym as Christiana began her morning workout. Her mother's words from the previous night, *"I entered his world and never looked back,"* still resonated. *If that's the secret to a successful marriage, how can I ever succeed in combining my demanding career with family?*

Later, when she arrived downstairs, she found her mother seated in the family dining room with coffee and the morning papers.

"Good morning, Mother."

Elizabeth responded, "Good morning, Christiana. Is my darling granddaughter up and about this morning?"

"She was still asleep when I slipped into her room before coming downstairs. It was a late night for her."

"Do you have time to join me for coffee?"

"Certainly, I have a little respite before our guests are down for breakfast. Is Father up yet?"

"He left at the crack of dawn with several guests to play golf at the country club."

Their conversation was quickly upstaged as one of the staff appeared at the door requesting Christiana's assistance. Preparations were underway to outfit the yachts for the afternoon and evening festivities. The crafts bobbed gently in the water as she made her approach. Looking out to the sea, she thought: *Father is the ocean. Mother is the port, the safe haven.*

Jonathan's yacht christened *Behold* measured one hundred ninety-two feet and had a cruise range of eight thousand five-hundred nautical miles. Christiana's ninety-eight foot Italian built AZUMIT was sleeker in design and named *Condessa*. Both boats were outfitted with an enclosed gym, a plunge pool and helicopter pad.

By midafternoon the majestic sun shone brightly on the shoreline mansions as the yachts cruised proudly out to sea. Once clear of the intracoastal, both father and daughter took control of their yachts and exhibited their boating skills. The boat excursion provided a lazy retreat following a morning of golf, tennis, swimming and shopping.

Later, as the guests nibbled on desserts, fine port, and coffees, Jonathan, in his trademark savvy swagger, due in part to his personality as well as the alcohol, clinked his glass to acquire the attention of his audience. "I will be brief. As a token of our appreciation, I am pleased to hand out your bonus checks."

"Thank you to Christiana and Jonathan,"—"Wow, this is fabulous!"—and "My wife forgives me for all her lonely nights," the accumulated comments and accolades resonated around the boat deck.

As the last of the guests departed Bellagio Sunday morning, Elizabeth and Christiana spent a few moments discussing the weekend. Hearing their discussion as he entered the foyer, Jonathan chimed in, "Let me thank both the ladies in my life. You are amazing." As he finished his comment, his telephone rattled to life. Retrieving the instrument from the pocket of his jacket, he said, "Please excuse me, I need to take this call," as he noticed the number on the digital read.

When he did not return, Elizabeth went in search. Jonathan was just ending his conversation and she caught only his last remark. "I will have the funds transferred tomorrow. *Yes*, it should be sufficient." He clapped the phone shut without a goodbye.

"Is there a problem, Jonathan?"

"Nothing serious, my dear," and in typical Jonathan modality, the subject was closed. Instead he offered, "Shall we go back to the yacht and finish our packing?"

By midafternoon, Palm Beach was a mere memory as the Barrington family took flights to their separate destinations.

CHAPTER 5 ... Later that week

"YOUR FATHER STILL HAS IT," he boasted as he slapped several newspapers down on Christiana's desk.

"Father, you are in a spunky mood today. Why such *modesty?*" she teased. He assembled the papers for her to see and guided her to the BHI feature stories. "You believe I spend too much time in Europe, leaving you here at Corporate."

"Father ... I ... I have never said that."

"True, not in so many words. As you read these articles, you will understand the importance of my presence in our European offices."

Captivated, she perused the stories. Setting the papers aside she asked, "How did you accomplish this? I am astonished a Saudi prince would place such an asset base outside the kingdom."

"We've held private discussions with the royal family for years but only recently did these conversations turn to brokered negotiations. Graham Cunningham, our CEO of Barrington Financial Services, is sniffing around Wall Street to lure top level analysts and managers to work for us here and in Riyadh."

"I'm speechless. Yes, Father, you *do* indeed still have it," she said, as she came around the desk to hug her father. "You will always be the master of negotiations."

Jonathan nodded and took his leave from her office.

Subtle knocking at the door almost went unnoticed. "Where would you like me to put these, Ms. Barrington?" One of her assistants was struggling with an oversized floral arrangement. Once the assistant left, Christiana picked up the card. "To the most beautiful woman in the world. Would you allow a humble bachelor to have the pleasure of your company for dinner this Thursday evening? Chad Nottingham. P.S. I will call you later this afternoon."

Several other gifts and bouquets arrived in short order with cards attached with similar requests for dinner. As Christiana was reading the note cards affixed to the bouquets, she was interrupted by her assistant Amanda.

"Christiana, James Langston is here to see you. May I send him in?"

"Yes, thank you."

James looked around and asked, "Did I miss your birthday?"

"Let's just say they are from some not-so-secret admirers."

"Not surprising, since your divorce has been leaked to the press."

"That explains the sudden interest in my social life."

"The media described you as the most eligible woman in the world."

"Eligible for what?" Christiana quipped. James simply chuckled.

"How did this get out to the press?"

"Because you are who you are—Christiana Lynn Barrington. There doesn't have to be another reason."

A meeting precluded her availability to take the call from Chad Nottingham, although she had several personal emails from additional men by the time she returned to her office. Shutting off her computer without replying to any of the messages, she placed a call to her publicist.

"Hello, Peggy Fairfield."

"Hi, Peggy, it's Christiana Barrington."

"Please hold, Christiana, let me cut loose my other line." Returning quickly, Peggy said, "Now you have my undivided attention. How may I be of assistance?"

"I understand the media has picked up news of my divorce and I've received voice and email messages from men around the world wanting dinner dates."

Peggy laughed. "I know many ladies, including me, who would envy that position. However, I am not making light of your situation. Let me see what we are up against. The only press on it I've seen were the celebrity news shows yesterday. Here is what's on my service. Two tabloids picked it up yesterday in addition; two other celebrity news shows will air it today as well as the tabloids in London, Paris, Rome and Tokyo."

"I suppose I'll just have to fend off this undue attention," responded Christiana.

"Nothing Christiana Lynn Barrington does or says is merely 'undue attention.' You are a media masterpiece and jobs depend on a big story like Barrington. Now if you tell me you are romantically linked to some fabulous fellow, I will blanket the airwaves and hopefully place a hard stop to the persistent males vying for your attention."

"Peggy, I haven't even thought about reactivating my social life. My efforts are focused on Jennifer as she really misses her father.

Fortunately, Michael has a new Broadway production and that will allow for frequent visits to Montrachet."

"Just make sure the media doesn't get wind that Michael is rooming at Montrachet. I can see the headlines now, 'Ex-husband back under her roof in Greenwich.'"

"Then let's make certain we keep a lid on it," retorted Christiana. "Absolutely!"

Spending a quiet weekend with Jennifer, she hoped to start to shape her new life as a single parent. Despite her efforts to the contrary, she missed Michael's influence but was determined to be the best mother—in spite of BHI and her father.

As the workweek commenced, Jonathan breezed into Christiana's office like a man on a serious mission. Amanda stood behind him with her arms raised palms up and silently mouthed, "I'm sorry."

"It's fine, Amanda," she said as she eyed her father. Impeccably turned out at all times, Jonathan was aging with panache and growing more handsome with the years. He maintained the utmost attention to self, family, and business. "Hello, Father, I didn't know you were around this afternoon."

"My meeting did not go as long as expected today, so if you have a little time," he said, taking a seat across from her desk.

"I'm just reviewing copy for the Jewels *by Barrington* ad campaign. In addition, I have just received both the print and TV ads. Take a look and tell me what you think," said Christiana as she motioned her father to the conference table. "Father, these are my favorites," she said, holding up two photographs of Jonathan faultlessly attired in a tuxedo and Elizabeth looking breathtaking in a sexy long, black, strapless gown. The first photo showed them holding hands and gazing into each other's eyes as the ad read,

Adoring, while the second photograph positioned Elizabeth with her back to Jonathan as he clasped a ten carat diamond necklace around her neck. The caption read, *Adorned. The world of perfection and beauty at one source—*Jewels *by Barrington.*

"Mother looks magnificent, doesn't she?"

"Stunning, absolutely stunning!" Jonathan couldn't take his eyes off the photos.

Perusing the photographs, Jonathan lifted one of Christiana descending a staircase in a long mink coat. The first caption pronounced, *Arriving,* while the second photograph revealed her at the base of the staircase, the mink coat open to her shoulders, a blond multi diamond necklace at her throat. The subtitle read, *Arrived. Make the right entrance with* Jewels *by Barrington.*

"You look pretty magnificent yourself," said a proud father.

"I'm pleased with the print advertisements, now let me show you the TV spots," she announced, switching on the wall-mounted television set.

"I like them, even the one with the cats and I'm not partial to felines," remarked Jonathan. The ad copy placed a large snow-white cat in the middle of a massive cushion facing a large jet-black cat on another cushion. An emerald bracelet spilled over the back of the white cat while a set of matching earrings luxuriated on the fur of the black animal. The cats were posed with faces toward the camera and the heading read, *Purrfection. A purrfect pair—*Jewels *by Barrington.*

"Father, as I have been researching advertisements, I've found something of interest." As Jonathan started toward her desk, Christiana continued. "It is Danielle Reynard, the world-class Swiss pianist, at a performance in Munich. She is wearing a necklace identical to the one you bought for Mother's birthday." The necklace looked stunning against Danielle's tanned skin and her trademark long, straight, raven-black hair. Her smoky mahogany eyes, perfectly lined with dark black eyeliner; her long neck; and the pout on her pink lips provided the sexy mount for the large diamond-studded necklace.

"Let me see that," Jonathan said, expressing his displeasure. "How outrageous, now I must return my gift and find something new for your mother. I will not have your mother wearing something flaunted by another celebrity. Would you mind if I take this page?"

"Of course not, Father, take the magazine with the article about Ms. Reynard in addition to the photograph."

"Thank you," he said and tucked it under his arm. "Are you free for a personal lunch?"

Christiana hesitated and Jonathan jumped in. "Save us both time, since you know I won't take no for an answer." Jonathan's boldness had genius, power and magic. He was correct, he would get his way. The comment brought a concerned look from Christiana. "Everything is fine; I didn't mean to startle you," he hurriedly replied.

"I would be delighted to have a father-daughter lunch."

As they were seated with menus in hand, Jonathan wasted no time in getting to his topic of discussion. "I've given much thought to Jennifer's schooling and it is time to consider enrollment at St. George's Academy. To expedite it, I've advanced a deposit to reserve a space for the fall term. It required some maneuvering, as you may imagine, along with a hefty financial contribution."

Chagrined, she allowed anger to take a firm grip. "How could you think of making this paramount decision? Jennifer will not be sent away to boarding school."

"Christiana, you must not be selfish; instead, consider what is best for Jennifer. She must be our first priority," he countered.

Indignant, Christiana charged back with more venom than she had ever displayed. "Jennifer is and always has been my first and only priority, thus the reason I will not send her to Europe for schooling. She needs the comfort and support of her family and she has a strong bond with her father. As her parents, Michael and I will determine what is best for our daughter."

"Christiana, you must not put your interests ahead of the betterment of your daughter. A fine education is tantamount to her proper development." He stopped and sat back, obviously not accustomed to refusal and disdain, and thrown by her outright condemnation.

Then they both spoke simultaneously. Jonathan deferred to Christiana. "Father, I know you have Jennifer's best interests at heart but as her mother, I understand her needs better than anyone. As such, I determine that she will stay in Greenwich and continue her studies."

Jonathan stiffened his upper lip and said, "Of course, darling. I understand. But Christiana, I will bring this up again in the future."

"Father, I know you will," she said, trying to feign a smile. "But understand I am adamant and will not change my mind."

"Yes, I know you are at this time." He then released the proposition and looked around to catch the eye of the waiter to order lunch. Lunch ended without further discussion on the subject.

Back at the office, her doubts surfaced; was her father correct? *Am I holding onto Jennifer because I am alone and don't want to lose her too?*

She was a single mother with a demanding schedule, which precluded her from spending enough time with Jennifer. And Michael certainly would not be able to dash over to Europe often enough to see his daughter.

Happily, she was interrupted by a call that was followed by a meeting and she tucked away her personal thoughts. However, Christiana returned home still haunted by the conversation with her father, and embraced Jennifer.

"Mother, there is a man here to see us. Grandfather brought him over a little while ago. They are waiting in the living room," announced Jennifer.

He must be parked along the side Porte Cohere, she decided. *Now what is Father up to?* Heading into the living room, she glanced from her father to the distinguished gentleman extending his hand.

"Christiana," said Jonathan, "this is Mr. Gerald Stedman, the head of St. George's Academy." Sending a glare in her father's direction, Christiana shook hands and replied, "It's a pleasure to meet you, Mr. Stedman."

"Please, call me Gerald, and may I call you Christiana?"

"Yes, of course."

Christiana's edginess was apparent but Jonathan pressed forward. "Christiana, I wanted to take the opportunity to have Gerald discuss the academic programming for Jennifer. It was auspicious he was in town for a speaking engagement and was able to come up to Connecticut this evening."

Propitious, all right. Why didn't he mention this at lunch? thought Christiana. "Yes, how fortunate," she answered with a hint of sarcasm.

She listened to his presentation, looked over the materials and asked several questions. He also added, "I'm sure your father has explained currently we have no openings but will accommodate Jennifer this next semester."

What sizable contribution must Father have made to the school? she wondered.

"Isn't that wonderful, Christiana?" Christiana did not acknowledge her father, but sat patiently listening to them talk about sending *her* daughter away to school—as if it were all prescribed.

"Gerald, I am grateful you have taken the time to discuss this with me, with us. I received a wonderful education at St. George's and the school played a vital role in my accomplishments and my outlook on life. My situation, however, was different than Jennifer's. I'm sorry, Gerald, but I am not going to make a decision at this time."

Running into the dining room, Jennifer tripped on the corner of the Persian carpet and careened forward. "Whoa, Princess, we don't want a visit to the emergency room," Jonathan said, strategically stationed at the end of the table as he helped break her fall.

"Sorry, I know I'm not supposed to run in the house," she said apologetically, "but I was excited because I can go to school where I can ski *all the time!*"

"Jennifer!" interrupted Gerald Stedman, laughing. "It doesn't snow *all* the time."

"I know, I know, but the pictures look *so* neat in the brochures."

"It is indeed a special place for the lucky students who come to us," he agreed.

The evening couldn't end quickly enough for Christiana and as she thanked her guest and closed the door, she gave a sigh of relief. Her father was still in the living room conversing with Jennifer when she rejoined them. "Marcia will be right down, sweetheart. Please gather up the brochures and say goodnight to Grandfather."

Once alone with Jonathan, she was determined to stand her ground. "I listened to him, Father, but am still adamant about keeping Jennifer in Connecticut. And I am distressed that you brought Jennifer in as if to make her your ally. She is not a pawn in your manipulation."

"You did listen and I am most appreciative. Jennifer is your child—yours and Michael's. I do understand, given your recent divorce, another separation would be most traumatic. My timing was wrong and my sensitivity way off. I am truly sorry." As Christiana looked at him all she saw was a false sense of innocence.

The subject of Jennifer's schooling did not resurface due in part to their travel and business schedules.

CHAPTER 6

LAUGHTER FILLED THE FOYER as Christiana arrived home early. Jennifer appeared content and happy. Searching for recompense, meaning and connection in the muddle and confusion that was Christiana's life, she wondered if perhaps Michael held part of the answer.

Once Jennifer was tucked in for the evening, Michael and Christiana enjoyed drinks on the terrace. "Michael, is the villa suitable to your needs?"

"Is there anything on this estate that is less than magnificent?" he chuckled. "Christiana, I didn't mean to upset you the other evening when I talked about your father."

Meeting no resistance, he continued, "I never wanted anything from you except *you*, and your love. The suggestion of the prenuptial agreement was mine, which even surprised Jonathan. I loved you ... I still love you and always will." She attempted to speak but he asked her to allow him to finish. "But as hard as it is for me to want to kiss you right now, I am resigned to having a relationship from afar for the sake of our daughter."

Feeling her cheeks redden at the inference, she merely replied, "Jennifer needs her father and you will forever be a part of our lives." Her gaze fell away from his piercing look.

Michael knew when to persevere and when to leave the subject alone. She was coated with the "Jonathan armor" and was virtually impregnable from penetration. Divorce set out barriers and distance. A couple who once shared everything, every bit of trivial banter, even felt each other's pulse, must now rely on chosen moments, prearranged meetings or circumstances and a margin of politeness, which until today had been all but forgotten, to make some semblance of what was once a family.

If Michael were acting this would be the most challenging role of his career and in dual positions of actor and director, he would cast himself as well as the others into roles that were unfamiliar. All divorces are not equal. Forget the financial stakes; the emotional toll could make one wish to "write a check for the difference."

After a few pensive moments, Christiana stated, "Michael, my parents are having a dinner party Saturday evening and have invited you to join us." Michael managed to turn his grimace into a smile, hoping she hadn't noticed.

"Oh, Christiana," he whined. "I don't know. Your father and I have never had a placid relationship. I can't imagine he would want to see me since we are no longer married."

Quickly, she added, "He knows you are staying at Montrachet and *he* was the one who extended the invitation. Michael, my father has never done or said anything that wasn't born of love and concern."

"I realize that is how you see it, Christiana, and I cannot change your mind," he said glumly.

"You may enjoy some of the other guests," she added, curtly.

"Okay, you win. I didn't mean to upset you again."

"Thank you, Michael. I'll update my mother in the morning."

"Christiana, since we are on the subject of parents, my mom and dad have expressed their desire to keep in touch with you and Jennifer."

"Michael, I've been so preoccupied with us and my family, I haven't focused on your family. I adore your parents and it so happens I am heading out to San Francisco next week to meet with Corinthian Properties, one of our companies. I will contact your mother to arrange dinner."

"Terrific!" Michael said, pleased.

Seeing Christiana stifling a yawn as she looked at the mantle clock, Michael took the lead, "Let's call it a night." Making his way to the guest villa, he looked back and watched Christiana ascending the stairway. He still enjoyed watching her fluid and graceful body and, like a sudden punch to the stomach, came the reality—she was no longer his.

At the office the following morning, as she reached for her coffee, her private line started to ring. Leaning over to see the digital read, she noted it stated, Private Call. That would eliminate Jennifer's cell, her mother, Marcia, and Michael. Two additional rings sounded before she lifted the receiver.

"Hello, my American princess," said the caller with a distinct French accent.

"Marc Philippe?"

"*Oui,* or yes," answered Prince Marc Philippe Boulanger, the aristocratic European playboy. Performance was his game—fast cars, fast boats and fast beautiful women. His relationship with Christiana was an exception to the "fast" women. He lived to play and played to live. A passionate polo player, he was slim yet muscular at six feet, with brown eyes and hair that always looked tousled, and a stubble of a beard—he wore a sexy, inviting presence. One of the heirs to the family fortune in shipping and steel, he was only marginally involved in the businesses.

"I come to understand, not by you, I might add, *ma Cheri* is once again, how do you say, single, available?" Before she could speak he added, "Marc Philippe requests dinner with Christiana Lynn Trent, or is it Barrington?"

Reluctantly Christiana responded, "Barrington."

"*Mademoiselle* Barrington, I will be in New York next week for meetings, and desire to see you, my lovely American princess."

Christiana responded, "Marc Philippe, I feel somewhat awkward going out for dinner, being so recently divorced."

"Christiana, we had a relationship before Michael and why not continue it after Michael? Remember our lovemaking?"

She remembered, he was an extraordinary lover—probably the best she ever had. "Okay, I will agree to dinner, but Marc Philippe, we need to take this slow."

"*Oui*. I understand," he said, while at the same time he was whispering sexy little nothings into the phone.

"Tuesday looks free at this point, Marc Philippe."

"Yes … yes, okay. Marc Philippe will be content to start with Tuesday. Now I will confirm my hotel and flight schedules. Until next week, *ma Cheri. Salut!*"

"*Au revoir.*"

The conversation left her in an upbeat mood and she was looking forward to seeing Marc Philippe. They had met while she was living in Europe and had maintained an ongoing friendship during the ensuing years. The only troubling item for Christiana was Marc Philippe's lack of ambition. When it pertained to business, he was a blank slate.

The termination of the call coincided with her father's arrival. In business mode, Jonathan launched quickly into the purpose of his visit. "I want to go over some documents before our afternoon meeting." But he appeared preoccupied and when she questioned him about it, he just brushed her off. Christiana let it slide, knowing with her father, you did not probe.

Their work concentrated on legal and financial information concerning a new interest—the potential acquisition of Sterling Hotels Worldwide. "I want Sterling, and I will get it!" bellowed Jonathan.

"Father," said Christiana, "I've never heard you so vehement." Toying with him she added, "I do believe you mean 'we, Barrington—BHI,' not just you."

Jonathan ignored her remark and continued, saying, "Acquiring Sterling for our portfolio will complete the hospitality empire I started as a young man."

BHI owned Westmoreland Hotels in the United States and Canada, Allemande Properties of Germany, Fleur de Lis Hotels of France and Belgium, Ashford luxury hotels worldwide and GTP hotels and resorts in Asia, the Middle East, South America, India, Africa, Australia, New Zealand and the South Pacific.

"Indeed, Sterling is the pinnacle in the hotel industry, although I didn't know they were considering a sale."

"I received a phone call from the investment banking firm starting to shop the deal. There are not too many serious contenders." Handing her a set of papers, he added, "Take a look at these numbers."

Christiana gasped. "Do you really want to take on an entity with this amount of debt?"

"Read on."

After reviewing the financial documentation, Christiana concluded, "This may well be worth the pursuit, although they want a fortune for the businesses."

"Yes, Christiana, they do and I'm prepared to pay it. With Sterling, BHI becomes the largest worldwide hotel conglomerate. It is finally within our grasp," he stated and sighed.

"Are you sure you want to pursue it at this time?" she again asked.

"It is exactly the time to pursue it. BHI has cash measured in the billions and unused borrowing capacity of an equal if not greater amount."

Finishing their business on an upbeat note, Christiana said goodbye to her father, adding, "Michael, Jennifer and I look forward to your dinner party tomorrow."

Promptly making a hurried exit from the office, Christiana headed to Greenwich for Jennifer's ballet recital. "Oh, honey, you are a beautiful ballerina," exclaimed the proud mother as she placed her briefcase on the foyer table.

The start to a perfect weekend.

CHAPTER 7

THE HOUSE WAS ALL BUT DESERTED Saturday morning as Jennifer and Michael had set out early. Christiana found herself missing the noise and laughter that had filled the house with Michael's visit.

However, by five in the afternoon, when she returned and opened the door, Christiana heard Jennifer's voice and saw them playing a game in the family room.

"Come see what Daddy bought me," exclaimed Jennifer.

"It looks like you two had quite a day," Christiana said, surveying the gifts and discarded food cartons.

"Sorry, Christiana, it was junk food delight and we had a blast," laughed Michael.

"I'm delighted you had a good time but I hope you didn't ruin your appetite for your grandmother's party this evening?"

"It's all icky grown-up food, there's never anything for me to eat. I'll ask Randall to make me something."

"All right, I'm sure that will be fine," replied Christiana, smiling. "Run along and get ready. We need to be there at seven." Turning to face Michael, she added, "I haven't seen Jennifer this happy in quite a while. Thank you."

"We have a great time together and I have missed her immensely. I guess I better shower and get ready to charm your father." He chuckled but noticed Christiana was not smiling.

Politely she instructed, "I'll see you here a little before seven."

Arriving punctually, they greeted Elizabeth and Jonathan. Elizabeth hugged everyone and Christiana watched Michael shake hands with her father. "It's good to see you, Jonathan. I appreciate being included in your dinner party," said Michael stiffly.

"Ah, Michael, Los Angeles agrees with you. You look terrific," Jonathan responded.

The women engaged in a discussion on Jennifer's ballet recital, leaving Michael alone with Jonathan. Patting Michael on the back, Jonathan commanded, "Michael, join me for a drink, since the ladies appear to be lost in their own world."

"Thank you, Jonathan. By the way, do I know any of your guests?"

"Well, let me think. There are the Conrads from New York and the Sherborns from Westport, social friends, really. The husbands are retired and spend most of their days on the golf courses. I'm not at that juncture yet, I'm afraid."

"I thought your passion was boating anyway, Jonathan?"

"Oh, it is, but again, not enough time."

Making their way to the library, Jonathan asked, "Are you still drinking scotch?" Michael nodded in the affirmative. "Then allow me to pull out my private reserve."

Michael found the guests familiar with his work and pleased to make his acquaintance.

"Well, I must admit, Christiana; I had a good time this evening," said Michael as they opened the door to Montrachet.

Michael merely had to co-exist with Jonathan for a few predetermined intervals. The competition was officially over. He had lost the best that was Jonathan—his daughter.

"Would you like a nightcap, Michael?"

"Sure, that sounds good."

The room was aglow; the brandy was warm as they sat comfortably in the large maroon leather wing chairs, gazing at the fire. Being in close proximity to Christiana was still brutally difficult. Reminiscing, Michael commented, "You look so beautiful in this setting. Do you remember our ski holidays? Although the skiing was good, the après de ski was my favorite."

"I particularly enjoyed our weekends at Stowe, but my ultimate ski destination was Gstaad. I will cherish those memories forever. We did have some good times together," she responded. Casting her eyes on the dancing flames in the fireplace, she struggled for an entree into the conversation about Jennifer's European schooling. As Michael finished his brandy, she felt the need to broach the subject before Jennifer inadvertently made reference to it.

"Michael, I'd like to discuss a conversation I had earlier this week with Father concerning schooling for Jennifer in Switzerland. Yes, I deliberately waited until after the dinner party because I didn't want you to have a confrontation with him."

"You have my undivided attention," he responded, as he walked over to the bar to refill his brandy snifter.

"As you know, I studied at St. George's Academy in Switzerland. The education and environment provided the foundation and discipline I have carried throughout my life. My father has been able to secure entrance for Jennifer for the next school term."

Neither spoke for what seemed like an eternity as Christiana reflected upon her earlier years. Finally, Michael blurted, "What did he do, pay for a new building to be dedicated in his honor?" At a scowl from Christiana, he added, "Sorry, I couldn't resist."

Reaching for the academy brochure and catalogue, she handed both to Michael. "Please keep an open mind and look over these materials to familiarize yourself with the school and its curriculum."

"Interesting how you have already obtained all this information," he noted unhappily.

"The Headmaster came by Montrachet earlier this week with Father."

"Really, was I going to be considered a part of this?"

"Yes, Michael, of course, no decision has been made."

"Are you finished, Christiana, because I can't listen to any more of your father's manipulation. Jennifer is *our* daughter and we both have the right and responsibility to raise her *as we see fit*. It's hard enough having her three thousand miles away. I sure don't want to add to that distance. Did anyone consider what this would do to Jennifer?"

"Jennifer warmed a little when she spoke to Mr. Stedman—but I honestly don't think she fully comprehended the scope of this."

"Christiana, your mother took an apartment near the school so she had the opportunity to see you at all permissible times; how could you arrange that on your schedule?"

"Yes, you are right, she did. I would not be able to handle the situation in the same manner. Please understand, my father only wants what is best for our daughter and views this as basic preparation for her eventual role at Barrington."

"Christiana, Jennifer is not *you!* She does not have an overwhelming desire to rush into Barrington and pay more attention to that eventuality than her childhood. God forbid if Jennifer doesn't want anything to do with Barrington. What would the precious Barrington dynasty say to that?" Michael was combative and relentless with his attacks.

"What do you mean? I am a product of that fine education and look what I have achieved."

"Christiana, I love you, and yes, you have achieved greatness in certain aspects of your life. But unfortunately, the controlling dominance of your father will haunt you forever and prevent you from total self-actualization."

Sidestepping his last biting remark, she offered, "Had you allowed me to finish, you would know I stood my ground and said Jennifer would not be sent to boarding school in Europe."

"And what did your dear father say?"

"I gave you the salient points, why the interrogation?" she snapped.

"Since you were ambushed by the Headmaster and your father when you arrived home that evening, it's hard to understand how you emphatically stood your ground."

"Surely you can understand the meeting was scheduled and could not have been cancelled at that late hour?"

"It provided another opportunity to manipulate you and Jennifer. Now that's the Jonathan I know so well," smirked Michael.

"The meeting had already been set up!"

"And we both know meetings are cancelled, postponed or rearranged all the time—and sometimes with much less advance notice. In this instance, I would venture a guess that a personal invitation to come to Greenwich was extended to Mr. Stedman on Jonathan's tab and Jennifer was the only potential candidate he was seeing on this junket."

"Okay, you are probably correct; I didn't gather the full details."

"What was his reaction? *Come on, tell me!* It's not like Jonathan to accept defeat so easily," Michael added with a mischievous grin.

Christiana hung her head and quietly replied, "He told me I was being selfish."

"Coming from the most selfish of *all* human beings, take that as a compliment."

"Oh, Michael, I don't think like you. Jennifer is not going away to school, she will stay here at Montrachet and there is nothing more to say. Now if you don't mind, I want to retire for the evening," she said with a strained voice.

"Go on upstairs and I will take care of the fireplace. Will I see you in the morning? I need to leave by ten as I have a lunch meeting before I head off to Kennedy."

"I'll bring Jennifer home from my parents' at nine, so that you'll see her before you leave." As she started to ascend the mahogany curved staircase, she looked back at Michael and said, "It meant very much to have you present this evening. Thank you."

"It was my pleasure and I enjoyed myself. Pleasant dreams."

After Michael's departure, she and Jennifer went out to lunch. Even a simple outing was a logistical stretch with bodyguards and the requisite measures taken for safety, but they both were used to the drill.

Montrachet seemed empty; Michael was already missed.

CHAPTER 8

"I DON'T FEEL WELL," moaned Jennifer as she slipped into her mother's bed, stirring Christiana to consciousness. She gently slid her arms around her daughter and tried to coax her back to sleep. But Jennifer whined, "My head and tummy hurt."

Pulling a silk robe around her shoulders, Christiana did a mother's mental checklist of children's symptoms with no alarming results.

"Daddy bought me some candy and I ate a lot before bed. I got a tummy ache."

"We will discuss the candy later, but for now, let's try to get some sleep."

The morning dawned gray and damp and it matched Christiana's somber mood from her fitful night. Jennifer's stomach ailment was gone but she was irritable and wanted to know when Michael would be back.

As she readied to leave for the office, her security team greeted her in the foyer.

Christiana was to be the spokesperson for Jewels *by Barrington* and due to her increased public exposure, she'd requested additional protection. Several fashion layouts were to be in discussion and in the works by the end of the long day. As Christiana was preparing to leave, her publicist called. "I'm checking to see if you are still hearing from the world's most eligible bachelors," asked Peggy.

"I have taken calls and responded to emails but kindly turned down the invitations. The timing just isn't right—but it may become so at some point."

"Good! I can't imagine the beautiful and talented Christiana Lynn Barrington sans a fabulous man for the rest of her life."

"Thanks for checking on me. Have you had any feedback from the interview with the *International Jewelry Magazine?*"

"Yes, they wish to do another story with you and Jonathan; of course, dripping in jewels, with some shots in the Fifth Avenue store."

Jonathan was a mile high over the Atlantic heading once again to Europe and Christiana would now miss having dinner with her daughter. Jennifer was playing in the bathtub when Christiana finally arrived home.

"Would you like me to leave, Ms. Barrington?"

"Thank you, Marcia, I'd like to spend some time with her since it's almost her bedtime."

Jennifer looked up as her mother entered the bathroom and said, "Grandfather called and wants to take me to New York and spend the whole day. He wants you to call him and tell him what time I can leave on Saturday."

"Grandfather is en route to London, so I will wait and contact him tomorrow," answered Christiana. "Come, Jennifer, it is time to get out of the tub and get ready for bed. You have school tomorrow," she added.

CHAPTER 9

HANDLING THE BULK OF THE corporate business due to Jonathan's absence, she had a frustrating day and barely arrived in time for her dinner with Marc Philippe. With not much time to spare, she untied her hair and let it fall gracefully around her shoulders. The emerald drop earrings coupled with the diamond and emerald necklace looked stunning with the low-cut cocktail dress, and she was pleased with her transformation.

Heads turned as the stunning couple was escorted to their table. "It is fantastic to see you, Christiana," said Marc Philippe as he leaned over to kiss her cheek.

Noticing Christiana's bodyguard, Marc Philippe laughed, saying, "Over in the far corner, sipping tonic water, is Robiere, my protector. We should give them a break; get them a table together and a good steak dinner."

"An excellent idea, but it isn't protocol—and we both know the Boulanger and Barrington families uphold protocol at all costs," answered Christiana.

"I know where we can go to escape the watchful eyes of our security teams," he said wistfully, with a lingering look.

"A tempting offer, my dear prince, but you are not going to get me into bed this evening."

"You cannot blame a royal for trying, my princess. And the night is not over."

Blushing, she navigated the conversation back to safer ground. "Marc Philippe, what brings you to New York?"

"I am officially working, my love," he said sans enthusiasm. "My father has given me operational responsibilities for a new joint venture."

Christiana chided, "I wondered what happened to your perennial tan."

"The only thing I haven't forsaken is race car driving but my father said he was tired of supporting my hobby."

"I have seen you race and you scared me half to death."

"Oh *Cheri,* you need to be more adventurous. You only live once."

Settling in with a rare bottle of wine, they chatted as old and dear friends. "I have taken on additional responsibilities and projects at BHI due to Jonathan's involvement in the European operations. I'm afraid I have a mother's guilt." Continuing, as she saw an email arrive, Christiana stated, "See what I mean? He is working even at this hour in Europe." *And he sees to it I am also thinking Barrington twenty-four hours a day,* she thought.

"Did Jonathan tell you I ran into him in a restaurant in Frankfurt? We spoke for a few minutes but I had to dash to an appointment. The man he was dining with reminded me of a younger version of Jonathan Robert Barrington, how amusing," he laughed. "He was handsome—European—but with an American attitude. I've seen his face somewhere."

The statement hung and Christiana's smile disappeared. She brushed aside the comment with, "My father has friends and business associates throughout the world."

Marc Philippe's European suit hung faultlessly on his well-defined body. His perfectly manicured hands gently clasped Christiana's as he gazed affectionately into her eyes. Their conversation, along with the meal, proceeded through its normal course—where Marc Philippe had been racing, which royal parties he had jetted off to, and then suddenly he flashed off like a light. Sitting quietly, collecting his thoughts, he finally announced, "I want to talk about business."

Christiana sat upright, startled, and noting his serious demeanor, she stated, "With pleasure."

"My father has given me an ultimatum, either I become actively engaged in the family businesses or I will lose my inheritance. He's convinced I would otherwise be a playboy, sorry, Christiana, forever. I'm finishing my MBA program and am working non-stop at the companies in Germany and France, but I feel totally overwhelmed."

"How may *I* help?"

"Christiana, under your father's tutelage, you were properly groomed to someday take over his worldwide holdings."

"Ah, yes, groomed from the womb," she once again quipped.

"We both have inherited commerce by birth, thus it is up to us to carry on the Boulanger and Barrington dynasties. Alas, sweet princess, I at least have a brother; two men to run the worldwide entities!" As Christiana frowned at the last remark, he quickly added, "Oh, *Cheri,* pardon me for that silly statement. You are more than capable of running the Barrington conglomerate. I am not a sexist, only sexy."

"No offense taken, Marc Philippe. In jest I have said to Jonathan, 'I am the son of my father.' As I was growing up, I wished I had a brother. All I wanted was marriage and family; but I have accepted the sad truth—my marriage is and invariably has been to Barrington."

"Ah, Christiana, you will have the opportunity to marry again. You are young and beautiful and when you are ready, I'm sure it will happen."

"Sorry for the digression. Let's talk about your business needs." She shuttered the previous conversation and would venture into it no further. He took her cue and said, "Christiana, you have a world-class reputation in business and finance and were driven to succeed. I'm totally dependent on my father's resources and until recently, I thought I deserved it, and approached life without a care."

"My father constructed my life to fit neatly within the necessary framework for BHI. I was not offered options since this indoctrination started at such a young age; I really didn't know anything else and stayed singularly focused on Barrington. Marc Philippe, you did not receive that same dictum from your father."

"Until now," interjected Marc Philippe. "My father is looking at a company in New Jersey and I would be expected to run it if we acquire the business. Although small, it provides a vital product to our manufacturing units in Frankfurt and Hamburg."

"Confidentiality precludes me from viewing any financial and other proprietary company information. You will need to supply me with materials that fall out of that realm. I will give you pointers by reviewing public records, 10k, the Annual Report, etc."

Marc Philippe smiled and replied, "That would be most helpful, Christiana." He then whispered, "Let's go to your apartment. I want to make love to you." It was all she could do to contain him during the ride back to her place.

"I told you I wasn't going to have sex with you this evening. I promised myself," said Christiana in a pleasant, albeit alcohol-induced, voice.

"Yes … yes, I heard the same thing before that second glass of wine. But your body movements said otherwise, my love, so relax. Marc Philippe is here to please. I will make you remember the old times, and I promise you will sleep like a baby."

In one long fluid motion he swept her up and carried her to the bedroom. Their love-making was magical and he never failed to satisfy. Words of commitment they could never substantiate were never uttered during the heat of passion. They both knew the boundaries of their relationship, and accepted the constraints.

"You were fantastic tonight, *ma Cheri!* You were like a tigress; where does this come from?"

Panting, Christiana rolled over and responded, "I really wanted you. I haven't had sex since my separation."

Marc Philippe took her in his arms and whispered, "Well, let me not disappoint," as they tangled their bodies for another round of passion.

When Christiana awakened the next morning, she saw Marc Philippe's signature rose lying on the pillow. The note read simply, "Another glorious night, my love."

She was more energized than she had been in months. Marc Philippe was the reason. He proved a wonderful diversion to the stresses of work and readjustment to single life. The tabloids splashed headlines: *The Newest Power Couple. Will Christiana Barrington marry the Prince? American Princess meets her European Prince.*

"You have certainly made a quick change from your life of solitary confinement, Christiana," Peggy observed as the business day began, prompted by Christiana's call.

"I saw one of the tabloids on my way into the office. What a pile of rubbish. Marc Philippe and I are old friends and he was in New York on business," she replied in a monotone.

"Sorry, Peggy, I need to cut this short," she said as she saw Jonathan walking into her office. "But please let me know if there is more inane media coverage."

"Good morning, Christiana," said Jonathan as he strolled in. "We need to discuss our pending offer for Sterling Hotels Worldwide." Hastily he added, "Apparently, Sterling has another suitor and I will not lose this unless it is by my own choosing. Find out where Marshall is on the financial review."

"Yes, Father. I will brief Marshall. Do you really believe Sterling has another viable offer?"

"We must proceed as if there is another serious contender until we know otherwise," commented Jonathan.

"Yes, of course, that is prudent. Father, on another note, Jennifer mentioned you wish to bring her to the City on Saturday. I've checked with Marcia and she doesn't have lessons this Saturday morning. So let me know what time she should be ready for you to pick her up."

"I'll be at Montrachet at nine. Thanks, Christiana."

Several days later ...

Arriving at the appointed time, and if his appearance in his tailored suit with Italian leather briefcase were any indication, Marc Philippe was poised for a serious business meeting. "*Ciao*, Christiana," he said, kissing her on both cheeks.

"Hello, Marc Philippe. I've set up my conference room for our meeting."

"I'm grateful we are able to review these files before my meeting tomorrow." With a pensive look, he remarked, "I cannot fail—my whole future is riding on this."

"Then let's get down to business."

When they had finished Christiana concluded, "You are knowledgeable on the company's profile, stock performance, shareholder value, product line and competition in the marketplace. Let me coach you on what to say and what to look for at the meeting."

By the time they parted, Marc Philippe exuded a sense of self-confidence and business acumen.

As Christiana arrived home for the evening, Michael surprised her with news of another trip to New York. Cautiously, she asked, "Will you stay with us at Montrachet?"

"That would be wonderful, I would rather drive to Manhattan and be able to see Jennifer on a daily basis."

Jennifer was thrilled her father would be back for another visit. Elizabeth was visiting her granddaughter and Christiana invited her to join them for dinner. The simple pleasures of the evening were upon them and the "ladies" all lingered over dinner discussing fashion, celebrities and other "girly" topics.

"I understand Jennifer and your father viewed a new children's exhibit in Manhattan then spent a fair amount of time at BHI," said Elizabeth.

"Jennifer enjoyed the exhibit although I didn't realize they stopped by the offices. I'm sure Father needed to retrieve some files or check on something, we both know his unbridled passion for Barrington."

"I'm sure that was the reason," answered Elizabeth, not seeming totally convinced. "Unbridled passion; yes, he certainly lives and breathes Barrington," she added, kissing her daughter goodnight.

CHAPTER 10

MICHAEL HAD A SHORT BUSINESS stay in New York, which permitted a quiet family dinner at Montrachet, reminiscent of the good times in their marriage.

"What brings you back to New York this time, Michael?"

"Several colleagues have written a play and they need a producer. I've read the script and it could be a major theatrical hit. I'll know more in the coming days."

"That sounds wonderful!"

"Thank you. And I'm grateful for your hospitality. I enjoy being around Jennifer and miss her so much. Montrachet is a special place."

"She's started modern dance and singing lessons and seems to be quite talented." Gazing at Michael, she added, "She takes after her father."

He smiled but turned serious with his next statement, "Listen, Christiana, I need to tell you something." After hesitating momentarily, he announced, "I've recently started seeing someone."

Reaching for words that would not come, she mumbled, *"Oh."* Feeling a shiver, she draped her sweater over her shoulders, allowing for a moment to regain her composure. "Please tell me about her," she said, forcing interest.

"Her name is Rachel Morgan and she's a young actress. We've only been out a couple of times but I wanted to let you know before you see us in one of the tabloids."

"Michael, we are divorced and many women will be focusing on you. I'm happy for you," she said, feigning a smile.

"Thanks, Christiana, I needed to reconfirm. Now, I have seen the tabloid headlines linking you with the prince."

"Marc Philippe and I have been friends for many years and his visits are business-oriented. Don't laugh, Michael; he is actively involved in his family business." Sipping his brandy, Michael waited for more. "But as far as a serious relationship, I … I haven't even thought about seeing anyone."

"You are too young and vibrant to be totally devoured by Barrington," Michael pointed out. "Use our relationship as the example of what not to do in the future. You need an enriching personal life, Christiana. God knows, I believe you wanted that with our marriage."

"Please, Michael, I don't have the energy to go down that path this evening," she said, sighing.

"You're right, sorry. I have an early flight back to LA so I probably won't see you in the morning. We'll talk when I get home," concluded Michael.

A couple of days later, as Christiana was staring in the mirror, the thoughts came … *Michael has moved on with his life. I need to move on emotionally and socially with my life as well.* Christiana went for a run to clear her mind. As she was untying her tennis shoes after her workout, the bedroom door opened. Jennifer came over and sat next to her mother on the settee. "I don't want to go away to school even though I told that man I was interested. I don't want to be far away from you and Daddy."

Embracing her daughter, Christiana assured her, "Sweetheart, you are staying here in Greenwich. Your father and I couldn't bear to have you that far from us."

"Do you promise?"

"I promise," answered Christiana, stroking her daughter's hair. "Why are you worried about this again?" *As if she had to ask—why would Father try to burden his granddaughter with ideas about being sent away to school?*

"Grandfather told me how much fun you had in Switzerland and that the school was the best in the world and it helped you with your job. He also said I have so much to learn to be able to work at Barrington."

"That's fine, sweetheart, but there is plenty of time to learn about Barrington."

"May I tell you something without you getting angry?"

Startled, Christiana answered, "Of course, you can tell me anything."

"I'm not sure I want to work at Barrington. I think I would like to be a doctor or maybe a veterinarian because I love animals so much."

"You have my blessings to pursue any career you desire."

"Thank you, but please don't tell Grandfather."

Her cell phone rang en route to Manhattan and she saw it was Michael's number. As he was not an early riser, Christiana quickly answered. "Michael, what's wrong?"

"Morning, Christiana, I'm fine but I spoke with my sister Veronica last night and I'm worried about her."

"What's the matter with Veronica?"

"Robert left her for another woman. She's devastated. Christiana, you have always been close with Veronica. Would you mind calling her to cheer her up?"

"I will call her this morning, Michael. I may have an idea that could benefit her. My car is pulling up in front of my office so I need to end our conversation. *Ciao.*" Formulating her thoughts as she rode the elevator to the executive floor, she figured her first call should be to Marcia, her current nanny.

"Marcia, I know it's your intent to finish school and move to the West Coast to start your nursing career. Michael's sister has had a change in her personal situation and she has a background in teaching. I would like to ask her if she would be interested in taking care of Jennifer, at which point you could expedite your studies. In turn, I will fund the remainder of your tuition along with a twelve-month separation salary if and when she would assume your position."

"Wow, I really don't know what to say besides thank you."

"You're welcome, Marcia; I will contact Veronica and keep you apprised."

Veronica apparently had been crying when she picked up the phone. "It's Christiana. I spoke with Michael and he told me the news. Is there anything I can do?"

"Oh Christiana, I'm fine. I mean … I'm better. It was just such a shock. This apartment is too expensive and a constant reminder of Robert. I'm not sure what I'm going to do. Who would have thought we would both be unattached at the same time?"

Intentionally ignoring the last comment, Christiana fell silent and Veronica sought to undo her blunder. "Christiana, my last statement did not come out the way I intended. I'm sorry; please tell me, how you are doing after the divorce?"

"I'm doing better, but it does take time. Thankfully, Michael remains a continuing presence in Jennifer's life. Enough about me; I may have an idea for both of us. Would you consider coming to live with us at Montrachet and taking on the child care for Jennifer? Her nanny is in school and will be leaving upon graduation."

"I am overwhelmed. I love you both but certainly don't want to be a burden."

"Veronica, have I offended you?"

"Heavens no, I am very touched by your generous offer. But I have so many decisions to make. When do you need an answer?"

"Veronica, I love you like a sister. Just tell me what would work for you."

"Okay. This may just be the fresh start I need. Yes, yes, I will come to Greenwich, but I must wait until the end of the school term."

"Wonderful! I understand."

"There is one small matter I hesitate to bring up, but would you pay me a little salary to help me get by?" Veronica held her breath.

"Veronica, my apologies, I should have mentioned this at the beginning of our discussion. The salary would be ninety-thousand per year plus full benefits, relocation expenses, and a car," Christiana assured her.

"That is most generous, Christiana. Would you mind if I tell Michael?"

"I know you will be wonderful with Jennifer and by all means, please tell Michael," Christiana said, concluding their conversation as Jonathan stepped into her office.

"Hello, Christiana," said Jonathan. "You look happy this morning." She then told him about the arrangement with Veronica. "She will be great with Jennifer, and you have always been close with Veronica."

"I think so, too. And yes, I adore Veronica," beamed Christiana.

Turning their attention to the reason for his visit, Jonathan began, "I need your help on these sales figures for Jewels *by Barrington*. Here, examine these reports. Sales and revenue are up for all locations except Phoenix. I've got to jump to a meeting. Do you have time to stop by my office before three to discuss Jewels along with a couple of other items? I'm heading to London in a couple of days."

Arriving at her father's office for the meeting, she found him chatting on the phone and he motioned for her to take a seat. He was conversing with William T. Marsh, a longtime business cohort. "Wonderful. I will see you tomorrow."

"Are you yachting tomorrow, Father?"

"No, William has two buildings on the West Side that no longer fit his portfolio of commercial investments. I told him about our beauty and skin care company and the need for more desirable space. Would you like to come along with me to see his buildings?"

"Yes, I would like that. Now the other business we should discuss before your trip to Europe concerns a new media campaign for Magnifique. Father, we haven't fully assimilated the last two acquisitions and you are out trying to win an even bigger prize," *and more work for me,* "with Sterling."

"I am a master at acquiring good companies and making them more profitable for the shareholders," said Jonathan in his cocky voice without a bit of hesitation or modesty. Switching thoughts, he continued, "Christiana, I'd love to see you as spokesperson for Magnifique. If we are to take on the beauty industry, BHI needs its best weapon—the epitome of beauty—Christiana Lynn Barrington."

"Father, our acquisition involved retention of the current management. Don't you think the PR and Advertising Departments should also be consulted in this decision?"

"Christiana, the endorsement has come directly from the company. Enough said, let's review some of the competitive advertisements." They critiqued their rivals' current TV spots along with print ads in *Vogue*, *Bazaar* and *Elle*. Then they studied the print advertising for Magnifique.

Deliberate in her response, Christiana said, "I need to be involved with a total overhaul before we sweep into a major media blitz." She added, "Barrington paid a premium for Magnifique and we need to gain market share *tout de suite*."

"Will you be the spokesperson?"

Christiana wanted to answer, *Father, do I have a choice when you have set the course,* but instead replied, "Absolutely, I will relish trouncing the competition when we are finished redesigning this company."

"Do whatever it takes, Christiana, you're in charge."

Focusing on the immediate, Christiana answered, "I've scheduled meetings with Allison Faulkner, President and CEO, and several Vice Presidents. I plan to analyze the products, review the sales data, reformulate a strategic business plan, and visit the offices and manufacturing plants in the next several weeks."

"Great, it sounds like we are moving in the right direction. Hopefully, the Sterling deal will show progress; I can't wait to take control and remove pompous Blake Eagleson from his throne as chairman," stated Jonathan decisively.

"Father, the other offer may be as appealing and your animosity with Blake is legendary, he may try to torpedo the Barrington deal."

"I have a meeting set up with Eagleson next week in Paris and in the end the greed factor will certainly win," retorted Jonathan.

Unable to contain her excitement, Veronica contacted her brother.

"Veronica, how are you?" Michael answered.

"Christiana called this morning and asked if I would be interested in being Jennifer's new nanny and live with them at Montrachet. What do you think of the idea? Please tell me you didn't orchestrate this?" Veronica was nonstop with her questions as Michael listened.

"No, I had nothing to do with this but I must say I'm excited."

"Michael, I do have a serious question, however. Since you and Christiana are divorced, will you find it awkward for me to be her nanny?"

Michael laughed as he answered, "You've got to be kidding! We'll be able to spend time together, which we haven't done in years."

Hours later, Christiana smiled as she read Michael's email thanking her for helping his sister. Settling into a fragrant lavender bath, she had just started to relax when the telephone pierced her solitude. Although she thought of letting it go to voice mail, she answered instead, "Hello, Father."

Thankfully, Jonathan was to the point. "Christiana, William needs to push the meeting up to nine tomorrow. Would you like to drive in together? I'll be by at seven."

"I'll see you at seven. Goodnight, Father." With her mood broken, she stepped from the tub and reached for a towel. Glancing at the mirror, she pondered, *Maybe I should accept a couple of dinner invitations. There's the Texas oilman, a plastics multi-millionaire, a young retired billionaire ...* but decided no conclusion was the best course, walked into the bedroom, slipped on her nightgown and went to bed.

Following their morning meeting, standing on the sidewalk facing William's commercial buildings, Jonathan asked, "Can you envision Magnifique in this space?"

"Absolutely! I asked William for the building plans and will go over them with Charley Taylor, our CEO of Corinthian Properties."

Back at Corporate, while she was coordinating her trip to the West Coast, she arranged for dinner in San Francisco with Michael's parents.

CHAPTER 11 ... The following week

LLOYD TRENT ROSE TO GREET Christiana as she approached the table. "It's delightful to see you, Christiana," said Lloyd, and Nancy echoed his sentiments.

"Thank you, I'm happy to see both of you. I have a little something for you." Christiana smiled, laying a photograph album and framed picture of Jennifer on the table.

"Our little Jennifer is growing up," murmured Nancy.

With the discussion focused on Jennifer, Nancy added, "We've heard wonderful news from Veronica and believe the move to Greenwich will put her life back on track. We're so grateful to you, Christiana."

"I think we're the fortunate ones. Jennifer and I adore Veronica."

Christiana was pleased to spend time with Michael's parents and vowed to return to the Bay Area soon for another visit, bringing Jennifer with her on the trip.

Corinthian Properties owned two distinguished buildings in the financial district of San Francisco. As they were fully leased with major anchor tenants, Christiana was anxious to see the newly completed renovations and meet with the Corinthian staff. However, her meeting with Charley Taylor was cancelled as she was called back unexpectedly to Los Angeles.

Without thinking, Christiana speed-dialed Michael's cell phone. Picking up on the first ring, he began with, "Hi, Christiana, my parents enjoyed having dinner with you."

"Michael, it was great to see your parents. On another subject, I may be in LA this afternoon and wondered if you were free for dinner this evening?"

"Christiana, I'm sorry. Rachel and I have a première; otherwise I would have loved to see you on my turf."

"I understand it is short notice." On that note, the call ended.

With a subsequent telephone call, she appended her travel plans and would now meet Charley Taylor in Denver tomorrow. Curling up on the sofa in the Presidential Suite of the Barrington hotel, she ordered room service and started to read the entertainment magazines. There they were, a perfect Hollywood couple, Rachel Morgan and Michael Trent seen leaving a trendy restaurant in Beverly Hills and attending a screening in Hollywood.

As she was preparing to board her flight for New York the next day, following a productive meeting in Denver, Michael called. "Are you in San Francisco or LA? Let me take you to dinner this evening."

"After our conversation, I shifted my meeting to Denver and met with the CEO today. I'm waiting to take off for Teterboro."

"Ah, Christiana, it's always Barrington first and foremost, but I'll cut you some slack since you're in Denver."

"Michael, that's not fair; I called you yesterday and you had an engagement. In hindsight, I'm glad you had plans since I had to cancel the trip."

Oblivious to her statement, Michael said, "So I can't convince you to change your flight plan? You are flying one of Barrington's corporate jets, aren't you?"

"No and yes," she replied and laughed. "No, I cannot fly to LA, and yes, I'm on one of our planes."

"Well, it was worth a shot. Have a good trip, Christiana. I've got to run to a meeting. I'll call you soon with the schedule of my next visit."

Once comfortably airborne, she quickly set to work through emails downloaded prior to departure. *Father wants to up the ante again for Sterling and has called an emergency board meeting. He will stop at nothing to get this company. It's good that he's stateside and wants an early morning meeting. I wonder how his meeting went with Blake Eagleson.* Reading emails regarding Sterling for the past several days, she noted BHI staff had prepared documentation for the hurriedly called meeting.

Finishing up with Sterling, she turned her attention to Magnifique. Christiana inherited an unhappy house and she might be facing a number of resignations in the near term if circumstances did not change. The course was crystallizing regarding Allison's tenure though she was reluctant to make a hasty decision.

Back in New York ...

Christiana and James were involved with the series of meetings at Magnifique. James had drawn a number of conclusions he shared with Christiana. "She's a tyrant. Allison is handing me demands; one would think Magnifique was the acquiring company, instead of BHI. While her last two employers raved about her creativity, her disposition and temperamental nature were overriding obstacles to her longevity. In addition, it's been rumored Jonathan may have a presence here."

Christiana laughed, "I have a swift answer for the second issue. Please inform the staff I will be the primary contact from Barrington. Now what to do about Allison will require more mind share," Christiana noted.

"I have been doing that, Christiana, but the thinking is 'like father like daughter.' It is going to take working with you to alter the misconceptions. However, I think part of the staff concerns center around Allison. She has not done much consensus building."

"BHI has been fortunate with other acquisitions, as the management teams have been outstanding. At Magnifique, it's a culture of status quo—creativity is at a standstill; the offices are unattractive and unwelcoming. Surprising for a company in the beauty business," mused Christiana. "Has Allison been working on the business plan?"

James sighed. "She informed me she is far too busy to get to it for several months. Christiana, she believes she is irreplaceable since Barrington is new to the beauty business. Remember, her father was the lead investor in the company."

"Lou Faulkner and my father have never seen eye-to-eye and have crossed swords on other business enterprises over the years. But we did get this without having to sign her with a multi-year contract."

"We both can champion Jonathan on that one. Lou realized he had a prime deal and was not about to have it crater at the eleventh hour," chuckled James.

"Yes, you are probably correct, but it does bring up the issue of what to do with Allison long-term."

"I think she'll have to go before we lose valuable staff."

"I'm also resigned to that conclusion."

As they pulled up in front of Magnifique, Christiana added, "We know what has to be done."

The diamonds on her Patek Philippe watch glistened, reflecting the sunlight streaming in from the window, as Christiana checked the time. They had been meeting for several hours. "Please excuse me; I need to make a telephone call. Allison, may I use the vacant office across the hall?"

"Five-forty-five should work. It will still be light enough to get a good view of the space. I'm bringing James Langston, our COO, with me. Thank you." Their meeting with Allison had a hard stop at five to allow the time needed to get through the cross-town traffic.

Settling into the car, James remarked, "Allison is going to balk at moving the offices, operations and manufacturing unit. I think we'll go ahead with the consultant for the business plan and start to seek her replacement."

"We are leasing space in a C-rated building and Legal indicated the lease obstacles will not be imposing. I'll withhold judgment until you look at these buildings. And James, please start a search immediately for Allison's replacement."

"You got it," he answered and averted further conversation as he turned his attention to studying the buildings.

"It's that one," pointed Christiana. "We also have the opportunity to purchase the building next door, for the manufacturing unit. Ah … there's William waiting in the vestibule."

Introductions aside, William escorted them to the top floor and after answering questions said, "Christiana, you are familiar with the property and unless you need me, I'll leave so you and James have the privacy to determine if the building fits your needs."

Christiana and James found themselves planning to reassemble Magnifique in these new surroundings with questions like, "What do you think of this?" "Have you seen the view from this direction over the Hudson to Jersey?" "This floor would make posh executive suites."

Reaching the second floor, they knocked on William's office. "Well, what do you think?" he asked as he sat back in his leather swivel chair.

Christiana deferred to James for comment. "I like it. I think it would suit our purposes quite nicely, William. Let's see the other building."

Completing their tour, James commented to Christiana, "This has been the highlight of my day. The two buildings provide ample space for the current business as well as future expansion. Thanks for setting this up with William."

CHAPTER 12 ... the business of Barrington

"I HAVE GRANT, MAX AND YOU in my camp. Roger will come around to our side. He's just exercising his fiduciary responsibility. I *will* get Sterling," snarled Jonathan.

"Father, I'm not in your camp; furthermore, I do not intend to vote to increase the initial offer for Sterling. Thus, you need Roger if you think you can win this one."

Jonathan backed off from further confrontation with his daughter and took leave to answer his cell. "Six months of painstakingly difficult negotiations, analysis and due diligence brought us to this juncture," said Jonathan on his cell phone. "Ah, the suits are coming around the corner, I've got to go."

Responding to the last comment from the caller, Jonathan confidently retorted, "Win this one? I have no doubts whatsoever."

Christiana approached as he terminated the call and in a show of unison he looked over to her and smiled, announcing, "Let's go buy a company."

Max Spencer from Sydney was holding on the line and the ring from London added Grant Pemberton to the conference call, when Jonathan breezed through the door to sit at the head of the table as CEO and Chairman of the Board of Barrington Holdings International. Jonathan Robert Barrington was one of those who define their space. Today he made no attempt to hide the truth that he was going to make his mark and obtain the results he was after.

"This isn't the time to pay a premium for this hotel entity. The BHI offer was and remains a highly attractive package," said Roger, one of the directors.

"I concur with Roger," responded another board member.

"With all said, ladies and gentlemen, look at the cash the entity is throwing off; let alone the equity play, which may be worth the trouble," said Grant Pemberton.

"Pemberton has a valid point with the equity," responded Roger.

"But they are playing to a seventy-five to eighty percent occupancy rate and given the changes in the economy, that percentage will decrease. I've been in the hospitality industry for most of my life," added Regina Wells.

"Jonathan, you met with Blake Eagleson. What's it going to take to get this done?" Max posed the question and several others echoed their sentiment and interest.

"Eagleson is one greedy son of a bitch. Sorry, ladies," extolled Jonathan. This was met with laughter and a roar from the Aussie, who added, "Are you sure you are not talking about yourself, Jonathan?"

Jonathan grinned at the comparison. "Okay, I admit, I want to beat him at his own game. The good news is he wants out and hopes to retire."

"It isn't a sound business decision for BHI to increase the offer because we appear to be in competition with Langley Properties and Holdings," added a director.

Promptly Regina responded, "Frankly, it's hard to believe LPH, as they are referred to, has enough financial clout to be our primary competition."

Christiana turned to Jonathan and asked, "Are you sure this is a legitimate bid?"

"It appears to be a legitimate offer. However, I can tell you Eagleson would prefer the acquiring company be Barrington and admitted to such when we met recently in Paris."

"BHI is the most financially sound company and this is an incredible deal for Blake," Regina responded.

"Apparently, Langley isn't going away and BHI could run the risk of losing Sterling completely," Jonathan stated emphatically.

"I think LPH will cave, Jonathan," Regina responded. "This acquisition would be a major stretch for them, even with private equity backing. They still need major bank financing. I don't think they can get it."

Christiana added, "I've reviewed all the financial data including the 10K on Langley, and I don't think they stand a chance at acquiring Sterling."

"Here is my take: Langley is too small. Their last attempt at an acquisition was 'Motor-the-Way Inns' and it was such a disaster they ended up spinning it off after one year. The next path was construction of new properties. Again, good attempt, lousy execution. The stock rating is still considered poor. So I would not be in favor of increasing the purchase price," Regina informed them.

"I agree with Regina," echoed Roger.

With no persuasive evidence from either the financial or legal information, the Board determined to leave their offer as previously submitted.

"I've a thought that might seal this deal for Barrington rather expeditiously. Although this is an operational and management issue, I believe it cuts to the heart of the issue," announced Regina. "Jonathan, you indicated Blake wants to run with the cash into retirement."

Jonathan took a moment before responding, "I don't remember his precise words; however, it is evident Blake and I could never work together."

Christiana took the floor with, "Why is it so evident, Father? He could continue to run Sterling and, in fact, he would be the answer to running our entire hotel conglomerate."

"It would never work," snapped Jonathan. "Anyway, I know he wants a clean break—that's why he's selling."

"Do not be hasty, Jonathan," interrupted Regina. "How much do you really know about Blake Eagleson?"

"What are you driving at?" Jonathan demanded.

"Blake's wife is dying of colon cancer and has only months to live. As tragic as that is, the situation is even worse. Their only son died at fifteen from a broken neck suffered in a high school football game as Blake and his wife watched from the bleachers. Let us say those are the salient points. The son's tragedy was front page news due to Blake's position, and he has been open about his wife's condition since it's affected his business and social commitments for years."

As the Board listened intently, Regina continued. "Work became, and remains, Blake's total redemption. I know what you are going to ask, Jonathan. Why sell? A good businessman knows when the time is right and Blake Eagleson is a keen businessman."

"Considering Regina's details, Blake might be exploring Langley to solidify a place with the combined entity," said Christiana.

Jonathan studied Christiana and for a moment seemed lost in thought.

"Regina, I had no idea of his personal situation. I just never considered an ongoing role for him if we purchased Sterling," said a now subdued Jonathan.

"So Jonathan, if you are hell-bent on wrapping this deal, you might consider less cash up front, additional BHI stock, and a lucrative employment contract for Blake," concluded Regina confidently.

"Is there any further discussion?" Jonathan asked.

"Blake is the marquee name in the hotel and hospitality industry. If we could secure him, it would bring additional value to the purchase of Sterling Hotels Worldwide," said a board member.

A revised offer detailing the cash purchase price and BHI stock allocation was discussed along with an employment contract for Blake Eagleson. A motion was made, seconded and affirmed by vote.

Following adjournment of the meeting, Regina held back and walked out with Christiana, who told her, "I'm stunned at the information you shared with us and could tell it affected my father. You certainly must be close to Blake."

Regina leaned in close to Christiana and whispered, "Please never tell Jonathan but …," her face reddened. "Blake and I had an affair for years. It was very serious. I would have left my husband for Blake. He and I have remained close friends and he has confided in me over the years. So I know the man; he's a workaholic and work has been his salvation. Christiana, Blake knows I sit on the BHI board, but we have never discussed this potential acquisition."

"What about you, Regina?"

"Do you mean as far as my marriage is concerned?"

"Yes."

"I've stayed married, Rob is a wonderful man, but Blake would have—could have been the one. I'll never know."

Curtailing further remarks, hearing footsteps, they turned the corner to find Jonathan, Marshall and David exiting the boardroom.

"Christiana, join us in my conference room. We need to finish the agreement that requires your signature," said Jonathan. Touching Regina's shoulder, he asserted, "Thank you. This is moving expeditiously due to your input."

"You're welcome, Jonathan. Now close the deal."

Christiana strode into Jonathan's conference room where the men were working. "Christiana, review these as I need to take a call from Graham." Jonathan hurriedly slid the documents to his daughter and sprinted to his office.

"What's that about?" Christiana quizzed the staff.

"There is a new wrinkle in the fund management deal with the Saudis. One of the Wall Street guys we hired wasn't adequately coached on proper Saudi etiquette."

"We'll hear about it soon enough. Meanwhile, let's get through this paperwork," Christiana decided.

"How do you think Blake and Jonathan will survive under the same roof?" asked Marshall.

"It's the best way to secure this acquisition and Jonathan was in full agreement," defended Christiana.

"Keep your friends close and your enemies closer," quipped David.

"If you were the lead on this, Christiana, and had Jonathan remain in the background, it may be more palatable," suggested Marshall.

"Blake will be the new CEO of our entire hotel empire," said Christiana. Segueing to her concerns about Magnifique, she lamented, "I wish we had someone like Blake over at Magnifique."

"Having more issues? That Faulkner gal is a real piece of work," exclaimed Marshall, scowling. "I've had several terse conversations with her as of late."

"James and I are coming to the conclusion she will need to be replaced," stated Christiana.

They hadn't noticed Jonathan's entrance but his grimace and clenched jaw told much of the story. "Jonathan, take a look at these papers as they require signatures from you and Christiana. You mentioned Eagleson was expecting our reply prior to their board meeting this week," said David.

"Yes, and Blake and I were to get together and go over the new terms before his board meeting. At this point, I'm going to ask Christiana and David to meet with him on Thursday since the board meeting is scheduled for Friday," said Jonathan.

Looking at her father, Christiana asked, "This is yours from the start; don't you think you should be the one to make it work with Blake?"

"Actually, Christiana, the best way to get this accomplished is to extract myself and allow you to secure it for Barrington," Jonathan replied intently.

"Father, it isn't like you to turn aside at a critical juncture in the negotiation process!"

"Relax, Christiana, I just got off the telephone with Blake and he's pleased to meet with you and David," assured Jonathan.

Once the meeting adjourned, Christiana remarked, "Father, I will do everything in my power to bring us this dazzling acquisition."

"I know you will. Is there anything else, as I promised your mother I would meet her for dinner?"

"Father, your mood changed abruptly when you returned to the meeting. What's really going on with the Saudi transactions?"

Consulting his Franck Muller watch, he replied, "I'll give you the quick version. Graham received a call that indicated a need to shore up relations with the royals due to arrogance and over-stepping of our staff servicing the account in Saudi Arabia."

"What needs to be done?"

"Graham sent over several more-experienced staff with a better understanding of the Saudi culture and business style to replace the moron who dumped us in this quagmire. Graham and I are leaving Friday evening for Riyadh and Jeddah to attend a series of meetings. That's the reason I need you to complete the Sterling deal."

"While this is disheartening, Father, I have the utmost confidence that you and Graham will turn the tide. Don't worry about Sterling."

"I trust you will take care of it, dear." Bounding out the door, he added, "Now I have to tell your mother I'm going to Saudi Arabia."

Heading back to her office, Christiana remembered her personal plans for the upcoming week. *Jennifer and I are flying to Bellagio on Thursday afternoon for some mother-daughter time.* Hoping to still catch David, she phoned his back line. "Hi, Christiana, what did I forget?" David never seemed irked or frazzled and maintained a professional demeanor even at the end of a long grueling day.

"You didn't forget anything, David. I want to reschedule the meeting with Blake."

"Morning would work better for me. Shoot me an email once you confirm. Goodnight, Christiana."

Wasting no time, she called Blake's cell number. Expecting his voice mail, due to the hour, she was surprised when he answered. "Good evening Christiana, I'm looking forward to meeting you. Jonathan is sending in the best at last."

"Mr. Eagleson, I understand that Jonathan mentioned he had an unexpected business trip develop precluding him from personally presenting BHI's proposal."

"Yes, he's off to Saudi Arabia. "I am making arrangements for him and the other gentleman at the Sterling Hotels in both cities. And it's Blake, not Mr. Eagleson. May I call you Christiana?"

"Yes," responded Christiana. "I apologize for the late call but I was hoping to reschedule our meeting from the afternoon to the morning, say ten?"

"Yes, Christiana, I'll move a couple of appointments around and make it work."

"Blake, thank you for accommodating us with the change in time. I believe Jonathan mentioned our Chief Legal Counsel, David Bradford, would be joining me."

"Yes, he did, and Sterling's legal team will be on hand too. I wish you a pleasant evening."

Perfect, she thought, zipping off a confirming email to David.

CHAPTER 13

"WHAT'S AN HEIR APPARENT," questioned Jennifer as Christiana kissed her forehead. On her daughter's computer there it was, an email from Jonathan.

Struggling for the proper response for her daughter, Christiana explained, "An heir apparent is a person groomed to take over either a position or a company. Grandfather was talking about preparing you to take over Barrington when I stop working. I've explained how he mentored me for my role at BHI."

"Yes, but what if I don't want to work at Barrington?" she questioned again. "Grandfather said I have no choice because there is no one else but me. He said you should have had another baby because if it was a boy he could work at Barrington and I could do whatever I wanted when I grew up." With this needless worry and undue pressure placed upon her daughter, Christiana could only counter with hugs, kisses and reassuring support.

Frustrated but unable to directly confront her father, she resorted to conversing with Michael once Jennifer went to bed.

"Hi, Christiana, can you hold a second? Rachel, get the door. Sorry, I'm having a dinner party, mostly Rachel's actor friends."

He muffled the receiver and shouted, "I'll be in shortly; offer your friends something to drink."

"Oh, Michael, I've caught you at a bad time. We can discuss this at a later date."

"It's a perfect time. I can only stand these pompous young actors so long. Let me get my drink and sit outside where I can have some privacy." Returning, he assured her, "You have my undivided attention."

"Michael, I'm not sure how to handle a situation between Jennifer and my father. He's been coaching her and taking her to BHI, trying, as she puts it, to ready her to work at Barrington. This evening, she and I discussed the term 'heir apparent.'"

Michael burst out laughing.

"Which part of this do you find funny, Michael?"

"Jennifer has been telling me this awhile. According to Jonathan, she has no choice but to work at Barrington since you will not be having any more children, especially a boy," said Michael wickedly.

"Her choice of words was different but the message was the same."

"This is too much information for a child to digest; and furthermore, this discussion should have come from you, not Jonathan. I have to chuckle at Jonathan's control factor in the statement that you will not be having any more children. Is that by design or direct order? I know you are looking for guidance and not criticism."

Ignoring the comment about children along with his sarcasm, she responded, "I have no one else to turn to."

"Although I don't condone Jonathan's methods, fundamentally he's correct in his assessment of Jennifer's career path. Imagine, Michael Trent in agreement with Jonathan Barrington. That's a first. But seriously, who else would be in line to run Barrington?"

"While you and Father are correct, I will not push our daughter to make a career choice she does not enthusiastically accept. I did and still do embrace Barrington with my heart and soul."

"Yes, we know you embraced Barrington, but this does not seem to be as simple for Jennifer. It appears she holds the big Barrington world on her small and fragile shoulders. There is no one else but her since you had no siblings and, unfortunately for both of us, she doesn't either."

Christiana started to speak but Michael cut her off, saying, "I'm sorry Jonathan has referred, inferred, or whatever, that a boy would have been his choice for our offspring to carry forth the legacy. Does your father really believe if we had a male child he would carry the Barrington rather than the Trent name?"

"I don't know what my father believes but I'm surprised he would say anything about a male sibling to Jennifer. He idolizes his granddaughter."

"We know he loves Jennifer, but I remember your insecurities about measuring up to your father's expectations. On more than one unhappy occasion you wondered if your father would have preferred a son instead of a daughter."

"Yes, I remember, and still have doubts at times."

The conversation continued longer than expected, allowing Michael to imbibe with his third drink. At which point, he shot off a remark he promised never to verbalize. "When Jennifer was born and I met your parents in the waiting room, I expressed our happiness about our healthy beautiful baby girl. Your mother did her usual joyful crying and hugged me. Meanwhile, Jonathan hung back and stared directly in my eyes then said, 'Are you sure it's a girl?' What did he think, that both the doctor and I couldn't tell the difference?"

"Why are you telling me this now?"

"He was hoping for a boy. It would have made things easier, I assume, in the world according to Jonathan. As far as revealing this now, I … I don't know. I promised never to say anything and I guess these martinis are stronger than I thought."

"It is okay, Michael, I've often wondered the same thing."

"Listen, Christiana, I should get back to my guests. One final thought, we need to deliver a consistent message and work with Jennifer to accept her predetermined course."

"While I'm surprised by your reaction, I'm in full agreement and will explain that to Father."

"Well, that's a start; although I doubt he'll pay much attention to our desires."

The following day …

"Father, here are the revised papers for your review and signature. I had a charming conversation with Blake and I'm looking forward to meeting him tomorrow."

"Just be careful. He's very disarming but as ruthless as they come."

"If you don't think I can handle it, Father, then why are you sending me into the lion's den?"

"The statement wasn't meant to demean your negotiation skills, Christiana. It was merely a word of caution."

When they finished with the documents, Christiana stated, "I have something else to discuss, it concerns Jennifer. Father, everything you do is born of love and concern for family and Barrington and I have never questioned your motives. However, I challenge your method of mentoring."

Jonathan squirmed, rubbed his hands together, and waited for her to open fire on this subject.

"That said, she's too young to be burdened with the enormity and complexity of this monster we lovingly call Barrington, although I understand your logic. Your mentorship is a great asset to further her development. Michael and I support your efforts."

"I certainly didn't see that coming from your introduction."

"Our efforts should be coordinated, not done solo or in a covert manner. Michael and I are here to assist and to ready our little girl for her eventual undertaking. I always knew I would end up here; she, however, has other plans. Apparently, you indicated she had no choice since I 'will never have more children,' especially a male child."

Apparently recognizing this would not permit a graceful exit, he remained silent.

"While I may not have the opportunity to have more children, why lay guilt on Jennifer? This is particularly alarming for two reasons. First, I would give anything to have more children. Second, this notion may instill the thought that solely due to her gender she does not measure up. Father, I trust that was not what you meant since *you* had a daughter rather than a son and I think I measured up pretty well."

Carefully calculating his words, he chose not to respond directly. Rather he stood to meet her eye-to-eye, with his steely blue gaze looking penetratingly at her, and answered, "Jennifer *will* be groomed for Barrington. She *has* no other choice."

CHAPTER 14

"IT'S A PLEASURE TO MEET both of you," said Blake Eagleson as he shook hands with Christiana and David. Blake Eagleson was a tall, slim man, about Jonathan's age, immaculately attired and possessing a deep golden tan. His face and eyes, however, betrayed his personal stress. "Welcome to Sterling Hotels Worldwide," he announced.

Using his home court advantage, Blake started the negotiations. "Please show me why Barrington should win this horse race."

Christiana smiled at the "horse race" comment while David handed the revised portfolio over to Blake. "Allow me to highlight the essentials of our new offer," she said.

"Blake, the substantial change is that the cash upfront is decreased by twenty percent and these figures are found on page three." Blake furrowed his eyebrows as he flipped to the page in question. "The gain is the increase of the number of shares of BHI stock granted to you as noted on pages three and four."

Christiana stopped briefly while Blake did his own formulations and as he deliberated she couldn't determine if his intense scrutiny was theatrics or serious calculation. "The third item is outlined on page six. It's an employment agreement in an expanded position with BHI." Silence reigned as Blake read over his "future."

"You mean to tell me Jonathan wants me at BHI? When negotiations commenced, it was with the express understanding I wouldn't be involved after the acquisition."

"This addendum came directly from Jonathan. Yes, he, we want you in the expanded role as CEO of all the Barrington Hotel entities."

"Honestly I hadn't contemplated this path, considering the relationship Jonathan and I've had over the years."

David pressed Christiana's arm before she could respond and took the floor. "Blake, our business philosophy has been to acquire sound companies and retain the excellent leadership already present there whenever possible."

"I never envisioned a role with either BHI or Langley." This was a coup and Blake obviously knew it.

"David, what did you think of the meeting? I found Blake a hard read."

"While I'm optimistic, I don't think we have this nailed. He was intrigued with the BHI stock allocation, and the employment contract is very rich and increases his present base salary by twenty-five percent. Now go and enjoy yourself with Jennifer and try to forget about Barrington, Christiana. We did the best we could do. Call me once you hear from Blake. I'll be available all weekend."

Replaying the meeting in her mind on the trip to Teterboro airport, she was lost in thought when her cell phone rang. "Christiana, it's Michael. I have business in New York mid-week and was going to fly in early to spend some time with Jennifer."

"Michael, I'm sorry, but I'm en route to the airport and heading to Bellagio with Jennifer and Marcia. Remember, we did speak about this trip."

"Yes, I remembered as soon as you mentioned it."

"Michael," she cautiously continued, "would you care to join us at Bellagio for a few days?"

"Christiana, I feel like an interloper since this was to be your time with Jennifer."

"You are Jennifer's father. You could never be an interloper."

"I appreciate the invitation and would welcome the Florida sun; it's been overcast in LA for the past several days. Let me see what I can arrange and I'll call you shortly."

Within forty-five minutes, Michael was back on the line. "Christiana, I'm taking the red eye this evening so I will see you tomorrow morning. I'll take a taxi and should arrive at Bellagio around seven-thirty in the morning."

"Nonsense, I'll have my driver pick you up, just email your flight information."

The following morning ... at Bellagio in Palm Beach

Taking her coffee and newspaper out to the sunroom, Christiana noticed Michael asleep on a chaise lounge by the pool. A call from her father, eager to hear the outcome of the Sterling board meeting, had focused her thoughts on business even before her second cup of coffee. With no word yet from Blake, Jonathan was not pleased.

Later, lunch was served poolside and when finished, Jennifer and her friend trotted off with Marcia to play croquet. Michael and Christiana lingered over iced teas and chatted. "You seem preoccupied, Christiana. I imagine it's Barrington?"

"We are working on a major acquisition and awaiting word on the outcome of a meeting. My father is out of the country and has called twice, anxious to hear the news."

"Christiana, you worry yourself sick about Barrington. Will you ever get out from under the grip of your father?"

"You still know how to hurt, Michael. This deal is of prime importance to BHI … and to me."

"I'm sorry; although I still wonder why you strive so hard to please your father," he amended, shaking his head.

"I appreciate your concern but you are not correct. I *do not* strive to please my father."

"Okay, I didn't mean to upset you." Gazing out at the pool, Michael segued, "How about a quick swim?"

"A swim would be delightful."

With the strength and precision of an athlete, Christiana was resting comfortably at the far end when Michael swam up. "You're still a strong swimmer, Ms. Barrington."

"Love the water—come, I'll race you to the other side." They took on a rhythm and swam several laps in perfect unison. Placing their arms on the edge of the pool, they heard clapping from their welcoming committee.

"Race again, race again!" cheered Jennifer. "I'll say ready, set, go."

"Whoa, honey," said Michael, panting. "We need a rest."

By late afternoon, the yacht was motoring out to sea. Michael and Christiana sipped champagne and enjoyed playing cards with Jennifer and Marcia. Excusing herself, Christiana took another call from Jonathan. "No, I haven't heard from Blake and it's now six Friday evening. Father, are you having a restless night? It is midnight your time."

"You could say that. Blake is making me squirm. If Langley gets this deal, I'll commence a hostile takeover of Langley."

"Father, please, I'm sure there's a valid explanation as to why Blake hasn't called," she soothed. "I'm afraid we are going to have to sit tight and wait. We did all we could. It's out of our hands."

When Jonathan responded, Christiana could sense he was preoccupied. "Yes, of course, we hold tight."

With determination she replied, "Permit me to conclude this transaction and allow him to come to me, as discussed at the meeting."

"All right, but call me as soon as you hear from him, regardless of the time."

When she returned to dinner with a concerned look, Michael poured her a glass of wine. "Come join us and take your mind off Barrington."

The next morning, Christiana and Jennifer slipped away for some mother-daughter time. Between a mouthful of food and a chuckle at Jennifer's funny expression, Christiana's cell phone rang. It was Blake Eagleson and Christiana put her finger to her lips to quiet Jennifer.

"Christiana, forgive me for not upholding my word and contacting you as discussed. I had a personal situation with my wife who has cancer and is down to her last struggles. Her chemo treatment was particularly difficult yesterday and my business day was lost. I'm sure Jonathan thinks it is gamesmanship and honestly, I wish it were."

"Blake, I'm sorry to hear about your wife's illness."

"Thank you, Christiana. Now to the purpose of this call. The board approved the revised offer. There is significantly more shareholder value with BHI."

"This is great news, Blake. I know Jonathan will be pleased."

"Yes, it's going to be good being on the same side as Jonathan after all these years."

"I'll contact David and get the paperwork started as soon as possible, Blake. BHI is proud to have Sterling join our ranks, particularly with your continued leadership."

"I appreciate the accolades, welcome the challenge, and hope I meet your expectations."

"I'm finished with my lunch. May I have some ice cream for dessert?" Jennifer asked as Christiana finished her call.

"Yes, sweetheart, whatever you want," said Christiana enthusiastically. "Honey, I need to call Grandfather but I won't be long." A large chocolate sundae appeared in front of Jennifer and she was lost in the pleasure of her ice cream.

"Father, good afternoon; we did it! Sterling is ours!"

"Fantastic! Did they accept our offer with no contingencies? And what about Blake, is he going to be working with us?" The zeal touched off by Jonathan's first sentence settled into a groan with thoughts of Blake working for Barrington.

"Yes and yes. I look forward to working with him with all his expertise in the hospitality industry."

"Did you forget where we started? Regal Plaza was my first endeavor before Eagleson was even employed in the hotel sector."

"I haven't forgotten our beginnings, but we are a worldwide conglomerate and do not have the years of concentrated knowledge in one sector."

Brushing her comments aside, Jonathan responded, "No need to dampen our enthusiasm over small operational details. We won the game and that's what matters."

"I beg to differ, Father. If you have major issues with Blake, trust me, they will not be 'small operational details.' Let me work with him, assimilate the structures, and define his position before you come in heavy handed."

"Run with it, Christiana, as I have too much going with Barrington Financial to step into the mix."

"We've been talking longer than I realized as your grand-daughter has devoured her ice cream sundae."

With a chuckle he added, "Go and enjoy our precious Jennifer."

"Elizabeth, where have you been? I've been trying to reach you for hours," inquired Jonathan.

"Darling, I'm tending to some personal items before I meet you in Europe."

"I have some wonderful news. Christiana closed the deal with Sterling. *It's mine!*" he bellowed.

"Jonathan, what a relief to have Sterling solidified. Darling, if I may change the subject …" Elizabeth prattled on for several minutes and when she concluded Jonathan just grunted. "Jonathan Robert Barrington, you weren't even listening."

Looking at his watch he said, "Elizabeth, as much as I would love to continue our conversation, I still have business reading this evening."

CHAPTER 15

"GRAHAM, WELCOME. Have you met my wife Ginger? Ginger, this is Graham Cunningham, the CEO from Barrington Financial Services." Peering past his guest to the porch, Grant called back, "Where's Barrington?"

"Not able to make it, last minute appointment."

Grant asked, "Did Jonathan say where he was headed? If his meeting doesn't take too long or isn't too far away, could he still join us?"

"I doubt it, Grant. He indicated he would be occupied for the evening."

"Ah, indeed. No need to call and leave a voice mail."

Meanwhile, Jonathan with security detail in tow stepped into his car, tossed an address to the driver and poured a scotch. He entered the concert hall from a private side entrance and made his way to his secluded box to watch the symphony. He fell captive to the music but one of the piano solos was peculiarly haunting. After the performance he continued to a reception and asked the piano soloist to join him for a drink on the terrace. Well acquainted, she obliged and they spoke about the performance.

"The last composition was superb yet unsettling, as if it was unfinished."

"Allow me to tell the story. Yes, purposely I left an edge to the conclusion, making the listener long for more. It's about a relationship between a man who is married and a woman who at the start of their affair is not. The relationship continues not for years but for decades. The woman eventually marries and divorces while the man remains with his wife. The woman still desires the one she cannot have, as the man already has his one true love," she said with emotion. Regaining her composure, she added, "I shall forward you the CD once it is released." Staring into the reception hall she declared, "I must get back to my guests. Will you stay for a while?"

As she reentered the reception hall, she glanced back toward the terrace and Jonathan was gone.

The following day ...

As Christiana returned from church Sunday morning, Bellagio was quiet except for staff preparing the yacht for the afternoon at sea. Sending Jennifer off to play, Christiana seized the moment to tend to business. "Good morning, David, it's Christiana. I'm sorry to disturb you on a Sunday morning."

"I've been hoping to hear from you."

"Sterling took our offer, as written, and I've apprised Jonathan. Blake asked me if we could expedite the paperwork and he will coordinate with you and Marshall."

"I'll have a draft of the relevant documents ready in the next several days."

Concluding her emails, she heard footsteps and turned to meet a tousled-haired, barefooted, half-awake man standing in front of her desk.

"Good morning," said Michael.

"I think you missed the morning."

"Wow, it must be jet lag. Have I ruined the plans for today?"

"No, the yacht is ready and we can leave anytime. Would you like some coffee?"

"Lead the way; I need a jolt of caffeine."

With two cappuccinos in hand, they strolled to the terrace as Michael's cell phone rang. Hurriedly, he walked into another room to take the call. In short order, he returned appearing more steamed than the cappuccino and muttered a few obscenities.

"Rachel wants to throw a party *this* evening and only now gets around to informing me. When I said no, she responded like a spoiled child."

"What did you tell her?"

"I'll spare you the exact response; needless to say, we will not be seeing each other anymore. I called my butler and put him on alert and called the security company and changed all the codes and gate entry. Why did I get myself mixed up with this bimbo?"

"Come on, Michael. We all make mistakes."

"Several weeks ago, I came home and she was having sex with two women. As exciting as it might seem from my point of view, *it was my house and my bedroom.*"

"Michael, you are a wonderful man and there is an equally wonderful woman waiting for you."

"Yes, Christiana, there was one wonderful woman out there. *You,* my dear. I will never again have a relationship like we had. You were—you are—and will always be, my one true love. Now that I have bared my soul, let's go have some fun."

Michael bounced back once they were out on the yacht but their earlier conversation was not revisited. At the end of the day, once Jennifer was in bed, Michael assisted Christiana as she packed away items in the kitchen. Just like old times, they moved effortlessly without speaking for several moments. Stepping on a stool to place a glass in the cabinet, Christiana lost her footing. Michael was standing behind her and, as she landed in his arms, she did not move. When their lips met she did not push away but hungrily continued in a long, open-mouthed kiss.

The penetrating Florida sun, the gentle rocking of the yacht at sea, coupled with rich food and alcohol, brought Christiana to new heights of relaxation and a lack of inhibition. She allowed the moment to carry her away but as she felt Michael getting hard she untangled herself from his embrace. "I … can't, Michael," she said, trying to convince herself.

"It's obvious I want you, but I won't do anything to upset you, now or later. The call is yours. I think I'll go for a swim." With that, he left the room.

She stood watching him in the pool and as he stopped to glance up at the perfect night sky, his eyes fell on her and he asked, "How long have you been out here?"

"Just a few minutes. You were in your rhythm." She had removed her bathrobe and was gliding into the shallow end of the pool. After a brief swim she announced, "This was perfect. I'm going to the pool house to shower."

A few minutes later, he entered the pool house and she rose from her dressing table. She turned the corner to hand him a fluffy bathrobe and found him standing naked. "My apologies," she said, but she didn't move; neither did he as she surveyed his body. "You've lost weight and developed your abs. You look amazing."

"Thank you, I hired a personal trainer," he said, now drying his hair.

Still holding the bathrobe, she was suddenly embarrassed and quickly handed it to him. He didn't bother to slip it on but rather turned and headed for the shower. Glancing back with a smile, he suggested, "Would you care to join me?" She remained in the doorway as he held out his hand and said, "Come, my love."

His finely sculptured body aroused feelings in her long removed from their relationship. Her bathrobe fell and they joined each other under the rainwater shower heads. Washing her back, he began nibbling her neck. When finished, he slowly turned her around, cupped her welcoming breasts and as water ran down her trim torso, his tongue circled her hardened nipples. Pressing her against the marble wall, they continued to explore each other's bodies.

Reaching the point of no turning back, Michael gasped, "No regrets, no second thoughts or we need to stop now."

"Take me, Michael. No regrets," she said as her body shuddered. "Follow me," she added, taking his hand as they went over to the daybed with its shimmering cool fabrics glistening in the soft glow of the moonlight.

Surrender was easy; the passion was hot and they made love for hours then drifted off to sleep in each other's arms. At the first hint of daybreak she woke.

"Michael," she whispered. "It's morning and we should get back to the main house before Jennifer wakes up and wanders into my bedroom. It's five and the staff comes on at five-thirty, so we need to get moving."

Once dressed, Michael embraced her and said, "What an incredible night."

"You were amazing, Mr. Trent. But come, we must not linger."

"Wow, I feel like a teenager sneaking in after being out all night."

"Shh, Michael, please. I'm serious."

Another passionate rendezvous did not present itself, either by choice or circumstance.

Waiting for their flight, Christiana took a call from Jonathan. "We have reestablished the account with the royals, but not without concessions and some groveling. Graham is staying, much to his chagrin, for several weeks."

"Sounds like your intervention worked, Father."

"Christiana, I had to eat a lot of crow—something I don't do well."

"That's an understatement, Father."

"So what's happening with Sterling?"

"All is moving along nicely. We are shooting for a meeting late this week."

"I'll be in Antibes this weekend and available by cell if needed. I'd better call your mother and have her bring some casual clothing for me. Let's talk tomorrow."

Back at Montrachet ...

"Good morning, care for some coffee?" Christiana was exhilarant as she bustled around the room.

"Sure. Are you heading out?" Michael was in his usual subdued morning mood.

"No, I have a conference call starting in about thirty minutes. But I wanted to mention that your insight was most valuable in our discussion with Jennifer last night. I can't believe our little girl is talking about boys already."

"The topic of boys has just started. Can't you remember the first time you discovered boys?"

"It was different for me since I was at St. George's and had no contact with boys."

"Maybe that explains why you were such a tigress when we first started to go out," he said. She would not participate in his carefree banter.

"Jennifer has several recitals and I have printed out a list of the events with dates so hopefully you might be able to join us," she stated, ignoring any thoughts of their romantic interlude in Florida.

Christiana found a suitable rhythm to her life during the ensuing weeks and months in no small part due to Michael's visits to Montrachet. But their one night of sexual intimacy in Palm Beach was not repeated.

CHAPTER 16 ... A couple of weeks later

"GOOD MORNING, when did you get back from Europe?" asked Christiana, glancing at her father striding into her office in his black pin-striped suit that accentuated his perfectly groomed thick silver hair.

"Your mother and I returned last evening. We need to get ready for the hotel meeting this afternoon," he said in his serious business tone of voice. Owning the largest worldwide hotel conglomerate made branding, marketing and consolidation critical.

Jonathan and Christiana were primed for this meeting and on their game. When the meeting concluded, Jonathan wore a wide grin. "That was a ballsy—sorry, Christiana, a sly move when you placed that signed document in front of them," he said, beaming. "I couldn't have done a better job. I've never seen you so assertive and hard-hitting."

God, I am my father's son, she thought. The best of Christiana, the loving, nurturing and feminine creature (the Elizabeth side of the composition), most often remained buried when she was around Jonathan. In the course of business her two selves collided, hard and often. Dismissing the notion, she acknowledged, "You gave me the ongoing responsibility of Sterling. I have given considerable time to understanding the breadth of this organization and how it will be assimilated into our hotel entity. I am merely doing my job, Father."

Veronica was to finally arrive.

Veronica busied herself sorting, packing and discarding items, along with the memories. The remaining few pieces of furniture and boxes awaited the moving company to carry them to her new life at Montrachet.

It had been some time since Christiana had seen Veronica but the strain of the divorce was evident in her gaunt face, sunken eyes and thin body when she emerged from the car and met Christiana and Jennifer.

"It's so good to see you," said Veronica, leaning over to hug Jennifer. As she resumed her standing position, her eyes met Christiana's. "I have lost some weight."

"Understandable," comforted Christiana. "The movers were here yesterday and your belongings are upstairs."

Pulling on her arm to show her aunt her new home, Jennifer took Veronica upstairs to her one-bedroom apartment with terrace overlooking lush gardens and fountains.

"It's just beautiful here and I can't thank you enough," she said, extending her arms to Christiana as she straightened her inexpensive and wrinkled dress, glancing at Christiana in head-to-toe couture.

"I have a couple of other items to discuss before I leave for the office. Shall we begin downstairs?"

There, Christiana walked over to a table in the foyer and handed Veronica an envelope. On cue, the butler opened the front door as Alex, Christiana's assistant, drove up in a black Mercedes SUV and presented Veronica with the keys.

"I can't possibly accept this, Christiana."

"Today, Veronica, you start your new life. The car and the new wardrobe are my special treats for you. I've arranged for my fashion consultant to take you shopping."

"I can't possibly, I need to unpack and organize, start my job—"

"We are the lucky ones, and we are family. Everything will be arranged by the time you return from your shopping spree."

Veronica embraced Christiana and with tears welling in her eyes, said, "I love you. Thank you. I will not disappoint you."

Within the first month Veronica gained some weight, color returned to her face, and she started to tone her body in the professionally equipped gym at Montrachet. Even the sad eyes started to twinkle. Jennifer was the catalyst and the two became inseparable.

Michael had made himself scarce, with no visits to Montrachet since the sexual interlude with Christiana in Palm Beach. But shortly after Veronica's arrival, Michael called.

"I just finished another movie that premières in Los Angeles and New York next week. If it bombs, my career may be in a whole different place."

"You are in your Trent worry mode. It'll be a blockbuster. We've missed having you at Montrachet. You'll be pleased to know Veronica and Jennifer are getting along well."

"Veronica sounds better than she has in ages," said Michael. "Thank you for taking care of my sister. On another note, Christiana, since I've just completed my last project, I would like to take Jennifer to Hawaii. I've rented a house at Mani Lani Point on the Big Island and was hoping to have her join me for a couple of weeks in late July."

"Michael, Jennifer will be thrilled."

"Christiana, would you mind if Veronica joined us? Since she is under your employ, I don't wish to be presumptuous."

"Your sister hasn't taken a vacation in years and it would be the perfect relaxation before she becomes entrenched in Jennifer's world. Michael, our daughter has just arrived so I'll hand her the telephone." She left the room and heard the squeals of excitement from Jennifer as Michael told her about the trip.

"Daddy wants to speak with you again. He's taking me to Hawaii and Veronica might go with us."

Retrieving the phone, Christiana relayed, "She sounds excited."

"Not as excited as me. I've really missed her."

"If you want to speak with Veronica this evening you might wish to call soon since she retires early."

"Yeah, you're right. One more thing, would you also like to join us? Before you answer, the house has five bedrooms."

"Michael, it's not appropriate. This trip is an opportunity for quality time with Jennifer and Veronica." The silence hung heavy over the line.

"Christiana, I've been distant since our rendezvous at Bellagio. It's part of the reason I've not frequented Montrachet. Have I offended you? Is it guilt? Please tell me what I have done?" In rapid succession, he fired off his questions, not allowing her time to respond or interrupt. "I tried to talk with you about it on several occasions both in person as well as on the telephone but our conversations veered almost purposely in other directions. I have no regrets and will always love you, yet somehow this has put distance in our relationship. I need to understand why."

Definitive and pointed in her response, "It was wrong and a mistake. Even though I told you no regrets, I have them. I can't help the way I feel."

"No, Christiana, *it* was not a mistake. A mistake is black or white. Our relationship has never been black or white. It wasn't when we were married and it still isn't, even though we have papers saying we are divorced. Christiana, admit it, you wanted me as much as I wanted you."

"Okay, yes, I wanted you, but it will never happen again. Never!"

"Why, Christiana? I've told you I can't get over you. You tore my world apart when we divorced."

"Michael, our marriage was not sustainable."

"I would have tried to hold it together even with the geographic distance."

"It was more than the distance; please, we've been over this many times. Our relationship is over and it's for the best—*for both of us.*"

"It's always black and white with you, spoken like a true Barrington."

"Don't go there, Michael, do not bring Father into this conversation."

"Wow, how absolute. I guess I wasn't expecting this ...," his voice trailed off. "I respect your feelings and decisions but please, Christiana, stop with the guilt. We were married, for heaven's sake."

"Michael, I wish it were that easy."

"Christiana, it doesn't make sense, but I don't want to jeopardize our friendship," said a contrite Michael.

"Thank you, Michael. I think you should call Veronica before Jennifer ruins the surprise with her enthusiasm."

The parting at the airport was harder for Christiana than she had anticipated. She would be alone for most of the summer while Jennifer and Veronica were with Michael in Hawaii. Of course, she had Barrington to keep her busy ...

CHAPTER 17

CHRISTIANA'S WORK DEMANDS mounted and the long hours coupled with the daily conversations with Jennifer eased some of her loneliness. But she counted the days until her daughter's return. Marc Philippe and other suitors filled some of the void and she seized the opportunity to travel on behalf of the Barrington charitable foundation.

Meanwhile, Jonathan jumped off to Europe and Christiana found herself questioning, *Why did Father feel the need to micromanage Grant?* It didn't make sense and Jonathan said nothing to alleviate her concerns. *Then there's Christian Luke, the newcomer to the London office, the Oxford graduate with the uptight English personality. He was so far down the corporate ladder,* she laughed as she thought about his arrogant attitude. *Why were the European operations so important to Father?* When pressed for an explanation, Jonathan summarily dismissed it with, "This is the opportunity for you to make your mark on BHI."

A dreadful feeling tugged at her that there was more behind her father's sustained trips and actions. As with so many things about Jonathan, Christiana sadly realized she would never really know the truth.

Lost in thought, but no longer muttering, as the elevator opened and without looking, she knocked into a man trying to enter. Startled, Christiana murmured, "I'm so sorry," and moved to the other side of the elevator. The stranger glanced over and inquired, "Don't I know you?"

"I don't believe so," and she turned forward to push the close button to continue the ascent to her floor. The stranger's attention remained fixed on her as she could see his reflection in the steel doors. He looked back as he exited; this time their eyes met and he smiled.

Fleeting thoughts aside, her work day precluded any meaningless daydreaming.

"Your father needs to speak with you and you have a meeting starting in fifteen minutes," said her assistant. With the time difference in London in mind, she immediately placed the call.

"Good evening, Father. Amanda said you needed to speak with me."

"Yes, I need to ask you a huge favor." Christiana remained silent. "Maximillian Spencer is in town and I was supposed to have dinner with him this evening. He is interested in selling his pink diamond business in Australia. Could you please meet him at seven at the Four Seasons Restaurant?"

"Father, I have an appointment this evening."

"The company is a syndicate with Spencer as principal. Several of the owners are available to meet us in New York next week. Do you think you might change your personal appointment?"

"Yes, Father, I'll change my appointment. Will you confirm with him or should I?" *I always do what you want.*

"Already done and he's looking forward to seeing you." Christiana just sighed.

Nursing his Belvedere martini, Maximillian Spencer looked up from his note-taking, flashed a wide smile as Christiana made her way to the corner booth. A broad-shouldered man, with the weathered appearance of an outdoorsman, along with the ruddy complexion of one who has imbibed too much alcohol, Max twisted his large frame around the booth to greet Christiana.

"Christiana, it is always a delight to see you. You are much more beautiful to view over dinner than Jonathan." He chuckled and Christiana, strained, managed a smile. "Thank you for meeting me this evening. I trust your time shall be well spent?"

"Good evening, Max," she greeted him and extended her hand as she moved into the booth. "I haven't seen you since the last board meeting. How are you?"

"No complaints. Doing a bit of fishing but I can't get my wife to accompany me. We purchased a place on Hayman Island and if we can put this deal together then I might spend more time up there," offered Max.

Drinks arrived and Christiana was eager to tend to the business at hand. When the waiter appeared for their dinner orders, Christiana reached for the menu and placed a hurried order, hoping the momentary distraction would segue to the sale of his business. "Jonathan gave me the preliminary financials along with the term sheet. With the pink diamond industry centered in Australia, your company is the leader," she stated.

"I will tender my resignation from the Barrington Board to avoid conflict concerns. Christiana, I've built a respectable business and if I can move it over to Barrington, the next generation of innovations will be harvested. Not bad for a guy from the outback."

"Max, we both know you and Jonathan met at Harvard," Christiana added with a little smirk.

"What do you think of Pemberton running the show?"

"Actually, I hadn't even thought of Grant since he is too vital to the European operations." Christiana wondered if Max and Jonathan had engaged in prior discussions over this subject.

"Yes, of course, Christiana. Maybe that younger gent, what's his name? Christian, CL, something like that. I'd bet Pemberton would be happy to have that brash arrogant youngster out of his hair."

Christiana sat digesting his words before she replied. "Jonathan's input is vital on operational and management issues and we certainly need to consider the present management structure."

En route to the office the following morning, Christiana updated Jonathan on the meeting with Max Spencer.

"Max and I discussed the business-growth potential along with the immediate capital considerations due to aging mining equipment. There has been a dip in revenues and projections indicate no significant growth."

"The company is not heavily burdened with debt and there is more than enough money available for the capital expenditures. Jewels *by Barrington* will also have to look at similar equipment purchases. Placing a consolidated order would drive down the costs," calculated Jonathan. "I've been interested in advancing our interests in the jewelry business to allow for assimilation of Max's company into our existing business model. Operations for Jewels *by Barrington* should end up with the Asia office."

"Father, I concur, and sense a smart fit with our product line. Interestingly, Max mentioned Grant or a subordinate," she would not say Christian's name, "heading up the operations. I am not sure if Europe can handle more, plus the Asia shop would be a better fit logistically. We will need Peter Chang involved."

"Max has requested we get down to Australia and view the operation firsthand."

"You may take the lead, Father. The mine is four-hundred miles southwest of Darwin, not a very civilized part of northwestern Australia," she added in a deliberate tone.

"Where's the sense of adventure? I have wanted to see his operations for a long time. This is a great opportunity."

"And I'm glad to have *you take this opportunity*—please invite Mother."

"She said the same thing, not interested in roughing it, and told me I could email her photographs. You women stick together."

The following day ...

"This package just arrived for you, Ms. Barrington," said Amanda. *The package is too small for additional business information from Max,* thought Christiana. Opening the delivery package, she was surprised to see two elegantly adorned boxes spill onto her lap. The attached card read,

"Please adorn yourself Aussie-style. One is an exotic pink while the other is sparkling champagne. All the best, Max Spencer."

Holding up two sets of exquisite earrings, she mused, *He must really want to ensure our attention is directed to his company.*

While focused on Max, she zipped an email to Jonathan and was surprised to receive an immediate response.

> *Can't wait to see the earrings; they sound fabulous. Have tentative plans to fly over next month. Max has freed up*

his schedule to accommodate us. I will be taking Christian with me. He will be in New York briefly before we fly to LA then on to Sydney. Due diligence is proceeding. —Jonathan

Christiana went numb. *What is he thinking? Christian! What possible involvement could he have with this acquisition? Why would Father even mention this to him?* She started to place a call to her father but was interrupted by her assistant.

Another opportunity to confront her father did not materialize and she thought it more prudent to broach the subject directly when he returned to the office.

CHAPTER 18

Lingering over breakfast with Jennifer and Veronica, Christiana noted that the normal routine had returned at Montrachet. Christiana was happy they were back; it had been a long lonely summer. While they were sharing vacation stories, Christiana's cell phone rang. Ariana Worthington, one of Christiana's girlfriends, inquired upon hearing Christiana's voice, "Are we still on for lunch today?"

"Yes, Ariana, I'm looking forward to it. Will Kathryn be joining us?"

"Yes, love, we will both meet you at twelve-thirty. *Ciao,*" said Ariana.

Ariana Worthington and Kathryn D'Egland were two prominent socialites whose worlds revolved around endless lunches sipping champagne or expensive white wine while picking at their salads sans dressing. They lived in their arenas of exclusivity petrified to venture outside the circle for fear of not being allowed reentry. Today the ladies had pushed for this luncheon and Christiana surmised they wanted her involvement with a fundraiser.

At eleven-thirty, Christiana's driver and security team converged at the entrance to her outer office to take her to the luncheon with her girlfriends. Arriving at the restaurant, she found the ladies already established at their "A" table engrossed in conversation and sipping from bottomless champagne glasses. Approaching the table, she heard them discussing their latest diets, as they spent their lives dieting in a vain attempt to stay young and desirable.

"Christiana, it's so good to see you. You look fabulous," the ladies cooed in unison.

"Waiter, please bring another champagne flute," called Ariana but Christiana caught the eye of the waiter and countered, "No, please, I'll have ice tea."

"Darling, we are here to celebrate. You must at least toast with us," Ariana said pouting, as she eyed the waiter to make sure he completed her directive.

"Okay, what are we celebrating? Ladies, what have you been up to?" questioned Christiana. *Why the suspense? Did one of them have plastic surgery or are they contemplating a little nip and tuck?* Christiana decided silence was the most prudent course of action.

The silence was broken when Ariana asked Christiana if she knew Jack Hamilton.

"Well, I know *of* him, if you mean the real estate tycoon."

"Yes, he's the one who just happens to be *the most eligible* bachelor in New York, possibly the whole country," Ariana quickly added. "He wants to meet you. Isn't it fabulous?"

Kathryn glanced at Ariana and interjected, "Darling, we must be sure Christiana isn't seeing someone, as the media has her linked with Prince Marc Philippe Boulanger. Do tell, Christiana?"

"You know Marc Philippe and I have been friends for decades. He is now involved with his family businesses that have a US component. Our relationship is and remains casual."

"Okay, we pronounce you single, available and ready to meet a new man," concluded Kathryn.

"Ladies, what have you been plotting? I'm not sure I'm ready to …," her voice trailed off. Stopping mid sentence, she remembered Michael had resumed his social life. Sighing, she stated, "I'm listening."

"Jack's in his early forties, never married, no kids, extremely successful and very wealthy. He's gorgeous, charming and intelligent. George and I have known him for years," purred Ariana.

"What am I committing to if I say yes?"

"A quiet dinner party, just the six of us, at our Westport home a week from Saturday," Ariana quickly informed her.

"Against my better judgment, I'll say yes," uttered a resigned Christiana, "and as much as I would love to continue this conversation, I will need to excuse myself and head back to the office."

Why would Jackson Hamilton want to meet me? Christiana wondered on her way back to Montrachet later that day. *Maybe Ariana was looking for a positive response from me then will serve it up to Jackson.*

Pushing the fantasy from her mind, she placed a call to Elizabeth. "Welcome home, Mother. How was your trip to France?"

"Hello dear, the trip was delightful. I was writing several thank you notes when you phoned. The weather cooperated to allow a charming couple of days on the yacht. How did you fare without Jennifer?"

"As you can imagine, life was full with Barrington. Thankfully, as Montrachet seemed so lonely without her. They had a marvelous time in Hawaii."

"That's wonderful news. Now that she is back, please come over for dinner soon."

"We will, Mother."

Changing the subject, Elizabeth began, "Your father mentioned you finalized negotiations for the Sterling acquisition. He's been boasting in normal Jonathan fashion."

"Sterling adds a new dimension to our hotel portfolio. I'm equally pleased Father was able to mend the breach in the Saudi transaction. He goes to Saudi Arabia to resuscitate one deal and is handed an equally impressive arrangement from another prince."

"Your father is a remarkable dealmaker."

"Mother, I'm in Greenwich, would you mind if I drop by for a few moments? There is something I would prefer to discuss in person."

After they exchanged kisses, they settled on the sofa as Elizabeth inquired, "Darling, is something troubling you?"

Pangs of embarrassment fluttered as Christiana hesitated before answering. "Mother, Michael joined Jennifer and me for several days during our last stay at Bellagio several months ago. Something happened and now it has affected our relationship."

"From your pained expression, I surmise you and Michael had a romantic interlude."

Blushing, Christiana nodded.

"You feel guilty and question yourself."

"Yes, I feel remorse, guilt, confusion … possibly interest, longing and loneliness. I've even questioned the reasons our relationship ended," sighed Christiana.

"You are concerned for the impact this has on your ongoing relationship with Michael. Have you discussed your feelings with him?"

"The subject was brought up recently on the telephone although he mentioned he tried to broach the subject on several earlier occasions. He still has feelings for me. I'm not sure how I feel. I told him I'm both guilty and tormented, which resulted in a rather terse conversation, but at least he listened."

Eyeing her daughter, Elizabeth waited for her to continue.

"Michael told me I view everything as either black or white and he reiterated our relationship had been neither. We've become friends and it was hard to get to this side with some of the bitterness of our divorce."

Elizabeth's nurturing support was the perfect prescription for Christiana. As they strolled hand-in-hand to the door, Elizabeth assured her, "Don't be so hard on yourself. It's up to you and Michael to decide the direction of your ongoing relationship."

Kissing her mother goodnight, she said, "I love you, Mother, and thank you for your sage advice." As she started down the stairs, she turned and added, "Mother, please let this remain between us."

CHAPTER 19

FOLLOWING AN INTENSE MORNING WORKOUT, Christiana wiped her brow and headed for the shower. As the shower jets kneaded her sore muscles, her thoughts went back to Jonathan's email regarding Christian's involvement with the pink diamond mine. Today she would finally have the opportunity for a face-to-face conversation with her father since they were driving together. His prolonged absences from New York had precluded much dialogue on the subject of Christian Luke.

Finishing his call on their ride into Manhattan, Jonathan acknowledged, "Graham's still in Jeddah. We really dodged a bullet with this account and Graham knows I place this mess at his feet."

"Yes, Father, but we didn't lose the account and you were able to walk away with a new portfolio of business."

"I'm both pleased and relieved," said Jonathan in a serious tone. Moving on to other matters, he asked, "Tell me about Magnifique? Have you hired a new CEO? Remind me of the name of the current gal?"

"Allison Faulkner is the current CEO. You know her father, Lou."

"Yes, I know, I just forgot her name. You didn't answer my question about her longevity."

"James has a confidential search underway but no viable candidates thus far."

"I see," replied Jonathan, half listening as he perused his email messages.

"Father, you haven't listened to anything I've said," she reprimanded.

"Yes, I have. The search is still underway."

"That part of the conversation was about five minutes ago. I also mentioned Corinthian Properties has a fifteen percent increase in net revenue."

"You have my attention. We need to consider taking the funds from the sales of the two properties in Denver and paying down the debt on Corinthian. I'll speak to Marshall."

Approaching the FDR highway heading into midtown Manhattan, she didn't want to waste another opportunity to confront her father about Christian. "Father, I would like to discuss Christian's involvement with Max's company. We need Grant's expertise at this juncture."

"I beg to differ with you, Christiana. While Grant's involvement will be paramount as we progress, there is no need for his high-priced talent with a site inspection. Furthermore, the trip has been pushed back for several weeks, and due to tax ramifications, Max does not want to close a deal this year. However, we will meet with the syndicate members."

"Father, I'm still not happy with the decision to let a mid-level employee become involved in these high-level negotiations. I feel adamant about this."

"While you may feel adamant, I believe you are putting your feelings in front of your reasonable business judgment, clouding your objectivity. This is so unlike you, Christiana." Jonathan managed to maneuver Christiana's offensive stance to a weakened defensive mode and she struggled to turn this around.

"I've expressed my opinions about Christian's arrogance on several occasions. Frankly, I haven't seen enough of his work to judge his business savvy," she responded in an icy tone.

"He's not been under your tutelage so allow me to make that determination," Jonathan said crisply, opening the door to the office building as his cell phone started to ring. Motioning to Christiana to go on upstairs, he stood in the lobby to take the call.

Settling into her office, she lifted the receiver of her phone as Jonathan wandered toward her desk. Hanging up the phone, she asked, "You had a concerned look as you answered your cell; is everything all right?"

Changing the subject at will, and side-stepping her question, he responded, "Did I hear you are staying in Manhattan this evening?"

"Yes, Father. I have a late meeting and then I am having dinner with Marc Philippe."

"Good. I want to see Jennifer and give her the books I purchased in Europe," he said, removing several bundles from his attaché.

"They are books on business, Father."

"I located them while in Switzerland. They are in English and geared for young minds. They will complement my mentoring sessions."

"Michael and I support you but remember, she doesn't have the zest and fervor I did for Barrington." Reflecting on his last comment, she questioned, "Were you in Switzerland on business?"

Jonathan dodged the remark in characteristic fashion with another question and on a different topic. "I saw a piece about your philanthropic trip to Africa on behalf of our foundation," said

Jonathan as he prepared for his exit. "Let Veronica know to expect me this evening around six."

"I'll let her know. However, there's one final item before you leave." Jonathan pivoted to face his daughter. "We are not finished with the subject of Christian," she stated with determination.

Jonathan turned to open the door but glanced back at Christiana, holding firm to the doorknob and pausing before responding to her statement. Then with his penetrating steely blue eyes on her, he said, "Yes, we are, Christiana." And he was gone.

Marc Philippe was preoccupied with his business concerns and instead of lingering over dinner, they hurried to Christiana's apartment. Exhausted from their hectic schedules, their lovemaking took on a slow and methodical pace and sleep followed rapidly. When Christiana woke she found the bed empty except for his signature rose. "To my American beauty. Hope you had pleasant dreams, Marc Philippe."

As Christiana was finishing her breakfast, she called Montrachet. "Good morning, sweetheart. Did you have a pleasant time with Grandfather last evening?"

"Yes, we played games and then he gave me some books."

"What kind of books did Grandfather give you?"

"Business stuff to help kids learn to run companies like BHI."

"Are you interested in learning more about what Grandfather and I do at BHI?"

"I don't want to do what you do, Mother. I want to be a doctor … I think," replied Jennifer. "But Grandfather tells me I have to work at Barrington. It will be my company some day. *I don't want to run your company!*"

"Sweetheart, slow down. First, Grandfather was merely discussing running BHI after I retire, which will not happen for a very long time." Again Christiana was left wondering why her father was placing undue pressure on Jennifer.

Arriving at the office after her meeting, Christiana was on a mission to locate her father, but he was nowhere to be found. Leslie, his assistant, said he was gone for the day and Christiana tried unsuccessfully to reach him on his cell phone.

By the end of the day she still hadn't spoken with him.

CHAPTER 20

A STREAM OF PERSONAL ATTENDANTS, a hair stylist, manicurist, masseuse, and makeup artist paraded through Montrachet on Saturday preparing Christiana for the Westport dinner party. Deciding on a capped sleeve, above-the-knee transitional season couture dress, she had her hair done in soft curls that accentuated her neck, shoulders and golden tanned skin. Chandelier pink topaz earrings, bracelet and watch finished her transformation. She was ready to meet Jackson Hamilton.

Veronica had the night off and Christiana was relieved her parents were in town and able to watch their granddaughter.

"Good evening," said Elizabeth, putting down her reading glasses and book. She came around the carved inlaid cocktail table and warmly greeted both her daughter and granddaughter. Jonathan remained where he was on the sofa and Christiana went over to sit next to him.

"Father, may I have a word with you before I head to Westport?"

Elizabeth took the cue. "Come, Jennifer, let's see what we are having for dinner."

Wasting no time, Christiana began, "Father, I am appreciative of your efforts to cultivate Jennifer's interest in business—or more directly, Barrington. However, your approach needs to be more subtle. I'm sure you understand this is a tremendous burden and responsibility for a child."

"Are you sure you're not overreacting?"

"I'm not. Jennifer does not have the desire to work at BHI."

"I'm not worried. I'll change her mind," puffed Jonathan. "I'm not doing anything different with Jennifer than I did with you, with the exception of the European schooling."

"Father, how many times do I have to remind you Jennifer is not *me!*" Christiana was provoked and realized they were at an impasse and segued to the issues about Christian. "Father, we have not concluded our conversation regarding Christian's involvement with Max's company."

"Christiana, may we discuss this at a more opportune moment than when you are on your way to a dinner party?" asked Jonathan.

Realizing she'd hit a wall on this topic as well, Christiana kissed her father and rose from the sofa to say her goodbyes to Jennifer and her mother.

"Good evening, Ms. Barrington, please follow me to the parlor. Mr. and Mrs. Worthington are expecting you." Glancing at the mirror in the foyer, Christiana moistened her lips as they headed to the living room. Engrossed in conversation with Ariana and Kathryn, Jackson touched Ariana's arm as Christiana entered the room. He stood as the ladies turned to greet their guest.

Coming around the cocktail table, Jackson extended his hand to greet Christiana. "It is a pleasure to meet you, Christiana, although we had an accidental encounter in an elevator several weeks ago."

Embarrassed, Christiana replied, "I remember the occasion; not my best first impression. Sincere apologies."

"Oh, but it was," responded Jack, "you looked beautiful that morning and enchanting this evening." Grasping her hand when first introduced, he'd held it during their entire discourse.

"Christiana, come and join us," coaxed Ariana.

Nursing his drink, Robert D'Egland remarked, "Kathryn and I haven't seen much of you, Christiana. Barrington continues to be front page news with its serious, high-profile acquisitions." Turning toward Jack, Robert continued, "Jack, this lovely lady is President of Barrington Holdings International, although you may have already been given that information by my wife."

"I'm familiar with the company as well as Christiana's accomplishments," Jack answered, looking intently at Christiana.

"Thank you both for the compliments. It's a pleasure to meet you too, Jack. Your business acumen and real estate deals are legendary. I'm intrigued to learn more about your interest in the New York marketplace, which you have shunned for many years due to pricing and competition, I understand."

"Christiana, you may recall Jonathan and I had some dealings several years ago. Fortune smiled on the Barringtons and you won the prize with the building on East 50th Street. I was disappointed circumstances did not present themselves with the occasion for us to meet during those negotiations."

"No, I was not involved with the transaction but the building was a sound investment for our company, Corinthian Properties. Knowing my father, it was probably best we were not introduced during those negotiations as we may not be enjoying this lovely dinner this evening. My father has a reputation of being ruthless when it comes to business, something he wants."

"Yes, he does and he was," remarked Jack.

"This conversation is getting *too* serious," said Ariana. "It's time for dinner. Shall we adjourn to the dining room?"

The guests followed Ariana and George, while Jack took Christiana's arm and whispered, "I can be just as determined— maybe not ruthless—when it comes to something I want." He squeezed her hand. Christiana clearly understood his message.

The Worthingtons were perfect hosts, allowing the flow of conversation on a variety of topics with all guests successfully integrated in the dialogue. Jack appeared well-versed and Christiana thoroughly enjoyed his company.

Christiana was the first to leave and Jack escorted her to the front door. "I've had a wonderful time, Christiana. May I call you next week to arrange dinner in the City if you're available?"

"I would like that very much."

As the butler summoned her car, Jack leaned over and kissed her on the cheek. "Goodnight, Jack," she said as she turned and walked out into the night. He watched her go and waited by the door until her driver and bodyguard tucked her safely into the car.

When Jack returned to the other guests he wore a wide grin and strode over to Ariana. "Thank you, Ariana. She was even more captivating than I imagined. Excuse me for saying this but she's so unlike Jonathan. Are you sure she's a Barrington?"

At which the group gave a pleasant chuckle and reaffirming nod. "Yes, Jack, she is pure Barrington. Fortunately, she has much of Elizabeth's fine pedigree," Robert clarified.

Early the following week …

The exquisite floral arrangement sat prominently on Christiana's conference table. A simple card was attached.

"It was a great pleasure to meet you Saturday evening. I had a wonderful time. Let us pick up where we left off over dinner, Jackson."

Smiling, she placed the card in the envelope and tucked it in her handbag.

"Ms. Barrington, Marshall is holding on line one and a Mr. Hamilton is holding on line two," informed Amanda.

"Please tell Marshall I'll be down in fifteen or twenty minutes. Put through the call from Mr. Hamilton."

"Good morning, Jack. Thank you for the gorgeous floral arrangement. I so enjoyed meeting you at the Worthingtons'. They are consummate hosts and their parties always include an erudite collection of friends."

"Yes, their parties are most eventful. I'm glad the flowers arrived. Pardon my interruption on a hectic Monday, but I didn't want the week to slip away without arranging a quiet dinner."

Glancing at her schedule, Christiana asked, "Would tomorrow work for you?"

"Absolutely!"

After she finished the conversation with Jack, she leaned back to savor the moment. *I must thank Ariana,* she thought, reaching for the telephone.

"Hello, *darling,*" answered Ariana, panting from her workout. "I need to take a break, Rex," she said to the fitness instructor. "Don't keep me in suspense—what did you think of Jackson? Darling, isn't he perfect?"

"He is charming, witty, and intelligent."

"Isn't he gorgeous? I just like looking at him; oh, don't tell George," laughed Ariana. "Would you consider seeing him?"

"I received flowers this morning followed by a telephone call. We are having dinner tomorrow evening."

"Marvelous! I'm confident Jackson is the man to help you get over Michael."

As Christiana concluded the conversation, Amanda approached and laid several messages on her desk. "Mr. Barrington needs some files you have regarding the Sterling acquisition," Amanda explained.

"I'll prepare the folder and ask you to deliver it to his office. Tell Marshall I'll be there as soon as possible and am sorry for the delay."

By late afternoon, Jonathan appeared at Christiana's office door. "I'm glad you had the final copy of the Sterling term sheet readily available as my hard copy must be in London. Eagleson's attorney wanted to clarify a couple of terms. I still can't believe we have Blake working for Barrington."

"It's just as you desired, Father."

"Indeed." In his usual rushed manner, Jonathan segued with, "Amanda said you needed to speak with me."

"Yes, Father." At hearing the firm tone of Christiana's voice, he took his cue and was seated. "Each time I mention Christian Luke you appear rankled. No more dodging the subject, Father." Watching Jonathan's body language, sensing the jaguar ready to pounce, she raised her hand indicating she was not willing to yield the floor. "Christian is middle management, yet on various instances he has been presented with highly sensitive materials and projects. You are giving him direction and overstepping Grant. Why, Father?"

"Christian is a valuable employee. I'm acquainting him with all aspects of our businesses, not only sales and marketing."

"It appears as if you are mentoring him. If he needs all this coaching, he isn't equipped for the job," she stated abrasively.

"Christiana, get to know him. Give it six months. Then let's revisit this conversation," said Jonathan, now standing, staring down at his daughter.

"So that's it?" she snapped.

"I certainly don't have anything else to add. Grant and I are working with him so your involvement should be minimal—with the exception of the Australia trip."

Christiana was relentless. "If you insist on sending him over to Australia then I suggest you send James. The three of you are more suited for the environment out at the mines."

"Very well, but I don't need James to be involved at this point. If there is nothing else, Christiana, I am late for a game of racquet ball."

Distracted with her thoughts from the tempestuous conversation with her father, she was startled as her private line rang. Answering it without looking at the incoming number, she was surprised to hear Michael's voice.

"Hello, Michael, are you planning another visit to Montrachet? Your daughter misses you."

"I need to be in New York next week and would love to stay at Montrachet."

"Jennifer will be thrilled. Michael, there is something I would like to mention," she said in a serious tone.

"Let me guess. You and Prince Charming are seeing more of each other—platonic, of course," he monotoned sarcastically.

"While I see Marc Philippe occasionally, I have started to see someone I met through a mutual friend. His name is Jackson Hamilton. You may have heard of him."

Waiting a moment before responding, Michael acknowledged, "No, can't say I have heard of him." But he quickly ended the discussion with, "Sweetheart, sorry, I need to take this call."

Bounding down the stairs when hearing her mother open the door, Jennifer exclaimed, "Daddy is coming next week. He wants to take me to see his new play in New York."

"That's very exciting," said Christiana, leaning down to kiss her daughter.

"Mother, I've finished my homework. May I watch television?"

Hearing footsteps, Christiana waited until Veronica entered the room before responding to her daughter's request. "Hello, Veronica, has Jennifer studied her French as well as practiced her piano lesson?"

"She's completed her French lesson but her piano teacher rearranged her schedule and is due here in about thirty minutes," stated Veronica.

Jennifer looked sheepishly at her mother who responded, "You heard Veronica, please go and get a little practice in before your lesson."

After Jennifer was in bed, Christiana wandered into her closet, pulling out several outfits and accessories, contemplating what to wear to dinner with Jack. Removing the bone-colored off-the-shoulder silk Valentino dress from its hanger, she held it up and examined herself in the full-length mirror. Catching a glimpse of Jennifer sitting quietly in the corner, Christiana remarked, "How long have you been there? I thought you were asleep."

"I couldn't sleep so I've been watching you with your dresses. Are you looking for something pretty for your dinner with that man tomorrow night?"

"Yes, honey, would you like to help me choose which outfit to wear for dinner with Mr. Hamilton?"

"Sure," said Jennifer, touching the fabrics and trying on her mother's shoes. "I like this one with the crisscross straps in the back," Jennifer decided, pointing to the Armani black beaded halter dress.

"I favor the Armani dress too, sweetheart. Let me ring the maid to pack an overnight bag and I'll be right back."

Jennifer was tucked in her mother's bed when she returned. "I don't want you to go out to dinner with Mr. Hamilton. You might fall in love and get married. I don't want you to be married to anyone but Daddy," she declared, frowning.

"Oh, Jennifer, I just met Mr. Hamilton."

"Did you tell Daddy you were having dinner with a man?"

"Yes, I briefly discussed it with your father on the telephone."

"Was he mad or upset?"

"No, sweetheart, your father told me to have a good time. Now please get some sleep. You have school in the morning," said Christiana as she turned off the lights and held her daughter until she fell asleep.

Jennifer's concerns from the previous night did not echo in the morning.

CHAPTER 21

A BEVY OF PERSONAL ATTENDANTS transformed Christiana's daytime professional look to evening glamour. Her hair stylist did an undone up-do with hair pieces sexily falling out at the back and around her face, revealing her tanned and toned shoulders and back through the crisscrossed straps of the cocktail dress. With her security team in tow she reached the restaurant to find Jackson waiting at the bar and he promptly relieved her detail, escorting her to their table.

"You are like an exquisite painting—one just wants to linger and soak in the beauty, interest and detail. And the dress is stunning," Jack whispered.

"Thank you. I've been looking for the perfect occasion to wear it."

Ariana had given Jackson advice on how to approach Christiana. *"She is fiercely loyal and extremely private. You have never heard a Barrington scandal. She will defend Jonathan to the limit so tread lightly in that area. Talk about Jennifer and you will climb to the top of the ladder. She will have nothing negative to say about her ex, Michael. She feels more to blame for the breakup of the marriage, although Michael blames Jonathan. And you should know going into a relationship with her that Jonathan is all-controlling."*

"You have led an extraordinary life, Christiana, and run an empire that would rival or equal the gross national product of many countries. Yet you are not the least egotistical, arrogant, or self absorbed."

"I believe you just defined my father, Jonathan Robert Barrington," she answered in jest.

"Possibly, but it hasn't rubbed off on you."

"I've been blessed with my mother's personality traits, the Matthews' softer personality. As for the running of Barrington; it is all I have ever known."

After placing their dinner orders, Jack continued. "I must confess, I've been a connoisseur of the Barringtons for years, well, particularly Christiana Lynn Barrington."

He saw the quizzical look on Christiana's face. "I've followed BHI's tremendous growth and its complicated mergers and acquisitions. And no, I'm not a corporate raider."

"BHI is an interesting company and I've heard we're referenced in a number of textbooks used in graduate schools of business," she replied.

"Much of the focus of the articles and news stories I've read centers on both you and Jonathan. The differences between the two of you are striking and definitive. One particular article, I think it was *Forbes*, profiled you and Jonathan as the feature story. The cover had you and Jonathan seated in wing-backed chairs at an angle—not facing inward looking at each other. The caption read 'Still seeing eye-to-eye on the future of BHI? Is Christiana still heading to the executive suite?'"

"How well I remember. While we may not be in agreement on every matter or decision, we are in perfect unison on all major transactions that affect Barrington. The comment about the executive suite is just ludicrous. God, I hope and pray every day my father is around and working for years. As a publicly traded company, we must endure additional scrutiny and regulations, as you know firsthand with your entities. Plus, the press continues to point to my more timid personality. I'm not perceived as having the bite, aggressiveness or arrogance of Jonathan. It's viewed as a major weakness."

"I hope you never change. You are captivating, intelligent and beautiful. The press cannot get enough of you," said Jack. *And neither can I,* he mused.

"But the comparisons to the legendary Jonathan Robert Barrington will always abound."

"You play it off very well."

"I've had years of practice. However, I draw the line with the media when they tread on my personal life. I'm a very private person who was born a Barrington and must live a highly visible and public existence. Here is one example. I was asked, during a business interview, if my father was the cause of the break-up of my marriage to the famous producer and director Michael Trent. The question was not answered and to this day I refuse to be interviewed or quoted by that journalist."

"Amazing how cavalier, irresponsible and insensitive the media can be at times. I've heard it referred to as 'The Barrington curse,'" Jack observed. While Christiana nodded in agreement, it was clear she was finished with this topic and Jack continued no further.

"If memory serves, Jonathan's first big break came with the purchase of a hotel that needed refurbishing."

"You do know a bit about Barrington business history. It was the Regal Plaza here in New York and we still have the property in our hotel portfolio. My father claims he will never sell it as it serves as a reminder of where he started."

"The Regal Plaza *by Barrington*, I know it well," commented Jack. "I tried to purchase it a few years ago and was met with an emphatic '*No.*' the property was not nor would be available for sale."

"I extend my apologies if you were poorly treated by any of our staff."

"Your staff was extremely professional, but the message was clear—Barrington had no interest in selling the hotel."

Switching the subject, Jack led in with, "Your ex-husband has become quite a talent on Broadway. I've had the opportunity to see one of his productions. I understand he has another play due to open shortly."

"Michael ... Michael Trent is a huge talent here and in Hollywood. The new play opens next week and he will be in New York to take our daughter to the première."

"I hope to meet Jennifer at some point; she sounds like a delightful little girl," responded Jack.

"She is the love of my life. Everything I would or could have imagined in a child, a pure joy."

"Are you grooming her for the Barrington throne?"

"Well, not intentionally; however, my father is of a different mind. He has been mentoring her for some time. Jennifer has her own aspirations and following in her mother's footsteps is not one of them. But with Barrington, your fate is pretty much sealed, although I'm hoping she comes to this conclusion on her own. This may be the real Barrington curse you alluded to earlier."

"Like you, I grew up knowing my destiny. But I was not as accepting to take the reins with my father."

"I never knew anything else, nor was I given a choice. Jack, I have dominated the conversation and I've wanted to learn more about you but time has slipped away."

"This means, if I may be presumptuous, there will be a next time and at that point, I will tell you more than you ever wanted to know about Jackson Hamilton II."

Their entrees arrived and they enjoyed the food with lighter conversation. She passed on dessert but nibbled on Jack's key lime pie while they sipped their coffees.

Saying their goodbyes, Jack turned and kissed her on the mouth. She did not resist.

Hoping to catch a glimpse of Christiana the next morning, Jack walked in the direction of BHI on the way to his office. Luck was with him, as he noticed her limo pull up to her building, and watched both driver and bodyguard make their presence known as they escorted her from the car. Within earshot, Jack called her name, resisting the temptation to approach and risk an unnecessary reaction from her security team.

Turning around, she saw Jack and waved. She asked security to wait and she approached Jack.

"I've not been able to get you off my mind. I do occasionally walk this way to my office and was hoping to run into you this morning."

"What a pleasant surprise. I've been thinking about our marvelous dinner."

"That's all the encouragement I need. When may I see you again? This time you will get chapter and verse on my life, albeit a life not as glamorous or ambitious as yours."

"Allow me to be the judge. Yes, I would very much like to see you again, Jack."

"I'll arrange something early next week as I'll be out of town for a few days."

"That sounds perfect," she replied as her cell phone rang. "Sorry, I will need to take this," she apologized, starting toward the building, but then looked back and smiled.

Finishing her business call with Corinthian Properties, she proceeded up to the executive floor and was informed her mother was on the line.

"Good morning, Mother, this is a pleasant surprise. Are you up at the Vineyard?"

Elizabeth and Jonathan sailed around Martha's Vineyard during the summer and biked from Oak Bluffs to Gay Head and Vineyard Harbor in the fall and spring. It was one of the few places where Elizabeth could get Jonathan to disconnect from his consumption of business. There was almost an unwritten rule on the island—no deal-making, no contract signing, no discussion of one's wealth, or even golf score. Instead literature, politics and social issues were the main topics du jour.

Walking on the beach, painting, and reading provided the mental and physical nourishment Elizabeth craved. While Christiana jetted off to Florida and preferred the blast of the tropical sun with casual beach attire and a perennial tan, Elizabeth found contentment strolling along the breezy dunes and the beach in jeans and a cable knit sweater.

"Yes, darling, I just arrived and am looking forward to some quiet time away from our fitful schedules as of late," responded Elizabeth. The wind had picked up and she was glad she had a light sweater to slip over her shoulders as she continued to speak with her daughter.

As she lingered for sometime on the beach after speaking with Christiana, the sand felt warm from the midday sun. Elizabeth took a long cleansing breath and continued to stare out at the sea.

Startled back to reality with the ring of her cell phone, she heard Jonathan command, "Elizabeth where are you? I called the house and the apartment and staff informed me you were out of town for a couple of days. Christiana said you're up at the Vineyard."

With a polite chuckle Elizabeth responded, "My love, we did speak about my trip and I asked you to join me but you declined due to business concerns in Europe."

"Ah ... I remember. I tried to persuade you to accompany me to London but you said the Vineyard was the change of pace you needed. The Vineyard is a special place; however, I am engaged in Europe longer than anticipated so would you please have the staff pack your bags and fly to Paris to meet me for a couple of days? I miss you, darling."

"Oh Jonathan, I miss you too. Let me call my secretary and see what social commitments I have for the next week or so."

As she spoke, Jonathan was instructing his staff, "Abbey, call the Sterling Hotel and change my room to the Presidential suite next week. Mrs. Barrington will be joining me in Paris." He caught his breath before returning to conclude his telephone conversation. "Elizabeth, I can't wait to see you."

"Jonathan, you are such an imp. No never enters your vocabulary," Elizabeth commented, going back to the house.

"We wouldn't be where we are today if it did, Elizabeth."

With the time difference, Elizabeth returned the call when it was late for Jonathan. "Darling, it sounds like I woke you, my apologies. Plans are all in order and I will see you in a couple of days."

Although he usually got his way, he never assumed so with Elizabeth. "I love you, Elizabeth. I will have pleasant dreams knowing I will see my beautiful wife soon."

"I love you too, Jonathan, I can't wait to see you." Feeling content, Elizabeth prepared a light snack and poured a glass of wine then called Christiana.

"Your father asked me to join him in Paris; as you know, business keeps him in Europe longer than anticipated."

"No, I was not aware he was extending his trip. He didn't mention it earlier."

"Something probably came up after your conversation with him," said Elizabeth offhandedly.

"I'm sure I'll hear tomorrow." She changed the subject.

"Mother, you adore Paris and the shopping. I'm sure you'll have a marvelous time."

Armed with a stack of files and sporting a harried look, Leslie barged into Christiana's office. "Sorry, Jonathan was adamant I get this to you before the end of the day. He wants you to review the board package before it is sent out tomorrow. Oh yes, I almost forgot, Jonathan will call you tomorrow morning at seven at Montrachet."

"Thanks, Leslie." Since Christiana was staying in Manhattan, she emailed her father requesting he contact her at her apartment in the morning. Perusing the files, Christiana realized she had four to five hours of work ahead. It was going to be a long night.

As she rode over to the Upper East Side apartment, she wondered if Michael was right. *There is only one man in your life and it's your father.* "Oh God, could it be true?" She heard herself talking out loud. The stars were clearly lining up in that direction.

CHAPTER 22

SIPPING HER SECOND CUP of coffee fortified Christiana with the adrenalin rush needed for her early phone call with her father. She wondered why he hadn't informed her of his plans to extend his stay in Europe. This was the week of the BHI board meeting in New York.

Precise as the Swiss movement of a watch, the seven o'clock call came through. "Good morning, Christiana. How are you and Jennifer?"

"She's fine but misses you and asked when you would take her to see her pony?"

"Ah yes, I'll take her just as soon as I get back from Europe."

Concerned he may sidestep her concerns, she began, "Father, I'm surprised you will not be present for the board meeting this week."

Not one for confrontation unless self-initiated, he batted back her question in typical Jonathan-style with another question, changing the playing field. "Did you have an opportunity to review the board package last night?"

"Yes, Father, wasn't that your dictum last evening?" she punched back.

At the apparent animosity, he attempted appeasement, "Christiana, you needed the necessary documents for review, consideration and change since you will be chairing the board meeting. I didn't have the opportunity to call since I was in a noisy restaurant with Grant and CL. I'm sorry you feel slighted, that was not my intention."

"Dinner with Christian? It's rather unconventional for senior management to have dinner with middle management."

"Christian's doing an outstanding job and Grant needs to take notice and promote him accordingly."

Exhaling loudly, Christiana shot back, "Shouldn't Grant make that decision? He works with Christian every day."

"Let's not go at this again, Christiana. You promised to get to know and work with him. I'm weary of these repetitive conversations about CL."

The famous *father-daughter* impasse impeded Christiana from responding to his last statement. Her father's micro-management bothered her as it was not Jonathan's modus operandi. Christiana inquired, "Is Grant in agreement to promote Christian?"

"Grant will come around shortly," he answered with an autocratic tone.

Each answer fostered additional questions and she rammed ahead with, "What type of promotion are you considering for Christian?"

"VP of Sales and Marketing Worldwide with a direct report to Grant," Jonathan answered matter-of-factly, leaving no doubt this was well-staged.

Thrown by the response, Christiana retorted, "Father, you can't be serious? Christian's too young, too inexperienced, and has not proven himself at BHI."

Fielding the volley of questions as it suited him, Jonathan replied, "With his expertise in sales and marketing, this promotion is a natural fit. My plans are to groom him to move into operations. And yes, I couldn't be more serious if he were my own …" and his voice trailed off.

Struggling to understand his reasoning, she asked, "What about Brian, Grant's choice for his successor?"

"Brian left the company," he stated flatly.

"Really? When? Why?" The questions flew like staccato notes as she wondered what other Barrington business he'd withheld from her.

Calmly, Jonathan responded, "It just happened and honestly, it's for the best. He wasn't cut out for the long term with Barrington." As the conversation unfolded, it appeared Grant had been maneuvered to remove Brian to make room for Christian.

"Are Grant and you in sync?" The question hung as if it were being washed slowly across the Atlantic.

At last Jonathan cleared his throat and replied, "I'm not sure. Time will tell."

Thoughts flooded her mind. *What is he really saying? Is he trying to sideline Grant after all these years?* "Who's replaced Brian? Who's handling operations in Europe? Is James involved in finding a replacement?"

"I will notify James today but I wanted to speak first to you. Since I'm in Europe so frequently we may leave the position unfilled, but I'll work that out with Langston."

"Father," she began, but was upstaged by Jonathan.

"We'll discuss this in detail when I return. But for now we have more pertinent matters to discuss." With the tense battle ended, at least for the moment, they pursued the other pending matters.

Concluding their conversation, Christiana sliced the airwaves by saying, "We will continue the first topic when you return, Father."

Not acknowledging her last comment, he responded, "We'll speak prior to the board meeting."

Unnerved by the conversation, Christiana pondered a trip to London. *But, do I really have a reason not to trust my father?* With resignation, she decided to listen to his full explanation in person.

Later at her New York apartment, Christiana prepared for her dinner date. She let her hair fall gently around her neck, enhancing the emerald necklace and simple black sleeveless cocktail dress. With some time before her departure, she turned on her computer to check her email. Nothing appeared urgent but there was an email from Christian Luke. The mere sight of his name evoked agitation and when she caught mention of Australia she sat down to read the entire message.

> *Hello Christiana:*
>
> *As Jonathan may have cited, I'm accompanying him on the due diligence trip to Australia. Jonathan mentioned that you have the bulk of the files and financial data in electronic format. Please forward all relevant information as soon as possible to allow me ample preparation time before I arrive in Australia. —CL*

Slamming the lid on her computer, she had no intention of complying with his request this evening or possibly at all. Looking up, she realized her butler was standing at the door. He hung his head and muttered, "Ms. Barrington, I'm sorry to intrude but your driver and security team are here."

"Thank you. I will be right out."

Christiana's public appearances never went unnoticed. Heads turned and several members of the media were standing guard waiting to photograph her arrival. Marc Philippe was quick to rescue her and escort her to the far end of the restaurant. Leaning over, he gave her a quick kiss as she slid into the booth. "Just another quiet dinner with Christiana Lynn Barrington! You draw more attention than I do in Europe."

"Marc Philippe, you know all too well what it's like to live in the public eye."

"I'm curious about a story and photograph of you and an attractive American man, ah, *Monsieur* Jack Hamilton. The press said you two are a real item," said Marc Philippe, his eyes locked on her intently.

"Oh, Marc Philippe, Jack and I just met at a mutual friend's dinner party."

"But are you dating or interested in this Jack Hamilton?" He noted Christiana's expression and was quick to add, "I know it's none of my business, *Cheri*, but it was quite an interesting article about you and the real estate tycoon. I must admit, you make a beautiful couple—not as spectacular as you and me—but quite exquisite. Do I still have a place in the life of my American princess?" He pouted.

"Yes, dear prince, you will always have a place in my life."

"Ah, close friends who happen to have romantic interludes now and then."

"Yes, that is certainly another side of our evolving relationship."

Shared laughter and a mutual sense of understanding proved the perfect icebreaker. Christiana noticed his signature rose in front of her place setting as Marc Philippe proclaimed, "Let me propose a toast to a memorable dinner with a mesmerizing and enchanting lady."

"Yes, to a memorable dinner. Since we haven't spoken in quite a while, please tell me about the New Jersey acquisition."

"Just look at me, Christiana. I'm now a working man, both pale and tired. My father wants me to run the company. I am a mess," Marc Philippe said, gesturing with his hands. He continued to lament to his attentive audience for a few moments.

"Well, now that you have indulged me, my dear, what is new at Barrington?"

While reluctant to mention her concerns about her father and Christian Luke, she was still rankled and decided to discuss her worries. "I do have a business issue and would like to get your read," she began.

"I'm honored you would ask the prince-turned-reluctant businessman for his opinion."

"BHI has a new hire in our London office who has been promoted with meteoric speed. He does not fit the 'Barrington mold.' He's arrogant, brash, and opinionated with no proven track record. I thought he would end up alienating enough of the staff to be terminated. But I was wrong. Now he's been promoted to VP of Sales and Marketing Worldwide reporting directly to Grant Pemberton, our GM. When I asked my father if Grant was in sync with this decision his response was, 'Only time will tell.' Apparently, my father intends to move him into operations."

"What is the name of this employee?"

"Christian—actually he goes by Christian Luke or CL," answered Christiana.

"That name sounds familiar. Does he look like the model that used to do the French fashion layouts?"

"I'm not sure I know who you are referencing, Marc Philippe."

Marc Philippe described Christian Luke in perfect detail. "Yes, that sounds exactly like him," she said in astonishment.

"Now I know why he looked so familiar. Remember, I ran into your father at a restaurant in Germany a while back and he was having dinner with a man? *That was the man, I would bet on it!*"

Brushing aside his last comment to conceal her chagrin, Christiana inquired, "Do you think I'm overreacting?"

"Do you think he is too inexperienced? Or are you upset you were not part of the decision-making process?"

"Both," she retorted. As she sat back, she added, "But I guess I'm not sure of Father's *real* intentions; and that is probably at the root of my frustration."

"I can tell you from firsthand experience, I never know my father's true intentions. Well, that is not exactly correct—his intentions were clear when he told me he would cut off my inheritance unless I became gainfully employed. What a dark day in the life of Marc Philippe Boulanger that was," he extolled.

"I didn't mean to turn our dinner into a drama about my petty business issues."

"Your issues are not petty and I think you have sound business judgment and exceptional intuition, and you may be correct about Christian. However, I think you should heed your father's advice and give the guy a chance. If my employees didn't give me a shot it would have been harder than it already has been, given my limited experience and skills set."

"You have a point, Marc Philippe."

Lingering over coffee and dessert, neither was ready to say goodbye to the evening. But since it was the middle of the week the parting was eminent.

Marc Philippe leaned over and kissed Christiana and thanked her for a wonderful dinner.

CHAPTER 23

THE FLOWERS' INTOXICATING FRAGRANCE greeted Christiana as she entered her office. Roses of every color and variety were strategically placed about the room. Amanda shook her head in amazement.

"You are certainly on someone's radar," James teased, surveying the bountiful arrangements. He had been waiting for her.

"Yes, I guess I am," she answered smiling, as she tucked the note cards in her pocket. She closed the door to her office as James started to speak.

"After spending a considerable amount of time at Magnifique, I've concluded it's futile, to believe we can overhaul operations under Allison's leadership and management. I've had a conversation with Samantha Jones and she may be interested in joining Barrington," stated James, as he sat back in his chair and waited for Christiana's reaction.

"Samantha Jones of Morgan Joseph? She's the cornerstone of that company and responsible for the turnaround. How do you think we can get her to jump ship and come to work for us?"

"Oh, yes, Christiana—*the* Samantha Jones, Tiger Lady of MJ fame. I've known Sam for years, and with the problems at Magnifique, we need someone of her caliber. Look at her results at Morgan Joseph."

"You have my attention."

He leaned over Christiana's desk and lowered his voice. "Now for an additional tidbit—apparently Morgan Joseph might be up for sale."

"Oh God, please don't tell Jonathan. BHI is overloaded with back-to-back acquisitions; we need to assimilate these entities before we pursue a competitor."

"Pardon me, Christiana, but I think Jonathan would be interested in this company. This entity could merge perfectly with Magnifique and we could see substantial growth in this sector more quickly. If I can get Samantha, I'm confident we could pull this off."

"It's certainly worth considering. Let's gather additional information about MJ."

"They're preparing an offering so I'll work with the investment banking firm. We should look at these as two separate pieces, the hiring of Jones and the pursuit of MJ."

"James, we couldn't touch Samantha if we became a contender in the purchasing of the company."

"She's currently without a contract, and if we are to do something, we may have to assertively chase her *now*. She's an asset to MJ, and if they are serious about selling they're going to lock her under a new contract to dangle to perspective buyers."

"Find out what it would take to get Samantha and make sure she is serious about leaving Morgan Joseph. There shouldn't be any mention to her of our interest in pursuing MJ," dictated Christiana.

"I want to move rapidly before Morgan Joseph tries to sign her to a new contract. At this point, she has no 'non-compete' clause.

She also mentioned she would welcome the opportunity to work with you."

"That's nice to hear; but from what I know about Samantha, she is *boss* of her domain. You tread lightly around her. She runs the show."

"Yes, and that is why she has been so successful," said James.

"We should arrange a meeting and could meet at my apartment either Thursday or Friday afternoon. We shouldn't arouse speculation from our staff."

James nodded as he made his way to the door. "On another note, I met with Peter Chang and apprised him of the potential Australian acquisition. Some staff restructuring and realignment may be necessary if Asia takes the bulk of Jewels' business, but he's confident they could assimilate the structure into their operations."

Desiring to get his reaction she asked, "Have you been told Christian will be accompanying you on the Australia trip?"

"I may have seen something in my emails, but honestly, I haven't paid much attention to the pink diamond deal at this early stage. Why do you ask?"

Pulling a Jonathan, she answered the question with another question, "Have you spoken with Jonathan since you returned from Singapore?"

"Not yet, but I understand he's looking for me," he replied, glancing at his watch. "I'd better get moving. I want to get a call in to Samantha Jones."

Once alone, Christiana carefully opened the note cards from her pocket to determine the sender.

The cards from Jackson read:

"White roses are for freshness—the beginning of our new relationship. J."

"Yellow roses are for friendship—I want to be your new friend. J."

"Pink roses are for the beautiful. J."

"Red roses are for the passion I hope will be in our future. Lovingly, Jack."

Rereading the cards, she hadn't heard Amanda step into her office; when acknowledged, Amanda conveyed the message that Christian had called twice and needed to speak with her as soon as possible. *I should speak with Father before I respond to Christian,* she thought, dismissing her assistant.

Reaching Jonathan at the London office, she came straight to the point, ignoring the normal pleasantries. "Father, I received an email from Christian requesting I forward the confidential files on the Australia deal. Do you wish him to have access to these files? Do you still plan on having him accompany you to Australia?"

"Yes, Christiana, to both your questions," responded Jonathan in exasperation. "It remains my desire to acquaint Christian with this potential acquisition since he has some responsibility with Jewels in London."

"I assume his only involvement is with the sales and marketing aspects of the business."

"It's not like you to question my judgment," Jonathan answered tersely.

"Christian reports to Grant, our GM," she chirped.

Jonathan sounded annoyed. "Grant has more than enough on his plate with Sterling's pivotal position in Europe. That's why I'm grooming Christian."

Not willing to drop the subject, Christiana pounced, saying, "Father, we are all playing a part in the consolidation and assimilation of Sterling."

Sensing she was not to be the winner in this round and before she leveled another insult, she surrendered. "You win, Father. As we speak, I've forwarded the files."

"Thank you, Christiana. You should still call Christian and make nice since he will be in New York in a couple of weeks."

God, there are times my father is IMPOSSIBLE, she thought. But in characteristic form, Christiana responded, "I'll call and exude my charm and charisma as the consummate professional you have come to cherish, your one and only darling child, Christiana Lynn Barrington."

"Good. I need to run as I'm late for a meeting. Love you," and Jonathan signed off not waiting for her goodbye.

As she finished leaving a voice mail for Christian, her cell phone rang.

"Christiana, it's James. Samantha will meet us Friday afternoon at three. Do you wish to discuss strategy before the meeting?"

"Sure, let's say one in my office and then we can drive together to my apartment."

Before she was sidetracked, she placed a call to Jack. "Jack, I'm overwhelmed with the beautiful floral arrangements but I was most touched by the cards. You have a lovely way with words—and with women."

"Ah, Christiana, not with women, just one particular intoxicatingly magnificent lady named Christiana."

"You're making me blush."

"I wanted to send them after our first date—but then I thought, let a little time go by, just in case she forgets about you," he chuckled.

"You are not easily forgettable."

Hearing telephones ringing in the background, Christiana took her cue, "You sound extremely busy and I'm late for a meeting." She lingered on the last words and Jack affirmed them.

"I'm consumed and asked my staff to work all weekend," he moaned.

"I understand. I've scheduled a meeting at my apartment Friday afternoon that will probably leave me in Manhattan Friday evening and unable to get back to Montrachet."

"You have given me a wonderful idea. May we separate from work long enough to have dinner together Friday evening?"

"Jack, I would love to have dinner with you. I'm just not sure what time my meeting will end. I believe a seven o'clock reservation would work."

"Christiana, cooking is one of my passions. I'd like to show you another side of Jack Hamilton so why don't you come over to my apartment and I'll make us a relaxing dinner? Then you don't have to be concerned with the time."

"Jack, it sounds like a welcome change from the paparazzi that seem to plague us in restaurants."

"I will have the champagne chilled awaiting your arrival."

CHAPTER 24

SAMANTHA JONES STRODE into Christiana's living room in head-to-toe couture. She oozed the sense of confidence of a highly charged and accomplished woman. Smiling, she leaned over to James and pecked him on the cheek and then, with her piecing chocolate brown eyes, turned squarely to her hostess and shook Christiana's hand as they were formally introduced.

"My apologies for not getting my resume over to you before this meeting," Samantha announced, handing each a copy of her vita.

"I'm familiar with your accomplishments, Samantha. Your creative endeavors and keen business sense have given Morgan Joseph a new image and taken the company to new heights," assured Christiana.

Not hiding behind modesty, Samantha responded, "Well, the creation of a new image was one of the items the company needed. But I've been instrumental in the total turnaround from operations, R&D as well as marketing and sales. If you look at the sales and revenue figures, I have succeeded. In addition, Morgan Joseph's stock price has had its best run up the past three years I've been on board."

"I have ... we have looked at the stock price and have been following the company for some time," said James.

"Of course," nodded Samantha, "Morgan Joseph's a formidable company and I have enjoyed my tenure. However, I've started to plateau and," looking at James, "I've put out feelers."

Christiana took the lead. "Samantha, why are you interested in leaving Morgan Joseph?"

"Christiana, my expertise and skill base is an asset to a growth-oriented company—even if it's fraught with problems. I fix issues, I know what sells, how to sell it, at what price point, and have enough research and development knowledge to ready new and innovative skin care products to blow away the competition." She added, with her no nonsense demeanor, "There are no real challenges for me at Morgan Joseph."

"I understand James has mentioned Magnifique definitely needs a makeover."

"I see it in the packaging, marketing, as well as the vintage product line. It's not a trendsetter," she continued smoothly with her edgy attitude. "I know your current CEO, Allison Faulkner, she and I worked together years ago at Vista Beauty. She is in over her head and frankly, I'm not sure she and I would work well together."

"Samantha, if you were to assume the role as CEO at Magnifique, Allison would be terminated unless you designate a role for her," offered Christiana.

"We'd like to give you some background on Magnifique and BHI's vision for its future," said James. "And you nailed it, Samantha," he nodded, "when you mentioned the vintage product line, outdated packaging and minimal marketing efforts."

Christiana interjected, "However, James, many of the older products are fantastic sellers and there still appears to be a viable market."

"I agree wholeheartedly, Christiana," said Samantha. "But I would bet each piece could be improved with new ingredients or formulations while some of the others might just need to be jazzed up with younger, trendier packaging and labeling," she continued briskly. "Christiana, I understand from James you might be involved as spokesperson for the company?" She paused for Christiana's response.

"It's more like she's been drafted," chimed in James. "Who better to represent the nouveau woman than Christiana?"

Before Christiana could speak Samantha took over. "I think it's a marvelous idea! In fact, I would take it a step further and try to start a line of men's products using the face of the new Sales VP in Europe. Um, James, help me, I can't remember his name. I saw a write-up about him in a London periodical. He's gorgeous and a dead ringer for the hunk that modeled underwear in magazine and billboard ads."

Fidgeting, Christiana attempted to break into the conversation but was upstaged by James. "You must be referring to Christian Luke who works in our London office."

"Yes, yes, that's the name. Christiana, I envision runaway success with you and Christian in the print and television spots. We could launch *The Barrington Collection!*" Samantha announced enthusiastically.

"I'm not sure I'm the right spokesperson and I'm certainly not a model," Christiana stated.

"Christiana, with you as the spokesperson, Christian's involvement in the men's line and the company under my reins, Magnifique would achieve the heights of ultimate sophistication and class," Samantha enthused.

"Thank you, but I think our first efforts are to resurrect a company and establish Magnifique as a major contender in the world of beauty."

"We may need to move on to some other matters," interjected James, his eye on the time.

"James, before we leave the subject, allow me to clarify one item. Given Christian's recent promotion, he will *absolutely* have no time for this type of involvement with Magnifique," Christiana stated coldly.

Giving Christiana a quizzical look, he sidestepped her remark, moving the conversation to items pertaining to Samantha's time-frame and availability.

Once Samantha had departed, James eagerly said, "I think she's a precise fit for BHI. I would welcome the opportunity to work with Samantha again. She's one hundred percent focused and driven to excellence." Reaching into his briefcase, he handed some papers to Christiana. "I've outlined her current compensation package as well as the additional items being sought with the new contract at Morgan Joseph."

"James, if you really want to bring her over to BHI, take whatever steps are necessary," granted Christiana.

"I'll draft an agreement and email it to you this evening. I suggest we speak tomorrow morning, as I leave for Asia on Tuesday." Looking at Christiana, he inquired, "Why are you opposed to using Christian to launch a line of men's products?"

"He has assumed more responsibility than he should at this point in his career with BHI."

"I must admit I was taken aback by my conversation with Jonathan. He informed me of Brian McCauley's sudden departure. It's hard to believe, since Brian never gave me any indication he was dissatisfied or unhappy at BHI."

As it became obvious there was more than Christiana was alluding to, James dropped the probing and moved to closure for the evening.

CHAPTER 25

Awaiting Christiana's arrival, Jack made a last minute visual inspection as he strode around his apartment. Satisfied that all was in order, he touched the Cristal Champagne chilling in the ice bucket on the cocktail table next to the Baccarat crystal flutes. Playing softly in the background was Shubert's Unfinished Symphony and the twinkling lights of Manhattan were starting to accent the skyline.

Walking over to the large expanse of windows with scotch in hand, he took in the unobstructed panoramic view of Central Park he commanded from his penthouse Central Park West apartment. With his myriad commercial ventures worldwide and perpetual travel, he wondered how this new relationship with Christiana was going to fare. Concluding that her professional and personal existence was just as exacting, if the relationship was meant to be, he'd work through the inconveniences.

After conferring with his household staff, he headed to the bedroom for a spray of cologne. Glancing in the mirror, he felt he still made a handsome impression with a full head of wavy sandy brown hair, graying only at the temples. His dark blue eyes were sexy; at least that's what he'd been told. At six foot three inches, with broad shoulders and a slim waist, he had the build of a man half his age.

Finishing her preparations, Christiana gave a quick telephone call to Jennifer and Veronica before stepping out for the evening. Sliding comfortably into the deep leather seat of her limo, she couldn't wait to see Jackson.

Breathing in the aromas of the city, she thanked Peter her driver and walked with her bodyguard up to the grand entrance of Jack's condominium. When the elevator door opened, Jack was waiting at his front door. Closing the door, shutting away the world, they kissed longingly. The Oscar de la Renta silk spaghetti-strap dress revealed her shapely form as he lightly caressed it. When she pulled away, he took the cue and motioned her into the living room.

"Here's to us and a wonderful evening," he toasted with the champagne.

"Yes," she smiled. "Your apartment is exquisite and the view is breathtaking."

"Wait here one moment," he said, heading to his study and returning with a gift.

As she eyed the small box, Christiana protested, "Jack, I can't possibly accept this from you."

"Relax, Christiana, it isn't jewelry. I wouldn't dare compete with Jewels *by Barrington.*"

An intricately designed bejeweled Jay Strongwater picture frame was nestled in the box containing a photograph of Christiana and Jack taken at the dinner party in Westport. He commented, "I wanted you to have a memento of our first meeting."

"Thank you. I am delighted that Ariana introduced us," she said and kissed him.

Taking her hand he invited, "Come, let's enjoy the city lights." Once they were seated comfortably on the sofa, Jack asked, "Now it is my turn to learn more about the hypnotically beautiful Christiana Lynn Barrington. What else complements your life besides family and BHI?"

"I enjoy sailing and boating as well as tennis and horseback riding. I'm fairly accomplished on the piano. In addition, I study languages and am fluent in French, Italian, Spanish and German. Collecting rare and first edition books is my real passion. I am fortunate to have purchased a first edition in contemporary binding of *The Lewis and Clark Expedition* in two volumes as well as a first edition of *Ulysses—The Shakespeare Company*—which is one of only 750 printed on handmade paper. Recently my broker was able to obtain a rare first edition in original cloth of Charles Darwin's *On the Origin of Species,* from London circa 1859," explained Christiana.

"I hope to have the opportunity to view this fine collection at some point."

Warmly, Christiana affirmed, "I trust that you will.

"Jack, now I want to hear about your pursuits. Please tell me about your collections, interests and hobbies."

"I have a collection of six hundred bottles of vintage wine, which is housed in a wine cellar at my residence in Aspen. My interest is skiing, thus the reason for the house in Colorado. I am fluent in French, Spanish and Portuguese as I have lived in France, Argentina and Brazil. During my time in Paris, I lived in Montparnasse where I learned to draw and paint. My bohemian era. Please allow me to show you my gallery." He took her hand and walked them down the corridor to the display. "In my mid-twenties, I spent two years in Paris as I was convinced a career at Hamilton Industries was not for me."

"You are very talented, Jack," she noted, viewing his art. "Did I mention my mother used to paint? She sold numerous works before she retired the paintbrush."

"Thank you for the compliment and no, I was not aware that your mother was an artist."

"A number of her paintings grace my homes. I hope someday she resumes her craft."

The household staff announced dinner and Jack escorted Christiana into the dining room. The composed salad of cured salmon and Oscetra caviar was placed in front of Christiana, while Jack poured the sparkling cuvee and toasted his guest. "I hope the food is half as delectable as the vision I have seated in front of me."

"If the presentation is a preview then the food is sure to be a masterpiece of tastes." Christiana took several bites and proclaimed, "This is delicious. The salmon and the caviar make a delectable combination."

Jack continued the previous conversation. "Ambiguity drove me to Paris since I wasn't convinced I wanted to continue under my father's tutelage, being the prodigal son. With a clearly delineated path, I commenced work at Hamilton upon graduation from MIT and Yale with degrees in Engineering and Business. Hamilton's biggest success was a small electronic component invented by my father. Moreover, he patented a component used for jet engines and we have several lucrative US military and defense contracts."

He paused as the plates were cleared and the next course of Pumpkin Risotto in a duck confit and parmesan was paired with a Bourgogne Rouge Burgundy.

"Jack, this is the best risotto I've ever tasted. The subtle taste of the duck complements but doesn't overwhelm."

Circling back to their main conversation, Jack continued, "I have two older brothers. Michael, the oldest, works side by side with my father and could be his clone—they look alike, talk alike, and think alike. He should, for all practical purposes, step into my father's shoes when he retires. Sound familiar? Todd, the middle child, is the creative genius. His inventions are too numerous to count, and he is happy to spend his life in a lab or doing research. Then there is me, the youngest. Todd and I spent much of our childhood inventing things so the Engineering degree from MIT was appropriate. However, I added an MBA as a fallback," he said as he stopped to enjoy his meal.

"Did you get your start in research and development?"

"Yes, R&D was my home and I'm credited with the design of an electronic component used by a large sector of the military. A newer version is still in play today."

"I've heard of Hamilton Industries; but that's not the company name on your business card?"

"So the story continues, Christiana. While it was exciting to design something with such significance to the electronics industry, I was bored. I told my dad I wanted a break. He was none too pleased. Thus I set off for Paris to live among artists and learn to paint. Sounds pretty silly, right? "

"Not silly at all," responded Christiana. "Brave and courageous come to mind. Many times I wanted to tell my father I needed time away from Barrington."

"While in Paris, I managed to sell some of my etchings and paintings and a couple of galleries displayed a few of the pieces."

Again Jack curtailed the conversation while the next course was served. "Allow me to explain this course. It's quail with sweetbreads, corn pudding and black mushrooms. It's paired with a Pinot Noir from my private cellar."

"It smells divine," she answered, taking a forkful of the quail, sweetbread and corn pudding. "Hmm, this is delicious. Are you sure you didn't attend Le Cordon Bleu while in Paris?"

"*Oui, Madame,*" he chuckled. "As the Jackson Hamilton story progresses, I soon got bored in Paris and set my sights on South America. At this point my father was irritated by my adventures and rambling lifestyle and demanded I return to Denver. Not quite yet, I said to him, and managed another year abroad. Living in Argentina and Brazil, I learned to cook and entertain on a grand scale as the wealthy gringo, and socializing was easy. Meanwhile, Hamilton Industries purchased a small company in Argentina, which I believe was intentional. My father asked me to 'check it out.' Baby-sit was what they really wanted, allowing me to ease back into the Hamilton environment even if it was six thousand miles away. But it worked. I became reenergized about the business and after a year returned to Denver. My interest still was not in the core businesses of Hamilton Industries. My father was tired of arguing and reining me in so when I came up with a proposal he agreed to a compromise. I suggested we set up a subsidiary, Hamilton Commercial Properties. Hamilton Industries had more than enough capital and collateral to make this a viable entity and I was willing to invest handsomely to help ensure its success. Now the family can take pleasure in talking about a more interesting side of our businesses. Electronics is not exactly the most stimulating cocktail conversation."

Smiling as he looked at Christiana's dinner plate, he said, "You enjoyed the quail but I hope my ramblings were not too boring?"

"Your culinary skills are extraordinary and I've been totally enthralled with your fascinating story."

"There's one small caveat," replied Jack. "For the first time I love what I'm doing. Hamilton Commercial Properties is the small dog in the Hamilton chain. That wouldn't bother me if circumstances were constant at Corporate."

"The playing field has changed?"

"Yes, in a matter of speaking. My brother Michael, whom I mentioned is the brains, has been groomed to become my father's successor."

Christiana's lips curved at the inference.

"A few months ago, he was diagnosed with a debilitating neuro-muscular disease. The prognosis links it to major restrictions on mobility, speech, and sight, and brain impairment."

"Oh Jack, I'm very sorry," said Christiana somberly.

They continued their conversation over cheese, mixed ber-ries and cream along with port wine. "So yes, it has changed the playing field. I'll eventually take over Hamilton Industries when Michael feels he can no longer work. Michael and I have always been close and this has been very hard ..." he said as his voice trailed off.

"I can only imagine the anguish your family is going through. Thankfully, you are back at Hamilton to work with your brothers and father to prepare for the eventual transition. You mentioned in an earlier conversation how you knew the time was right to resume your career at Hamilton, possibly receiving a nudge from above." Glancing at her watch, Christiana concluded, "I've had a wonderful evening, Jack. You are an amazing cook! However, it's getting late and I must be heading home."

Escorting her to the door, he draped her wrap over her shoulders and summoned the elevator and his car. Jack caressed her shoulder but they fell silent for most of the ride over to the East Side. Entering her apartment, she placed her belongings on the foyer table but as she turned to say goodnight, the strap on her dress accidentally fell as Jack was preparing to set forth into the night.

She whispered, "Don't go." In one fluid movement, Jack shut the door, lifted Christiana into his arms and ascended the mahogany staircase.

Laying her softly on the bed, Jack removed his clothes and kissed her. With abandon, he removed her clothes, whisked the hair from her neck and shoulders and began kissing her body. Lost in a long passionate kiss, he could feel her svelte body arch, ready for lovemaking. Their intimacy was eagerly anticipated.

When they finally succumbed, Jack spoke. "In the passion and moonlight I didn't get a chance to see your gorgeous body. Please let me look at you."

Christiana obliged her lover and turned on the bedside lamp then stood up in full view. She shook her head and her tangled hair fell loosely around her shoulders and danced around her breasts. Jack knelt on the side of the bed and pulled her hair away from her breasts then stood silently in awe of her.

"You have taken my breath away again this evening."

Tumbling back into bed, they made love slowly and fell asleep in each other's arms. Jack stirred in the middle of the night and awakened Christiana.

"Sweetheart, I hate to leave but I have a meeting this morning and need to go to my apartment," Jack said. Christiana pulled on her robe and walked him to the foyer.

"What an incredible night. I'll call you later, my darling."

CHAPTER 26

B Y LATE MORNING, Christiana had completed her call with James and was heading to Montrachet. Reflecting on her night with Jack, she almost missed a telephone call from her father.

"Father, it's good to hear from you." Moving ahead to the business at hand, she continued, "James is presenting an offer of employment to Samantha Jones before heading to Asia. We had an excellent meeting with her yesterday afternoon and we're convinced she's the turnaround agent needed to advance Magnifique."

"Splendid! I know you and James have been none too pleased with Allison."

"It was clear during our interview that, if Samantha takes the position, Allison may be terminated shortly thereafter unless Samantha finds a spot for her on the management team."

"Good, yes, of course, that makes sense," responded Jonathan distantly.

"Father, you sound preoccupied?"

"I just missed two telephone calls. Sorry. What else were we speaking about?"

"That was it. Father, since you called me, what's the purpose of *your* call?"

Not responding directly to her question, he replied, "Sorry, Christiana, I need to take this call. We'll resume our conversation later. My love to you and Jennifer."

By the end of the day, she was surprised her father had not called back but pushed the thought from her mind as Jennifer was having a sleepover party.

As promised, Jack called that evening. "I can't get you out of my mind," he whispered. They chatted unhurried until Jennifer poked her head into the room, taking her mother's attention. "Jack, my daughter is having a sleepover and the girls need my assistance with a project, as Veronica has the night off. I'm afraid I'd better get back to them."

"Of course, I'll call you tomorrow from Denver. Have a good time with Jennifer. Goodnight, darling."

"Goodnight, Jack. I look forward to seeing you next week."

With the preoccupation of the girls' slumber party, Christiana had managed to push work from her mind for most of the weekend. However, after Jennifer was in bed Sunday evening, she sat down to peruse her emails and saw a message from her father. As she read the email it became clear why he had not telephoned her since Saturday morning.

> *Christiana:*
>
> *Christian Luke will be at Corporate this week. Please show him around and give him access to the Spencer file on the Pink Diamond Mine. Take him to lunch or dinner or both and please try to make him feel comfortable. Have the sales and marketing staff of Jewels brief him on the new marketing campaign. Acquaint him with the thrust of*

our companies and the corporate structure of Barrington.
—Jonathan

Shaking her head, she emailed the response:
  As you wish. —Christiana

An interesting week lay ahead …

Christian arrived at the New York headquarters for BHI with his usual flair and bravado. He smiled and breezed by the two front receptionists in the lobby. The ladies looked at each other and all they could mutter was, "Oh my God. Did you see him! He must be the guy from the London office." Realizing they had allowed a security breach, one receptionist went sailing down the corridor to locate the entrant, but Christian was nowhere to be found.

Making his way up to the executive floor, Christian was ogled by every young and not-so-young staff member of both genders who greeted him. By the time he landed at Christiana's threshold he had a posse. Amanda gave him a smile and glanced behind him to see the onlookers.

"You must be Christian. We have been expecting you. I'm Amanda, Ms. Barrington's assistant. Please have a seat and I will tell her you are here."

Amanda noticed that Christiana had finished her telephone call so she went inside to speak with her boss. Moments later, Christian was escorted into the office. "Amanda Worth, this is Christian Luke … ah … this is …. Excuse me, but I don't know your last name, Christian?" Christiana stopped and stared at him.

In his patrician manner, he answered, "I go by Christian, Christian Luke or CL. I do not use a last name."

"Oh," exclaimed Christiana. "Sorry, I should have known that bit of information."

"Apology accepted, Christiana, and Amanda and I have already met."

Introductions finished, Christiana proceeded to take Christian through the offices to meet appropriate staff. Setting him up in a temporary office suite, she noted, "Amanda will bring you the files on the potential Australia acquisition as well as the revised sales and marketing plan for Jewels *by Barrington*. Lunch is scheduled at twelve-forty-five followed by a three o'clock meeting at our beauty company Magnifique. I'll fill you in on that later as I need to attend another meeting."

Amanda was arranging files and new messages on Christiana's desk when she returned to her office following her meeting. "Thanks, Amanda. Please make lunch reservations at the Four Seasons for one o'clock—party of two—my usual table."

"Certainly, Ms. Barrington." Amanda paused for a moment before exiting and ventured, "May I ask you something?" Christiana nodded. "What is Christian Luke's position at Barrington? He reminds me of a model. I don't suppose he's single. Sorry, it's none of my business. He works for us anyway, what a shame. Oh, I don't mean it like that, it's just that I couldn't have a relationship with him, oh, he probably wouldn't even be interested in me anyway …" rambled Amanda.

Christiana rescued her with, "Christian works in the London office and started in the sales department. He has been given additional responsibilities at BHI and that's the thrust for his visit to Corporate." Cutting short the conversation at the business reference, Christiana did not acknowledge the personal question and turned her back to her assistant to gather her belongings. Amanda left the office without further mention of CL.

Ignoring the stares and the hushed remarks, they entered the restaurant and were led to Christiana's table. The deliberate attempt to guide the conversation along BHI issues succeeded until Christiana answered a business call.

Lying in wait, at the conclusion of her telephone conversation, Christian took command of the conversation. "Christiana, please explain what I have done to garner such disdain and disgust? Our business interactions are minimal and I know Jonathan has requested we try to develop a respectful business relationship."

So Father mentioned this to him. Gathering her thoughts, she dabbed her mouth with her napkin before speaking. "Christian, I have neither disdain nor disgust; however, you display a degree of arrogance that I find totally inappropriate at Barrington."

"That which you call arrogance, I designate to be drive and ambition. I'm working hard to succeed," and looking her squarely in the face, he added, "and doing whatever it takes to get ahead at BHI."

Raising her brows, but quick to respond, she answered, "Be careful with your choice of words, Christian. 'Whatever it takes to get ahead'? Talent, drive and ambition are rewarded and sought after at Barrington. But an overbearing, self-serving attitude and a cavalier approach to business scruples will bring people to the exit door. We have an interesting culture at Barrington, which I trust has been instilled by Grant and Jonathan."

At the impasse, Christian contritely added, "It's certainly not my intention to alienate anyone at the company, especially you. I plan to make my career with BHI."

We shall see about that, she mused.

At her obvious discomfort, he changed the subject. "Christiana, I admire the way you handle the press. You appear unflappable. The paparazzi hound you incessantly, but there's never a scandal. You've been linked romantically with the most iconic men in the world and live in the public eye twenty-four hours a day."

She answered, "The public overexposure is what I deem The Barrington Curse. I have learned to display only my public persona. My private life remains permanently off limits." Christiana signed off on the subject as well as the check. Lunch had come to a close. Business conversation resumed until they went their separate ways back at BHI.

As they were heading to Magnifique by midafternoon, Christiana asked, "Christian, how long is your stay in New York?" She was trying to gauge her time commitments with him for the week.

"Um, I'm not quite sure," he responded.

"I want to make sure we address the most critical and salient matters," she answered pleasantly.

"I'm sure we'll have time to discuss all relevant matters. Thanks for acquainting me with the pink diamond mine deal before the trip to Australia."

The remark passed without comment as Christiana sharpened her focus on their pending meeting at Magnifique. "Please listen closely to what Allison has to say about the company and be mindful there is a particular sensitivity about change."

"Duly noted; her father owned the company and brought her in to run it, from what Jonathan has told me," relayed Christian.

"That's a quick summation. Look at the current product line and give me your thoughts on the changes James and I have proposed in the draft of the business plan."

"Will Allison be staying on as CEO?"

"Barrington acquires sound companies and allows management operational autonomy with minimal involvement from Corporate."

"But I have to believe not every executive fits the Barrington profile," he snickered.

Ignoring his last comment, Christiana commanded, "Since we don't have much time this afternoon, I'd like you to meet with Allison and get a feel for the product line. Were you able to arrange a meeting with James Langston?"

"Yes, he filled me in on the major issues. I'm anxious to delve into this mess."

"That approach will not play at Magnifique," returned Christiana in a reprimand.

A call from James prompted Christiana's departure from the meeting with Christian and Allison. "We have a deal with Samantha with one small caveat. She feels Allison's presence will undermine her authority and direction and wishes she be dismissed pronto," said James.

"Before we address that matter, are the other items, salary, merit bonus, stock, and expense package, the same as we discussed?"

"Yes. Her timeline is three to four weeks depending on when MJ wants her gone. Samantha insists the personalities will get in front of the logic and they will throw her on the street rather quickly. That's why she's pushing for Allison's quick termination."

"Is she waiting to give notice until we make the move she requested?"

"The short answer is yes, Christiana. I've conferred with Legal on the termination issues and Allison is working without a contract. They suggest the easiest route may be to eliminate the position as Co-President. She may still fight and we may burn up attorney fees, but we will win. The severance package is being reviewed as we speak."

"In order to expedite, we should have the conversation with Allison ASAP?"

"Yes, I plan to speak with Allison tomorrow morning," sighed James.

"Christian is conferring with her now. Should we pull him away?"

"Let him continue—he's doing an assessment for Barrington."

"I want to get back with Samantha to allow her to move forward with her extraction from MJ."

As Christiana entered Allison's office, Christian turned and said, "Your timing's perfect, we've just finished as Allison had an appointment. Do you need me for anything else, Christiana?" They were soon in the elevator with the security team heading to the waiting Barrington limo.

CHAPTER 27

STIFLING A YAWN, Christiana answered the telephone. "Hello, Father. Even for you this is an early hour to be calling New York."

"Good morning, I'm sorry, not paying attention to the time, did I wake you?"

"No, Father, it's fine. My personal trainer arrives at six."

"How did your day go with Christian?"

"Father, honestly, you're calling at five in the morning to ask me about Christian? We spent the morning at Corporate and the afternoon at Magnifique. He met with Allison yesterday and will meet with the sales and marketing department today."

Before Jonathan could respond, she coolly added, "My impression remains the same. He is arrogant, pompous and cavalier. We did manage a civil lunch."

"I was much like Christian in my earlier days, arrogant and pompous. Look what I have accomplished," chuckled Jonathan.

"Your earlier days? The arrogance and pompous attitude is still very much alive in you, dear Father," she quipped.

"Don't underestimate Christian. He's handling operational responsibilities well."

"I await his assessment of Magnifique. While on the subject of Magnifique, James indicated Samantha Jones accepted our employment offer. The only glitch is she wants Allison Faulkner gone before she starts. Legal has been advised to prepare a severance package."

"Use Christian if you can since James will be in Asia. CL needs to understand the full extent of our operations to be valuable to BHI."

"Who uses only a single name besides some of the celebrities like Oprah or Cher? He must not be very proud of his lineage and background," she sniped.

"What makes you say that?" retorted Jonathan.

"Father, there is no reason to be defensive."

"The purpose of my call was to tell you that the Australia project and site visit has been pushed up to next week. Our operations team will arrive next weekend but I have a problem with my schedule."

"What is it, Father?"

"I need to make a quick trip to Riyadh," said Jonathan without elaboration.

"Father, if you are hinting that I head to Australia, consider sending either James or Grant. James will be in Asia and could easily fly on to Australia."

"Without *our* direct involvement, this deal with Max will not go forward."

"Then reschedule the meetings to allow time to fly from Saudi Arabia to Sydney," answered Christiana flatly. "I understood Max wasn't in any hurry to ink a deal."

"While that is true, we need to push this along or remove ourselves from the process. I guess I could fly on from Riyadh. Let me speak with Max and check my schedule as well as Christian's," said Jonathan abruptly.

"Still intent on having *him* travel to Australia?" Christiana added with dismay.

"If by him you mean Christian, then yes I am. Christiana, how many times do we need to rehash this issue? This brings up another point. While he is in New York, please acquaint him with Sterling and discuss the long-term strategy of Sterling under Barrington Hotels & Resorts International."

There isn't enough time to educate this brat on everything he needs to know. "How long is he here, Father? I asked Christian but he was evasive."

"Not sure, maybe a week, but it depends on when I have him fly over to Australia," Jonathan added, obviously thinking out loud.

I have him for the whole week!

As Christiana walked into the sales and marketing meeting, she observed Christian chairing the session. As she watched the slide presentation and listened to the remarks from the sales team, it appeared he'd hit a positive chord. She sat in on the presentation until the vibration of her cell phone prompted her exit. Stepping out of the office after completion of the call, she caught a glimpse of James heading in her direction. He pointed to the office she had just vacated and they went in and shut the door.

"It's done, almost as if Allison expected it since the Barrington purchase. I explained the active search for a CEO, thus the reason for the elimination of the Co-President position. I don't think she had any interest in staying with Barrington," said James with a bit of laughter. "She'll work with us but would like to be out within four weeks. In addition, I've received an email from Samantha and she has given her notice. She'll be here in three to four weeks, which should allow for a brief changeover."

"When will we receive the signed employment contract from Samantha?"

"I have the signed contract in my office. HR is meeting with Allison this afternoon. Is there anything else before I run off to my apartment and pack?"

"Jonathan called regarding a change of date for the site visitation in Australia. This poses a conflict due to his meetings in Saudi Arabia. I suggested having you continue on to Australia since you are familiar with the proposed acquisition," Christiana advised.

"Where is Jonathan? Still in Europe?"

"Yes, and due back here in a couple of days. He has meetings in Riyadh and Jeddah and thought he might fly from Saudi Arabia to Australia."

Scratching his head, James said, "Okay, I'm glad you gave me a heads up. I will add boots and outdoor gear to my suitcase in the event I get the call to go down under."

"I'll let you know as soon as I have the definitive word from Jonathan."

Back in the hallway, she found Christian waiting to speak with her.

"Would you mind if we postpone our meeting until tomorrow? I would like to finish up and write my sales and marketing assessment," asked Christian.

"That works better for me too," agreed Christiana. "Let's meet in my office at nine tomorrow. You will have the opportunity to meet Blake Eagleson from Sterling."

"Perfect. I look forward to meeting him. Jonathan has mentioned his name a number of times."

I can only imagine what Father had to say about Blake, she mused.

The call almost went unanswered as her cell was buried deep in her purse and she didn't hear the muffled ringing. Finally managing to retrieve it, she assumed it was Jennifer and answered without thinking, "I'm on my way, sweetheart. I should be in by seven."

In his sexiest voice, Jack responded, "Terrific. I will chill the champagne!"

"That will teach me to check caller identification." They shared a laugh.

"Sounds like your day was as frazzled as mine," continued Jack.

"Probably so. I'm looking forward to seeing Jennifer. Where are you?"

"I'm at the Miami airport waiting to fly to Atlanta and took the chance of catching you on your ride home. I can't wait to see you, I've missed you," he said.

"I've missed you too, Jack. When are you back in New York?"

"Tomorrow evening. What does your weekend look like?"

"I'd love to arrange something although I'm not clear on Jennifer's activities this weekend."

"I'll drive to Greenwich, if that works better. I just want to see you," offered Jack.

"I like that idea, although I should add Jennifer's father, Michael, may be visiting and he usually stays in the garden villa. I hope that's not too awkward?"

"It's not uncomfortable for me if you are okay with both of us there? In fact, I would like to meet Michael and Jennifer."

"Wonderful! I will call you tomorrow with the particulars," said Christiana.

CHAPTER 28

"Good morning, Christiana," greeted Christian, as he continued arranging his presentation when Christiana arrived at the office. "I've spent most of the night finishing up this assessment and would like to give you the full presentation," he stated confidently. He then inquired, "What happened at the staff meeting yesterday at Magnifique?"

Fielding the question with a quick response, Christiana said, "Allison will leave in four weeks and Samantha Jones will be on board by that time."

"Good, I look forward to working with Samantha as I have several ideas on updating the packaging. Presently, my concern is the major advertisement campaign ready to be launched, which could be catastrophic. First note these three slides. They embrace the essence of the campaign as it stands now. This was used in nationwide ads three times in the last two years. And it did not increase sales." He pushed several sheets of sales figures and graphs in front of Christiana for review. "Sales actually went down in corresponding time sequences with the hardest hitting time periods of the ad placement."

"Sales and revenues have been sliding for a while, Christian. It was one of the reasons Lou Faulkner wanted to sell."

"Yes, however, this campaign isn't going to revive the ailing numbers in such a saturated market. I strongly recommend pulling the plug or shelving it until Samantha comes in. She'll have a field day with this."

As Christiana mulled over their choices, he continued, "Apparently this campaign needs to be snuffed by Friday before Barrington starts to rack up serious expenses with the contracts for the television spots."

"Our major decision at present is the pending ad campaign?"

"Yes, I would sideline the present campaign before Allison gives carte blanche to everything as she is sailing out the door," warned Christian.

"I agree, let's delay the ad campaign. Please speak with the Sales Director at Magnifique today and suspend the campaign indefinitely."

"Consider it done. I'll see you in your office at eleven, Christiana," he concluded and smiled. She turned to leave, but he had more to say. "Thank you for your input. Jonathan has recognized my business acumen and places complete faith in my opinions and judgment. In sales and marketing, I am a force to be reckoned with. I'm glad we are on the same page with these points."

She wasn't sure whether to be annoyed or appreciate his directness. She replied, "We are in lock step with the marketing problems at Magnifique. I appreciate your read on the company and your assistance during this transition period."

He nodded with a fresh sense of cockiness but as he prepared to exit the conference room Christiana parted with, "Don't allow your ego and arrogance to get in front of you. And let me forewarn you about Blake Eagleson: His ego is even bigger than yours. However, it comes with major business successes and more than thirty-five years of experience." Her voice carried a hint of disdain.

"Point well taken; see you at eleven," he replied and made a quick exit.

At the appointed time, Jonathan and Blake walked into Christiana's office engrossed in conversation. "Good morning, gentlemen. Father, I didn't think you were due back until tomorrow?"

"I flew back last evening as my plans changed after we spoke yesterday," answered Jonathan. "Blake and I've been discussing space issues and how soon we might house Sterling's corporate offices and the reservation center in our building with Barrington Hotels."

Gathering up papers and files to proceed to the conference room, Christiana inquired, "When do you foresee moving operations to this building, Blake?"

"The executive department will move next week; the accounting as well as the sales and marketing departments have already started to come over. It's the technology and reservation side that may take the longest due to technology challenges." Laughing, he added, "I love my corner office. I never had a Manhattan view like this at my old building."

"We're glad you're satisfied and pleased to have you at Barrington," assured Christiana. Looking around, she noted, "I'm not quite sure what's keeping Christian." Almost on cue, Christian waltzed into the room brimming with confidence.

Jonathan made the introductions. "Blake Eagleson, our CEO of Sterling Hotels Worldwide, this is Christian Luke, our VP of Sales and Marketing Worldwide from our London office." He also introduced Christian to the rest of the sales and marketing personnel from Sterling.

"Blake," began Jonathan, "we should give Christian some background on Sterling before we discuss marketing, branding and the assimilation of the Sterling and Barrington products." Blake handed Christian collateral materials and brochures as he proceeded to tell the Sterling story. At several junctures, Christian interrupted with questions and comments. Blake appeared peeved with Christian's exaggerated sense of self importance. Jonathan was the only one who remained oblivious to Blake's pointed remarks. Blake concluded his overview, saying, "Make sure you work closely with the VPs as they have been with the company for years and know the product cold. You will learn much about our marketing and branding philosophy."

Following further discussion by the conclusion of the meeting, Christian appeared set for close collaboration with the Sterling team to prepare a new advertisement campaign that would stress *"The utmost in luxury—Sterling and Barrington offer you a world of choices."*

As Christiana was preparing to leave the meeting, her father asked, "Would you care to join Blake and me for lunch?"

"Thank you, Father, but I have plans," responded Christiana as she departed.

Christian was packing up his folders as Jonathan leaned over to say, "Good meeting, would you care to join us for lunch?"

"Yes, thank you. Let me just fetch the other files from my office as I am heading over to Magnifique this afternoon," replied Christian.

"Mother, where are you? We haven't spoken in a couple of days," asked Christiana when she placed a call to her mother after returning from lunch.

"Darling, I'm up at the house on the Vineyard painting, and just lost all track of time. The Chelsea Gallery in London, where I displayed my works years ago, received a request from a client. I'm very excited."

"Mother, that's wonderful! How long will you be at the Vineyard?"

"Another week, I hope. The last time I made that statement your father called and I left instantly for Europe. I'm trying to convince him to come here, but you know more about his travel schedule than I."

"*Sometimes.* He surprised me today at a meeting with Blake Eagleson."

Laughing, Elizabeth responded, "He surprised me as well yesterday; unfortunately, he had to spend the night alone at Sur La Mer."

"Mother, would you be up for some company?" Christiana asked cautiously. "I'm not sure this will work but I would love for you to meet Jackson Hamilton." Contemplating the idea a moment she then apologized, "Oh, Mother, forgive me, I didn't inquire about your plans, you are there to paint and this would surely interrupt your creative processes."

"I would love your company and welcome the opportunity to meet Mr. Hamilton. Would Jennifer and Veronica be coming as well? I'd love to see my granddaughter. I'll watch her so you and Jackson can enjoy some time together."

"If you are up for it, I'll telephone Jack and finalize with you this evening."

"I would be thrilled to meet your mother and daughter. I can't imagine anything better than to spend the weekend with you on Martha's Vineyard. Honey, I'm free after one at the latest," said Jack.

"I'll have my jet ready at Teterboro for a three o'clock departure. We are going to have a wonderful weekend," responded Christiana with excitement.

Rapidly she hit the speed dial to her mother's cell phone. "Mother, Jack will be joining us. You will have all of us—Jennifer, Veronica, Jack and me. We should be arriving by late afternoon tomorrow. Shall I bring anything?"

"No, sweetheart, Isabel will take care of the details. Now if your father would grace us with his presence, all would be perfect."

CHAPTER 29

T HE CRACKLING SOUND OF TIRES on the gravel driveway stopped Elizabeth in mid-brush stroke. Glancing out the window of her artist's retreat, she watched the car door open and her granddaughter bounce from the backseat.

She cleaned her brushes, removed her smock and opened the door, waving and calling, "Hello, I'm over here."

Jennifer was the first to respond. "Grandmother, I have a present for you."

"Jennifer, come and give Grandmother a big hug."

Christiana and Jack joined the others and waited for Elizabeth to lift the lid of the yellow ribbon-festooned gift box revealing a silver frame holding a photo of her granddaughter. "Jennifer, you look so grown up. I have the perfect place for your picture. Thank you, sweetheart," she added, kneeling down to hug her granddaughter. When she rose, Christiana kissed her mother and introduced Jackson.

After introductions, Elizabeth motioned them into the main house. "Come; let's sit comfortably in the sunroom with some ice tea." Elizabeth led the way to the room overlooking the ocean.

"Ah, what a fabulous view, Elizabeth," said Jack, entering the sunroom. "I can see why this environment is so inspiring from an artistic standpoint. It is my understanding you have been commissioned to paint several works for a private client of a London Gallery?"

"Yes, Jack. I have just completed one painting that was crated and shipped to London this afternoon. It is the reason I have tried to spend so much time here, it is indeed my inspiration." Elizabeth sighed. "I have some unfinished pieces in my studio I may complete once I finish the job for the British client. Let's have our tea and if you are interested, Jack, I will show you my projects."

"Elizabeth, I was hoping you would invite me, yes," he said, picking up a sugar cookie and walking over to the window to admire the view.

"Will Father be joining us this weekend?" inquired Christiana.

"Yes, dear, when I told him you were coming up he said he would fly directly from a last-minute business trip," said Elizabeth, sounding pleased.

"I look forward to seeing Jonathan in a personal setting rather than across the table during a negotiation," responded Jack.

"Jack, allow me to take you to my retreat. Christiana, would you care to join us?"

"No, Mother, I'm going to help Veronica settle in with Jennifer. Please take your time."

Giving Jack a tour of her studio, Elizabeth showed him a number of artworks. Her earlier pieces were cataloged and they leafed through the volume as Elizabeth noted poignant meanings to each of her creations.

"Elizabeth, I spent a couple of years in Paris in my twenties, where I learned from the locals living in Montparnasse. First I learned to draw then I took up painting."

"I would very much enjoy seeing some of your art," Elizabeth replied warmly.

"I would welcome an assessment of my limited skills."

Their conversation took on an easy cadence until Elizabeth looked toward the setting sun and said, "Jack, I didn't realize how long I've kept you here."

"Kept me? I'm delighted to have seen your work. You have amazing talent; your use of color coupled with the complexity and the substance of your paintings is captivating. Elizabeth, once you are finished with your current project, I would like to commission you to paint a large canvas, a foyer piece, for my new office building in Dubai." Before Elizabeth could answer, he touched her shoulder and added, "I won't take no for an answer. And you will have plenty of time."

She simply said, "We should be getting back to the others as I need to advise the staff on a dinner item." They strolled back to the house in silence and found Christiana sitting in the living room lacing up her running shoes.

"Jack, would you care to join me for a run on the beach before dinner?"

"Sounds like a great idea. Do you mind, Elizabeth?"

"The weather's perfect this time of the afternoon. Please, enjoy yourselves."

"We will return shortly. Jennifer and Veronica are out by the pool if you wish to join them, Mother."

"Be back in a flash," announced Jack, bounding up the stairs to change clothes.

The repetitive pounding of their tennis shoes against the sand was the only sound as they ran in rhythm. Jack finally broke the silence. "Your mother is a talented painter. The way she captures light and shadow shows the depth, excellence and professional nature of her style. It's a shame the world has not seen more of her works."

"Life with Father has been more than a full time endeavor," Christiana responded.

"Fortunately, she has resumed her creative pursuits," noted Jack.

"The commission from the British client provided some concise measurement of her time. I'm not clear on her plans once she completes these two projects."

"She showed me several unfinished paintings that she indicated she might finish."

"I had no idea. My mother never fails to amaze me."

"I asked her to design a foyer piece for my new building in Dubai. She didn't say yes, but she didn't say no either."

"You will not be disappointed if she agrees."

The setting sun cast its orange glow over the beach. "Okay, let's pick up the pace. I'll race you back to the house."

"You're on," Christiana answered, starting to sprint. Finishing briefly ahead of Christiana, Jack waited in the driveway to tease her.

"Not bad, been waiting about five minutes."

Her hands on her knees and breathing heavily, Christiana exhaled before responding. "I timed us, maybe thirty seconds at the most!" Slipping his arm around her shoulder, he kissed her on the forehead as they followed the pleasant aromas emanating from inside the kitchen.

Veronica and Jennifer were engrossed in a game of Monopoly on the patio when Christiana and Jack returned from the guest house following their quick showers. At seeing Christiana glancing around, Veronica stated, "Your mother went inside to take a call from your father."

Christiana turned toward Jack to say, "Hope his plans have not changed. I want him to meet you again, and he so loves the Vineyard."

Overhearing the conversation, Elizabeth answered, "Your father will arrive tomorrow morning. Come, let's sit down for dinner."

As they savored the al fresco dining and cool breezes, a muffled cell phone ring broke the sounds of the ocean. "Relax, Christiana, it's Friday evening, what could be so important?" asked Jack.

"I'm not sure," she responded and located the digital read, "but I plan to let it go to voice mail and will check after dinner." Several minutes later the telephone rang again.

Tapping her mother on the arm, Jennifer whispered, "Your phone is ringing again." It was another call from Christian Luke and with annoyance, she snapped off the ringer, placing the phone on the table to resume her conversation.

Jack poured wine for Elizabeth but when he asked Christiana she started to nod with an affirmative response until she looked down at her telephone and noticed receipt of several emails. "No thank you," she merely responded.

Waiting for the first opportunity to excuse herself, she stayed until the entrée dishes were removed. The voice messages as well as the emails were all from Christian. *What is he doing at this time of the evening?* she wondered.

> *I need to speak with you as soon as possible. Time does not matter. Call me. —CL*

The table was now filled with ice cream, sauces, nuts, candies and dishes for do-it-yourself sundaes. "I want chocolate, *a lot of chocolate*," squealed Jennifer. Christiana took the group's preoccupation with dessert as an opportunity to leave the table.

"Honey, you barely touched your dinner. Would you like Beatrice to make you something else?" inquired Elizabeth, as Christiana stood.

"No, Mother, the food was delicious," as she made a stab with her spoon into the ice cream sundae. "Please excuse me while I tend to a couple of urgent messages."

"Now?" asked Elizabeth. "Look at the time; who could possibly be working at this hour? I've already spoken with your father."

"It's Christian." Jack shot her a look and she glanced away.

"Hopefully, I will return soon. However, it depends on the full extent of these voice and email messages," said Christiana in a flat tone of voice.

Elizabeth patted Christiana's hand, saying, "I understand. We will be playing board games, so please rejoin us when … if … you finish."

Since it was almost ten in the evening, she determined an email response to be the most prudent. But when she reread his last email, she became more agitated. "What is he talking about?" she said out loud.

> *Christiana:*
>
> *Since I have not yet heard from you, I am forwarding this email. I need the following information: 1. Latest media/ advertising program for Jewels; 2. Budget for next year on Jewels by Barrington; 3. Contact information on the sales and marketing staff for Jewels; 4. Marketing and advertising program notes on Sterling Hotels; 5. Complete list of the hotels acquired, along with sales and marketing and personnel contact information; and 6. Financial statements from Sterling. I will be working all weekend. Need to get a jump on this with all the work that must be done. —CL*

Sitting at her computer, she fired off an email first to Grant.

> *Grant:*
> *I'm sorry to disrupt your weekend. I have received a flurry of communications from Christian requesting all PR, sales and marketing details and contact information for both* Jewels *by Barrington and Sterling Hotels. He will meet the office staff of* Jewels *in South Africa in the next couple of weeks and the sales/marketing departments for both entities while here in NY. I will forward all relevant sales and marketing materials to him but am not clear as to why he should have access to the financial statements of Sterling?*
> *Thanks, Grant. Let me know your thoughts. Please give my love to Ginny.* —Christiana

After reviewing the requested files, she appended the necessary but not confidential materials to an email:

> *Christian:*
> *Per your requests, I have attached the following: Proposed marketing and advertising plans for* Jewels *by Barrington. Represented are the latest revisions from meetings here last week.*
> *I'm available Monday afternoon if you wish to discuss any of this with me. With regards to Sterling: Your involvement starts and stops with overall coordination of sales and marketing efforts, thus no financial data will be forthcoming.*
> *What happened during your sales/marketing meetings with the Sterling staff? And have you contacted the sales people at* Jewels? —Christiana

As she was shutting down her computer, the door opened and Jack entered the guest house. "I've just finished. Thank you for being so understanding, sweetheart."

Leaning over to kiss her, he whispered, "Hope you're not too tired for me."

Meticulously undressing, they savored every moment of caressing and kissing. Tumbling into bed, they took each other with heated passion and then slept soundly until Christiana awoke at dawn's first light. Jack snored softly as she disentangled from his arms and slipped out of bed.

Tiptoeing into the front room, she switched on her computer to check emails and was relieved to find no further correspondence from Christian.

However, Grant Pemberton did respond:

> *Hello Christiana:*
>
> *Never a bother to hear from you; give my regards to your mother. I think you did well by forwarding the sales/marketing information regarding Jewels by Barrington. That should give him enough to start. As for Sterling, I haven't given him any work regarding the Hotel entities. Check with your father since much of Christian's time pertains to duties given to him by Jonathan. Enjoy your weekend. —Grant*

Christiana thought, *Maybe Christian was trying to pull a fast one but I'll check with Father. If my suspicions are correct this could be evidence enough to let him go. I wonder if they discussed anything the other day after I left the meeting for lunch.*

Contemplating that unpleasant notion, she gazed out the window and noticed the light on in the kitchen of the main house.

Silhouettes of the staff scurried around the kitchen and then she gazed toward the sunroom and saw her mother sipping coffee and reading the newspaper. Jack was still asleep as she stepped back into the bedroom so she slipped on a pair of jeans, sweatshirt and loafers and left to speak with her mother.

Entering the house through the kitchen door, Christiana poured coffee and proceeded to the sunroom. Elizabeth smiled, glancing up from her newspaper, and commented, "Good morning, darling. You are up early."

"Yes, I wanted to check my emails regarding that work issue last evening."

"Has everything been resolved?"

"Not entirely. Something is puzzling and I need clarification from Father."

Not one to easily venture into BHI matters, Elizabeth offered, "Would you care to discuss the matter?"

"There is a new hire in London named Christian who has been quickly promoted to VP of Sales and Marketing Worldwide per Father's instructions. This advancement has not been totally championed by Grant. The prickly situation last evening concerned a request for confidential information that prompted me to send an email to Grant. Grant's email response said to check with Father since 'much of Christian's time pertains to duties given to him by Jonathan,' quote unquote."

"I see, but I sense more behind this than that to which you have just alluded."

"Christian Luke is one of the most arrogant, brash, and ruthless people I have ever encountered. I sense he has his eyes set on the GM's spot and I find it difficult to comprehend why Grant actually hired him. This was a cataclysmic shift from his earlier career as a top male model in Europe."

"Model turned businessman. Please tell me his name again?"

"Christian—but he goes by CL or Christian Luke with no surname. Currently he's in New York and at Father's request I am acquainting him with all our business entities. Father envisions an expansive role for him in Operations, which is ludicrous."

"Christiana, you seem quite biased, which isn't like you."

"I'm not alone as a number of staff has also had problems and issues with him. Ironically, with his bravado and arrogance, you almost feel at times you are dealing with Father. It's like seeing a clone of Jonathan Robert Barrington."

Elizabeth inquired, "How old do you think he is?"

"Oh, I would guess a year or two younger than me. I got side-tracked on CL's personality traits instead of telling you the perplexing issue. Christian forwarded a barrage of email and voice mails last evening asking for proprietary information and data on Sterling Hotels Worldwide. I replied with the non-proprietary information and explained that financial and proprietary materials were beyond his job scope."

"Your father is due shortly so you will have the opportunity to speak with him directly," offered Elizabeth. "I'll bring fresh coffee," she added.

Armed with steaming hot coffees, Danish and muffins, Elizabeth placed the tray on the ottoman, saying, "Jack is well-versed on a variety of subjects and is most entertaining, especially with Jennifer. He's delightful and charming. I enjoyed his company last evening."

"Mother, I'm glad you approve. We are having fun although finding time to be together has proved challenging."

"Honey, don't cast doubts on your horizon. You appear happy and content."

"I'm not sure I should have a serious relationship, with my demanding schedule."

"Please remember, Christiana, Jackson is not Michael. Don't compare the relationships or the men. The personalities, the ages, and the egos are very different."

Their private conversation ceased with the arrival of Jennifer and Veronica, allowing Elizabeth to retreat from the sunroom. The conversation with Christiana prompted her to advance the trip to London so she forwarded emails to the Chelsea Gallery and a few friends. Then she sent one to Grant Pemberton.

> *Dear Grant:*
>
> *I have travels to London next week. After years, I have completed my first commissioned painting and am anxious to get it to the Chelsea Gallery.*
>
> *Are you available for lunch Wednesday?*
>
> *My love to you and Ginny.*
>
> *Elizabeth Matthews Barrington*

CHAPTER 30

ARRIVING WITH HIS NORMAL GUSTO, Jonathan made his entrance and joined Elizabeth, Veronica and Jennifer by the pool. Greeting everyone, he asked the whereabouts of Christiana and Jack.

"They set off to bicycle to town and picnic along the beach," answered Elizabeth. "They are due back midafternoon. Would you like something to eat, Jonathan?"

Jonathan nodded and excused himself to change into more comfortable clothes.

A peck on the cheek roused Jonathan from his nap in the chaise by the pool. "Ah, Christiana, I must have dozed off after lunch. How was your bicycle ride?"

"We found a lovely deserted beach and had a pleasant picnic lunch. Father, I would like you to meet Jackson Hamilton, although I understand you already met some time ago," she said as Jonathan stood to shake hands with Jack.

Drawing a blank, Jonathan stared several seconds before Jack rescued him. "We were introduced briefly over negotiations for the office building on East 50th Street in Midtown. I was sorry to lose that piece of real estate, but it was to a very worthy opponent."

"Ah, now I remember. You were an ardent contender in rather contentious negotiations. I think I would prefer a personal relationship with you."

"I agree, Jonathan; this setting far surpasses the confines of a conference room. If you would excuse me, I'm off to take a shower and change clothes before dinner."

As Jack headed back to the guest house, Jonathan leaned over to his daughter and asked, "Is your relationship becoming serious, sweetheart?"

"I hope so. Jack is wonderful and makes me happy." Jonathan patted his daughter's hand. "Father, while we have the opportunity, I need to speak with you about BHI. Thankfully, Mother is not around to reprimand me for polluting the beautiful island atmosphere with the likes of business matters." Both laughed at the suggestion. Christiana cut to the chase, "While we were dining last evening, I was interrupted by several urgent calls and emails from Christian."

"He was probably working late, didn't realize the time," said Jonathan, ignoring her tenor.

"He demanded I forward sensitive financial data and statements regarding both Jewels and Sterling. I complied partially with his request and forwarded relevant sales and marketing information, but did not include the financial data on Jewels and Sterling."

"Maybe you misunderstood the nature of his request? He's working on ad campaigns for both entities and probably needed past costs for various products such as print ads, television spots, and so on," answered Jonathan, seemingly bewildered by her accusations.

"No, Father, I most certainly did not misunderstand the nature of his request. You might ask Christian, the erudite Oxford graduate, if he comprehends the difference in financial statements for a company versus costs and expenditures associated with sales and marketing activities," she retorted.

"Well, there may have been some misunderstanding," he acquiesced. "However, it didn't appear so when we were discussing it over lunch with Blake," he muttered.

"You asked Christian to have lunch with you and Blake after I declined?"

"He heard us talking about going to lunch," snapped Jonathan, raising his voice. "Besides, it makes for good public relations with the staff."

"That was to be a social lunch with Blake. I was hoping you and Blake might bury the hatchet and develop an amicable work relationship."

"I will have a word with Christian before I head to Saudi Arabia. Your mother has invited guests for dinner and they are due for cocktails at four," said Jonathan as he sprang up from the chaise lounge and headed into the main house, effectively ending the discussion.

Once the guests had left and the family retired to their separate quarters, Elizabeth and Jonathan enjoyed some private time. "Lovely evening, darling, it was good to see Cindy and Alan Wallace. Jack and Alan spent time discussing commercial real estate. I had not connected Jack with Hamilton Industries Inc.," said Jonathan.

"Jack and I had occasion to become better acquainted last evening when Christiana was called away to handle the business of Barrington. I like him, Jonathan, and hope it becomes a solid relationship for Christiana," replied Elizabeth.

"I'm glad Christiana is seeing someone. She must maintain a more balanced existence as it is starting to affect her business life," said Jonathan, as he moved to open the bureau and remove his pajamas.

"What's been affecting her?"

Sloughing off the comment, Jonathan merely added, "She's been fairly tense lately and rather caustic and abrupt with some of the staff."

"Are there any staff members in particular with whom she is at odds?"

Sighing, Jonathan replied, "Elizabeth, you don't know many of our employees."

"With Christiana's personality, I find it hard to believe that she has difficulty with anyone. She has a sixth sense and it's my bet she is spot on in her judgment."

Wrapping his arms around Elizabeth's waist, he nuzzled her neck, murmuring, "Shh, that's enough about Barrington for the night. Remember, we don't discuss business while we are on Martha's Vineyard—Elizabeth's rule."

"My rule has an exception when our daughter appears agitated, does not finish her meal, and spends the evening in the guest house working on a business issue."

"It was probably of her choosing."

"It's not really a number of staff she is having difficulties with; it is one person, Christian Luke. Am I correct, darling?" Elizabeth replied coldly, pulling away.

"Well, I can't recollect the others, but yes, Christian Luke is one she has in her crosshairs," he answered nonchalantly. With interest mounting he asked, "What has she told you about CL, I mean, Christian Luke?"

"He's arrogant, brash, opinionated, and, my dearest Jonathan, he sounds a lot like you. Christiana was quick to admit he's very bright, impeccably attired, focused and detail-oriented—the profile of the Barrington employee."

Jonathan groaned, tired of this tedious conversation. He started to chide his wife as he tried to cuddle. "Do you really find me arrogant, brash and opinionated?"

"Yes, you are most certainly arrogant, brash and opinionated, but I knew that when I accepted your proposal of marriage. Now what I find endearing, my love, is your drive, ambition, zest, and irrepressible personality. Jonathan Robert Barrington, you are one sexy man," she answered and kissed him longingly. The conversation concerning Christiana and Christian Luke was soon forgotten.

After breakfast the next morning as the family was preparing for its departure, Elizabeth advised Jonathan of her travel plans to London.

"I didn't realize you needed to head to London so soon. Why don't you accompany me this evening? I will be in London until Tuesday then I will be flying on to Jeddah," said Jonathan.

"I would enjoy that, my love."

As they settled in for their short flight to New York, Jack turned to Christiana and whispered, "What a wonderful weekend. I am so happy to have met your family. Jennifer is a delight and I understand why you want to rush home every evening to be with her."

"I am blessed to have such a lovely daughter. Thank you for being here with me and meeting my family," responded Christiana joyfully.

Winging their way to London on the Barrington jet, Jonathan kissed his wife on the head as he moved to the bar to refresh their cocktails. "Great weekend, sweetheart, but I'm surprised you wanted houseguests since you went to the Vineyard to finish your paintings."

"I do not consider our family houseguests. I treasure my time with Christiana and Jennifer," said Elizabeth, lounging on the sofa with a plush maroon throw over her legs.

"Tell me about the painting you just finished. Didn't you send another piece earlier this week?" inquired Jonathan.

"The client is a British fellow who has a weekend home on the Isle of Jersey. He asked me to capture the essence of the Isle in a painting to hang in his central London office. During my last visit to England, I went over to Jersey to see and sense the colors—the lifestyle of the people, the sights and the smells of the island, to heighten my creativity," cited Elizabeth. Lifting one of her bags, she thumbed through her files and pulled out a large photograph then handed it to her husband.

"Elizabeth, this is exquisite. You've rediscovered your passion," he stated as he handed back the photo. Then he asked, "How long will you be in London?"

"My plans are to stay just a few days as I must be back in Greenwich by the end of the week. Do you still plan to go to Saudi Arabia on Tuesday?"

"Yes, but my conundrum is whether to head from Saudi Arabia directly to Sydney to meet with Max Spenser or to first come back to New York."

"This site inspection is what has Christiana so upset."

"Elizabeth, if you mean her concerns over my selection of one particular person to accompany us then yes, her feathers are ruffled," said Jonathan in a matter-of-fact tone.

"Is *that* one particular person Christian Luke? By the way, what is his last name?"

"He doesn't go by a last name. He may have had it legally changed or something," said Jonathan, visibly bothered by the topic. "Regarding the other question, yes, I asked him to go to Australia. Elizabeth, I'm sorry to cut you short but I need to finish this report. May we continue later?"

"Of course, Jonathan, I'm going to have dinner and take a nap," she replied.

"Have Christy place my dinner tray on the table and I'll nibble while I'm working."

Awakened by turbulence, Elizabeth could see Jonathan still seated at the desk. "Honey, you haven't touched your dinner."

"I've eaten some of the appetizers. How much more flying time do we have?"

Looking at her watch, Elizabeth answered, "We should be landing in ninety minutes. Why don't you try to take a nap, Jonathan?"

"I'm too wound up to sleep. The stakes are high with these portfolio investments for the Saudis," answered Jonathan, joining her on the sofa with a drink. "Graham Cunningham and I have a meeting Wednesday since he has been in Saudi Arabia the last couple of weeks."

"I see," said Elizabeth. Broaching the subject of their earlier conversation, she stated, "Jonathan, I've always taken a *very* back seat with all business concerns of BHI. However, seeing Christiana distraught the other evening over Christian Luke, and your agitation at the mere mention of his name, I must say, I just don't understand."

With a heavy sigh, Jonathan said, "What is it you don't understand, dear? By the way, I was not agitated over discussing CL; I'm just preoccupied with meatier matters." He moved from the sofa and sat back at the desk chair.

"If you have finished 'the meatier matters,' please tell me why Christiana is upset with him?"

"Elizabeth, why don't you ask her yourself?"

"I have and expressed those concerns to you in our earlier conversation," answered Elizabeth, not letting go of the discussion.

"Yes, I've heard the same things—Christian's arrogant, brash, and opinionated and his behavior borders on rude. Yet she'll admit that he is extremely bright and articulate."

"There are many extremely bright and articulate individuals who might blend better with the Barrington culture," responded Elizabeth.

"Christiana has had limited dealings with him and I have asked her to get to know him over the next number of months."

"There is something about Christian that bothers her and I believe you should listen to your daughter, Jonathan."

"I have and I'm quite sure I will continue to listen to Christiana about this subject," Jonathan responded.

"Is Grant in full agreement?"

The question hung for an interminable amount of time.

"Let's just say we are not in lock step."

"Jonathan, I'm surprised to hear that, after you've worked with Grant all these years. If you are not in agreement with him on this matter, I would believe there is good reason. Does Grant have issues with Christian?"

"Elizabeth, Elizabeth, I've never heard you so interested in Barrington. You need not worry your sweet head with the business of BHI; suffice it to say I will handle it. Grant and Christiana will come around eventually."

With a determined look, Elizabeth retorted, "And what if they don't?"

Steepling his hands, he pondered her question. His response was slow, "Honestly, I have no answer. I hope over time they do. Christian is an asset to Barrington and I have every intention of retaining him."

"Even over objections from Grant and your daughter?"

Before dodging the question, he received a reprieve, as Captain Dennison's voice came over the loud speaker requesting them to prepare for landing. At that point, Christy came into the main cabin to collect the trays and then strapped herself into a seat within earshot of the Barringtons, which precluded further conversation on the issue.

Once on the ground, with the security team, they exited the aircraft and were greeted by the porters and their private car. Thankfully for Jonathan, the subject of Christian was not reintroduced. It was late, they were tired and they rode in silence the distance to their flat. When Elizabeth entered the bedroom after preparing to retire, Jonathan was snoring peacefully.

The next morning he was gone when she awakened and the subject of Christian Luke was not revisited before Jonathan left for Saudi Arabia.

"Elizabeth, how wonderful to see you," remarked Grant Pemberton. He leaned over and kissed her cheek as she sat in the high-backed red-cushioned booth at the Grill Restaurant in the Dorchester Hotel.

"Good to see you, my dear friend. It's been a while—Florida, I believe, at Christiana's house," said Elizabeth, smiling across the table. Eyeing Grant, she noticed he had gained some weight, appeared tired, and his hair was decidedly grayer.

"I hear you have resumed painting and head to Martha's Vineyard whenever you can slip away. I'm glad you are starting to take care of Elizabeth for a change."

"The Vineyard has been my sanctuary for years. I've even dusted off some old canvases and finished several works in addition to the commissioned pieces that have brought me to London. When I emailed you, I was on the island with the family and Christiana's new beau. I was flattered he asked me to design a foyer piece for the building he is constructing in Dubai. I'm not sure I have the time but he seemed genuinely interested in my work," explained Elizabeth.

"Indeed a wonderful compliment and well-deserved."

Bothered by the weathered look of her friend, she softly touched Grant's hand and asked, "Are you feeling okay? You seem tired; not your usual charismatic self."

"I'm okay but work is exhausting and all-consuming. I don't have to tell you what it's like to have Jonathan around all the time." They chuckled. "I've thought of retiring, for the first time, although Ginny isn't ready to have me around full time. I admire your husband; he runs circles around even the youngest staff."

"Jonathan is tireless; however, I do worry."

As they were finishing lunch, Elizabeth lifted a small framed art piece from her satchel. "Grant, here is that piece I promised you years ago. It complements the other work I designed for you."

"Elizabeth, you finally finished it. This is extraordinary! Ginny will be thrilled. Thank you," he said as his face lit up with a wide grin.

"It was a labor of love for a man whose friendship means so much to me," responded Elizabeth. "You are most welcome."

After Grant wrapped the painting, he retrieved a manila folder from his briefcase and handed the envelope to Elizabeth. He simply added, "You will understand."

Clutching the folder, she glanced at the package then over to Grant for validation. He nodded, saying, "You were correct in your suspicions, I'm sorry to say."

"Me too. Thank you, Grant. Now I must go."

As they hugged when leaving the restaurant, Grant whispered, "I am here for whatever you need me to do."

"I know, Grant. Thank you," she sighed, patting his hand then walking away.

CHAPTER 31

CHRISTIANA'S TACTIC HAD BEEN "hands off" at Magnifique to allow Samantha Jones to take the reins. She was asked, however, to test the new product line and was impressed.

One frigid morning after the holidays, Christiana received a call from Samantha and was pleased to hear from her CEO. "Christiana, I believe we will have a 'magnifique' new year," Samantha laughed. "Have you tried the new products?"

"I've used everything according to your instructions. I even had a close-up photo taken prior to commencing the new Magnifique regimen," replied Christiana. "Samantha, the products are incredible. The rich and silky feel of the night moisturizer is amazing. The day cream is a perfect balance of creaminess and protection. The piece de resistance is the anti-aging line. Samantha, these are the best products I have ever used."

"I am ecstatic. I so value your judgment and opinion."

"You have every reason to be ecstatic; the products deliver!"

"Do you have time today to preview the new ad campaign?"

Looking at her appointment schedule, Christiana replied, "I'll see you at eleven."

Entering the lobby of the new headquarters for Magnifique Beauty, Christiana was impressed with the surroundings. The renovation showed, and showed well, befitting a company named Magnifique, and the staff appeared as polished as the marble floors. Samantha hit the pavement at marathon speed and hadn't stopped.

"What do you think of the offices?" Samantha beamed.

"They capture the elegance of a company in the beauty business. You've done a great job," replied Christiana.

"We used the Corinthian Properties design team," explained Samantha.

"Have they finished work on the building next door yet?"

"It's nearing completion and I can hardly wait to have our manufacturing unit there," said Samantha. "If you have the time, we can walk over after our meeting."

"I would like that."

"We are pleased you like the new product line, Ms. Barrington," remarked Alexis Stevens, VP of Marketing.

"Here's the 'before' photograph you requested, Samantha," responded Christiana, reaching into her handbag to pull out the picture.

Both employees studied the photo for several moments and Samantha moved around the table to take a better look at Christiana's skin. "You are gorgeous, regardless. But I do see a difference in the overall texture of your skin and improvement in fine lines around your eyes and neck," remarked Samantha.

"Please unveil our new packaging, Alexis," announced Samantha. Moving to the credenza behind the conference table, Alexis lifted coverlets from the gold-lined peach-colored jars and containers for the new skincare line.

"Stunning, absolutely stunning," Christiana murmured. "Have you given consideration to the name of this line?"

Alexis anxiously responded, "Yes, Ms. Barrington, we have given much thought to the branding of this collection."

Samantha exuberantly announced, "We wish to call the new line *The Barrington Collection,* or *Barrington Beauty and Skin Care.*"

"Oh," said Christiana, with a momentary pause.

"Barrington is the epitome of class, elegance, beauty, success," praised Alexis.

Samantha interrupted, "Alexis, please show Christiana the new perfume collection," and Alexis handed perfume testers to Christiana.

"It's a floral scent with an exotic ingredient I can't quite place," said Christiana.

"This one has the frangipani flower essence, a plant native to Hawaii, Mexico, Central America and Venezuela," responded Alexis.

"How do you wish to brand the perfume collection?" Christiana inquired.

"We want to call it *Christiana,*" Samantha answered.

"I'm flattered," replied Christiana.

Picking up another perfume bottle, Alexis remarked, "This is the new men's cologne," she explained, spraying the blotter and handing it to Christiana.

"We would love to call this *Christian,* after Christian Luke, the gorgeous former model who is now our worldwide head of sales and marketing. You may recall, I mentioned using him in some of the advertising before I came on board," offered Samantha.

Feeling anguish at the mention of CL's involvement, Christiana said, "Ladies, I'm impressed with the products and new packaging but reticent to give my endorsement on the product names. It's an interesting marketing strategy, one that proved beneficial for us with Jewels *by Barrington.*"

"I remember those. One featured your mother and father holding hands and gazing at each other," responded Alexis.

"Yes, the caption on the first piece read, *Adoring,* as they stared into each other's eyes, and then the second stated *Adorned. The world of perfection and beauty at one source*—Jewels *by Barrington.* I loved that piece, Christiana, as well as the ad with you descending the spiral staircase in a luscious mink coat with the caption, *Arriving,* and then segued in the second photograph with you standing at the bottom of the staircase with the mink open to reveal an exquisite necklace. The caption read *Arrived. Make the right entrance with* Jewels *by Barrington.* We would like to achieve that magic again with our ad campaigns," sang Samantha with unbridled enthusiasm.

"As we look to brand the men's cologne, either *Jonathan* or *Barrington* should be the choices considered. I'm partial to Barrington since most of the premier fashion designers who have expanded their reach into fragrance use their prominent last names—Valentino, Gucci, St. Laurent," stated Christiana.

At an impasse on that subject, Samantha moved on to say, "Christiana, please consider being the spokeswoman for the skin care collection. You would be perfect."

"I will consider a role as spokesperson for Magnifique and my namesake for the fragrance collection. I'll discuss this and the use of the Barrington name with Jonathan."

"Please understand; this was not a slight to Jonathan. Fragrances are most successful when they are connected to a familiar personality and the Barrington name and its cache blend beautifully. That is why I saw a whole campaign centered on Christian as the new hip businessman of today," explained Samantha.

"I'm fascinated by what I have seen today and the progress made at Magnifique. We should have quick resolve on my concerns with one exception. Christian's contract precludes his present involvement with this company. However, at some juncture, if sanctioned by Grant and Jonathan, we might launch a fragrance with his name under the Magnifique label, but not under the Barrington name or collection."

Pausing to permit her audience to both receive and digest her message, she curtly added, "He is not a Barrington."

"Of course, we understand and most certainly could separate the products," Samantha swiftly concluded. "Let me add this—time is short, as you probably know from CL; we pulled the old advertising several months ago in anticipation of this new launch."

"Yes, we must make these determinations soon," said Christiana, shaking the proffered hand of Alexis as the VP left the room. Turning to Samantha, Christiana added, "The progress you have made in your short tenure at Magnifique is remarkable."

"Thankfully it was done with minimal bruising, and now we have a dynamite collection to launch. Please do consider being our spokesperson and using your name for the collection," said Samantha with a lilt to her voice. "Your skin looks amazing, Christiana. I smoke and over the years have developed fine lines around my lips and use the anti-aging serums on those areas. I'm impressed with the results."

"It's good to have firsthand knowledge about your products. One final note, would you please send several bottles of the men's and women's perfumes and a complete set of the skin care collection to my office this afternoon?"

Once Christiana had left after they visited the other building, Samantha reflected on the meeting. *I hope I convinced her to be the spokesperson. I bet we go forward with The Barrington Collection. Maybe there is a way to incorporate The Barrington Collection as well as Barrington Beauty and Skin Care. But that's not what bothers me,* she thought. Reaching into her purse, she took out a pack of cigarettes and lighter, grabbed her coat and stepped out on her terrace to smoke. *Something bothers Christiana about CL. I've seen it twice in meetings. Damn, I was hoping to have reason with the ad campaign to foster more frequent dealings with him, but Christiana has nixed that.* Feeling a chill, she took one final drag of her cigarette, snubbed it out in the ash tray, and went back into her office.

CHAPTER 32

"H ELLO, MY AMERICAN PRINCESS, I'm back in New York,"
announced Marc Philippe as Christiana answered her mobile
phone.

"It's wonderful to hear from you. You must be busy with the
Jersey Company."

"Busy, so very busy, *Cheri*. Poor Marc Philippe, he does not
get enough sleep, worrying all the time about business. Too little
rest," and he added with a chuckle, "too little sex. Not good for a
man like Marc Philippe."

"Oh, I think you still get by okay, my dear prince. But as I
recollect, I haven't seen you cavorting on the covers of the tabloids
recently."

"There, you see what I mean. It's all just work for Marc Philippe,
flying back and forth all the time; I am *so* exhausted. But not too
exhausted to see you, Christiana. How about I pick you up for dinner this evening around seven?"

"As much I would love to have dinner with you, Jennifer
is expecting me. I too have been traveling and quite busy with
Barrington."

"While I am saddened I cannot see you this evening, I understand."

Since they were speaking, she took the opportunity to ask, "Marc Philippe, you mentioned some time ago you saw my father in a restaurant in Frankfurt with a man who looked vaguely familiar. Do you recall our conversation?"

"Yes, yes, of course. Jonathan was dining with a younger very elegant man. They were engrossed in conversation as the maître d' escorted me to my table. He was a model in Europe for a number of years and that is why he looked familiar, Christiana."

"That part I now understand. Do you know anything else about him?"

"I seem to recall he had a contract with Bregaux, the Swiss watch company, for several years. He was everywhere in the print media then it was as if the sponsors dropped him or his contract expired, he was just gone. Why do you ask, *ma Cheri?*"

"He now works for BHI. When did you stop seeing his magazine spots?"

He pondered her question for several moments before responding. "Oh, let me see. I would say it's been over a year. Oh, no, it's been longer … a couple of years."

Not desiring to reveal her concerns, she brushed off his earlier question with, "Just curious, no real reason." Trying to cover her tracks, she said, "He's made a very successful transition from fashion and modeling to the business world." *That would fit perfectly with the time he joined the employ of Barrington,* she thought.

"Happy to assist, although I do my best work in the pleasure department. You do remember, *Cheri?*"

"I well remember. As much as I would love to continue our conversation, I've just arrived at my office." As the Rolls Royce Phantom coupe pulled in front of the Barrington building, Christiana ended with, "Marc Philippe, please call me when you are back in New York and I promise we will get together. I miss seeing you."

Striding through the corridors at BHI, Christiana passed Jonathan's office. Noticing the door ajar, she glanced in to see him working at his desk. "Father, do you have some time, I would like to discuss a couple of items regarding Magnifique."

"Please come in and sit down, Christiana. I just need to double-check some figures before I forward them to Marshall. You mentioned Magnifique?"

"I've just had a lengthy meeting with Samantha and Alexis, the VP of Marketing. The renovations on the main building are superb with subdued elegance in the décor. The executive suites are smart and chic. Please take time to go over and take a look."

He nodded and asked, "Does Samantha seem to be settling in?"

"Yes, James has indicated she is results-oriented and quite a taskmaster."

"Great. Bring me up to date on the progress."

"Samantha's been instrumental in a smart and modern packaging for the existing product line. Additionally, they've created a new skin care system with anti-aging products as well as a fragrance line for both men and women. Samantha asked me a couple of months ago to sample the collection. This new skin care collection is amazing."

"You have flawless skin, but I admit you have a new radiance and glow."

"Thank you, Father. With that as my preface, I'll give you the takeaways from our marketing meeting. First, they want to name and brand the new skin care line either *Barrington Beauty and Skin Care* or simply *The Barrington Collection*. They have asked me to launch it and be the spokesperson."

"I concur with Samantha. Sales skyrocketed when you did the ads for Jewels. You'd be perfect as the face for skin care."

"In addition to the skin care line, Magnifique wishes to launch a fragrance line. The women's collection would be called *Christiana*. The men's line would be either *Jonathan* or *Barrington*. Which do you prefer?"

"With your appeal and recognition, I think *Christiana* is an excellent choice. I prefer *Barrington* for the men's cologne under *The Barrington Collection*."

As they spoke, she contemplated discussing Christian's involvement and thought, *I'd best say something about Christian before Samantha does.*

"Father, there is one final item before we leave the discussion on Magnifique. Samantha was aware of Christian's modeling career and thought he would be perfect as the new face for the men's fragrance line."

"Sorry, I must be missing something. You just indicated a world launch on a collection of skin care products that will be called *The Barrington Collection* as well as new fragrances named appropriately *Christiana* and *Barrington*. Is there a third product they also wish to launch called *Christian*?"

"I must be honest, *Barrington* was my idea and they acquiesced. Staff had pushed to launch the products as *Christiana* and *Christian—The Barrington Collection*. I told them we might get Christian involved in the future with another fragrance named *Christian* marketed solely under the Magnifique banner, thus leaving no confusion with the Barrington products or our name."

"I understand your concern with the proprietary nature of the Barrington name, although I don't see it as in the same vein," remarked Jonathan. "I think an ad campaign for the fragrance collection featuring both you and CL was ingenious. It would be high profile, high glam and probably high profit."

"So you don't think there would be any confusion with the name even though he's not part of the family?"

Steering clear of her last comment, Jonathan stated, "It appears you have handled it with the pass off to a later product and his namesake under Magnifique. However, I would advance the time frame for development and launch, as Christian may soon not have time for this project. More importantly, we should capitalize on his name and face while he's still known in the worlds of fashion and modeling."

"You were aware of his modeling career?"

"Yes, Christiana, both Grant and I were aware of his past pursuits," he answered in a testy tone.

"What a fascinating change in careers. How long did he model?"

"I don't know, Christiana, I suggest you ask CL rather than me as I have more pressing issues that require my time and attention," answered Jonathan, visibly annoyed.

"If we make him the new face of Magnifique, it is *my* business," she replied with an icy stare.

In typical Jonathan fashion, he changed the subject and gingerly appealed, "I'm pleased Magnifique is in capable hands with Samantha Jones."

Sensing his distraction, she peered over the stack of materials on his desk and caught sight of the pink diamond files open. "Father, what's the latest with the potential acquisition of Max's company?"

"Yes, about that, damn it. I didn't want to involve you since you have enough on your plate, but this deal isn't going in our direction."

"I've been out of the loop since the site visit. However, I thought we were proceeding with due diligence," she said, surprised.

"That was the initial assessment. The deal is much more convoluted than I believed at the onset of negotiations due to the position of the syndicate."

"The syndicate smells big money with Barrington's interest."

"Probably, but it's more complicated than just the financial consideration. The diamond mining business has been losing momentum and we knew that when we made our major purchase, but we didn't overpay. Max and the syndicate have started to mine iron ore in Western Australia, which shows promise, according to our team from Namibia. However, the other diamond mine part of this acquisition is relatively virgin. It may require seven to ten years before it produces."

"We envisioned the long-term horizon from a financial standpoint when we purchased the Jewels entities. The profit margins are large and we own some of the finest quality stones. Sales have increased substantially in China, India, the Middle East and Russia," replied Christiana.

"That's the take from Remi, our CEO at Jewels. Where is Remi?"

"In Singapore and heading to London," announced Christiana.

"I need his insight on this," said Jonathan, reaching for his cell phone.

"I'll take my exit and hopefully will see you later at Sur La Mer with the new skin care and fragrance samples from Magnifique."

Waiting in the living room, Elizabeth warmly greeted her daughter. "Christiana, you look wonderful. I love your outfit but I don't recognize the designer?"

"Mother, it is a design from your dear friend Carolina Hunter."

Placing her satchel on the carpet, Christiana removed the products from the elegantly designed velvet bags and presented the collection. As she described the daily skin care regime, Elizabeth leafed through the brochures.

"Do you really believe these products have made a dramatic difference?"

"Yes, Mother, my skin has a silky texture and the fine lines have virtually disappeared."

"Your skin has a definite glow."

"I think so too, as does Samantha Jones. She has started to transform the tired old company into the beauty powerhouse we anticipated when BHI acquired Magnifique. In addition, they asked me to be the face and spokesperson for the new line."

"There is no better representative for a line to be called *The Barrington Collection* than Christiana Lynn Barrington. You dazzled in the advertising for Jewels."

"My parents were amazing in those ads, too."

"It was fun to do those media spots with your father. He's such a ham," she chuckled. "Seriously consider the opportunity, Christiana. You sell product."

"I'm feeling more comfortable and confident after using the products and await your feedback."

"Francine will be here later this week for my regular facial. I'll acquaint her with the new line, although we have been devotees of that French line for years."

"What I need is your assessment," replied Christiana. Reaching for her satchel, she removed the perfume and sprayed a paper blotter then handed it to her mother. "Let me show you the new fragrance as well."

"Lovely smell—exquisite bottle," sighed Elizabeth. "What's it called?"

"They want to name it *Christiana*."

"How could I not love a perfume called *Christiana?* I now understand the branding potential of *The Barrington Collection.*"

As the mantel clock chimed six-thirty, Christiana prepared for her departure just as her father arrived home. "Father, here is the sample of the men's cologne we wish to name *Barrington.*"

"I like the scent," said Jonathan. He sprayed some on his neck and inquired, "Elizabeth, what do you think?"

"It smells wonderful on the namesake," answered Elizabeth.

"Then *Barrington* it is!" exclaimed Jonathan.

CHAPTER 33

SIPPING THEIR MORNING COFFEES in Samantha's office at Magnifique, Christiana wasted no time in moving ahead with her agenda. "Samantha, let's brand the skin care line and the two fragrances as *The Barrington Collection*. We shall market the fragrances as *Christiana* and *Barrington*."

"Perfect," said Samantha. "Will Jonathan assist in the launch of *Barrington*?"

"He will be coming by Magnifique to meet you and view the renovations. Be direct with him regarding his involvement in the advertising campaign."

"I will, and am most eager to meet Mr. Barrington. Christiana, have you given more thought to your involvement?"

"I'll be involved with the first series of advertisements and the launch of all new products. However, I hesitate to commit on an ongoing basis due to time constraints."

"I couldn't ask for more. It goes without saying; we work around your schedule."

"There is one open item from our last meeting regarding Christian Luke and a new men's cologne. First, we'll launch *The*

Barrington Collection. Second will be the campaign for the contemporary businessman featuring Christian Luke branded and marketed under Magnifique."

"I will get R&D on it immediately," responded Samantha. "Should I contact Christian to discuss his involvement?"

"Jonathan said he would handle it," stated Christiana as she prepared to leave.

Back at Corporate as Christiana exited the elevator, she found Blake heading in her direction. "Good morning, Blake."

"Morning, do you have time for me?"

"Let's go into my office." Christiana placed her crocodile attaché on the credenza, slid her Hermes purse into the desk drawer, and sat down to face Sterling's CEO.

"We've started converting the brands to the new name, *Sterling— The Luxury Collection by Barrington Hotels & Resorts International*. It's had broad appeal in the hospitality industry," commented Blake.

"The Sterling name and brand has and shall continue to be the apex of the luxury line and the crown of Barrington Hotels," stated Christiana, her smile bright.

Blake nodded. "Our central reservations system and call centers are working well in Asia. The technology side is progressing flawlessly. Peter Chang is amazing."

"Peter is that and then some. He's a tremendous asset to BHI," agreed Christiana.

"He told me he has been with BHI for years."

Grinning, Christiana responded, "Peter and I met at Harvard and developed a close friendship. I suggested to Father that we hire Peter. When he took the reins it helped solidify our dominance and permanence primarily in the electronics arena. The Asian operations are well-run, consistent in their forecasts and highly profitable."

"Peter and I visited a couple of our hotel properties in Hong Kong. He suggested converting the Barrington hotel to a mixed-use space since there is a shortage of residential units in that part of the city, and we have two properties in the area."

"Coordinate with Charley Taylor from Corinthian Properties," suggested Christiana.

"Peter mentioned a meeting with him in Singapore in the next couple of weeks."

Grinning, Christiana corrected, "Charley Taylor is a lady. I guess Peter failed to tell you that."

"Thanks for the heads up," he laughed.

A while later ...

Preparing to head to Palm Beach, Christiana felt a surge of excitement. *Concentrate on Jack,* she reminded herself. Five fabulous days in a place she loved with the man she adored. Jack had been making overtures about "falling hard" for her.

"Mother, Daddy's on the telephone. I asked him to come to Bellagio."

Thoughts of Jackson quickly evaporated as Christiana responded to her daughter, "Honey, you should have talked with me first." *There's probably no harm since Michael will be too busy anyway,* she contemplated.

"You promised I could see Daddy whenever I wanted."

Sidestepping the comment, she picked up the phone. "Hello, Michael." Before she could articulate the next sentence he commandeered the conversation.

"I was coming to New York but Jennifer tells me you are heading to Bellagio."

"I mentioned it several weeks ago," said Christiana with a hint of exasperation. "Some friends are having a party for my parents and have invited Jack and me."

"I didn't realize the social commitments when I was speaking with Jennifer. Who is having the party?"

"Megan and Paul Montgomery are social friends of my parents. They are retired and spend their winters in Palm Beach. She is the consummate Palm Beach socialite. Megan and my mother love to trade party tips, etiquette breaches and town gossip."

With reluctance, she extended the invitation to Michael, but was quick to add, "You might be spending most of your time with Jennifer and Veronica."

"Oh, my sister is coming too? It would be great to see Veronica as we didn't have much time on my last trip to Montrachet."

"So I take it you will be joining us?" Christiana inquired.

"Sure, if you don't mind," he said smugly.

"No, it's fine, but don't ask me to finagle an invite to the Montgomery party."

"Oh darn."

"By the way, where are you?"

With a laugh, he answered, "I'm working in Miami. I'll arrive at Bellagio before you."

"We are dining al fresco at eight, so we'll see you for cocktails around half past six. On another topic, I have business in Los Angeles the last week of the month and was considering having Jennifer accompany me as she has a school holiday. Are you in town?"

"Yes! Will you stay in Malibu?"

Hesitating, Christiana answered, "I'm not sure of the location of the meetings," not willing to commit to staying at Michael's home.

"Outstanding. I have a première and would love for Jennifer to accompany me. I'm also doing a shoot in LA and Jennifer has been bugging me about a role as an extra."

"The movie première is fine but I forbid you to involve her in one of your features," Christiana said pointedly.

"You *forbid* me!" he shouted and added sarcastically, "How 'Jonathanisque.' The last I remember, I'm still her father and have a say in the rearing of our daughter. She likes the entertainment industry."

"Young girls fantasize about being movie stars," retorted a very unhappy Christiana.

"Christiana, get over it. You might need to face the fact that Jennifer is not willing to be molded into the likeness of you and your father. What are you going to do, ship her off to school in Europe?" He cut a nerve with his comments and he didn't care. "Jennifer may not be your eager heir apparent."

Then he tossed out another stinger. "Maybe you and Jack should get married and have another child; maybe a son this time. The whole Barrington dream come true," he said, his voice dripping with sarcasm.

Not reacting to his vicious remarks, in a subdued voice, she replied, "I don't have time to continue this conversation, Michael; I must finish preparing for a conference call and head to the airport."

Knowing he hit at the core with reference to the venerable Barrington family—Jonathan in particular—he changed his delivery and tone. "Christiana, I didn't mean to upset you. I'm sorry for my sharp words. I was being a jerk; maybe I'm a little jealous of you and Jack. Do you wish to rescind the invitation?"

"No, Michael, we look forward to seeing you this evening. *Ciao*," said Christiana, hurrying off the phone.

The conference call lasted longer than expected and she rushed her final trip preparations. Resting for most of the flight, Christiana was awakened when she heard the captain announce their landing in West Palm Beach. Whisked away in their limousine, Jennifer, Veronica and Christiana chatted like schoolgirls for the duration of their ride.

Looking out on the terrace as they entered Bellagio, Christiana noticed her parents and Michael enjoying cocktails and was thankful she had forwarded quick emails mentioning Michael's inclusion. "We're here!" Jennifer shouted enthusiastically and raced to greet the family.

After welcoming her guests, Christiana along with Veronica slipped upstairs to freshen up before dinner. Glancing at her Patek Philippe watch, Christiana saw she had just enough time to change from her New York black "uniform" to more suitable Palm Beach dressy casual evening wear before Jack arrived. With the final touch of removing the chignon and allowing her hair to fall gracefully around her shoulders, she was ready for the evening.

As she descended the staircase, she noticed Jack standing in the foyer. "You look beautiful, my love," he murmured as he kissed her.

"I'm so happy you are here. I've missed you. The staff will show you to our room and I will meet you on the terrace with Jennifer, my parents, Veronica and Michael. He called this morning and Jennifer invited him. Coincidently, he was in Miami working on a film. I hope you got my voice mail?"

"I like Michael and yes, I did get your voice mail." Jack was clearly not about to say or do anything that would ruin their time together.

Christiana leaned over to kiss her parents and as she strode around the table to sit next to Jennifer and Veronica, Michael kissed her hand. In short order, a stylish Jack appeared with cocktail in hand and greeted everyone at the table.

Michael's tempestuousness from their earlier telephone conversation retreated and his charming and gregarious personality resurfaced, adding to a pleasant dinner that included a lively interchange of topics.

Once the dessert dishes were removed, Michael announced, "Jennifer and I are going to the pool. Veronica, come on. We'll race like we did as kids."

"I, ah, I don't think so, Michael," answered Veronica, embarrassed.

"*Please*, Aunt Veronica. It'll be fun," urged Jennifer.

"I'll watch but I'm not going swimming," she said reluctantly.

Meanwhile, Jack and Jonathan resumed their conversation centered on business while Christiana and her mother took their coffees and moved to a settee on the covered terrace to view the pool area.

"It's nice to have some mother-daughter time," said Elizabeth, comfortingly, patting Christiana's hand. "I wanted to give you my reaction to the skin care products. I am very impressed as well."

Christiana beamed. "Samantha will be thrilled since this line is her brainchild."

"Francine said she would use the line in her spas when Magnifique is ready to distribute *The Barrington Collection*. When do you launch the new advertisements?"

"In a few weeks, according to Samantha."

"I look forward to seeing the spots—especially the one with your father."

"Father is perfect in front of the camera. His charisma is apparent even when he doesn't say a word," stated a proud daughter.

As if on cue, Jonathan and Jack strode over to the ladies and sat in the accompanying chairs. "Did I hear someone mention charisma?" Jonathan asked in a lighthearted mode. "I didn't mean to monopolize Jack for the entire evening; my apologies, Christiana."

"I'm pleased you and Jack are enjoying each other's company, Father. Mother and I were chatting about the launch of our new skin care line and I mentioned you are very photogenic in the advertisements for our men's cologne *Barrington*. You exude charisma even without speaking."

"Maybe I best keep my mouth shut more often," Jonathan laughed, but quickly chirped, "Ladies … I know what you are thinking."

Just then Michael called up, "Christiana, why don't you and Jack join us in the pool? Maybe we can even coerce Veronica to get her feet wet."

His eyes on Christiana, Jack replied, "Go ahead; I'd rather talk with your parents."

Michael was now out of the pool, displaying his rock-hard body as he toweled off. Christiana quickly looked away before Jack could see her staring. "Jennifer, ask your mother to come swimming," called Michael.

"Mother, *please,* I want you to race Daddy. I will say on your mark, get set, *and go!*" Jennifer shouted.

"Jack, are you sure you don't mind?"

"Honey, please go, you love the water," answered Jack, smiling as Jonathan handed him a brandy.

Leaning over the balustrade she called out, "I'll be right down."

The casual familiar sounds of a family at play echoed up to the terrace. The intimate banter once shared in marriage, although not outwardly displayed, was still present. Jack keenly sensed the closeness that remained between Christiana and Michael.

At Jack's sudden quietness, Elizabeth turned the conversation to her commissioned art piece for his building in Dubai. He was glad for the distraction and they talked for much of the next half hour.

"Again, I'm sorry about my comments this morning on the telephone. I was way out of line," said Michael.

"Thank you, Michael. I hope we stop verbally hurting each other as you will always be a major part of our lives."

"You're right," he said, but instinctively leaned forward to embrace his ex-wife. Christiana quickly jerked away. "Sorry again! I hope Jack didn't see *that* stupid move."

Positioned on the sofa with full command of the pool area, Jack blinked, clenched his teeth and stiffened his posture.

When the pool party dispersed, Veronica took Jennifer upstairs to prepare for bedtime. Michael went off to shower and Christiana slipped on a cover-up and proceeded to the terrace. Elizabeth sat alone sipping her tea. "Mother, what happened to the men?"

"They're in the library as your father wanted to show Jack something on the Internet regarding navigational equipment and boat engines."

"Mother, sorry, I didn't mean to leave you alone."

"I've enjoyed watching everyone in the pool. Jennifer's quite a strong swimmer."

"Yes, she shares my love of the water but her swimming abilities can be attributed to Michael's assistance," said Christiana.

"Yes, you have both the indoor and the outdoor pools at Montrachet," Elizabeth responded curtly.

Picking up on her mother's tone, Christiana glanced about to ensure privacy and quietly asked, "Did you notice Michael lean over to hug me?"

"Yes, Christiana, I noticed." And before she could inquire whether Jack witnessed the action, Elizabeth added, "Yes, Jack did too."

"I will let Jack know Michael had just apologized for rude remarks he made on the telephone earlier today. The hug was automatic and he even apologized for that, too."

"Christiana," said Elizabeth shaking her head, "the relationship you and Michael have is none of my business, but it does seem to concern Jack. It is hard enough for any man to be seriously involved with you and have to contend with BHI and your father. One man couldn't succeed; I hope you don't give another even more reasons to leave."

Sighing, Christiana responded, "I certainly don't want to ruin what I have with Jack. He is the first man, since Michael, I could truly love."

"Does Jack know how you feel?"

"No. He has told me he is falling in love …." The words hung. "I am afraid of failing with this relationship just like I did with my marriage."

"Jack is not Michael. If you really are serious about him, go after him, my darling. I want to see you happy and in love again," said Elizabeth, reaching over and hugging her daughter. "Let's go inside. I'm ready to call it an evening."

"Ah, here are the two visions of beauty," said Jonathan as the ladies entered the library.

"Come along, dear, it's getting late," said Elizabeth, starting to escort her husband out to the lighted walkway leading to the yacht.

"Yes dear. Jack, our tee time is at seven."

"Great! See you in the morning, Jonathan. Goodnight, Elizabeth," Jack replied.

"Oh, by the way, Christiana, I called Megan Montgomery earlier this evening and she is delighted to have Michael and Veronica join us tomorrow," smiled Jonathan.

Startled, Christiana replied, "Oh! Did you give Michael the good news?"

"Yes, everything is arranged, including childcare for Jennifer."

"Very well, Father."

Freshly showered and lying on the crisp blue Egyptian cotton sheets, Jack waited patiently for Christiana to arrive upstairs. He fantasized about making love but as quickly as the mood arrived, it left as Christiana opened the door wearing a scowl.

"What's the matter, sweetheart?"

"My father should not have contacted Megan Montgomery to have Veronica and Michael invited to their party."

"I don't really see the issue. If Mrs. Montgomery did not wish to enlarge her party, I'm sure she would have told your father."

"My father has the power of persuasion. It's going to be uncomfortable having Michael there," she pouted.

"Relax, it's only a dinner. I'm okay with having Michael present. After all, you are there with me," he assured her. Trying to evoke an erotic mood, he nibbled her ear. "I've been waiting all evening to make wild passionate love to you, Christiana."

Quieting the alarm buzzer at six, Jack rose and prepared for his golf game. He brushed the hair from her face and kissed her as he tiptoed out of the bedroom.

The ladies spent the morning shopping Worth Avenue and were displaying their purchases over tea on the terrace when the roars of the men entered the compound.

"He's a handicap golfer too, Christiana," exclaimed Jonathan.

Embarrassed, Jack responded, "You're being kind, Jonathan, since you failed to mention you won with a birdie on the eighteenth hole."

Elizabeth chided, "And you thought you were rusty."

"I should spend more time practicing at the Club to compete with these guys."

"We are expected for cocktails at six so I shall excuse myself to get ready," said Elizabeth. "Megan has just had the house redecorated. It's been featured in *Palm Beach Life* and *Architectural Digest*. Please make a fuss. This is Megan's world."

"I'd rather discuss the house décor than listen to Paul complain about his poor golf game," Jonathan chuckled.

"I've never been to a Palm Beach High Society party," Veronica said, sounding like a schoolgirl. "I can't thank you enough for the beautiful outfit," she added, finishing her conversation with Christiana and closing the door to her room.

As Christiana stepped from the shower, Jack appeared at the entrance to the bathroom, "Don't suppose we have time to play?" he asked, oozing boyhood charm.

"As much as I would love to hop into bed with you, unfortunately this is not one of those functions where we can be tardy," replied Christiana.

"I understand. Paul Montgomery is a classy guy, I like him. Tell me a little more about the other guests."

"The best way to describe it is Palm Beach High Society. I despise that term, but to this group, it is of monumental importance."

"Do you fit in with this fluff and stuff? I hope I am not offending you?"

"I'm not down here enough to really fit in, given my work schedule. I financially support several philanthropic endeavors. To really be included, you need to volunteer your time. Peel away the 'fluff,' as you call it, and you'll find that these women are some of the most accomplished, intelligent and caring people I have ever met." As they glanced at the clock, Christiana remarked, "I'd best get ready."

Jack was dressed as she was applying her makeup, and said, "I'll meet you downstairs. It smells too feminine in here for me."

As Christiana made her entrance, the men were ensconced in the library.

"Palm Beach chic," said Michael with a wink. Christiana shot Michael a glare then promptly turned away, hoping Jack had not noticed.

"The off-white in your dress sets off your lovely tan," commented Jack.

"We're waiting on Veronica and your mother," said Jonathan, pacing.

"Veronica's going over some details regarding Jennifer with the staff," responded Christiana. "Michael, would you like to say goodnight to Jennifer?"

The Montgomery home was magnificent and it was easy to rave about the new décor. Megan delighted in escorting the ladies on a tour while Paul led the men to the terrace bar.

One's eyes were drawn to the vaulted ceiling and carved alabaster fireplace in the living room as the ladies commenced their tour. Seating areas were stationed about the room and the rich colors of fabrics, draperies and furniture brought warmth and comfortable elegance. The dining room had an intricate ceiling design and *trompe l'oeil* mural. "Christiana, we've missed you in Palm Beach this year," Megan remarked.

"I hope to spend more time here in the coming months," replied Christiana.

"The *trompe l'oeil* is remarkable," exclaimed Elizabeth, moving to the other side of the dining room to take a closer look. "This is some of the best work I have ever seen; the objects really do appear three-dimensional. Please give me the artist's name, Megan."

"Elizabeth, that's a true compliment, coming from an artist. Of course, I would be happy to give you his name," cooed Megan. "Now come and see my favorite room—the master bedroom suite." There, the large expanse of windows revealed the beauty of the water. Megan was thriving on the praise and attention. "I do hope you enjoyed my tour. Our other guests have seen this transformation but the darling Barringtons have been scarce this season."

"The men haven't even missed us," said Veronica, watching the men engrossed in serious conversations in various spots around the massive travertine terrace.

As the ladies dispersed, Christiana saw Jack advancing in her direction. "Great party," Jack said. "Let me bring you a glass of champagne."

"Your ex has found an appreciative audience," whispered Megan as she waltzed past Christiana. Glancing nonchalantly over her shoulder, she found Michael camped out in a sexy pose leaning against the balustrade gesturing theatrically to several ladies. *Must be talking show business,* she thought. She noticed two voluptuous, surgically enhanced ladies making their assets known to Michael. He appeared to be giving them careful consideration as he bobbed his head side-to-side and up-and-down. *Oh Michael, must you be so shallow?*

As he returned with champagne, Christiana introduced Jack to her friends and he engaged in conversation, allowing her a timely exit. On her way to the powder room, she was approached by April, one of the women Michael had been speaking with out on the terrace. "Your ex-husband is charming. I love his work and have followed his career. I did some modeling and acting before I married," she confided.

And it didn't seem to Christiana she was pleased with the demise of her career. "Your new perfume *Christiana* and *The Barrington Collection* are divine. You are stunning in the advertisements."

"Thank you," responded Christiana.

"Who is the male model for the new men's cologne called *Christian?*"

Trying to hide her disdain, she answered, "The model's name is Christian Luke and he now works for BHI in our London office."

"Is *he* at the party this evening?" purred April, surveying the guests.

Not a chance. "No." With her monosyllabic answer Christiana snapped the conversation to an abrupt close before April asked any more questions. Turning deftly to another subject, Christiana stated, "I know your husband Clifford. My father and he have been business associates for years."

"Oh, everyone knows my Cliffy," she said with a little laugh. "Cliffy is consumed with business. He's probably still in the same corner where I left him; ah yes, I see the plume of smoke from his stogie."

Clifford's trophy wife—bedecked in jewels and all the plastic surgery money can buy—those breasts belong to a twenty-year-old, thought Christiana.

"That is a lovely necklace, April."

"Another gift from my Cliffy. It's a piece from Jewels *by Barrington*, of course," she giggled.

Placing his arm on Christiana's shoulder, Jack rescued her from the superficial conversation. As they turned to leave, April whispered to Christiana, "The two most handsome men of the evening have eyes only for you."

Christiana gave her a weak smile as she and Jack headed in for dinner.

"Did I miss something?"

"No, Jack, honestly, you didn't miss a thing," responded Christiana. *I feel sorry for her husband,* she mused.

As dinner was called, Michael sauntered up to Christiana and put his arm around her waist. As she arched her back, he retreated accordingly. "Sorry, you just look amazing from the back side," he whispered. Although Jack had been sidelined by conversation, he did see the gesture.

With the sumptuousness of the décor in the dining room as background, Megan maintained simple settings accented with unscented candles of varying heights placed along the center of the tables and large leaves from her garden as placements sprinkled with exotic flowers as decoration. It was a perfect Florida presentation.

When everyone was seated, Christiana locked eyes with Michael at the adjoining table. His mischievous twinkle and sly grin played her every time she looked his way.

"Did you enjoy the evening, Christiana? I thought Megan's designer did a superb job. She gave me the name of the French artist who created the *trompe l'oeil* mural," said Elizabeth on the ride back to the estate.

"Yes, Mother, the party was lovely. Are you contemplating having the artist design a mural in one of your residences?"

Before Elizabeth could answer Jonathan stated, "I think she wants to do something at Sur La Mer." Elizabeth nodded.

Jack commented, "I would welcome the opportunity to meet the artist."

"Jack, I'll arrange for him to come to Sur La Mer and would be delighted to have you join us. Apparently he splits his time between his flat in Paris and country house in New Hampshire."

"That would be wonderful. Thank you, Elizabeth," returned Jack.

"Father, did you enjoy the party?"

"Yes …" Jonathan said, lost in thought. "There's an intriguing business proposition for Barrington Financial. I need to speak with Graham."

"Father, do you ever stop living and breathing Barrington?"

"Christiana, you more than anyone should know *THAT* answer," blurted Michael, and realized no one was amused.

Elizabeth rescued Michael with her quick segue. "Since your golf outing, Jonathan continues to mention his desire for more time on the golf course."

"I look forward to a rematch," said Jack. Michael nodded in agreement.

Returning to Bellagio, the ladies retired for the evening. Meanwhile Jonathan, still energized, went into the library and invited the gentlemen in for a nightcap.

"I won't be long, sweetheart," Jack said to Christiana as she left the room.

Still reading when Jack entered the bedroom, Christiana looked up as Jack remarked, "Your father has the most phenomenal knowledge base. He's fascinating to engage and he was genuinely interested in Michael's latest project."

"I'm happy to see everyone getting along so well."

"Why do I sense you are not all *that* happy?"

"No, of course I'm happy," she said but the frown told another story.

"But? It must have something to do with Michael," said Jack, with an edge.

"Well, yes. I'm not sure he should have come to the Montgomery party. Veronica was entirely out of her element and Michael left her alone far too long."

"I had some pangs of jealousy several times this evening as he seemed to be preoccupied with you. I don't understand Michael's intentions."

"Sweetheart, I'm not romantically interested in Michael. We've discussed my relationship with him and how often he stays at Montrachet to see Jennifer."

"Christiana, I believe you. I really do," reaching out to hold her hands. "But darling, you cannot be that oblivious. Michael is still in love with you," Jack stated in a somber tone. "He placed his arm around your waist to escort you into dinner and stared at you through the entire meal."

"Michael and I have a complicated and convoluted relationship and because of Jennifer, he will always be a part of our lives. We'll remain close and I'll always love him but I am no longer in love with him."

"Christiana, I sound like a jealous fool. I'm sorry."

"You have no reason to feel jealous, sweetheart."

"That's what I wanted to hear, since I'm falling in love with you. *NO,* not falling in love, I am in love with you and have been for some time. And if you desire to resume your relationship with Michael, I don't want to further complicate your life."

"Jackson Hamilton, you are the only man I am interested in," Christiana said firmly as they embraced. As the intensity rose, Jack hurriedly undressed while Christiana lifted the camisole over her shoulders and slithered out of her panties. With their bodies entangled, they rolled onto the bed and continued their long sensual kiss.

Jack fell into a deep sleep after they made love, while Christiana lay awake bothered by her inability to express her feelings. *Oh my God, could Michael have been correct when he said, "No man will ever be able to compete with your father"?* Quietly, she slipped out of bed, pulled on a bathrobe, and headed down to the kitchen to warm some milk.

Deep in reflection, as she stood at the stove, she heard footsteps and turned. "Couldn't sleep either?" Michael's hair was tousled and his bathrobe open, revealing his toned chest.

She nodded. "Care for some warm milk?" She averted her eyes from his bare chest and again faced the stove.

"Sure, I'll get the mugs."

They took the mugs and sat on stools at the kitchen counter. "Are you still mad at me?" he asked, his eyes on her as he sipped the milk.

"Jack's in love with me."

"What's the problem? The relationship's been heading in that direction."

"There is no problem, and yes, the relationship has been heading that way."

"You're not sure where you want the relationship to go, or you don't share the same feelings?"

"Michael, I really don't know. When he says he loves me, I can't echo the same words. Why am I telling *you* my thoughts?"

"Does he ask if you are in love with him?"

"No, he remains silent."

"Well, I hope the sex is good." She turned "Christiana red" and he knew better than to continue.

"He asked me about you," she said with hesitation.

"Really, during sex?"

"Oh, why are you so difficult," she scolded, shaking her head. "I told him it was a mistake to have you at the party."

"Wow. I was extremely sociable and on my best behavior. Remember, it was your father who invited me."

"Yes, I remember. Granted, you were charming, but wrapping your arm around me to escort me to dinner—Michael, what were you thinking? Then you compounded the problem by staring at me for most of the meal. Furthermore, you abandoned Veronica for the better part of the evening. To top it off, Jack noticed your actions. This prompted me to elaborate on our rather unconventional relationship and your frequent visits to Montrachet. Tonight, I awoke haunted by a statement you made when we divorced, 'No man will ever be able to compete with your father.'"

"Well, I can't help you with that one—although I tried for years. Don't allow it to sabotage your relationship with Jack."

"There's one other issue. Jack believes you are still in love with me."

"Jack is a very intuitive man, Christiana." With that he got up and took the empty mugs to the sink and simply said, "Goodnight, Christiana."

The note on the pillow read, "In the gym, need to maintain my stamina to keep up with you in bed, Love J." Christiana slipped on her exercise clothes and made her way to the gym to find Jack.

"Good morning, Sleeping Beauty," Jack said, wiping his face with the towel.

"You're up early," she answered, pecking him on the cheek.

"Slept well and wanted to get some exercise."

"Me too," she agreed, heading to the Pilates machine. "We are having breakfast with my parents on their yacht before attending church service."

"What time is the dinner party here this evening," asked Jack, sipping some water.

"Cocktails will be served at five in the gardens around the pool area. We will have a dinner cruise on my father's yacht. Thank goodness for my mother and our party planner. They are probably huddled together right now working out the final preparations for the event."

Jack and Christiana crossed paths with Veronica and Jennifer as everyone was making their way downstairs. "Veronica, are you joining us for breakfast?"

"Thank you, but I have some work to do this morning."

"Good morning everyone," Michael said in a loud voice.

"Good morning, Daddy," chirped Jennifer. "Come with us to Grandfather's yacht for breakfast?"

Michael looked to Christiana and she nodded approval. "Sure, Jennifer, I'd love to join you for breakfast," said Michael. Jennifer started to tug at him as he leaned down and said, "Hold on, sweetheart, I need to talk with your mother for a moment."

Jack took the cue and escorted Jennifer down the path to the boat.

"I won't be joining you this evening as I plan to take Veronica and Jennifer out to dinner and a movie, if you have no objection."

"Would you mind attending the cocktail reception, as there are some people I would like Jennifer to meet?"

"I'd be happy to. I'm not sure I can drag Veronica."

"Please try to change her mind," said Christiana.

"I'll try, although she's not much of a party person," he answered.

Christiana found Jack and Jonathan on the bridge. "Good morning, Father. What a glorious day!"

"Good morning, Christiana. Apparently a number of the electronic components on this boat come from Hamilton Industries," informed Jonathan.

"Interesting."

"Tell your mother we will be right there, just want to show Jack something I bought for *Behold*," said Jonathan. Christiana proceeded to the forward deck.

"Christiana, you look lovely and relaxed this morning," exclaimed Elizabeth.

"I know why," taunted Michael.

Ignoring his comment, Christiana responded, "Michael, would you mind if I have a word with my mother?"

"Of course, may I bring you ladies some coffee?" Elizabeth shook her head no and Christiana accepted his offer.

Taking a sip of her tea, Elizabeth waited for Christiana to present her news.

Christiana leaned close to her mother and confided, "Jack is in love with me."

"Oh, darling, it's wonderful to be in love," said Elizabeth. "I'm thrilled!"

"Mother, I'm not sure *how* I feel. Am I being ridiculous?"

"Be governed by your heart, my dear. When the time is right, you'll know; your feelings will become clear. You can't hurry love."

"Oh Mother. That's an old Supremes song, 'You Can't Hurry Love.'" Their seriousness broke into laughter at the same moment the men came on deck.

"That song was a little before your time, Christiana," teased Michael.

"What are my ladies talking about this beautiful morning?" quipped Jonathan.

"Just girl talk," said Elizabeth, and motioned for the group to sit at the table.

Michael deliberately placed himself at the far end of the table to avoid ongoing eye contact with Christiana. The conversation was easy and light-hearted with Jennifer as the primary focus.

"We're going out to dinner and to a movie tonight," said a beaming Jennifer.

Turning to Michael, Elizabeth inquired, "You are not going to join us this evening?"

"Jennifer and I will be at the reception and then go out with Veronica," he replied.

The party planner caught Elizabeth's eye and she said, "Please excuse me. Christiana, would you join me for a moment?" When the ladies returned, Michael and Jennifer were alone at the table.

"Jack and your father headed back to the house. Listen; go ahead and spend the afternoon with Jack. Jennifer wants to swim and play badminton, so have fun. You're not needed here with 'Mr. Party Perfect.'"

Christiana rolled her eyes and responded, "It's Christopher Fleur."

"Well 'Fleur' to you, too," Michael teased.

"Do you ever stop acting like a child? Seriously, I would like some time with Jack. Thanks," she answered.

"Even attending church with the Barringtons is a major event," Jack said quietly to Christiana, now dressed for the Sunday occasion.

"A sizable donation has eased the pastor's concern about our circus performance at his services. Be prepared for the onslaught of those who want to get close and talk with Jonathan Robert Barrington after the service," she lamented.

Jonathan managed to untangle from the group chatting with him after the service as he took Elizabeth's arm and escorted her to their waiting car. Christiana too was bombarded with interested parishioners and had learned the proper way to exit courteously at precisely the right moment.

As Elizabeth and Jonathan left for their luncheon, Christiana and Jack drove back to Bellagio. The house was quiet. Stepping out onto the main terrace, Christiana caught sight of Jennifer and Michael splashing in the pool.

"Are you up for a bike ride?" Jack asked as he watched her.

"That sounds wonderful," Christiana answered as she turned to Jack. "I'll dash upstairs and put on some shorts. Would you mind asking one of the staff to retrieve the bikes and bring them around to the front of the house?"

"My pleasure," he said, bounding off in search of the household help.

The light ocean breezes and temperate afternoon temperature—sans the Florida humidity—granted Christiana and Jack a chance to bike for a longer period. Rejuvenated and energized, they returned to the estate. Bellagio had been transformed into a festive party environment. Christiana found her mother walking the grounds with Christopher while her father lounged poolside with Jennifer.

The evening was a charming reminder of the balmy and pleasant outdoor living that exemplifies the Florida lifestyle. True to his word, Michael was present at the cocktail reception but sprinted off with Jennifer and Veronica for their own fun-filled dinner and movie date. Jackson was more at ease this evening and his previous agitation over Michael's presence seemed to dissipate.

"I understand why you enjoy Bellagio so much, my love," said Jack as they sat out on Christiana's boat after the party enjoying the night lights reflected on the water.

Jack sighed as he stroked her hair and added, "I hate to call it a night but I have an early tee time."

As they wandered hand-in-hand through the gardens back to Bellagio, Jack stopped to embrace Christiana and kissed her under the star-filled sky.

"I'm sorry we have to leave tomorrow," murmured Jack.

"Darling, let's come back soon. Bellagio awaits our return," whispered Christiana.

CHAPTER 34 ... Several months later

THE URGENT TELEPHONE CALL went to Christiana's assistant since Christiana was ensconced in an all-day meeting and her cell phone was out of reach. The call prompted Amanda to scurry into the conference room and whisper the news to her boss. Christiana controlled her emotion and fear, in true Barrington fashion, and politely excused herself, turning the meeting over to James.

"Christiana, the school said they tried your cell phone and there was no answer. Thank goodness Jennifer was not kidnapped. The school assured me Jennifer is fine and waiting in the principal's office for your arrival. The police are en route," said Amanda as they walked from the conference room. "I've sent for your car."

"Thank you, Amanda. See if Peggy Fairfield is available to accompany me to Greenwich. I'll be in my office on the phone." Christiana speed-dialed her sister-in-law's cell. "Veronica, I've just heard what happened. Are you sure Jennifer is all right?"

"Jennifer is faring well. My heart is still racing; I've never been so frightened. It happened in an instant. Jennifer walked out behind one of the parents and due to her small size, no one saw her. She said she was coming to greet me. Thankfully we were close enough to react and change the course of the event as we saw the suspect attempt to grab her. Jennifer's right here; let me put her on the phone."

Sheepishly, Jennifer answered, "Are you mad at me since I walked out without Aunt Veronica? I really thought I saw her before this strange lady started to pull on my arm. I yelled really, really loud. Everybody heard me—but the person ran away."

"No, sweetheart, I'm not mad at you. But I am most concerned about your safety," she responded, tamping down the fear in her voice.

"I'm okay—but it was scary, Mother. I don't ever want to go through that again."

What would I do if something happened to her, Christiana reflected. "Please don't worry about that, my angel. I'm on my way to your school and will see you shortly."

Still waiting for Peggy and her driver, she phoned the school to consult with the principal. "Good afternoon, Mr. Newcomb, this is Christiana Barrington."

"Ms. Barrington, first let me assure you Jennifer has not been harmed and is waiting in my office."

Thank God. "I spoke with Jennifer and her nanny before I called your office."

"Good. We have eyewitness accounts of the incident. The security guard first noticed the suspicious woman as she attempted to grab another girl, a classmate of Jennifer's. We have reason to believe this was a random act or even a prank. Greenwich police have been notified and are due momentarily," he stated.

"Thankfully, neither Jennifer nor her classmate was abducted. The school has a protocol for release of the children. Veronica Trent, her nanny, as one of those named responsible for her pickup and her security detail were there today. Thus, I am wondering why she was in a vulnerable area without adequate supervision."

"Ms. Barrington, I was told that Jennifer thought she saw Ms. Trent and walked out behind another student and her mother and was not seen by the staff. Please understand, I'm not minimizing blame or the severity of the situation; I am merely reporting the compilation of facts. The school's response team acted expeditiously and responsibly according to school procedures. Unfortunately, it was not sooner."

"Mr. Newcomb, this was a potential kidnapping. Has this ever happened before at your school?" asked Christiana in cold detachment.

"No, Ms. Barrington." As a follow-up, he added, "I've been informed the police will want to question your daughter. Hopefully you will be here by that time. The captain also said they wish to speak with several students, faculty, Ms. Trent, your daughter's security guard, and our security team."

By now, Peggy Fairfield was standing in Christiana's office. "I should be at the school within the hour to meet you and the Police Chief. There is one last item. Under no circumstances should this be leaked to the press."

"Yes, Ms. Barrington. We have the eyewitnesses in the vice principal's office awaiting the police."

"Thank you, Mr. Newcomb," said Christiana as she hung up the phone.

Christiana conversed with Peggy on relevant details for the next few minutes in preparation for the ride to Connecticut. "Keep track of the news broadcasts and make sure we stay out of the press," commented Christiana.

She nodded then added, "Have you contacted Michael?"

"No, I will," answered Christiana but was interrupted by an incoming call from Alex Snow, her personal assistant. A meeting had been arranged for that evening with the Head of Barrington Personal Security to determine increased security measures. Two additional guards had been placed on 24-hour surveillance at the compound.

"Thank you, Alex. Take all your conversations on the private line—no cell phones. This is to remain confidential. In the event of a press leak, Peggy Fairfield will speak on behalf of the Barrington family."

"Understood. I'm here, and will stay as long as you need me. I'm thankful Jennifer is okay," replied Alex.

Before she decided what to say to Michael they had reached the school. Several unmarked police cars were stationed out front. Christiana noticed one detective searching the foliage as they entered the campus and made their way to the principal's office. Another detective was interviewing the security guard and a faculty member.

As they entered the outer office of the principal's suite, Christiana saw Veronica and Jennifer sitting pensively. Jennifer hurried over to kiss her mother.

"I really thought I saw Aunt Veronica and I just wanted to surprise her. It's my fault," lamented Jennifer.

"Darling," said Christiana, "it's not your fault and I'm not angry with you. I'm just happy you are safe."

"I'm okay, but Aunt Veronica and Mr. Newcomb said this was very serious."

"Yes, Jennifer, this was. Stay here while I speak with Mr. Newcomb."

Glancing at Veronica, Christiana queried, "Have you spoken with the police?"

"Yes, I've spoken with one of the detectives."

Before Christiana could ask another question, the principal's assistant appeared and said, "Ms. Barrington, please come this way." Christiana introduced Peggy Fairfield to Glen Newcomb. "Ms. Fairfield is the public voice for the Barrington family and I have asked her to attend this meeting," stated Christiana.

"Very well, let me bring you ladies up to date," announced Mr. Newcomb. "Detective Brooks has been in to see me and is speaking with some of the eyewitnesses. When finished he will swing by my office. As we discussed on the telephone, we have reason to believe this was a random act and Jennifer was not targeted. Eyewitness accounts revealed the assailant was a white female, probably in her early twenties, nicely dressed. Thus, she did not arouse suspicion since most nannies and child care personnel are light-skinned European girls. A forensic artist has been sent over to construct a composite drawing from information we've gathered."

"Hopefully that will conclude with a quick arrest," said Christiana.

"I understand how upsetting this is, Ms. Barrington. Rest assured, we will use all our resources to assist in the apprehension of the suspect," assured Mr. Newcomb.

"Is the girl seated in the waiting room the student who was grabbed?"

Mr. Newcomb nodded and said, "Detective Brooks asked them to remain in case you wished to speak with them."

The chief was soon to arrive and brought Jennifer, Veronica, the other student, and her mother into Mr. Newcomb's office. "We still believe this was a random act possibly from a local youngster, even a relative, sister or friend of one of the students. We'll have a preliminary drawing soon and ask if you recognize her. It's only a sketch; the finished composite will take some time to complete.

But it might give us something to go on," said the chief. "While we are waiting, I would like to ask the girls a couple of questions."

As the girls left the room to be interviewed by the police chief, Christiana and Veronica spoke with the mother of the other student. With only slight variations, primarily from their distinct vantage points, the girls' stories were consistent and complementary. The woman came out from nowhere and grabbed Sandra Smith from behind, which precluded the student from getting a good look at the attacker. Reaching for Sandra, the perpetrator accidentally tumbled, releasing her grip. As the suspect fell away from the first student, Jennifer came into view trailing behind the parent. With the commotion set off by Sandra's screams, the response team went into play. The suspect scurried away from Sandra and reached for Jennifer. As the security guard was quickly approaching, Jennifer was released and the suspect fled to the waiting car.

As the girls reentered the principal's office, Christiana asked, "Did anyone get the license plate number of the vehicle?"

"I understand the plate had been removed from the back of the car," replied the chief. "It may have been deliberate. We did get a good description of the vehicle and have put out an All Points Bulletin, APB, within the tri-state area, which may be extended if we don't pick up a trail in the next couple of hours."

Christiana had been scrutinizing Sandra since she had reentered the room. The girls possessed basic similarities, thought Christiana. Each was wearing a lavender sweater and similarly colored pants. They were almost identical in height and hair color and both were sporting pigtails. But something was disturbing to Christiana and she couldn't put her finger on it.

With a knock on the door, the detective produced the sketch for the group to view. No one uttered a word as they stared at the facial rendering. The silence was broken when the chief asked, "Have you seen this woman around school before today?"

All parties responded *no*. He had turned up empty-handed with the other eyewitnesses as well. As he was about to continue his questioning, his cell phone blared. Swiftly answering, he turned his back with a few hushed words to the caller.

The chief excused the girls with Veronica while he finished speaking with the parents. Then a second call came through. When he answered the call he stated, "Sorry, I need to take this in private."

When the chief returned, his face held a grave expression. "I have additional news." With nervous anticipation, Christiana sat upright.

"The getaway car has been found," he began. "It was abandoned in the parking lot of a strip mall in the outskirts of Danbury. No sign of the suspects. Police are talking with shop owners and anyone who may have seen the suspects leave the car." The room remained silent until he continued. "The search is now for the suspect and her accomplice or driver of the getaway vehicle."

He paused but only momentarily, as Christiana sat forward on the edge of her chair. "But this is where it changes dramatically. We've searched the car and found a ransom note crumpled under the front passenger seat. This has been a targeted attempt to kidnap Jennifer Barrington-Trent. The ransom was twenty million dollars."

Christiana shuddered and Peggy placed her arm around Christiana's shoulders.

"Both girls were wearing similar clothing with their hair in pigtails. The girls resemble each other from the back so the kidnapper may have assumed it was Jennifer," the chief reported solemnly.

"This has always been my worst nightmare," said Christiana, trying to control her emotions. "They may continue to stalk her until they find her in a vulnerable position."

"Due to this significant change, the high profile nature of this case and the significant ransom demand, the FBI has been contacted. The assistant director and his field agent will meet you at your home at seven this evening."

Numb, all she could do was nod.

Once the police had left, Christiana turned to Principal Newcomb and commented, "I wish to have Barrington security at the school tomorrow with Jennifer."

In mild protest, Mr. Newcomb replied, "But Ms. Barrington, with the school security there really is no need for a bodyguard. It will alarm the student body."

"Principal Newcomb, I know you will make an exception since this is an unprecedented situation," she said with clear determination.

He nodded and merely replied, "Have Ms. Trent bring the agent to my office."

A somber mood hung over them on the ride back to Montrachet. Once home, Veronica and Jennifer went upstairs while Christiana went to her study to contact Michael.

"You caught me heading out for a late lunch. May I call you back from the car?"

"*No*, Michael, this can't wait and we need to speak on a hard line."

Hearing her urgent tone, he responded, "Oh God, what's happened?"

"Jennifer was the target of a potential abduction at school but it was thwarted by the quick response of security personnel. At first they believed it was a random act as another student was first grabbed. Thankfully neither of the girls was harmed. Subsequent details have revealed, however, that it was not a random act. Police found a ransom note in the abandoned getaway car."

"What? Jennifer was almost kidnapped?" When she finished retelling the drama, Michael responded, "Let her come here and stay with me awhile."

"You think she'd be safer in LA than Greenwich?"

"As of right now, yes," he answered. Softening his tone, he said, "Christiana, I don't mean to add to your anguish. I agree with your idea of a security guard, but *my God*, how horrible for a young child to be burdened like this. There must be alternatives?"

"Michael, I *have* no alternatives. I must and will protect our daughter. Due to the high profile of the case, the FBI is now conducting the investigation and will be here this evening."

"Christiana, call me as soon as the FBI leaves, I don't care what time it is."

Precisely at seven that evening, as the doorbell chimed, Christiana followed the butler to the front door. Anticipating the FBI detective, she was startled to see her father. Jonathan brushed past the butler with a customary nod and grasped Christiana's hand, leading her to the living room.

"I take it you've heard what happened to Jennifer at school today."

"Veronica contacted your mother when she was unable to reach you by cell. I came here directly following the phone call from your mother," said Jonathan with a worried look. "Where's Jennifer?" Just as he completed the last sentence the doorbell sounded and the FBI agents were escorted into the living room.

"Tom Mitchell," said Jonathan with a sense of relief. "I'm glad to see you're in charge. Tom, this is my daughter Christiana."

"Mr. Barrington, it's good to see you but I'm sorry it's under these circumstances. I'm pleased to make your acquaintance, Ms. Barrington. This is John Franklin, who will be working the case with me."

Jonathan asked, "Tom, what do you have so far?" Not waiting for an answer, he continued, "How could this happen at a private school in Greenwich? Pull out all the stops to apprehend these suspects immediately. I'll put up the reward money."

"I cannot speak for the security efforts of the school; you'll need to ask Mr. Newcomb," stated Tom Mitchell.

With a penetrating stare, Jonathan said, "This is my grand-daughter. Jennifer will have all the protection possible from our side. She will never be put in a vulnerable position again."

"This is an FBI investigation and I trust you will let us do our jobs."

Touching her father's arm to silence him, Christiana commented, "Assistant Director Mitchell, we understand. You will have our full cooperation and we'll do everything in our power to help protect Jennifer and assist the FBI in a quick resolution to this investigation."

Perched at the edge of the sofa, Jonathan remarked, "Christiana's the polite Barrington. I'll be relentless until these predators are behind bars!"

"Mr. Barrington," Tom cautioned.

"Tom, we've known each other too long, drop the formalities," added Jonathan.

"We've been down this path before so I'll cut to the chase. Here is what we have so far."

Before Tom Mitchell could continue, Christiana turned to her father. "What does he mean; you've been down this path before?"

Clearing his throat, Jonathan explained, "Your mother experienced a similar incident years ago. Her bodyguards thwarted the abduction. The suspect was caught but before sentencing, he took his own life in prison, the coward."

"So Jennifer was not the first Barrington to be targeted?"

"Sweetheart, I've worked feverishly to protect you and the family *at all costs*," said Jonathan, now holding both his daughter's hands. "Okay, Tom, apprise us of the developments in the case."

"A late model silver Ford Explorer SUV was found abandoned in a strip mall on the outskirts of Danbury. The SUV belongs to a businessman in Westchester who reported it stolen two days ago from his company's parking lot. While we have no reason to believe there's a connection, we are conducting a background analysis on him. The ransom note has been turned over to our handwriting experts."

"Can you give us any information on the man?" asked Christiana.

Tom Mitchell retrieved papers from his bag. "His name is Peter St. James and he appears to run a legitimate Asian import/export business. No criminal record."

Tom Mitchell continued. "The primary suspect blended in with the other au pairs and nannies so she didn't draw attention. In addition, eyewitnesses identified a male as the driver of the car. The male was Caucasian, a bit older, say, mid-thirties with shaggy blond hair and a cap. The vehicle was parked directly in front of the school and almost hit another car in its hasty retreat."

"I recognize that name St. James from somewhere," mused Jonathan.

As they deliberated, Tom Mitchell received a call and stepped away. Returning with news, he called out, "Mystery solved. He worked at Barrington for several years."

Another phone call interrupted Tom Mitchell's discussion and as he left the room, Jonathan also followed him out to contact Barrington's Head of Human Resources. Fortunately, he found Meredith Chen still in the office. Meredith had been with BHI for twenty years. She expressed her concern but kept the conversation short and professional. The St. James name also had immediate recognition to her.

When all three were reunited, Tom Mitchell said, "We've lifted fingerprints and DNA samples from the vehicle. I have some further information about Peter St. James. He worked for your hotel conglomerate in Manhattan in a sales capacity."

Jonathan interrupted, "I spoke with the Head of HR for BHI and she is due to report back to me with the particulars of his employment and departure."

"Good," answered Tom Mitchell. "That should prove to be worthwhile information, although we have no reason to suspect Mr. St. James, except that his vehicle was used in the course of a crime. Several storekeepers at the strip mall where the vehicle was dumped have assisted with information on the suspects. Both proceeded to walk in a northerly direction toward the interstate. The APB has just been expanded to all of New England. Law enforcement agencies in states to the south and west have also been contacted as well as the Canadian border officials."

The ringing of Jonathan's phone halted further explanations. "Barrington. Yes, Meredith. Please give me the salient points, I'll read the email attachment later. I have you on speaker so Christiana and the FBI can hear this as well."

"Peter St. James was a sales coordinator for Barrington Hotels & Resorts International at Corporate. He had several run-ins with supervisors and was passed over for a promotion. He was known to have a temper and it was questioned whether he had a substance abuse problem, although never confirmed."

When Jonathan started to interrupt, Meredith admonished, "Wait, Jonathan, there's more. Apparently you had a heated argument with him. You were heard to say this would be documented with his supervisor as well as HR. You walked away without further comment. St. James retorted, 'Mr. Barrington, you will pay for this.' The employee who overheard the conversation still works for us."

As Jonathan read through the file on his computer, Tom Mitchell asked, "Do you recall this incident with St. James? Did *you* hear him make the threat?"

"No on both counts," replied Jonathan.

"Hearsay evidence is not going to help us."

"Wait, Tom, Meredith mentioned that the person who heard him make the threat is still employed with BHI. We should be able to get a statement," said Jonathan.

The FBI agent nodded.

"Do whatever it takes—*whatever*," replied Jonathan.

"It would be helpful if I could speak with Jennifer briefly," said Tom Mitchell.

Concerned, Christiana answered, "Assistant Director Mitchell, Jennifer has been through so much today, does this have to be done tonight?"

Before he could answer, Jonathan placed a comforting hand on his daughter's arm and said, "Christiana, let Tom speak with Jennifer while everything is fresh in her mind. She may have remembered something since the inspector and Greenwich police spoke with her earlier today." Christiana wasn't convinced but noting the intent look on Tom's face she conceded and went upstairs to locate Jennifer.

When they returned, Tom said, "I think this might be easier if Jennifer and I spoke privately," as he motioned toward the dining room.

Left alone in the living room, Christiana had the opportunity to question her father on the experience her mother had years ago. "Father, you never mentioned Mother's potential abduction. Why was I not informed?"

"It was your mother's wish. You were safely tucked away at school in Switzerland and she did not want you to worry. Now I've broken my promise to your mother. Not another word about this. This chapter is permanently closed." Jonathan rose from the sofa and poured a double scotch.

Returning to the sofa with his drink, Jonathan handed Christiana a glass of sparkling water. He asked, "Would you like me to call Gerald Stedman and see how quickly he can accommodate Jennifer at St. George's? Or would you prefer to make the telephone call?"

"Although not convinced that's the best solution, I'm not as adamantly opposed to the idea as I was before. However, the decision rests with Michael and me and, to some degree, Jennifer," she answered.

"What will it take to change your mind, Christiana? Does Jennifer have to be kidnapped before you realize she is a target due to our wealth?"

"Father, you need not remind me of that, as I live in fear every day."

"Thus it appears obvious she should be moved to Switzerland for schooling. I will pull some strings and have her enrolled even though school is in full session."

"*No,* Father you will not call Mr. Stedman. Please, Barrington Security is waiting to speak with me and I must call Michael as soon as possible."

Looking at his distraught daughter, he enveloped her with his arms. "Sweetheart, I'm here to do whatever you decide," Jonathan whispered.

"Thank you. Father, I know in your heart you want what is best for Jennifer."

Opening the front door to leave, Jonathan added, "Sweetheart, Tom Mitchell is the best. As a young man, he pulled out all the stops with your mother's case. Now he is the seasoned professional; we will get a speedy resolve."

"I hope you're right, Father. I'm afraid and can't display my fear to Jennifer. What if Peter St. James is somehow involved and this was all a vendetta between a disgruntled employee and Barrington?"

"Try to relax, Christiana. Let the FBI do their job. Your mother is probably a wreck with worry so I need to head home," said Jonathan as he strode out into the night.

Concluding the meeting with her security team, she went upstairs to find Jennifer asleep. Hearing Christiana down the hall, Veronica opened the door of her apartment and the women discussed the salient points of the investigation.

Once finished, Christiana entered her bedroom in time to find her private line ringing. "Christiana, what happened? Did the FBI come by Montrachet? What do they know at this point? How's Jennifer?" Michael quickly threw out his staccato questions.

"I was just preparing to call you. The meetings with the FBI and Barrington Security took longer than I anticipated." Dropping down on a padded chintz chair, she brought Michael up to date with the status of the investigation, including the possible connection with the disgruntled former Barrington employee. Initially, she skirted revisiting the topic of Jennifer's schooling in Switzerland, but as the conversation proceeded, she raised the issue. At the mention of her father, Michael blew up.

"Gee, what could he be thinking? He happens to have the Head Master's number on speed dial and could place a call immediately and enroll our daughter at St. George's in Switzerland before I'd have a chance to say goodbye. But my God, our daughter was almost kidnapped today," sparked Michael in frustration and anxiety.

"Yes, he briefly brought up the subject of the European schooling but nothing has changed except that I'm not as opposed to the idea as I once was." Quickly turning the focus, she filled him in on her mother's experience and the suicide of the assailant. "Michael, you must promise not to mention this to anyone—*I mean anyone.*"

"You have my word. I adore your mother; thank God she was not harmed. How painful to hear this news on top of everything else you have been through today."

"It's difficult to comprehend the magnitude of these events. This gave me a newfound appreciation for Father's concern about Jennifer's well-being." Looking at the clock, she concluded, "Michael, I'm drained and need to get some rest."

"Of course, but before I let you go I have an idea. I'll change my schedule and come back to stay with you and Jennifer. My next project for Broadway could gear up and I'll place the film on the back burner. Jennifer needs the protection and support of her father until we see what comes from this investigation," said Michael.

"Thank you, Michael. That would be comforting," she whispered.

CHAPTER 35

DOGGING THE INVESTIGATION with daily telephone calls to Tom Mitchell, Jonathan was persistent in his pursuit. Due to their relationship and the high profile nature of this case, Tom Mitchell took his calls even when there was nothing new to report. He consoled, questioned, refreshed, and refigured with Jonathan on a regular basis. If he did not, he knew full well Jonathan would pull rank. The Director of the Bureau in Washington was a close personal friend of the Barringtons.

Peter St. James had not surfaced and this was stalling the investigation. An APB had been sent out as he had not returned to his Westchester residence since the kidnapping attempt. His house was placed under 24-hour surveillance and in short order the FBI secured a search warrant.

Then the case got interesting.

"Boss!" yelled the agent to Tom Mitchell. "Come down to the basement, I think we found something."

Maneuvering the steep staircase to the basement of the St. James residence, Tom Mitchell found his agent retrieving information from a desk at the far corner of the room. Covering two walls were photographs and Tom remained silent, looking over the array.

"What do you think of this?" the agent asked.

Peter St. James had a vendetta against BHI, or more pointedly, against Jonathan. A diary revealed plot scenarios including the use of weapons and bombs. Pages had large Xs scribbled with notes—"not workable at this time," "not enough range." However, as Tom Mitchell continued to read, he found a plot not crossed out, unfolding the kidnapping scene in graphic detail. On the side of one of the pages, St. James wrote, "Jonathan, your granddaughter is the love of your life. What better way to get revenge than to take your precious little Jennifer and destroy her. Sorry, Christiana, I actually liked you but your miserable prick of a dad made everything impossible. I can't take it anymore. Jonathan Barrington has ruined my life. Now it's payback and he must lose Jennifer."

Chilling details were found in other writings and photos of the Barrington dynasty. Clippings and photographs of the Barrington family filled several desk drawers including several of Jonathan, which appeared intentionally ripped at the head, leaving only his trunk. A photo of Jennifer was taped over a picture of Jonathan with a note attached, "I will take her from you *soon*. Sorry, Christiana."

"It's hard not to speculate Jonathan was his prime target. With the tight Barrington security and Mr. Barrington's travel schedule, it would be problematic to get him in his sights. On the other hand, his granddaughter goes to school every day with time and location a constant," said Tom Mitchell as he scratched his head.

"With the veil of privacy and security that protects the Barrington dynasty it's puzzling how a lowly employee would know about Jennifer's school. But she was obviously the easier target. Christiana also travels with bodyguards and would be less vulnerable. And it appears St. James liked Christiana." The agent paused to look at his boss.

"Tom, your hunch may be correct, Jonathan was the main target. Peter St. James needs to be found and brought in for questioning."

"Have the neighbors been thoroughly questioned?" The agent gave an affirmative nod. They gathered and removed the evidence from the house and as they were heading back to the office, Tom stated, "I want to keep 24-hour surveillance on this property. I sense Mr. St. James is going to return home, and soon."

Back in the FBI office, Tom Mitchell placed two telephone calls requesting a meeting with Jonathan and Christiana the following day at the FBI offices.

Meanwhile, Michael had settled into Montrachet and added an extra layer of protection for Jennifer. Montrachet and Sur La Mer became fortresses.

Jack's travel schedule and family issues precluded Christiana from discussing Jennifer's potential abduction. When she reluctantly mentioned it to him several days after the event, he exclaimed, "My word, why didn't you call me? What can I do? Shall I come and stay with you at Montrachet?"

"Jack, I didn't want you to worry; you're busy enough with your own family and business concerns. Michael flew back a couple of days ago for an indefinite stay. He is taking Jennifer to and from school. Thank you, though."

With a bite of jealousy in his voice at the mention of Michael staying at the mansion, he answered with, "I wish I could hold you and make all your troubles go away. Hopefully, Michael's presence will help alleviate some of your concerns."

"Yes, it has. Father also has been steadfast but remains extremely agitated and stressed since there has been little movement in the case. The suspects remain at large and there might be a link with a former BHI employee who had a vendetta against my father. This potential link compounds the issue."

"It's almost too much to comprehend. I feel helpless; I want to do something, anything. Is there a possibility you are also a prime target?"

"I don't think so, but honestly, I'm not sure of anything at this point. We have a meeting with the FBI tomorrow. There's some significant evidence that has just been obtained and hopefully will prove beneficial." Sighing, she continued, "I have always tried to keep Jennifer out of harm's way. Now I just don't know. This has shaken me to the core."

"Christiana, please call me after your meeting with the FBI. Better yet, I'm going to drive out to Greenwich tomorrow afternoon." Before she could protest he gently insisted, "You can't stop me. I love you and want to be with you."

"I love you too, Jack. Thank you."

CHAPTER 36

CHRISTIANA TURNED WHITE; Michael murmured obsceni-ties; and Jonathan clenched his jaw, narrowed his eyes as Tom Mitchell presented the new evidence. He unveiled the pictures, the diary and other Barrington reference items taken from the St. James residence in Westchester.

"My God, Peter St. James *is* the prime suspect. He was willing to harm my granddaughter to get to ME!" Jonathan exclaimed. Christiana started to cry and Michael wrapped his arm around her shoulder.

Turning his chair to face Tom Mitchell, Jonathan bellowed, "Tom, for the second time in my life, my family is at risk and for no other reason than because they are related to *me*. Look, the bastard even writes that he likes Christiana, it is just the father she has that's the problem."

Tom Mitchell interrupted the tirade, "We will get him, Jonathan, and bring him in for questioning. He will resurface soon. We have his house under surveillance; it is only a matter of time. St. James now appears central to our investigation and when we find him we should also find the two accomplices, the woman and the man."

"I won't just stand around and do nothing," stated Jonathan, punching the table with his fist. "I'll hire my own private investigator to hunt this son of a bitch."

"Father, your involvement could compromise the investigation, and as much as I understand your feelings, we must allow the FBI to do their job."

Tom Mitchell cautioned, "It's prudent the entire Barrington family maintain tight security until we apprehend St. James and the other suspects."

"Security has been intensified at our estates and I'm carrying a piece around again," groaned Jonathan as he opened his jacket to reveal a gun and holster.

"Hope you have a permit for that, Jonathan," admonished Tom Mitchell. Jonathan flashed the permit.

Moving back to the main topic, Tom asked, "Is there any additional information that might shed light on this case?"

Jonathan bullied with, "Tom, I warn you, if you don't—"

"No threats, Jonathan. We know this has taken a toll on the entire Barrington family and of course I include you, Michael, as Jennifer's father. I understand your frustration, anger and concerns. We want to bring these fugitives to justice."

"Thank you. We are here to assist in any way possible," said Christiana, who had been virtually silent during most of the earlier conversation.

Arriving back at BHI, Christiana demanded in no uncertain terms, "You *will* never come near Jennifer or Montrachet with that gun. I hope that is clear, Father?"

"Yes, you are perfectly clear, Christiana," he responded, avoiding a confrontation as he marched out of her office.

Michael smirked at the testy relay between father and daughter and stated, "I'm heading back so I will be at Jennifer's school before dismissal. I'll see you later."

"Jack will be having dinner with us this evening."

"Would you like me to vanish?"

"It's a family dinner, so you are most welcome," answered Christiana.

Michael and Jack were engrossed in conversation when Christiana arrived. Jack rose to kiss Christiana while Michael watched them embrace with a gulp of scotch.

"Christiana, would you care to join us for a drink?" Michael asked.

"No, thank you, I'm going upstairs to see Jennifer," responded Christiana.

"She's finishing her homework," said Michael.

Jack and Christiana were happy for some private time but the stress of the FBI investigation had taken its toll on Christiana. She was emotionally spent and as the clock chimed ten, Jack placed his coffee cup on the bone china saucer, and said, "Although I hate to leave you, I should get going. You need some rest." They embraced for a long while, neither needing to speak. Goodbye was not easy as Jack reluctantly left.

Heading into the kitchen for tea, Christiana found Michael having a snack and she sat down with him at the kitchen table. "Jack's a good man. I see why you like him," said Michael. "He's concerned and protective of both you and Jennifer."

After chatting easily with her for some time, finally Michael said, "You look exhausted, my dear." He touched her cheek softly and she did not pull away.

"Yes, I guess I should try to get some rest," she responded, pushing back the chair and going over to the sink with her teacup.

"Pleasant dreams, Christiana. I'll turn off the lights and lock up."

"Thank you for being here for us, Michael." And with that she was gone.

CHAPTER 37

"WHAT DO YOU THINK OF Samantha," asked a beaming James Langston as he and Christiana headed back to corporate headquarters following a meeting at Magnifique.

"She's quite impressive. With lightning speed, she has established her presence, and is clearly making her mark. The synergistic feeling in the room and the support and excitement of the staff were evident," replied Christiana.

"Give her running room and you will continue to be impressed. Accolades have been forthcoming from a number of our prominent customers and vendors. Right person, right time, right fit, I would say," bragged James.

Christiana sat down at her desk after finishing up with James, as her private line started to ring. "Mother, this is a pleasant surprise."

"Darling, I'm sorry to bother you at work but I am really worried about your father. He hasn't slept since the kidnapping attempt. I made him take a sleeping pill last night," sighed Elizabeth. "He continues to blame himself and as you know he has started to carry a gun. Most distressing, he wanders aimlessly muttering that *he* will find Peter St. James and bring him to justice. I was hoping you might speak to him."

"Of course, I'll speak with Father, although I'm not sure it will do any good. We discuss the subject daily. He wants to look St. James in the eye when he is apprehended by the FBI," said Christiana with concern.

"That worries me. He might try something foolish," voiced Elizabeth sadly.

"I firmly believe Father would never imperil us, BHI or himself," assured Christiana.

"I pray you are right, dear. I've never witnessed him so distraught," continued Elizabeth. "He's obsessed with Mr. St. James."

"The FBI's expanded the investigation and Tom remains confident we should have a break in the case soon."

"I respect Tom Mitchell's abilities and know he will not rest until this case is solved. However, there is the less patient man named Jonathan—one who plays by no rules but his own." Elizabeth's statement left no further comment, concluding the call. Preparing to place a call to her father, Christiana noticed an email from Christian. *Well, maybe this will shed some light on the Aussi project,* she thought. However, that wasn't the purpose of Christian's email, as she soon discovered.

Christiana:

I'm sorry to hear about the kidnapping attempt on Jennifer. I know how worried and anxious you must feel. Jonathan informed me neither of you are doing any but the most essential of travel.

Thus on behalf of the company, I will be attending the global Sterling meeting in London. Need you to forward a number of documents on our hotel and resort entity.

I will need the following ...

Not bothering to finish reading his email, she punched her father's office number. Jonathan was not in and had left no information with Leslie. Even his cell phone went unanswered. To circumvent Christian's maneuvering, she fired off emails to Grant and Blake specifying her intention of attending the Sterling meetings. Furthermore, Christian's presence would not be necessary and no proprietary files need be transferred to him. Blake fired back an immediate confirmation with a "right-o."

Listening to his voice mails, Tom Mitchell winced when he heard a message from Christiana. He *so* wanted to bring closure to this case but no additional information had been forthcoming. Fortunately, Jonathan had not been riding him today. Checking his watch, he called his surveillance team.

"Nothing new to report, Tom," said Agent Mendez.

"I have that sinking feeling something is about to happen. For St. James not to resurface or have any other comings or goings at the property ... it just doesn't compute," surmised Tom.

"But Boss, he's probably figured the cops are on to him, with the stolen car hoax and all."

"The police interactions have only been to leave him messages regarding the abandonment of his vehicle," responded Tom.

"So you think he'll be checking in at some point? A neighbor could have tipped him off about our search of his residence," replied the agent.

"Clearly, but the house sits back far enough on the property to discourage much visibility to the neighbors. And yes, I believe he will return, even if it is for a change of clothes, a passport, or some other necessity."

"Well, all I can say is its pretty darn quiet out here. I could use a little action."

"Be careful what you wish for, Agent Mendez," cautioned Tom.

Meanwhile, Christiana was speaking with Jack, unaware Tom Mitchell had returned her call. A knock on her office door prompted the conclusion of their conversation. "Hello, Father," Christiana greeted. "I've been looking for you," she said, noting a sullen and distressed Jonathan settling into the wing chair in front of her desk.

"I've left two voice messages and haven't heard from Tom," bristled Jonathan.

"I left him one as well earlier today." As they spoke, she noticed her message light blinking and reached over her desk to retrieve the communication. Returning Tom Mitchell's call while her father was present brought them both current with the investigation.

As the conversation concluded, Christiana acknowledged, "I look at you and see your pain, Father. It's almost incomprehensible what you went through with Mother's thwarted abduction. Now for a second time you are living this nightmare."

Leaning forward, Jonathan responded, "My first priority has and remains the security of the Barrington family, *at all costs.*"

"I know, Father, but you must not blame yourself. I thought I was prudent with both safety and security issues for Jennifer and me. This has taught me a valuable lesson."

"This should not have happened. It was entirely *my* fault!"

"It's your fault one mentally unhinged individual was employed by BHI? We are more fortunate than most, due to our hiring and internal controls. With your vast wealth and, sorry, Father, your at times abrasive personality, you will invariably be a target, unfortunately. I plead with you to be patient and allow the FBI to run the investigation."

"I'll try to be patient. This doesn't mean, however, I wouldn't welcome the opportunity to bring St. James to his knees," chewed Jonathan.

"Father, you would never do anything to legally jeopardize yourself or your family," she stated in a firm tone of voice. Jonathan chose not to respond to his daughter's comments and moved on to BHI matters.

"Let me bring you current on the Spencer acquisition. The African and Asian teams will have their findings and assessments presented next week. Unless there is something new or unsettling, we will proceed with the acquisition," Jonathan replied confidently.

"Father, you will know if it's a sound investment for BHI," replied Christiana. "On another matter, I received an email from Christian requesting information regarding Sterling and Barrington Hotels & Resorts International, since he has been instructed to attend the Sterling meeting in London. Why does Christian know about Jennifer's attempted kidnapping? We agreed not to inform people due to the security issues."

"Christiana, we haven't been traveling and I didn't think you planned on attending the London meeting," commented Jonathan.

"Father, I'll make that decision. At this point, I plan to be present at the series of meetings and Blake and I have discussed some agenda items," she stated, rather miffed.

"I see. I do hope we are further along in this investigation, enough to put your mind at ease being thirty-five hundred miles away," he admonished.

"I appreciate your concern, Father, but let's not assume my plans or schedule unless we have spoken directly."

Before Jonathan was able to spin a caustic barb, Amanda buzzed and pronounced, "Please pardon the interruption. Leslie is looking for Mr. Barrington."

"I'm heading to my office." With those words, he made an expeditious retreat from his daughter's office. As he closed her office door, he parted with, "I'm sorry we can't finish our conversation but you still seem too bothered by Christian. Get over it."

Christiana chose not to dignify her father's remarks with a reply.

The ringing of Tom Mitchell's telephone breached the silence of the night. His wife stirred, groaned and turned over, as Tom lifted his cell phone and stepped out from his bedroom.

"Boss, Lambert here. Sorry to wake you but we have a situation at the surveillance site in Westchester," reported the FBI agent.

"Go on, John," yawned Tom, wiping sleep from his eyes.

"Local police and fire departments responded to a call from me about thirty minutes ago. There was a massive explosion at the St. James residence."

"Oh shit," responded Tom.

"I received a call for backup from Agent Mendez. A taxi dropped St. James off at the residence about fifteen minutes prior to the explosion. No confirmation whether he was consumed by the fire or managed to escape. Air and ground teams are combing the area."

"I'm on my way," responded Tom. "I'll call you from the car. Thanks, John." Out the door in ten minutes, Tom drove in silence for sometime until he contacted his agent.

"Boss, the fire is under control and Arson is on the way."

"John, it's going to be dawn soon and that place is going to be swarming with reporters, neighbors and spectators. Keep them at bay. No comment from anyone," instructed Tom.

"You got it, Boss."

Theorizing, Mitchell drove on deep in contemplation. *Peter St. James arrived home; went downstairs to discover his "stash" of sordid Barrington clippings and articles had been confiscated. But where did he get all the explosives? We searched the premises. He couldn't have planted everything in fifteen minutes, could he? You sneaky cowardly bastard—don't go and die on me now.*

Tom's arrival at the former St. James residence-turned crime scene took forty-five minutes. By the time Tom finished conversing with his team, daylight graphically displayed the destruction. The house was incinerated; only a few smoldering embers remained. Air and ground law enforcement teams were unable to spot anyone fleeing or in the vicinity of the property after the explosion.

"I have reason to believe the homeowner may have perished in the blast and his body will most likely be found in the basement area of the house at the northwest corner of the property," indicated Tom to the Arson inspector.

"Was there anyone else at home at the time of the blast?" asked the investigator.

"The property has been under surveillance for the past couple of weeks and we had a search warrant and combed the inside," replied Tom. "The suspect entered the premises approximately fifteen minutes before the explosion, according to my backup team," Tom answered.

"The morning rain has helped cool things considerably. But this doesn't look like it will be a fast operation. Ah, here comes the canine squad."

CHAPTER 38

Engrossed in conversation with Jackson as her car pulled under the Porte Cochere, Christiana observed Michael stepping out from his automobile. She finished her call as Michael waited to walk with her into Montrachet.

"Where's Jennifer?" questioned Christiana nervously.

"Relax, dear, Veronica picked her up and Jonathan asked to take her to dinner. Your mother has some philanthropic endeavor this evening."

"Father has been so tormented over the situation; I'm pleased they're spending time together." Placing her briefcase on the foyer table, Christiana continued, "Father blames himself for everything and I've never seen him so shaken—"

Michael stopped her mid-sentence as the butler approached, requesting time to serve dinner. "Would you care to join me? It's just the two of us this evening."

They resumed their earlier conversation as they were dining. "I'm giving careful consideration to sending Jennifer to school in Montreux. Maybe Father was right."

"If someone is out to ruin the Barrington dynasty, they will stop at nothing. You know that, Christiana. We will protect our daughter—together—here and not shut her away in Europe."

"Oh Michael, emotionally I agree but rationally I'm not sure anymore. I have never been this afraid in my life," she added, choking back tears.

"I give you my word; I *will* protect her. Christiana, you have done everything possible to reduce the risk," said Michael, gently touching her hand.

"I pray you're right, Michael."

"Have you had any news from Tom Mitchell?"

"No, and I was hoping for a break in this case before I travel to London next week."

"I'll be here to watch over our daughter." Focusing on his schedule, he added, "I need to jump to LA for a few days but I'm flexible, so let's coordinate."

"Excuse me, Ms. Barrington; you have an urgent call from Assistant Director Mitchell of the FBI," said the butler.

"Henri, we will take the call in the library," she answered as they both hurried to the phone. "Good evening, Tom. Michael is here with me."

"Glad you are both there. I'm sorry to bother you this late but we have had a major turn of events, so to speak. Early this morning, the surveillance agent summoned the backup team to the St. James residence. As they approached the property there was a large explosion and resulting fire." He recounted the facts and concluded, "The conflagration was so intense it has taken the better part of the day to sift through the remains."

"What happens if Peter St. James died in the inferno? If he was killed we may never have the answers we need to solve Jennifer's case," lamented Christiana.

"Let's not get ahead of ourselves. If it was Peter St. James who entered the residence, he may have made a speedy exit out the back. The possibility of surviving the blast is next to nil. I'll have the results from the search by tomorrow morning, since the structure was too hot for the animals earlier today."

"Maybe the accomplices were closeted in the residence and perished in the fire," voiced Michael.

"At the time of the search warrant, we found no one present at the residence. Now if there was a hidden door or tunnel system, it's possible but not likely, according to the agents who conducted the search. Let's wait for Arson's findings," urged Tom. The Assistant Director's cell blared and he said, "Sorry, I need to take this call. Ms. Barrington, please convey this new information to your father."

Michael pulled Christiana close with a supportive hug. "People have been hurt; people have died, all because of hatred and a fixation with my family. Father will be upset too when he hears this news," she moaned.

As he walked past the library, Jonathan peered inside to ask, "What will I be upset about, sweetheart?"

"Father, we need to speak with you. Where's Jennifer?"

"Veronica met us at the door and took her upstairs." Jonathan questioned again, "What's going on?"

"Assistant Director Mitchell just called to discuss the latest developments."

Christiana and Michael teamed up to explain the breaking news. When they concluded, Jonathan rose from the leather wing chair and poured a drink. He stood for some time with his back to them. She expected an eruption from her father, but none came. Finally Christiana spoke, "Father, you've been far too quiet."

Slowly Jonathan turned to face them and with a tone of total detachment answered, "I wanted to look St. James directly in the eye and tell him what a bastard he was. Why didn't he try to take me out, the miserable son of a bitch?" He gulped the last of his drink, kissed his daughter, shook Michael's hand and left without another word.

"Boy, he's looking for revenge," said Michael, chagrined.

"Father has been through too much recently, and views this as an assault on his family."

"His response was pure Jonathan," Michael pointed out.

Christiana was still emotionally charged and Michael handed her a drink. "I'm worried about you, Christiana."

"Thank you, Michael, but Father also deserves your compassion," responded Christiana.

"You're right, Christiana. I'm sorry, I know Jonathan is hurting. I'm going upstairs to say goodnight to Jennifer and Veronica. Try to get some rest, Christiana."

"Goodnight, Michael," she said as she shut the library door. Reaching for the telephone, she dialed Sur La Mer. The butler answered, saying Mr. Barrington had not yet returned home. Concluding the conversation, Christiana punched in her father's cell phone number. "Father, where are you? I just called the house."

"I decided to drive out to Westchester to see what was left of the St. James residence," responded Jonathan. "Stop worrying; you are as bad as your mother."

"You shouldn't be there," she reprimanded but Jonathan had already hung up.

Christiana and Michael crossed paths upstairs. "I just reached my father on his cell. He is driving out to Westchester right now!"

"Whoa, that's a twist, but the same thought has crossed my mind," responded Michael.

"Curiosity is one thing, but you don't carry a gun," she lamented.

"Law enforcement has the place covered. Your father won't get anywhere near it. Anyway, St. James probably died in the blast," he said with reassurance.

"I hope you're right."

CHAPTER 39

To her surprise, Christiana slept through the night, but upon awakening, her thoughts turned to her father. As soon as the hour was appropriate, she called his cell. "Father, good morning, I've been worried about your little escapade."

"I told you there was nothing to worry about. It's impossible to believe someone could survive that blast, unless he managed to slip out the back door," offered Jonathan.

"Please, Father, stay away from there and permit the FBI to solve this case."

"You have my word. Don't mention this to your mother."

Jennifer and Veronica were heading downstairs when they caught sight of Christiana. "Hi, Mother, see you tonight at my recital," chirped Jennifer.

"What time is the recital, Veronica?" Christiana questioned.

"Ballet recital at seven," responded Veronica. "After the recital Jennifer and I are going to New York with Michael to see his play tomorrow."

"Yes, that part I did remember."

"Does Jennifer have clothes at your apartment or should I pack a suitcase?"

"She does have some clothes, but I would pack an overnighter."

As Christiana settled into the car for her drive to Manhattan, her cell phone rang.

"Good morning, darling. Did you finally get some rest last night?"

"Good morning, Jack. Yes, I slept better, probably due to our conversation."

"I love talking with you late at night. Dinner reservations are for six this evening."

"Oh, Veronica reminded me this morning of Jennifer's ballet recital this evening. Jack, it totally slipped my mind. I'm afraid I will have to cancel," but a thought struck and she added, "unless you would like to accompany me to a child's ballet recital? I'm alone this weekend as the family is heading to Manhattan to see Michael's new play. We'll have Montrachet to ourselves," she purred.

"I would love to see Jennifer's recital. And spending the weekend with you, that's irresistible."

Jack was still at the apartment so he pulled out his luggage and packed.

As he did, he remembered a recent conversation with Ariana Worthington. *"Jack, my dear, no relationship with Christiana will be easy."* Michael seemed to spend more time in Greenwich than Malibu, Jack thought. "How can I compete with that?" he'd asked Ariana.

"You don't compete. Although they are divorced, Christiana has made it quite clear that he will have a dominant role in the raising of Jennifer. So you simply accept Michael's presence. Darrrling, is she

worth it or not? Only you can make that determination. Remember, I explained the pitfalls of any involvement with Christiana Lynn Barrington. Michael knows them only too well. Oh, Jack, I didn't mean that the way it came out. I think their relationship was doomed from the start since Christiana didn't care for the entertainment industry and Jonathan didn't much fancy Michael Trent as a husband for his daughter," she'd said with a chuckle.

"I get the feeling Jonathan Barrington doesn't fancy any man for his daughter," Jack had retorted.

"Well, *my adorable friend, just take it slow and stop obsessing about Michael. That was the past—you are the future," affirmed Ariana.*

The Ferrari arrived at his office that midafternoon, and Jack slipped into the magnificent machine with thoughts of Christiana, as he maneuvered through the snarled Manhattan traffic. Traffic was nightmarish as well on the Cross Bronx Expressway heading for Interstate 95 North to Connecticut. Glancing at the two bouquets on the passenger seat (red roses for Christiana and yellow for Jennifer), he grinned.

Traffic eased as he made the changeover to the Hutchinson River Parkway. Not expecting to hear from Christiana as his cell phone rang, he answered, "Jack Hamilton."

"It's Christiana. Are you on your way to Montrachet?"

"I'm on the Hutch and should be there in about forty minutes. Where are you?"

"We're just entering the exchange to the Hutch. Jack, there has been a change of plans for this evening. Michael will be attending the recital."

Gripping the steering wheel, he grimaced before responding. "It's great that Michael is able to see his daughter's performance."

"See you soon, my dear," said Christiana.

Laughter filled the house as Christiana entered the foyer. Jennifer ran over and hugged her mother and Jack stood waiting for his turn. Michael had excused himself and headed out to the guest villa to change for the evening.

"I'm thrilled you are here, sweetheart," she said, squeezing his arm.

"I enjoy your family, they are a part of who you are," Jack answered.

Not anticipating other guests for the evening, Christiana looked to Veronica when she heard the doorbell. "I invited your parents to Jennifer's recital," said Veronica.

To Jack, Christiana stated, "It appears we have the entire Barrington clan this evening. I had no idea, as you can tell."

"Ms. Barrington, dinner is served," said one of the household staff.

Michael reentered and shook hands with his former father-in-law and kissed Elizabeth. Over dinner, Michael, Elizabeth and Veronica were engaged in a discussion about Jennifer's recital and Michael's new Broadway play the "Trent family" would be seeing tomorrow in Manhattan.

Kisses, hugs and accolades were bestowed on Jennifer following the evening ballet recital. "Who wants to go for ice cream?" Jonathan questioned, embracing Jennifer.

"Me! Me!" exclaimed Jennifer.

"Jonathan," said Michael, "as much as we would love to join you, the long drive to Manhattan is going to make it a very late night for Jennifer."

Glancing at his watch, Jonathan reluctantly conceded, saying, "You're probably right. Jennifer, you and I will go for ice cream next week, okay?"

"Okay, Grandfather," pouted Jennifer.

Shedding their coats once back at Montrachet, Christiana asked Jack, "Would you care for a nightcap?" With the warmth of the brandy and cozy surroundings, it didn't take long to ignite their passion. Christiana took Jack's hand and led him upstairs where they hurriedly undressed, fell into bed and made love.

Later as she awakened, Christiana slowly untangled herself from Jack's arms and went into her bathroom. As her skin tingled from the pulsating jets of the shower, she sighed with contentment. Jack was a master at lovemaking and with him she had found new avenues of pleasure.

"Mind if I join you?" Preoccupied with her thoughts, Christiana had not seen Jack, his hair falling onto his face, standing at the far end of the enormous shower stall.

"Jack, I didn't mean to wake you."

"Honey, you didn't wake me. *Wow,* you do look amazing."

"So do you. Come and join me, you gorgeous, sexy man," she said seductively and held out her hand. They played briefly but the steamy warm shower and the late hour pushed them rapidly back into bed and immediately to sleep.

A little before eight, the private staff intercom stirred her to consciousness. "Ms. Barrington, I'm sorry to disturb you this early but you have just received an urgent telephone call from the Assistant Director of the FBI. He and his chief investigative agent are on their way to Montrachet and will arrive in approximately thirty minutes," reported the day butler.

"Thank you. Please set up coffee service in the living room and I will be down soon," Christiana said, reaching for her robe.

"Oh, Ms. Barrington, one final note. Assistant Director Mitchell notified your father and Mr. Barrington will also be joining you for the meeting. Will there be anything else?"

"Yes, please prepare breakfast for Mr. Hamilton in the family dining room."

Jack slipped on a pair of jeans and loafers waiting for Christiana to finish her telephone conversation. Placing the telephone back on the cradle, she turned to face Jack. "I guess we'll know something now. Assistant Director Mitchell contacted Father and he will also be here this morning," she concluded.

"There must be a big break in the case. Due to the high profile of this investigation and his relationship with your father, he probably thought it best to discuss it in person." He encircled her with his arms.

Christiana entered the living room and found her father already seated and enjoying coffee and pastry. "Good morning, Father. I understand Assistant Director Mitchell interrupted your golf game."

Wiping his mouth, Jonathan responded, "Good morning, Christiana. I suspect there have been some major developments. Sit down and have a cup of coffee. Don't allow anxiety to rule, Christiana. I feel good about this meeting and you should, too."

As the men from the Bureau entered Montrachet, Christiana tensed. Jonathan whispered, "Relax, our patience has finally been rewarded. I can feel it."

Assistant Director Tom Mitchell, singularly focused, took command of the meeting. "Thank you both for seeing us on such short notice," he opened, glancing at Jonathan in his golf attire. "I'm sorry for taking you off the course on such a beautiful morning. But I think you both will be intrigued by these recent developments."

"Yes, we are. You have our undivided attention," replied Jonathan.

"The Arson Investigation Unit found the remains of a body in the area of the house that was once the basement, which contained the files and pictures of your family along with a diary. Fortunately we were able to obtain a DNA sample from the charred remains." He stopped momentarily to sip his coffee. The room fell silent in anticipation.

Tom continued, "The DNA results and dental records identified the remains to be those of Peter St. James. We surmise he went to check on his 'little occupation' downstairs and realized someone had rooted through his coveted materials. It's my guess he either figured his time was up and he was going to go out with a bang or he was interrupted by a knock or ring of the doorbell from Agent Mendez. The explosives had been planted several places in the house and the gauges for ignition were found close to the body."

"St. James got exactly what he deserved," growled Jonathan.

"No additional bodies were found in the remains of the property, and the air and ground teams concluded their searches without locating anyone trying to make a quick getaway," stated Tom Mitchell.

"If Peter St. James is dead and the additional suspects have not surfaced, how will the case be closed?" inquired Christiana with apprehension.

"I would like to defer to Agent Wits for his update," said Tom Mitchell.

Wits cleared his throat and rifled through his files before he commenced. "As you recall, the SUV seen at Miss Barrington-Trent's school was found abandoned in Danbury shortly after the aborted abduction. The car was impounded and we obtained fingerprints as well as DNA samples from a beverage bottle. We canvassed the area with the composite drawings but had no positive identification until a couple of days ago from a shopkeeper. He informed us that a woman resembling the composite drawing had come into his store, purchased several items and retreated to the motel across the street. He observed her several times outside pacing in the parking lot as if she was waiting for someone to arrive. When we approached her for questioning, she maintained no knowledge of the explosion. However, when we indicated the positive identification of the charred remains of Peter St. James, she began to cooperate. She was *indeed* outside waiting for someone, Peter St. James, who was almost two hours late to fetch her for their getaway to Canada."

After fielding questions, he rolled on, "We found some incriminating evidence inside the motel room linked back to Peter St. James. St. James drove the getaway vehicle while she was the one at the school."

"Is there a possibility there were others involved?" asked Christiana.

Tom Mitchell fielded this question. "We have reason to believe she and Peter St. James were the only suspects. She has been thoroughly interrogated, and even passed a lie detector test asking that particular question. She's being held without bail facing arraignment. We have a full confession so we should be able to proceed fairly quickly. I am confident this case will soon be closed. However, I would still adhere to the highest security measures at all times. This has now happened twice to your family and your wealth, position and power will unfortunately remain a draw to this unthinkable behavior."

"Duly noted, and Barrington Security has been primed. What a relief, Tom, I knew I could count on you," Jonathan announced with confidence. Christiana smiled in appreciation.

"We were just doing our jobs, but thank you," acknowledged Tom.

As the gentlemen prepared for their departure, Tom asked, "Jonathan, I'm just curious, what did you expect to find the night you drove out to the site of the explosion?"

Jonathan quipped, "Just wanted to see the total destruction for myself."

With a little chuckle, Tom added, "That was the scene of an ongoing investigation and you should not have been around there *under any circumstances*. Lucky for you I was out there that evening, otherwise you would have been arrested, my friend."

Shutting the front door, Christiana hugged her father with relief. As they were conversing, Elizabeth appeared.

"Darling, I didn't know you were here. Did you hear the news? The nightmare is over!" Jonathan exclaimed with exuberance, hugging his wife.

"A heavy burden has been lifted, I am thankful to God," sighed Elizabeth.

"Please join Jack and me for breakfast," Christiana said to her parents; then added, "I need to call Michael first so I'll meet you on the terrace in a few minutes."

"Michael, good morning, I have amazing news. Did I wake you?"

"No, Christiana, Jennifer did that about ten minutes ago."

"The FBI just left and the case will soon be officially closed," exclaimed Christiana.

Michael answered, "That's wonderful news. What broke the case? Tell me!"

For the next few minutes she unfolded the story for Michael. As the conversation was concluding she asked, "Would you mind if we both share the news with Jennifer upon your return?"

"That's an excellent idea. Enjoy breakfast with Jack and your parents. You have made my day. No, you have made my weekend. Thanks for the call."

CHAPTER 40 ... Several weeks later

WITH THE SUCCESSFUL CLOSURE of the kidnapping case, Christiana had revived her social life. As she was staying in Manhattan for the night, she was able to meet Jack for drinks at the St. Regis Hotel Bar at seven-thirty. A quick ride brought her to the hotel at the same time Jack was stepping out of his limo. Jack's strength and comfort the last number of months had drawn Christiana closer to him and she was deeply in love.

Relaxing over drinks, Jack commented on his travel to Denver for a series of meetings. As he was speaking, the topic was curtailed as her cell phone rang. Viewing the caller ID signaled her mandatory and prompt response, "Good evening, Father." Jonathan replied, "Grant Pemberton is taking early retirement due to health concerns."

"I just spoke with him late last week and he never mentioned anything to me."

Jonathan said it was necessary for him to stay in London longer than expected. She in turn had an impromptu out-of-town meeting tomorrow and a couple of urgent phone calls to place immediately. Jack allowed her privacy and walked over to the bar to order a round of drinks and appetizers. When she was finishing the calls, he joined her tableside and commented, "Your call sounded serious."

"Father informed me Grant Pemberton, our GM in Europe, is taking early retirement due to health issues. This follows shortly after the unexpected leave of the second-in-command of our European operations. Father is staying in Europe for the foreseeable future." As the words poured out she suddenly thought, *Oh my God, he wouldn't dream of elevating Christian? I hope he hasn't mentioned Grant's resignation to him?* "Now I wonder if Christian is posturing for Grant's position," she said aloud.

"You really believe he's that conniving?"

"I think he will stop at nothing to reach his goals," she stated emphatically.

Sipping their drinks and nibbling hors d'oeuvres, Christiana was not truly engaged or ready for a relaxing dinner. "You're not with me this evening," he commented.

"I'm sorry, Jack. It's probably just my imagination, and you already know my feelings regarding Christian Luke. Recently he accompanied Father to Australia regarding the purchase of a company."

"I recall, the Pink Diamond Mine Company owned by a BHI board member."

"Yes, it was the site visit to Northwestern Australia with our assessment teams to determine if it was a valuable and strategic investment for BHI."

"Okay, possibly sound investment, but that's not your real concern. It's Christian's involvement in this and other high-level dealings within Barrington."

"Yes, he should have no viable role in any acquisition. When I mention this to my father, he responds that Christian is being primed for a significant role in Operations. The last time I brought up the subject with Father, he brushed off my concerns with a cursory response that 'Grant will come around.' Tonight I hear that Grant is retiring."

"Do you think your father has orchestrated this without Grant's sanction?"

"I have no doubt and that's why I know there is more behind Grant's sudden desire for early retirement. Grant has been with BHI since its infancy and built this company up into the distinguished position it holds throughout Europe. I know Grant too well; he would never just walk away from Barrington without a clear path of succession."

"The playing field would be dramatically altered if Grant had a recent health scare. But to your other concern, why would Jonathan promote Christian if he was not ready to assume the position?"

"I feel my father is sharing too much of the business with Christian. When they were in Australia, I did not have the usual frequency of communication with Father. Our contact was reduced to email where he touted the praises of Christian."

"Considering the time difference, email makes sense, Christiana."

"Time differences have never bothered Father. When he needs to reach me, as just witnessed with his call from London, he does not hesitate."

"Dear, you are sounding a little envious of the close working relationship Jonathan seems to have with Christian," teased Jack.

"I sense there is a back story here that has yet to fully present itself."

"Jonathan Robert Barrington is one of the shrewdest businessmen in the world. I doubt you need to worry he would compromise or disclose high-level company affairs with Christian," Jack said, kissing her softly on the cheek.

"I'm sure you're correct; but there is still something I don't like about this relationship." As she finished her statement, she thought, *I'm ashamed to admit I don't have the unconditional trust in Father I once had.*

"Have you discussed your apprehensions with your father? What about Grant, are you clear on his view? A word of caution—if your suspicions are correct, are you prepared to live with the consequences?"

"Yes, I have spoken with my father on numerous occasions and he doesn't understand my misgivings, thinks I just don't like Christian."

"Don't you trust your father?" As the words rolled out, Christiana advanced with pinpoint accuracy. Her tone was cold and aloof when she answered, "I have never intimated I distrust my father." *God, I hope I am correct and I have not been lied to by my own father,* she thought. "But I do believe he is misguided when it comes to Christian Luke."

Searching for a pleasant segue, Christiana made for a graceful exit. "I will take your suggestion and speak with Grant. That's enough about Barrington. You mentioned on the phone you wanted to discuss something this evening?"

"Before we leave this topic, Christiana, I apologize for overstepping my bounds with my comments."

"There is no need to apologize," she replied. But it was clear there was an emotional distance between them on this subject.

"What I wanted to discuss with you was the possibility of you joining me in Denver for the weekend, but after listening to you, I realize the prospect is remote."

"I have put a damper on our evening."

"I need to head to Denver tomorrow and will be gone for several weeks. My parents are throwing a party this weekend and would like to meet you."

"Oh, Jack, I would be delighted to meet your parents but …."

"As much as I would love to show you off to my family, friends and colleagues, I understand your obligations," he said earnestly. "There will be another time, dear," he added as he reached for the check and placed his credit card on the tray.

With her security entourage and driver waiting, she slid into the backseat of the Rolls Royce and blew him a kiss before the door closed and the car sped off to her Upper East Side apartment.

Every couple goes through periods when they are not in step with each other. Damn, Ariana was right; I ventured into the great abyss when I mentioned Jonathan. What was I thinking? He is totally off limits. One does not criticize nor judge the man. Michael, the ex-husband, found that out the hard way. I don't want to become the ex-boyfriend. This is a slippery slope to climb to win the heart of his only child—Christiana Lynn Barrington, he contemplated.

Deep in thought, staring out his apartment window at the glowing city below, Jack didn't hear the house phone ring. Sprinting to the kitchen to retrieve the phone by the fourth ring, he answered, catching his breath.

"Hi, it's Christiana. I'm sorry for calling so late. Jack, if the invitation is still open for this weekend, I would love to meet you in Denver."

"Wow, are you kidding? Of course the invitation is open; I would be honored to have you with me this weekend."

"I want and need you, Jackson Hamilton. You center me and bring balance to my life that I forfeit too often in the name of Barrington. I made that mistake once in a relationship and vow not to repeat it. I love you, Jack," she said.

"Darling, I love you too. I want you in my life, Ms. Barrington … more and more every day."

The subject of Barrington was put aside, at least for the weekend, as Christiana jetted to Denver to meet Jack and the Hamilton family.

Walking in the moonlight on the grounds of the Hamilton estate, Jack took Christiana in his arms and kissed her. "My parents like you, as if I had any doubts. My mother hasn't stopped talking about you since last night."

"They are a dynamic couple. I see where you get your quirky personality, Jackson," she said, squeezing his hand.

"Yes, my father and I are the pranksters of the family. And to think we are here together when just a few days ago I thought I had permanently driven a wedge through our relationship. I was presumptuous with my comments about your father. I crossed the line and even a wrecking ball couldn't have sustained more damage. I was soul searching when you called."

"I was contemplating how I've managed to have BHI, or more accurately, my father, orchestrate my every move. A failed marriage was proof of that. No, Jack, you helped me discern that while Barrington is my world, it cannot be my life. I want the life we design together and it was with those thoughts I realized how much I love you."

With unabashed spirit, Jack lifted her off the ground and twirled her around. "She loves me. She loves me! Christiana Lynn Barrington loves Jack Hamilton and he loves her."

CHAPTER 41

Eturning from Denver, Christiana eagerly embraced her welcoming committee at Montrachet. "Jennifer has been asking to see her grandmother so I invited your mother to stay for dinner," said Veronica. "Your father has a late meeting this evening."

Jennifer took her mother's hand and led her out to greet Elizabeth. "Mother, this is a lovely surprise. I'm glad you are joining us for dinner."

"Thank you, darling. Jennifer and I had a wonderful afternoon at dance class. Your father has business this evening before heading to London."

"We spoke several hours ago and he didn't mention London," stated Christiana.

"Until a suitable replacement is found for Grant, I'm resigned to seeing less and less of your father," lamented Elizabeth.

"My plans are to fly to London to assist Father in the interviewing of the candidates for the GM spot as soon as I can free up my time," reassured Christiana.

"Thank goodness he has you. You are like the son he never had. Oh Christiana, I'm sorry, that did not come out the way I intended."

"Mother, I've often wished you'd had a son; possibly someone who could better measure up." Looking compassionately at her mother, Christiana added, "Mother, I know you would have liked to have had more children."

The dark secret had long been buried by Elizabeth and she certainly did not wish to open up the deep wounds on this pleasant evening with her daughter. Christiana need not know it was not Elizabeth's inability to conceive but Jonathan's finite and unilateral decision not to grow his family.

"I have you, sweetheart, and my darling granddaughter. My world is perfect."

The pain Elizabeth had shut away was resurrected with Christiana's comments and then it all came back again.

Why did it still grip her so unmercifully after all these years?

Shortly after Christiana's first birthday, Elizabeth had wanted another child and broached the subject with Jonathan. Jonathan loved Christiana but was not ready for a second child. He told Elizabeth, "*You will be more tied down, even with nannies, and I need you with me.*" Elizabeth placed her wishes on hold for the moment. She would never try to deceive Jonathan and "accidentally" get pregnant. She knew him all too well. As Christiana approached her second birthday Elizabeth's desire for more children was bubbling to the surface.

This time, however, Jonathan did not put up a fight. She remembered him saying, "*Elizabeth, if this is what you want, I would welcome another child. We will certainly enjoy the process.*"

Six months later, with a determined regime, Elizabeth was still unable to conceive. Frustrated, she went to a specialist who concluded after administering the prerequisite tests there was nothing physically wrong with Elizabeth. She was elated and couldn't wait to tell her husband. Jonathan said nothing. Elizabeth brushed aside his indifference, thinking he was just preoccupied with Barrington.

Then Elizabeth began to suspect the problem rested with her husband. She suggested he see a doctor. He refused. At this juncture, Jonathan became distant, moody, more geographically inconvenient and unavailable.

However, avoidance of the issue was short-lived as Elizabeth surprised him in London adorned with sexy lingerie and other erotic items. Jonathan was not thrilled, rather said he felt conned and cornered. But at last they spoke. She remembered well the conversation. *"Elizabeth, please sit down. I need to tell you something."* Her heart stopped and she sat, motionless. She prepared to hear the words, "I'm in love with another woman," "I'm having an affair," "I want a divorce." As Jonathan spoke she remembered holding her breath. *"I've had a vasectomy. We will not have any more children."* As it began to register she cried, *"Why? When? Why didn't you discuss this with me?"* Jonathan seized the moment. *"One child is enough for this family. I had the procedure done almost six months ago and didn't think it was a big deal."* He felt no guilt or remorse, she recalled.

The totality of his decision was a crushing blow to her. Without considering her feelings, Jonathan reached for Elizabeth and said, *"Let's go to bed and let me take off that beautiful negligee."* Elizabeth rushed tearfully into the bathroom to compose herself. She clearly was not in the mood to make love and felt relieved when she heard the phone ring and realized it was his business line. Jonathan was gone when she awoke in the morning leaving a note in the bathroom. "My love, you looked so peaceful; I didn't want to disturb you. Don't be mad at me. I'll make it up to you. Buy yourself something pretty to wear and meet me at seven at the Connaught for dinner."

Elizabeth met Jonathan at the Connaught for dinner determined to understand the reason he had not discussed having a vasectomy. *"Was there a physical problem that prompted you to have the surgery? Why did you not discuss this with me beforehand?"* Her words hung in the air as Jonathan composed his response.

"Elizabeth, you would have tried to talk me out of it and I was determined to have the procedure. My decision was not predicated on medical issues. Elizabeth, I believe our family is complete with Christiana and we do not need more children. I love you and hope you will find the way to forgive me."

"But Jonathan, you said you wanted a son to carry on the business," how she remembered those words as well as Jonathan's response, *"Elizabeth, do not worry your pretty head with business. At the appropriate time it will all work out."*

"A marriage is built on trust and honesty, Jonathan. I'm afraid it will take me awhile to get over this." Sadly, she knew she would never get over it.

Concluding the terse conversation, Jonathan slid a small box in front of Elizabeth and said, *"Let this gift in some small way pave the way to my forgiveness."* She managed a smile as she focused on the exquisite diamond earrings. The chapter was finished and the book was closed as far as Jonathan was concerned. He set his sights on locating his waiter to order wine and dinner. Jonathan worked best with people when emotions were not exposed. Elizabeth had learned the lesson early in their relationship and it was brought home once again that evening.

"Mother, you seem lost in your thoughts," Christiana said, strolling back into the room.

"No … not at all, dear." Changing the subject, Elizabeth asked, "Are you and Jack planning to attend the political fundraiser at Sur La Mer on Sunday?" Elizabeth Matthews Barrington was the consummate party-giver. Each of her events was always a "must attend." Christiana and Jonathan loved to tease Elizabeth that she not only knew what one was thinking—but in what language.

"Yes, Mother, we will be there." Mother and daughter sounded like girlfriends as they continued chatting about the party, the guest list, and their attire for the upcoming occasion.

When Jennifer appeared with her boundless energy, she snuggled up on the sofa between her mother and grandmother. Three generations of Barrington ladies, each with her own sense of style, grace, confidence and polished elegance.

After dinner, Christiana escorted her mother back to Sur La Mer and gave her a hug and kiss. "I'll say goodnight here, Mother. Thank you for this evening."

"Goodnight dear," said Elizabeth as she watched her daughter leave. Elizabeth removed her jacket as she heard Jonathan's voice coming from the library. When he hung up the phone, he glanced at his wife standing at the threshold of the room. "Did you have a nice evening with Christiana and Jennifer?" he inquired.

"Yes, I so enjoy spending time with them. How was your board meeting?"

"Over, thankfully. Explain to me why I sit on that board?" Jonathan was pouring himself a brandy and asked, "Darling, would you care for a nightcap?"

"No, thank you, I have an early day tomorrow. Will you be coming to bed soon?"

Pulling her close, Jonathan whispered, "Do you want me? Elizabeth, wear that sexy little black number you bought last week." He winked. "I want to see it on the floor in the morning."

CHAPTER 42 ... Christiana goes to London

THE SEARCH FOR GRANT PEMBERTON'S replacement was still underway. Jonathan maintained any candidate must be ready to "live and breathe" Barrington Holdings International. And as far as he was concerned, the day-to-day operations were running smoothly with Christian Luke's involvement.

This rhetoric was making Christiana concerned whether a serious search was really underway. When she pressed her father for answers, Jonathan replied, "I have not found the right candidate to fill Grant's shoes." Maybe a new perspective was needed, she said during one of their telephone conversations. Reluctantly, Jonathan agreed to involve her in the hiring process. Then she planned her trip to London.

As she cleared Customs at Heathrow, she glanced around the airport terminal and found her father and Barrington Security coming toward her. Jonathan handed her a stack of resumes to review on their ride to central London. "I've made dinner plans for seven," he stated as they headed into his flat.

"That should be sufficient time to read these vitaes," she said as she went into the guest suite.

"Travel definitely agrees with you. You look lovely," said Jonathan, looking affectionately at his daughter as she entered the living room prepared for the evening.

"Thank you, Father," she said, smiling as they strolled to the waiting Rolls Royce.

Comfortably seated at the restaurant, Jonathan was ready to talk business. "I'm not thrilled with these candidates. Haven't found the right fit for BHI," he grumbled.

"Father, don't be so hasty. Let's discuss the resumes and potential candidates."

"I have no desire to hold second interviews with any of the prospects. You may wish to interview them but I'm sure you'll arrive at the same conclusion," stated Jonathan with an air of disdain.

"Have you considered hiring a new search firm, Father?" suggested Christiana.

"Not at this stage. I'm beginning to think you don't trust my judgment?"

"The issue has nothing to do with your judgment, Father," she snapped. "But we must persevere since we no longer have a proper succession plan after Brian left."

"There are additional resumes back at the office sent over by the firm. No interviews have been scheduled due to my upcoming travel. Let's pick this up tomorrow when you are in the office. I have an early conference call so I need to retire for the night."

Christiana's primary business focus was the recruitment issue and she seized on the task with determination. She spoke with Executive Recruiting and conducted a number of interviews.

However, one day with a lull in her schedule and a perfect London afternoon, she decided on some fresh air and ventured into Knightsbridge to do some shopping. As she turned the corner, she noticed Grant Pemberton leaving a small antiques shop. Christiana called to him and he turned and smiled. He stopped, waited for her to cross the street and they warmly greeted each other.

"You look well. How are you feeling?" she asked cautiously.

"Well, I'm fine. Why do you ask?" answered Grant in bewilderment.

The truth dropped like an anchor. "Your retirement was not due to health reasons," she deduced.

"You're correct, health reasons did not precipitate my retirement; Jonathan did. He asked me to keep it quiet. My life at BHI was fine until the arrival of Christian Luke. I should have seen the clues; the young brash whiz kid brought in to eventually take over European operations."

Her need to know more kept her feelings of betrayal by her father in check—at least for the time being. She asked Grant to continue.

"Barrington was my life, my home. I never tried to usurp Jonathan and remained his staunch, trusted and loyal lieutenant." Christiana was visibly shaken as Grant offered her his hand. "Perhaps we could continue over tea?"

"Why would Father keep this from me?"

Although she'd posed a rhetorical question, Grant answered, "Jonathan always has his reasons and private agenda."

They ordered tea and scones with Devonshire crème and sat by the window of a small café overlooking the back of Harrod's Department Store. "Christiana, I have accepted the situation and am moving into retirement a very wealthy man thanks in no small part to Jonathan. Barrington served me well but I still miss work. However, now I can spend time with Ginny and we just purchased a country home. I'm in London today to bring a period piece in for restoration." As Christiana listened he reached for her hand, saying, "Christiana, you have always been like a daughter to me. You are the best treasure Jonathan has and you add a caring and compassionate side to Barrington."

"Thank you, Grant. I've learned so much from you throughout my career."

"I will miss working with you, Christiana, very much. I just wish I felt as confident as Jonathan about Christian's abilities." He continued, "He's too much like Jonathan, his actions, his temperament and bravado. Brian spent twenty years with BHI and still remains my choice for General Manager. He was bitter when Jonathan turned on him and forced him to tender his resignation. "

Christiana had no reason to doubt his story as credibility and honesty were foremost with Grant. It also didn't sound like sour grapes. "I'm still not clear why we hired Christian Luke?"

With his typical British reserve, Grant answered, "Jonathan has known CL for years. As you are now acutely aware, Christian had a rather flamboyant and quite successful modeling career in Europe. Although he could have continued that pursuit, at least for a short horizon, he started to look for other career choices, according to Jonathan." Grant stopped to sip his tea and ran his hand through his wavy hair.

"Interesting leap from modeling to business," she commented bitterly.

"There are a number of highly successful models-turned-business titans."

"Yes, Grant, but most founded their own companies, and didn't land a plum position in one of the world's largest conglomerates, without preparation."

"Christiana, there's a peculiar synergy between Christian and Jonathan; if you need more of an explanation you need to speak with your father. I did not agree to hire CL nor did I approve his subsequent promotions," replied Grant tersely.

"I'm in London to accelerate the hiring process of your replacement, although we can never replace you. Father and I are not seeing eye-to-eye on any of the most eligible candidates."

"Christiana, I would bet you will not bring in an outside hire. You are fighting a losing battle with Jonathan. He will tell you no one is suitable and just leave the position vacant for the foreseeable future."

As the conversation was unfolding, Christiana found it more difficult to come to the defense of Jonathan, so she merely affirmed, "You may be right."

"I believe Jonathan has a plan in mind and will not be persuaded otherwise. The most qualified of candidates will not pass the 'Jonathan test.'"

"Grant, what are the major stumbling blocks to finding your replacement?"

"There is only one major, all-encompassing stumbling block—your father."

"Would you ever consider coming back to Barrington?"

"I would, but it isn't my decision. It's Jonathan's."

Desiring to flex her authority, she confidently responded, "Grant, I will handle this one. It's clear we have not found a suitable replacement. It is in the best interest of the company to rehire both you and Brian as quickly as possible."

"Christiana, please don't go down this path. Just leave it alone, for both our sakes."

"I'm not sure I can."

"You must trust me with this, let it go, at least for now," pleaded Grant.

Sensing the seriousness of both his tone and demeanor, Christiana promised she would not bring up the issue with her father. They turned the conversation to a lighter subject just as Grant looked out the lace-curtained window of the café and noticed the proprietor of the antiques shop waving him over. "Ah, Christiana, I'm going to have to find out what the cost is to repair this blasted piece Ginny so adores."

They hugged outside the café and she watched him walk across the street, still impeccably attired in his sports coat and customary ascot, even to run an errand.

Unnerved by their conversation, she lost interest in shopping and promptly returned to the office. On her desk was a note from Jonathan indicating he would be out of the office for the remainder of the day. Under the handwritten message, he had placed several new resumes. After reviewing the applicant files, she contacted Executive Recruitment to set up an interview schedule.

As she was terminating the call, Christian poked his head into her office.

"Hi, you're back? May I have a few minutes?"

With his more appeasing approach, she responded, "Yes, of course, Christian."

"I'll be brief, Christiana. Have you seen the new Magnifique ads for the men's fragrance using just my initials?"

"Yes, but I'm not clear why we had to change the name of the product. I'll discuss this with Samantha," answered Christiana.

He explained, "Both Sam, I mean, Samantha and I thought *Christiana* and *Christian* sounded too similar. There have been some consumer confusion and brand identification issues. *CL* has a nice ring to it. It sounds like today—hip—exciting—a man on the move."

Man on the move is correct, may be a move out of Barrington, or at least out of my sight, she mused. But as she pondered the issue, the more she admitted, "The similarity in the names could certainly give rise to brand identification issues. It was the right call."

"Good, Sam wanted to make sure you were on board before we launch."

"And marketed under Magnifique, not Barrington," she added tersely.

"I understand the figures for *The Barrington Collection* are out and they look impressive," he said, changing the subject. "You'll be pleased. I hope the *CL* fragrance line proves as successful for BHI."

"I do as well," she acknowledged.

Jonathan in his exercise attire and tousled hair was minus his usual vim and vigor when he and Christiana met for breakfast the following morning at his apartment.

"Father, I'm surprised you're not ready for the office. Are you ill?"

"I'm just tired. I didn't sleep well last night." Pushing to the business at hand, Jonathan stated, "I have set up another meeting with the Aussi syndicate to meet with us in New York." He handed her a piece of paper and added, "Here are the particulars. There are hurdles to jump due to the complex ownership position of the syndicate."

"Is Max's company still a strategic and prudent move for Barrington?"

"Christiana, the short answer is yes, but I need all the facts," replied Jonathan.

As breakfast was concluding, Christiana switched to the topic of candidate interviews. "Father, I have reviewed the resumes and added some notes. The search firm has scheduled interviews for later today and tomorrow."

Without acknowledging her comments, Jonathan merely added the appointments to his scheduler. Rising from his chair was indication both the breakfast and the meeting had concluded. "I'll see you at the office," he announced.

She caught her father's disdain for the topic of hiring a replacement for Grant and she was reminded of Grant's remarks.

CHAPTER 43

"Y ou've been pensive since we finished the interview, Christiana. What did you think of Anton Beckjord?"

"He is well qualified, right schools, impressive background; ah, I can't put my finger on it," she responded, lost in thought.

"He lacks the Barrington pizzazz. The large conglomerates he ran don't have the international presence or the public exposure we do. He's not our candidate."

"We definitely need to continue our search."

"We need another Peter Chang," said Jonathan.

"No, we need Grant Pemberton!"

Sidestepping that landmine, Jonathan merely shrugged and commented, "Tell me about the other candidate we have scheduled."

"We have two scheduled. Give me a minute," she said, leafing through the file of job applications. "The morning appointment is with Armand Schroeder and the afternoon belongs to Hollis Mann."

"Armand Schroeder, interesting! I've had a number of dealings with him. Which company is he currently with?" asked Jonathan.

Christiana slid the resume over to her father. "Global Titans, of course, now I remember. He's a hell of a negotiator, one shrewd businessman. I'm surprised he would want to come over to us. I'm going to do my own background check on him. He might be too much of a maverick," answered Jonathan. "Who's the other applicant?"

"Hollis Mann. I only know him by reputation," noted Christiana. Glancing at the download of an email on her phone during a lull in the conversation, Christiana sat back and grinned.

"Did I miss something?"

"Just an intriguing email from Samantha Jones regarding a topic briefly mentioned before she was hired."

"What does she want, an S-class Mercedes?"

"No, Father, she isn't talking about personal perks—an S-class Mercedes, how nice. However, that was not the intent of Samantha's email. Morgan Joseph is officially for sale. Are we interested in trying to acquire the company?"

"Have her forward me the prospectus from the investment banking firm. It's not going to be a steal and having Samantha under our wing might prove detrimental in negotiating with the principals of Morgan Joseph. I remain intrigued and appreciate Samantha apprising us."

"I'll speak with Samantha after our interviews. Now to our more immediate concern, I've been mulling over the alternatives on this hiring and I think we should rethink our strategy, Father. Instead of hiring a GM, let's concentrate on filling the number two spot first. It would allow me time to develop a working relationship with the person and help mold that candidate for the job."

Jonathan had turned to assemble some files and questioned, "You would consider leaving the GM post open for a period of time? What's the logic?"

"This is one of the most senior, visible and pivotal positions in the entire corporate structure. Thus far we have empty conclusions on each candidate. I'll reserve judgment until tomorrow, but I'll bet we agree. We really should be interviewing for the number two spot."

"I sense more behind those words, my dear. It's as if you think Grant is going to walk back into Barrington," chuckled Jonathan.

"If only he would, Father. It is not in our best interest to settle for anything but the best fit—after all, we are Barrington!"

Jonathan smiled at his daughter's last comment. Segueing from that, he stated, "I must be on my way to meet your mother back at the flat. Are you sure you can't extend your stay in Paris for an additional day? Friday evening, we are hosting a gathering for Barrington Financial in the renovated Grand Ballroom of the Sterling Hotel. You and Jack should really be in attendance."

"I haven't seen Jennifer all week."

"It's one additional night, Christiana. I miss my granddaughter but she has Veronica and I thought I heard you say Michael was at Montrachet. Jennifer has the whole Trent clan at this point."

"Yes, Michael is there. But I seem to see the least of her and I'm her mother."

"This will allow you the opportunity to be more visible at Barrington Financial as well as have some quality time with Jack," Jonathan added, continuing to push his point. "While I can't make this decision for you, reconsider, as it's just an extra day. It would mean a great deal to me to have your presence at the party."

Considering her father's proposal, she murmured, "Jack and I have not spent much time together in London and he is already in Paris on business." With conflicting thoughts and guilt, she reluctantly relented, saying, "Okay, I will try to work it in. Goodnight, Father. Give my love to Mother."

The flickering candles, soothing music, and scented bath crystals relaxed Christiana as she soaked in the luxurious bath. She had tuned out the world, at least for a few moments.

The ring of the cell breached the tranquility but it was Jack and she smiled as she answered. "*Bonsoir,* Christiana. How are you? I miss you, sweetheart!"

"*Bonsoir, Jack. Tres bien, merci. Comment vas-tu?*

"*Bien, Cheri.*"

"*Je desire mon amant, Jack.*"

"*Je voudrais, Christiana, maintenant.*"

"*Je prefere Paris avec Jack.*"

"*Je prefere un rendez-vous a demain.*"

"*Bien. Je arrive d'hôtel elegant Sterling en Paris a quartre heures de l'apres-midi.*"

"*Repetez, s'il vous plait. Je ne comprends pas.*"

Christiana laughed and said in English, "I thought we were doing so well. I will be arriving in Paris tomorrow around four in the afternoon."

"As we speak, I am walking around the penthouse suite at the Sterling Hotel admiring these beautiful surroundings and thinking of you, my darling Christiana."

Her body warm under the bubbles, she cooed, "I cannot wait to see you, darling. Jack, my father has asked if we would attend another function Friday evening. It is a client party for Barrington Financial in the Grand Ballroom at Sterling."

"It sounds like fun and we could have another day in Paris. But I thought you needed to be back in the states by this weekend?"

"I did promise Jennifer I would be home Friday and I'm feeling tremendous guilt at the moment."

"Honey, for what it is worth, you're a mother and guilt goes with the territory. Thus I cannot render you guilt-free, but I'm here for comfort and support. I just want to be with you, the location doesn't matter."

"Jack, please give me time to place a few telephone calls. Thankfully, Michael is staying at Montrachet this week, so it alleviates part of my anxiety, but I'm not clear on his demanding schedule." She couldn't help but imagine Jack's grimace at the mention of Michael, and the thought of his frequent visits to Montrachet. But it wasn't in his tone as he ended the conversation with, "I await your call, my love."

Michael was set up for a conference call and did not have long to talk. "Of course I don't mind. Jennifer's been bugging me about taking her out to see her horse. Enjoy yourself; we'll see you when you return."

"Thanks, Michael. I'll be there in a couple of days."

With the family obligations satisfied, she phoned Jack to give him the news. Jack and Christiana had a sexy conversation in anticipation of seeing each other within twenty-four hours in Paris.

CHAPTER 44

ARMAND SCHROEDER WAS SEATED and conversing with Jonathan when Christiana entered the conference room. Introductions aside, the interview commenced and remained focused since Jonathan and Christiana were tightly scheduled with interviews and had pending afternoon flights to Paris.

Hours later they were shaking hands with Mr. Schroeder as he left the conference room. As they took a breather between interviews, they compared notes on the earlier candidate. "He has extensive global expertise and an impressive background," Christiana affirmed.

"While that is certainly true, I'm not sure he'd be a team player. He's known for having a tremendous ego—which has led to problems with staff retention in a couple of instances."

"Those could be insurmountable issues. Although he is very polished I sensed the arrogance and the 'my way or no way' mentality," agreed Christiana. "I tried to probe on a couple of issues with his past places of employment and I was not satisfied with his answers."

"Yes, he was clever in his packaged responses," Jonathan remarked. "I need to make a quick call. One of the assistants is sending in lunch for us."

By midafternoon, Christiana and Jonathan were headed to the airport going over their interviews. "Even I could work with Hollis Mann," chuckled Jonathan. "I would be very surprised if you find much of a blemish on his career. He catapulted two companies into the ranks of the Fortune 500 by his careful orchestration. Moreover, he has extensive experience in most of our core businesses."

"He didn't seem to be concerned about title."

"The man knows the spot would be his in due course and to work at Barrington would be the pinnacle of his career," gloated Jonathan. "I'll bring him back for a second interview then fly him to New York next month."

"Sounds good. I like him, Father." The car was approaching the private airfield and they started to assemble their belongings to exit the vehicle. Elizabeth was standing on the tarmac and greeted her family as they left their private car.

Two of Barrington corporate jets glinted in the afternoon sunlight.

Getting the nod from their pilots, Jonathan leaned over and said, "Christiana, you don't mind flying alone, do you?"

"Of course not, Father. I'll see you and Mother at the car when we land in Paris," she responded as she strode toward her plane.

Intently focused on a business call when Christiana entered the hotel suite, Jack blew her a kiss. Christiana accompanied the bellman with her luggage into the bedroom, allowing him privacy to conclude his conversation.

As she finished unpacking, she went into the bathroom to place her toiletry bag on the marble countertop. Glancing in the mirror, she noticed Jack behind her, smiling. "I have been waiting all day to see you," he said.

They washed each other's bodies in the shower following their lovemaking. With no time to spare, they dressed for the gala.

Jack was responding to emails when Christiana entered the parlor wearing a red silk, gathered, one-shoulder Valentino gown. "I am the luckiest man in the world to escort you, my darling. You are dazzling," he said, as he shut down his computer.

"You look perfect, even with your clothes," she teased. "Let us go meet French society." She nodded to her security detail and they headed down to the Grand Ballroom.

"This place has been transformed," said Christiana as they made their way through the crowd.

"It is beautiful, but not as gorgeous as you, my love."

Heads turned, people smiled, while others continued to meet or say hello to Christiana while her security team elbowed their way through the crushing crowd of well-wishers. She spotted Blake Eagleson and wanted to give him accolades on this renovation. Luckily, he spotted her, extracted himself from his present conversation and moved in her direction. After introductions and greetings, Blake raised his hands to gesture around the room and asked, "So what do you think of this place?"

"Absolutely breathtaking," responded Christiana.

Blake was the star of the evening so after a fleeting conversation with Christiana and Jack, he continued to circulate amongst friends, colleagues, employees, guests and dignitaries.

"Blake is the marquee name in the hospitality industry. Jack, I'm pleased you had a chance to meet him." Looking around the room, Christiana inquired, "Have you seen my parents?"

"With the throngs of people, it is hard to spot anyone," offered Jack. Christiana's bodyguard leaned over and stated, "Ms. Barrington, your parents are in the foyer."

"Thank you. We will try to make our way over to greet them." As they worked their way through the crowded reception area they were stopped every few feet by guests.

"I love your gown," a man whispered. Not immediately distinguishing the voice due to the noise level, she turned around and found Christian with a recognizable model attached to his arm.

"Good evening, Christian," she said. Hiding her surprise at his presence, she quickly added, "Jack, this is Christian Luke. He is Vice President of Sales and Marketing Worldwide from our London office."

"It's a pleasure to meet you, Christian."

"May I introduce Reece Springer, although *she* needs no introduction," said Christian, beaming. The foursome exchanged casual banter as Christiana scanned the room hoping to locate her parents. An interruption promptly surfaced when a female guest asked Christian for his autograph. "I bought your cologne for my boyfriend. I love your advertisements, especially ..."

Christiana and Jack used the moment to make a hasty retreat. "He does have an ego," commented Jack.

"Don't remind me," snapped Christiana. "Magnifique's fragrance *CL*, launched some time ago, is doing quite well. He's relishing the renewed celebrity. But autographs at the Sterling Hotel unveiling? He has stepped over the line once again. Where is my father?" she fumed.

"He certainly has a sense of self-importance."

"This was tame compared to his usual behavior," Christiana scowled, now on a mission to find her father. "Jack, there is someone very special I would like to introduce," spotting Grant Pemberton in the distance. "Grant Pemberton was Barrington's former GM in Europe."

Grant caught Christiana's gaze and remained planted as she and Jack moved through the crowded ballroom. With his warm embrace of Christiana, it was evident Grant was a dear friend with the roots of a relationship that bridged the boundaries of employment at Barrington.

"Jack, I would like to introduce my dear friend and colleague, Grant Pemberton. Grant worked for Barrington most of his career and has just recently retired, I am sorry to say. Thankfully for BHI, he remains on our board. Grant, this is Jackson Hamilton, the real estate developer," she said, touching Jack's arm.

"It's a pleasure to meet you, Jackson. Any connection to Hamilton Industries out of Denver? Great company," stated Grant.

"Thanks for the kind acknowledgement; and yes, it's the family's business."

Turning to face Grant, Christiana said, "I am so pleased you are here for the unveiling of Sterling Paris. Did Ginny accompany you?"

"She would have enjoyed this but her mother is in town this week."

"What do you think of the transformation of the hotel?" asked Christiana.

"For years I was a frequent guest at this hotel but she'd grown tired and forlorn the last number of years so I changed my allegiance. Blake said it would be a complete makeover, and he was correct."

"A total renovation; they took her down to the studs," said an excited Christiana.

Grant caught sight of Elizabeth and Jonathan approaching. "Good evening, Grant," Jonathan greeted him.

"Good evening, Jonathan," returned Grant as he hugged Elizabeth.

"Mother, you look stunning," said a beaming Christiana as she kissed her parents. Addressing her father, she remarked, "Father, may I have a word with you?"

"Can't it wait?" he asked. As she was adamant in her request, father and daughter retreated.

"Father, it is most inappropriate to have Christian signing autographs in this setting. He is putting on a sideshow."

Surveying the room but unable to locate CL amongst the sea of guests, Jonathan replied in the absolute, "*I'll* handle this, Christiana. I will return shortly."

Finding a quiet, well-lit corner, Jonathan sent a terse text message to Christian. "*Curtail the autographs. Highly inappropriate, this is not your show. Jonathan.*"

James Langston crossed paths with Christiana, who was wending her way back to Jack and her mother. "Hello, James. Sterling Paris is a glorious achievement for Blake and BHI."

"Impressive! Speaking of Blake, his wife passed away last week. He asked to keep it quiet until after the reopening of the hotel," conveyed James.

Christiana nodded in affirmation. "Although I've known she was terminally ill, Blake does not readily discuss his personal life."

"True; however, he has considered mentioning her in his speech this evening and I didn't want you to be caught off guard. I haven't found Jonathan; would you mind mentioning it to your father?"

Christiana nodded as James hurriedly segued, "I'd like you to join me if you have a little time to meet the presidents of two of the major distribution sources for Jewels?"

"Lead the way," said Christiana.

Accompanying James to the far corner of the grand room, Christiana observed Samantha Jones locked in an animated conversation with Christian. His date was downing another glass of champagne with a look of total boredom. Off to the other side of the room, Christiana spotted Blake in the intimate zone of conversation with Regina Wells, on the Board of Directors at BHI.

Following several minutes of cocktail chitchat, sprinkled with a couple of savory bites of business talk, Christiana took her leave from James and the businessmen and headed to the ladies room. Passing the main terrace, she caught Samantha's eye and waved. Taking one last puff of her cigarette, Samantha snubbed it out, excused herself and hurried inside in pursuit of Christiana.

Christiana was reapplying her lipstick as Samantha exclaimed, "Fabulous party! This place is magnificent."

"All accolades belong to Blake and our teams from Sterling and Barrington. Yes, the place is 'Magnifique.'" Both women laughed.

"Christiana, I've received the prospectus on Morgan Joseph from the investment bankers. James and Marshall have been given copies."

"Thank you, Samantha. I'm due back in the office the first of the week and should have the opportunity to read through it then," commented Christiana. At the conclusion of their discussion, Christiana searched for Jack and found him engrossed in discourse with several high profilers. Elizabeth was speaking French with a couple of French socialites, while Grant and Jonathan were holding court with the magnates who personified the "Who's Who" of world business and finance. Seeing all involved in conversation, Christiana went in search of Blake.

Blake warmly greeted Christiana, "We are receiving rave reviews about the property."

"You have done a superb job. She is divine!"

"She was always one of the true gems of the entire Sterling collection. Now Sterling Paris has regained her luster and shine," he returned, glowing with pride.

"Indeed," she echoed but promptly turned serious. "Blake, you have my sincere sympathies with your wife's recent passing. James just informed me."

"Thank you, Christiana. Although expected, it's still a jolt when it happens. I'm consoled by the fact that the entire family was with her at the end."

"Blake, if there is anything I, we, Barrington, can do, please don't hesitate to ask. Whatever you need, just let us know."

"Thank you, Christiana, but work is probably the best medicine. I'll take a few days off when I return stateside." They conversed until the lights started to flicker, indicating time for dinner. Then Christiana found her father and quietly revealed the news about the death of Blake's wife before they sat down. Hearing this, Jonathan bolted forward trying to locate Blake before the commencement of the evening's program and dinner. Jonathan expressed his condolences. "Whatever you need, ol' buddy. You are a part of the Barrington family."

"You and Christiana have been most understanding and considerate. Thank you. Now, we must get on with the reason for this dinner—our beautiful new hotel; the legend is reborn," said Blake, patting Jonathan on the back as he approached the stage.

Artistically designed gift bags were placed at each table setting. The bags held a Lalique crystal paperweight with the inscription:

Sterling Hotel Paris

The Legend Reborn

The Sterling Collection by Barrington Hotels & Resorts International

"Good evening, ladies and gentlemen. Welcome to the Sterling Hotel Paris. It is indeed an honor to have the President of France and his wife here this evening to share this momentous occasion. At this point, it is my privilege to introduce Monsieur Robiere Chaumont," announced Blake.

Thunderous applause accompanied Monsieur Chaumont as he made his way to the podium. Once the applause ceased, Monsieur Chaumont spoke in French for several moments. Jack gave Christiana an appreciative nod in response to his understanding of the speech.

The President then delivered his speech in English, "Dear invited guests, on behalf of my wife and myself, I welcome you to France. As most Parisians know, this venerable hotel has been a continuing part of the fabric of this celebrated city. Through the extensive efforts of Sterling and Barrington Hotels & Resorts International, she is even more beautiful now. I express a special thank you to the CEO of Sterling and Barrington Hotels, Monsieur Blake Eagleson and to my dear friend, Monsieur Jonathan Robert Barrington, the CEO of Barrington Holdings International, and his lovely wife Elizabeth. My commendations would not be complete without acknowledgement to the President of BHI and another dear friend, Christiana Lynn Barrington."

Jack squeezed Christiana's hand as the President mentioned her name. His speech continued for several more minutes, concluding with, *"Viva La France—Viva D'hôtel Sterling a Paris."*

Blake and Monsieur Chaumont shook hands as Blake resumed his position at the podium. "Monsieur and Madame Chaumont, you have honored us with your presence and in some small way I hope the new Sterling Hotel will exude the best and beautiful that Paris and France give to the world. Now I would like to take the opportunity to acknowledge several other distinguished guests." He went through a short list of high-ranking French government officials, high-level CEOs and the elite of French society.

Simon and Maurice Robard, the architects, were introduced and given a standing ovation. Blake added, "You'll see more as I run a short video presentation that will show you the painstaking efforts and challenges of this project. A fairly significant development occurred shortly after we shuttered Sterling and started preparations for the major renovations. Sterling was acquired by Barrington Hotels & Resorts International. The strength, stature and capital investment brought by BHI has given us what we are witnessing this evening. The ultimate in luxury, Barrington style." Blake paused to allow the applause of the crowd.

"I owe a round of gratitude to the principals of BHI, Jonathan and Christiana Barrington. Sterling indeed found the right home with Barrington." As he looked down into the audience at his bosses, Jonathan gave him a salute and Christiana blew him a kiss.

"This hotel holds a very special spot for me as this was where my wife and I honeymooned thirty years ago. Numerous other happy occasions throughout our life together were spent in these spacious and grand surroundings. She accompanied me here a month ago for the soft opening. The transformation brought tears to her eyes as we reminisced on our pleasant times here together. My dear wife passed away last week of colon cancer and this was to be her last trip. To witness this place resume her former grace has truly been my inspiration. Before I leave the stage, I would like to request the lights be dimmed and ask you to watch this presentation on how Sterling Hotel Paris, the Legend was reborn."

Grant leaned over to Christiana and whispered, "I feel for Blake. He mentioned about two months ago she didn't have much time."

"There is no easy way to ease that pain," returned Christiana.

Back in command when he resumed his Master of Ceremony functions, Blake brought the evening to a successful close. It was another hour before all the fanfare ended and guests departed. Christiana and Jack were still on the adrenalin rush as they went back to their penthouse suite. However, it was not a restful night for Christiana. By early morning her body jerked and she moaned quietly. She stirred and in turn woke Jack.

"Bad dream?"

"Yes, it was an absolutely preposterous dream. I was in a large gathering similar to last night and all I could see were Christian's autographs everywhere—on the walls, the floor, the ceiling, the tables. He was running around signing his name with a large black marker, laughing at me as I stood watching, seemingly unable to do anything. I cannot believe I allow him to get under my skin."

Noticing Jack stifling a yawn, she glanced at the alarm clock and it read five in the morning. "Oh Jack, now we are both awake and we went to bed very late."

"Come, lie down next to me and let's fall back to sleep," he comforted. Wrapping his body around her allowed sleep to return and they didn't rise until almost nine.

After breakfast, strolling hand-in-hand, they viewed a new exhibit at the Louvre. They lingered over lunch in an intimate Parisian bistro and added a little shopping before returning to the Sterling by midafternoon.

"You look tired, sweetheart. Why don't you take a short nap before this evening's function?" suggested Jack. "I have work to do."

She was sound asleep when he entered the bedroom and so he stretched out on the sofa to read but soon he too fell asleep. The sounds of running water woke him and he wandered into the elegant marble bathroom. Washing her hair in the shower with her back to the door, she hadn't noticed Jack enter the room. As she reached for the conditioner, she smiled at her lover watching her intently. He was draped in a plush white terry robe provided by the hotel.

"Would you care to join me?"

As the robe fell to the floor, his enthusiasm was evident. Jack was a sensitive and compassionate lover and he knew how to please Christiana. They both needed cold showers when they finished their sexual romp. Thankfully they felt rejuvenated before the long evening ahead.

Jack rose from his chair when she entered the living room dressed for the dinner. The sexy ensemble from the previous evening was replaced with a simple black cocktail dress and jacket. Baring the shoulders and cleavage was not the order of the evening with the Saudis and the other conservative guests and clients to be present. She did, however, add her touch, with several new pieces of jewelry from Jewels *by Barrington.*

"No matter how you try to hide your femininity you are still one gorgeous and sexy creature," Jack said, mesmerized.

Protocol required Christiana's attendance in the Barrington receiving line. Jack, meanwhile, positioned in a keen spot near the entrance watched the notables introduced and proceed through the reception line. Each client and guest was presented by name and title as they made their way down the line meeting the Barrington Financial hierarchy: Mr. and Mrs. Graham Cunningham, Christiana Lynn Barrington and Mr. and Mrs. Jonathan Robert Barrington. The Saudis were cordial to Christiana but it was clear their focus and business discussions were centered with Graham and Jonathan.

Watching her parents host the evening, Christiana commented to Jack, "My mother is pure perfection; sophisticated, cultured, refined, intelligent and so comfortable speaking a multitude of languages. I don't believe my father would be half the success he is without my mother by his side."

"They make a dynamic couple," Jack responded.

Several of the attendees turned out to be customers of Hamilton Industries and added an interesting flavor to the dinner.

This evening was not as demanding as the previous one and they returned upstairs by ten-thirty happy for some quiet time. Once seated in the living room, Jack began the conversation with, "Grant Pemberton was certainly one of the most engaging people I've met the last two days. Why did he leave Barrington?"

"I'm not totally objective when it comes to Grant. I adore him. His guidance and mentoring helped prepare me for my role at Barrington. Interestingly, my mother brought Grant to my father's attention as they had been friends since childhood. A trusted ally, friend and astute businessman, Grant is or was the reason the European operations are so important and strategic to BHI," she answered.

Jack remained silent, waiting for further revelations.

"Then one day, Grant was gone, retired, due to health reasons. I thought it odd but I accepted Father's explanation. But then I started thinking. About two years ago, Christian Luke assumed a middle management sales position in our London office. Christian rubbed me the wrong way from the beginning. A small dose of his arrogance and flagrant disregard for protocol was evident last evening with the autograph signing. It seems Christian has been propelled up the Barrington corporate ladder diligently empowered by Father. The more I protested the more Father rushed to his defense. I figured if Grant and my father were in sync then maybe I was missing something about Christian's abilities and assets."

"So Grant was not in sync with Jonathan?"

"No, he was not. I ran into Grant while I was in London recently. We went to a café and as we were conversing, I learned that his retirement was not for health reasons but rather was a forced resignation by Jonathan. Grant and his chosen successor Brian McCauley both left Barrington in short order. Moreover, he had nothing to do with the hiring of Christian and contends Jonathan has plans to groom Christian to take over the European shop."

"But say that's true; why would he want both Grant and Brian out of the way until Christian was ready to assume the position?"

"I haven't yet figured it out. Grant surmises we will interview but not fill the position of GM. He believes Jonathan will continue to oversee the European operations for the time being."

"Why don't you confront your father with your suspicions along with the substantiated information from Grant?" questioned Jack.

"Unfortunately, Grant asked me not to. His exact words were 'You must trust me on this, leave it alone … at least for now.' I promised him I would not broach the subject—at least for the time being."

"Intriguing, but I can't figure out what Jonathan has to gain. You will eventually assume the reins at BHI, so your thoughts, opinions and decisions should be paramount to this issue," mused Jack out loud.

"You would think so," Christiana lamented. This topic delivered more questions than answers and since tomorrow was an early travel day, they closed the discussion for the night.

CHAPTER 45

A S THE HAMILTON INDUSTRIES corporate jet landed at
Teterboro, Christiana and Jack were busy coordinating schedules. Their relationship had intensified on the European trip and
they parted with reluctance.

"I'll call you this evening. Thank you for a memorable trip,
my love," said Jack.

Jennifer looked up as her mother came through the front door. She
was undoing her riding boots and with childhood excitement, she
nearly tripped on her boot, racing over to greet her mother.

"Whoa, sweetheart," said Christiana, breaking her daughter's
fall. "How was your riding lesson?"

"It was great, Mother. I'm learning so much from my trainer.
I love my horse."

"Maybe we can go out to the stables next weekend so I may
see Tulip." Looking around for Michael, she asked, "Where is your
father?"

"Oh, he just went to the kitchen to get something to drink."

"Hey, you're back, it's good to see you. How was your trip?" Michael asked, entering with beer in hand.

"The Sterling Paris Hotel is exquisite and the parties were fun. Jack and I managed some brief sightseeing and shopping. But it is wonderful to be home."

"Make any headway in finding a replacement for Pemberton?"

"We have two candidates under consideration. After Jonathan conducts the second round of interviews, I may have them come over to Corporate."

Changing subjects, Michael said, "I thought I would take Jennifer out to dinner. Care to join us?"

"Yes, that sounds nice. When were you planning to leave?"

"Around five-thirty," said Michael, finishing his beer.

The dinner was a pleasant diversion from Christiana's harried business life and she and Michael focused their attention solely on Jennifer. When they returned to Montrachet, Christiana tucked Jennifer in for the night and was heading to her room when she heard the phone ring. "I can't get you out of my mind," Jack greeted her.

"My thoughts are with you too, my love, but I was delighted to see Jennifer."

"Sweetheart, I need to head to Denver tomorrow and will be there until the end of the week. That will push back a time for dinner until the weekend, but I will know more in a day or two," he said. "I'll call every chance I get."

"I look forward to hearing from you."

The ringing of another phone prompted Jack to say, "Honey, my father is on the line and I need to take it. If I arrive early enough in Denver tomorrow, I'll give you a call. Goodnight, sweetheart, I love you."

"I love you too, Jack. Safe travel."

CHAPTER 46

AMANDA CAUGHT CHRISTIANA heading back from a meeting and asked her to call Jonathan in London as soon as possible. She was glad to hear from her father as they had not spoken since the dinner for Barrington Financial in Paris.

Phoning him straightaway, she greeted him with a lilt in her voice, "Good evening, Father."

"I trust you and Jack had a good time. Sterling Paris is an outstanding achievement and Blake appeared well satisfied. I'm just sorry he was coping with the death of his wife at the reopening of the hotel," responded Jonathan.

"Blake said he plans to take a little respite before settling in to a new BHI project once he returns stateside. He did a remarkable job; the hotel is exquisite. And yes, Jack and I had a marvelous time."

"I'm happy to hear that. On another matter, I wanted to inform you second interviews are scheduled for Hollis Mann and Armand Schroeder."

"I didn't think you were interested in Armand."

"I was speaking with Langston in Paris and he knows Schroeder. James believes we should bring him on board," replied Jonathan.

"Are the candidates aware we are interviewing for the number two spot?"

"Yes, Christiana, and both expressed their interest in the scope and depth of this position."

"Sounds like we have some traction," said Christiana, pleased.

Cautiously, Jonathan delivered, "We shall see where this all leads."

Taking his cue the topic was now closed, she changed the subject. "I have read the prospectus from Morgan Joseph and scheduled a meeting later this week with Marshall, James and Samantha. Do you wish me to forward you a copy?"

"Go ahead, but I'm not sure I'll have a chance to read it. You and Marshall should take the lead on this."

However, Jonathan's continued involvement with the European Operations precluded his return to New York the following week. The second series of interviews were postponed due to his travel schedule. Christiana considered flying to London to conduct the interviews but when she questioned her father he told her to leave it in his court. She wondered how Christian might be fitting into the equation.

"Hi, Christiana, do you have a second?" asked Jonathan late one weekday afternoon London time. "I finally reviewed the prospectus and memorandum of sale for Morgan Joseph. The asking price is too high from what I see."

"I agree," she responded, gazing at the Manhattan skyline and tapping her pen on her notepad. "Marshall has run the numbers and the ratios don't add up. I'll forward accounting's computations."

"I think we should sit back and wait for them to: A. get more realistic with the sales price; or B. get desperate," stated Jonathan.

"I concur, but Samantha believes it would be a great fit for us," noted Christiana.

"Samantha needs to get her ego in check. Her motives are far from pure. She wants this primarily to prove something to her former employers. Confine her to turning Magnifique around," sniped Jonathan.

"I'll tell her it's being handled within Corporate."

"The less you say the better. I'm not interested in Samantha's agenda until I need her," said Jonathan firmly.

"Understood," responded Christiana. "When will you be home?"

"I'm not sure, but you will be happy to know I have rescheduled the interviews. In addition, the references for both candidates are very impressive. I'm getting the high sign from Dennison. I need to board my plane now. Love to you and Jennifer."

"Goodbye, Father. Have a pleasant flight." *Grant's assessment might be wrong. Father did reschedule the interviews,* she thought.

"Christiana, your two o'clock appointment is waiting. Marshall asked to speak with you ASAP and Michael Trent is holding," buzzed Amanda.

"Give me a minute with Michael, and then put Marshall through. Please tell my appointment I won't be long."

"Hello, Michael, I have an appointment waiting but I wanted to take your call."

"I'll be brief. There is a reception and première for the opening of my new play next Wednesday and I would love to take Jennifer. You and Jack are invited too if you're available."

"Oh Michael, that sounds terrific. I will do my best to have the stars align from this side. Now I really must go. *Ciao.*"

"*Ciao, Bella.*"

Concluding her meeting, she walked to Marshall's office. "One of those 'Barrington' days," he grumbled. "How are you, Christiana?"

"Better than you, it seems," said Christiana, sipping the water she'd brought.

Glancing at the stacks of files on his desk, Marshall sighed, saying, "Where are those sales figures from Jewels? I just had them before I took my last call. Here they are," he announced, handing the data to her for review. "The first set of figures reveal regional market trends. On page four you will find our manufacturing costs and page five estimates costs for major equipment purchases. Since the acquisition of Spencer's company is on hold we need to address these capital expenditures."

"More due diligence was needed following the last site inspection and the meeting with the syndicate. It doesn't seem Max is in a hurry to sell. So let's discuss our own equipment purchases," commented Christiana.

"Our capital investment needs, apart from the pink diamond mining business, are twenty-five million dollars. I have spoken with Remi to gain his perspective as CEO of Jewels *by Barrington*, and he concludes the same. We have taken full depreciation on the equipment in the mines for our companies in Botswana and South Africa but not India," said Marshall.

"Let's set up a conference call with Remi tomorrow afternoon," Christiana decided as she rose to leave the CFO's office.

Christiana went back to her office to gather up files to take home when her cell phone rang. "*Bonsoir, ma Cheri.* I'm in London and would like to see you. Where are you, my American princess?"

"Oh, Marc Philippe, I've been back in New York for a couple of days."

"The prince is sad, my princess. Now I must be serious, Christiana. I see your pictures everywhere in magazines and the tabloids, with the headlines, *Has Christiana Barrington found a new love? Is Christiana Barrington in love? The dashing real estate baron has eyes set on Christiana Lynn Barrington.* Is it true, princess, you have a relationship with this tycoon? Mr. What's-his-name, Jackson Hamilton?"

Not precisely clear what she wanted to say to Marc Philippe regarding her relationship with Jack, she hesitated momentarily. "Yes, Marc Philippe, I have a fairly serious relationship with Jack ...." And her voice trailed off.

"Is he in love with you?"

"Yes, he is in love with me," she responded.

"Ah, but more important, are you in love with him?"

"Oh Marc Philippe, yes, I think ... I hope so."

"Oh *Cheri,* until you tell me unequivocally you are in love, there's still a chance for Marc Philippe."

"You darling man, we've always respected the boundaries of *our* relationship. I don't know where this alliance with Jack will go but I want to nourish it and allow it to flourish."

"But we may still have dinner, right?"

Laughing, Christiana answered, "Of course, we may have dinner, the next time you're in New York."

"*Cheri,* it will be extremely difficult to keep my hands off you," he pouted.

"Our relationship continues to evolve. A couple of years ago who would have thought we could spend hours discussing business and finance," said Christiana, in an attempt to cheer him up.

"True, *ma Cheri,* but afterwards we looked forward to sex."

"Marc Philippe, I too will miss the great sex."

"Just don't forget your dear prince?"

"You are most unforgettable."

"I will be in New York in a couple of weeks; I will call you. Christiana, one final thought. If this relationship between you and Mr. Jackson Hamilton is real, then I wish you all the best, my American princess."

"Thank you, Marc Philippe." *I hope it's real—I really do.*

Not hearing the normal chatter when she arrived home, Christiana headed up to Jennifer's room. She could hear Jennifer practicing her French lesson with Veronica. *A trip to France would certainly aid in Jennifer's mastery of the language. Maybe Jack would also join us,* she daydreamed.

"Your pronunciation is perfect, sweetheart. Do you enjoy French?"

"I think so, sometimes. Well, I like it better than studying the icky business stuff Grandfather wants me to learn," said Jennifer, turning up her nose.

When Jack called later in the evening, Christiana mentioned her idea of a trip to France. He said he would welcome the chance to expand his language skills; however, finding the time to make the trip may prove harder than learning the language.

CHAPTER 47

CHRISTIANA'S WORKLOAD MOUNTED the next several weeks, and any thoughts of a brief romp in France were sidelined. Moreover, Jonathan had not returned to New York. Even Elizabeth grew weary of this lengthy absence and headed to London.

As she had not been briefed on the outcome of the second interviews Jonathan was to hold last week, Christiana called the London office. To her surprise, she was informed Jonathan was traveling for the next several days.

Dialing his cell phone, she said, "Father, good evening. Where are you?"

"I'm in Switzerland, heading to Frankfurt tomorrow."

Not focusing in on the reason he was in Switzerland, she charged forward with her pressing question, "What was the outcome of your second interviews with Armand Schroeder and Hollis Mann?"

"I had to reschedule both interviews to the end of the month. I'll forward the particulars later," he said, sounding tired and distraught.

"Father, we need to hire someone in Europe *soon*, you can't continue at this pace," she said in a tender voice.

"You're right; but on another note, we have some highly lucrative new business for Barrington Financial. Graham is meeting me in Frankfurt tomorrow."

Hearing but not acknowledging his last statement, she returned to the reason for her call. "The second interviews have been pushed back for at least four weeks?"

"Yes, Christiana, my mind is wrapped around this deal at the moment due to its size and complexity. I did, however, personally contact Armand and Hollis. They understood the reason for the postponement."

"I do hope we don't lose them in the interim," she said, not willing to put the topic to rest.

"I'll take my chances, Christiana," and he quickly concluded the conversation.

She was irked by her father's nonchalance over the interview schedule as she was responding to voice and emails; then she saw two messages from Christian who was in Germany. *What is HE doing in Frankfurt? He has nothing to do with Barrington Financial. There was a Sales and Marketing Symposium for the hotel industry in Germany, but I didn't think it was in Frankfurt. I'll check the location,* she thought but the notion left her mind as she was interrupted by Amanda.

"Ms. Barrington, James is heading over to see you," her assistant announced.

As she readied for the COO's arrival, her private line started to ring. Smiling, she answered, "Jack, it's wonderful to hear from you."

"I'm back in New York driving to my apartment. My meetings concluded early so I took the opportunity to come home. Any chance on dinner this evening?"

"I could arrange an early dinner but I can't stay in the City tonight as Jennifer has a school function in the morning."

"An early dinner it is! I have an afternoon meeting near the Barrington building. Why don't I swing past your office and pick you up a little after five? I love you."

"That should work perfectly. I look forward to seeing you. And I love you too."

Her pleasure of hearing from Jack was short lived as James entered her office with a scowl on his face. He did away with pleasantries and placed several photographs on her desk. He stood quietly waiting for her reaction.

"James, where did these photographs come from?"

"Samantha informed me you sanctioned these for the next ad run for the men's cologne, *Christian,* or *CL,* or whatever it's called under the Magnifique umbrella," responded James with an edge to his voice.

"I've not had conversations with Samantha regarding these ad campaigns for Magnifique and I certainly would not approve these photos of a scantily clad Christian. We are not doing underwear commercials or advertising for a fitness program," she scoffed.

"Samantha was told by Christian you had signed off on these," James persisted.

"When did Samantha start to take direction from Christian Luke?"

"I've already dealt with her," he sternly replied. "I reiterated all advertisements must be signed off by you or me. That didn't set too well with Samantha."

Choosing not to comment on his last remark, Christiana merely stated, "I'm glad you caught it before it went out."

He nodded his agreement. "Now, for a bit of good news, take a look at Magnifique's sales figures for the last two months."

Studying the data for several moments, she finally remarked, "Samantha was the right fit at the right time. I'm amazed by the figures for *The Barrington Collection* in particular."

"You and Jonathan are icons. The Barrington name sells," he replied with a grin.

She smiled at the compliment and as James prepared to leave, Christiana stated, "I'll handle this situation with Christian."

As he shut her office door, she immediately fired off an email to Christian.

> *Christian: cc: Jonathan*
>
> *I am in receipt of several almost nude photographs to be used in the next round of media advertisements for the CL cologne campaign. Samantha understood that I had sanctioned these shots to be used in the campaign. Allow me to be very clear: I did not nor would I give permission for this type of advertising. If you prefer to resume your modeling career leaving the employ of Barrington, then possibly we could contract with you to be the face of the men's cologne as long as you abide by our professional standards and ad guidelines. —Christiana*

A quick response was not forthcoming from either Christian or her father as she finished her work day and prepared to meet Jack for dinner.

As they conversed over drinks in the restaurant, her cell phone vibrated. Glancing at the phone in her open purse, she saw Christian's number and ignored the call but her eyes lingered, anticipating a prompt text message.

Touching her hand, Jack said softly, "Forget business awhile, darling."

"You are absolutely correct," she said, forcing a smile. Raising her wine glass, she remarked, "To the most handsome man in the world—and the love of my life."

"I'm not sure about most handsome but I like the 'love of my life' part," he murmured, leaning over to kiss her.

As Christiana rode in the darkness on her way to Montrachet, she felt disappointment that their short time together was none too exciting. Reaching into her purse for her cell phone, she dialed Jack's number. He answered on the second ring. "Jack, I wasn't much company this evening. Darling, you deserve my entire attention when we are together."

"Sweetheart, no apology is necessary. Do you wish to talk about it?"

"It almost seems too trivial to mention," she sheepishly answered.

"Nothing is too trivial to mention, I am here to listen," he assured her compassionately. They conversed until she approached the gates of Montrachet, but she remained quiet on the subject of her annoyance with Christian.

Jonathan's email message the following day expressed the same concerns regarding Christian's ad photographs for Magnifique, indicating he would have a word with Christian while they were in Germany.

Decked out for his première, Michael fidgeted while waiting for Jennifer and Christiana to arrive downstairs. An unexpected business crisis forced Jack to cancel at the last minute, but Michael convinced Christiana to still attend the function with him and Jennifer.

"Wow, Daddy is so popular. Is he more famous than you, Mother?" Grinning at her daughter's comments, but unable to respond since

363

they were standing in the crowded foyer following the première, Christiana watched Michael, now very much in his element. He was heading to an after-party following the backstage meeting of the actors, which allowed Christiana and Jennifer their needed exit to head home.

Sleep was not forthcoming, so Christiana curled up in bed and got lost in a book. A gentle knock made her look up from her reading to find Michael standing at the entrance of her bedroom.

"I saw the light under the door and figured you were still awake. What did you think of the play?"

"It was fantastic. You have a way of instilling such depth and personality into each of your characters," said Christiana, pulling her robe tightly over her shoulders.

"Thanks. Two Broadway critics were in the audience and approached me after the play. One applauded the storyline and character development while the other said I nailed the accuracy and delivery of the timeline of the story," he said with satisfaction.

"That should translate into rave reviews. I enjoyed the evening and believe you will have a huge Broadway success," Christiana replied.

"From your lips, let it be so," he smiled. The alcohol he'd consumed at the reception had apparently given him the nerve to knock on her bedroom door, and momentarily hesitating before departing to his villa, he seemed hopeful she might invite him to stay. As she said nothing, he mumbled, "Goodnight, see you in the morning."

"Goodnight, Michael."

CHAPTER 48

STILL CONCERNED BY HER FATHER's stalling on filling the open European position, Christiana forwarded an email to Jonathan suggesting she conduct the interviews in New York. Surprisingly, by midafternoon, Jonathan had responded positively to her handling of the interviews. Christiana set the wheels in motion with calls to both Hollis Mann and Armand Schroeder. She told them they would be hearing from Human Resources for travel schedules within the next two weeks.

"Hello, sweetheart, I'm back in New York. Are you on your way to Connecticut?" Jack inquired.

"Yes, Jennifer and Michael are waiting to have an early dinner before he and I head over to Jennifer's school for an Open House," she explained.

Michael is still at Montrachet. Tightening his jaw, he took a deep breath and cordially inquired, "How was the première? I am sorry I was unable to attend."

"The play has been acclaimed a major hit by the critics. One described it as Michael Trent's best work to date. The only missing ingredient of the evening, my darling, was you," answered Christiana.

"Please extend my congratulations to Michael." Segueing to another topic, Jack said, "I trust we are on for tomorrow? I have a gourmet feast planned just for you."

"I wouldn't miss another masterpiece from my favorite chef. Until tomorrow, my darling," Christiana replied.

The next day ...

With the business in Saudi Arabia concluded to their satisfaction, Jonathan and Graham were relieved to be heading back to London and New York. The rigors of the negotiations left little time for updates with Christiana so Jonathan placed a call as he settled into the London office.

"Father, it's good to hear from you. Are you still in Riyadh?"

"No, I returned to London earlier today. Graham and I had a successful series of meetings in Saudi Arabia. In addition, I made contact with a very prominent German investor and the size of the Baron's portfolio made Graham's eyes glaze over."

"Was that one of the dignitaries you met at the Sterling events in Paris?"

"Yes, and I think we have a great shot at landing this due to our structure, which complements the complexity of some of the transactions. Now, bring me current from your side," he said, tilting his desk chair back, sipping a tumbler of Glenlivet.

"Have you handled the issue with Christian regarding the ad photographs?"

Off-put by her preoccupation, Jonathan returned, "I told you I would handle it."

"All right, Father. Interview schedules and travel arrangements have been set up for Hollis Mann and Armand Schroeder. Meredith Chen is conducting the background and reference checks on both candidates."

Jonathan concluded the call, "I'm glad you and Meredith have everything coordinated. I'll be back in New York next week for the board meeting."

Several days later ...

The conversation between Jonathan and Grant Pemberton had been turbulent, much like his airline flight to Geneva. Although Grant remained a member of the board at BHI, his friendship with Jonathan was strained due to his forced employment resignation. The advancement of Christian remained a cornerstone of their mutual discord.

"Are you sure you really want to do this, Jonathan, and why now? You are not ready to retire. It's not in the best interests of the company. You've already promoted him well beyond his experience and expertise," said Grant. "You advanced him against my operational judgment and authority, you son of a bitch," muttered Grant under his breath as they concluded the conversation. Jonathan caught the comment.

Replaying the conversation in his mind, Jonathan took the liberty to use the head as the turbulence subsided. As soon as the plane landed, Jonathan checked his messages with one phone and rapidly dialed a local Geneva phone number with another cell phone. Getting no answer at the local Swiss number, Jonathan snapped the phone shut.

Where is she, he fumed. *She knew I was flying in this afternoon.* Tapping his fingers on the armrest, he shifted in his seat, anxious to leave the aircraft. *At rehearsal, it is opening night,* he assured himself.

"Good afternoon, Elizabeth, it's Grant," said the voice with the impeccable English accent. "I'm sorry to trouble you on your cell phone but I thought it more prudent." Grant rarely called Elizabeth and never on the cell phone.

"Good afternoon, Grant. Jonathan's not home."

"Yes, I know. I just finished speaking with him before his plane departed."

Feeling her hands tighten around the receiver of the phone, she made no acknowledgement of his last remark. "Is there a problem, Grant?"

"I must speak with you about Christiana," said Grant pointedly. "It concerns BHI and I feel we should discuss the matter in person. I will be in New York for the board meeting. May we meet in Manhattan on Wednesday?"

Her voice quivering, Elizabeth answered, "Yes, of course, Grant, but I have one question. How serious is this?"

"It's very serious, Elizabeth, and please refrain from any mention of this conversation or our meeting to anyone, especially Jonathan."

"You have my word."

"Please jot down this address in the City. I know it's not one of your usual haunts but I think it will be more discreet."

"I know the location. I'll see you Wednesday at noon."

As her eyes welled with tears she cursed, *Damn you, Jonathan. You never ended your relationship with Danielle.* Dabbing her eyes with a tissue, she noticed the illuminated light indicating a voice mail on her private phone line. Pressing the voice mail button, she played Jonathan's message. "Hello, sweetheart, I'm still in London but will be back in New York in a couple of days. I can't wait to see you. I'll call you tomorrow as I have a business dinner that will probably run late. I love you."

Oh Jonathan, she sighed. *Was Danielle somehow involved in why Grant urgently needed to meet?* Pouring a glass of sherry, gazing at the Baccarat crystal glass, she contemplated her next move. Finishing the aperitif, she poured another and purposely strode to her safe. Nimbly turning the combination, when it opened, she carefully removed several large envelopes. Laying them on the desk, she sat down and removed the contents of each envelope. She lost track of time in her review until she heard a knock at the door. "Please come in," Elizabeth called, tucking the papers and folders inside her desk drawer.

"Mrs. Barrington, your dinner is ready. Would you prefer to eat in the family dining room or shall I bring a tray to the study?"

"Please set it up in the family dining room in about twenty minutes. Thank you, Martha." As the maid retreated, Elizabeth reached into the drawer and retracted the files. After careful deliberation, she thought, *Yes they are all in order, updated and signed.* Placing them in sequence and chronological order, she returned them to the safe, finished her aperitif, turned off the light and locked the door.

She was ready for the meeting with Grant.

CHAPTER 49 ... The following week

THE CAR DROVE SLOWLY down the street as Elizabeth searched for the address Grant had given her. Out of the shadow of the arched front entrance, Grant appeared, motioning her into the parking lot that adjoined the building. He met her at the car and locked the gate across the parking lot as they walked silently back toward the building.

Grant was the first to speak as he noticed Elizabeth surveying the area.

"I own the building. I'm in the midst of a total renovation and have tenants lined up awaiting a move-in date. This part of the City is becoming very trendy."

"It has been going through a renaissance for several years," responded Elizabeth. Stepping into the lobby, she exclaimed, "This is a handsome remodel, Grant."

"Credit goes to the design company and their quality work. Let's use this suite, which is already furnished," he said, guiding her to the door on the left.

Obviously noting her uneasiness as she dropped down in the suede wing chair, he offered, "Thank you for meeting me here, Elizabeth."

Handing her a cup of coffee, he cleared his throat and said, "You need to know what Jonathan is planning to do—"

Before he could finish his sentence, Elizabeth sparked, "Do you know where he is?"

The question took Grant by surprise but he continued with his prior subject. "Elizabeth, I asked you to meet me to discuss BHI. I've never felt comfortable discussing Jonathan's personal whereabouts even when given firsthand knowledge."

Elizabeth's icy stare told him she already knew. "Geneva," she said flatly. It was not a question, merely a statement of fact.

"Yes," Grant said, and hung his head.

"I have just one more question. *Please,* Grant, I need to know—is he still seeing Danielle?"

With resignation in his voice, he said, "Yes … the affair never ended." At this affirmation, along with the knowledge of Jonathan's intent to change the BHI succession plan, Elizabeth sat upright, pulled the portfolio of papers from her briefcase and handed them to Grant.

"I think you will find the paperwork in order," she announced. Declaring that, she stood, kissed Grant on the cheek, and added, "You are a dear friend, thank you. Let us now do what must be done."

With that she headed for the door. After his seeing her safely to her car, they parted and he stood, watching her drive away. She had spent the day sans Barrington Security; it was another first for Elizabeth.

As she headed along East End Avenue, she had the sudden desire to stop at Bergdorf's. Traffic inched as she made her way onto Central Park South and she almost reconsidered her decision but had soon arrived at Fifth Avenue. She managed to park in a garage on West 58th and entered the department store.

Moving through the shoppers, she rode the escalator to couture. A couple of sales associates immediately recognized her and soon were escorting her like military personnel. "Mrs. Barrington, it's lovely to see you."

"I'm looking for …" and her voice trailed off. "That!" She pointed to a red Chanel suit.

When the sales associate appeared at the dressing room, she said, "That is a real showstopper, Mrs. Barrington. I have never seen you in that shade of red."

That's what I intend to do—stop the show, mused Elizabeth.

Heading to Connecticut within an hour, *Mission accomplished,* she thought. She'd missed a call from Jonathan, who was coming home tonight. "Don't wait dinner, darling. I will probably not be in before nine."

Considering her watch and the time of his message, she knew Jonathan was in the air at this point. *Good,* she thought, this would give her extra time to prepare.

CHAPTER 50 ... The next day

"THE REVISED BOARD AGENDA has been placed around the conference table, Mr. Barrington. Is there anything else?" questioned his assistant.

"No, thank you, Leslie." *The rest is up to me,* he surmised.

Jonathan was joined by board member Max Spencer on the elevator ride to the boardroom. Max dispensed with his normal pleasantries. He looked directly at Jonathan and questioned, "Are you absolutely sure about this, Jonathan?"

"Absolutely," responded Jonathan, with the steeliness of a metal blade. The elevator opened before Max could continue, eliminating any chance of further questions Jonathan did not wish to field.

Jonathan proceeded to meet several other board members, extracting himself from Max. He made the rounds shaking hands but moved on, not bothering to listen to responses to his greetings.

He slowed, however, when he passed Grant, who was heading for a seat at the far end of the conference table—as far away from Jonathan as possible. "Grant, I wasn't sure you would be here today."

"I'm here, Jonathan, that's about all I can say," Grant retorted.

The members took their seats as Jonathan readied himself for the meeting.

Closing the door quietly, Christiana moved to her assigned seat and glanced down at the agenda in front of her. Her eyes fixated on the agenda item regarding management changes. Although it was unusual, she paid it no mind.

The meeting was on course and fairly mundane as it headed into the last part of the agenda. "Ladies and gentlemen," Jonathan began, "we are now at the last yet most important item of this meeting. I stand before you today as both Chairman and Founder of Barrington Holdings International. The successes of BHI are in part a result of the diligence, intelligence and excellence you have brought to your positions as directors of BHI. I trust I have served you well as Chairman and CEO."

The audience was hushed as Jonathan continued. "Now it is time for Barrington to set the stage for its next evolution and to tap and implement its leadership transition. BHI is set to exceed last year's forecasts by twenty-five percent. *Fortune Magazine* and the *Wall Street Journal* have consistently praised the stock valuation and believe it will not falter in the future."

The board members, now on the edge of their seats, waited apprehensively. "During the next twelve to twenty-four months, I will share the executive suite with the person who will take over as Chairman when I retire."

What is Father doing? I haven't been briefed about this item, Christiana thought. The last reference to the succession of BHI was in broad terms without specific timelines.

Jonathan paused only slightly, and rambled forward. "That moment has arrived and for some this may come as a complete surprise. A company the size of Barrington needs a clear line of succession. In this line of succession Christian Luke will be groomed to take over as Chairman and CEO of BHI as I transition to retirement." As if orchestrated, Christian Luke entered the room from a side entrance and took his place at the empty seat on the left side of Jonathan. Christiana and Christian now flanked both sides of Jonathan.

Christiana sat motionless, staring down at her hands shaking in her lap. The undercurrent of voices and surprise didn't register as she turned her head and focused directly on her father.

"My God—'son of my father'?" she said out loud, locking eyes with Christian.

"Why, Father?" was all she could muster. Swallowing hard, she stood to exit the room and tersely added, "What happened to 'groomed from the womb'?"

Pandemonium prevailed with this startling announcement and went on unabated as board members protested with concerns and objections.

Jonathan, too preoccupied with the proper delivery of his momentous announcement, had failed to see Grant rise and open the side door. There, a subdued Elizabeth waited patiently in the vestibule. "Come," he said. "It's time."

As Elizabeth entered the boardroom, Grant touched her shoulder and whispered, "Good luck. Be strong. Use me if you need to but I have no doubt you will deliver."

"Please go back and sit down, Christiana," Elizabeth stated, her fire-engine red Chanel suit capturing the attention of the entire room, as she made her way to the head of the conference table accompanied by two attorneys.

Then suddenly the noise level started to dissipate.

Jonathan didn't witness Elizabeth's entrance, as he had bent down to tuck some papers into his briefcase. As he resumed a sitting position, he noticed his wife's unmistakable legs, close to his right side.

The room fell silent as Elizabeth spoke. "I request permission to address the board." She looked squarely at Jonathan as he glared at his wife. The vastly different trajectories of their lives had intersected for one deadly encounter.

With consent rendered, Elizabeth began, "Christian, would you please properly introduce yourself to the board?"

"Mrs. Barrington, it is indeed a pleasure to finally meet you. However, I am acquainted with most of the people in this room," he said in his suave manner.

"Are you?" she coldly snapped back. Their eyes locked. Christian did not respond.

"Ladies and gentlemen, since Christian does not wish to introduce himself, please allow me," addressed Elizabeth.

"Elizabeth, this is outrageous," proclaimed Jonathan.

"Jonathan, I am upholding my fiduciary responsibility to Barrington Holdings International," stated Elizabeth. "If I may continue with my introduction," she ordered, flashing a look of "get out of my way" to Jonathan. "Christian Luke Reynard is Christian Luke Barrington, the illegitimate son of Jonathan Barrington and Danielle Reynard."

"Elizabeth, how dare you barge into a board meeting like this?" barked Jonathan.

"How dare I? With due respect to all, please note I am the largest shareholder and maintain voting control of BHI," Elizabeth added with indignation. "It was never my intent to play this hand but I will not allow *your* illegitimate son to take over this empire. Christian Luke will not assume the roles of Chairman and CEO of Barrington Holdings International."

Gazing up at her mother, Christiana asked, "Mother, is this really true?" Sadly, Elizabeth merely nodded, but then continued with purpose.

Measuring the momentum of her delivery, Elizabeth presented the mysterious pieces of the puzzle for those seated in the room. Her eyes on Jonathan, she acknowledged, "Yes, Jonathan, I know the truth. I've kept the secret all these years and would have taken it to my grave if you would have spared *our* daughter. Christiana is the rightful heir to the chairmanship of BHI and we may either do it by vote or I will use my leverage," Elizabeth declared as she stood unwavering at the table.

"*Please Elizabeth,*" pleaded Jonathan, moving to the other side of the room. Heads ricocheted from Jonathan to Elizabeth. Elizabeth placed her hand on Christiana's shoulder in a show of solidarity. Jonathan shot a hard glance at Grant as he now paced behind him and angrily snarled, "How could you?"

"Sorry, old chap, this is in the best interest of Barrington," Grant retorted.

The normally sedate and erudite BHI board meeting had become a spectacle. With voices raised and questions flying, Jonathan tried unsuccessfully to regain control of the meeting with an unrelenting plea, "Please, please, I can explain everything."

"No, Jonathan, you can't," growled Grant. "Elizabeth, please continue; the board has the right to know the truth."

"Thank you, Grant." As Elizabeth propelled forward, the attorneys opened their briefcases and began to distribute the carefully prepared documents to all assembled. "BHI was founded thirty-five years ago with my family's money." The room again became silent as Elizabeth spoke. "Yes, Barrington started and continued for many years with Matthews money and as such operated with very clearly stated requirements, which you will find detailed in the package presented to you by counsel."

The documents were a real page-turner and assisted Elizabeth as her conquest continued. "The largest shareholder remains Elizabeth Matthews Barrington, not my husband, Jonathan Robert Barrington. Jonathan was appointed Chairman and CEO and I was never to have an active role in the running of Barrington—with one exception. I ask you to turn to page four, paragraph five.

"The sole heir to Barrington Holdings International (BHI) shall be Christiana Lynn Barrington, the only legitimate and biological child of Jonathan Robert Barrington and Elizabeth Matthews Barrington. Any subsequent children conceived either inside or outside wedlock will have no claims to the inheritance of BHI."

"That item was struck years ago, Elizabeth," smirked Jonathan.

"No, Jonathan it was not," responded Elizabeth in an icy tone.

Turning red in the face, Jonathan stood up in protest. "But I have the paperwork right here!" Fumbling through files until he located the legal instrument in question, he realized the shell of his legal defense was about to crater. He bellowed, "There must be some mistake. I need my attorney, *now!*"

"I thought you might," added Elizabeth. Grant, the keeper of the side door, motioned Jonathan's personal attorney into the boardroom.

"Brandon, what is the meaning of this?" Jonathan was visibly shaken.

"Jonathan, I'm sorry, but Elizabeth is legally correct. The referenced document legally required only her signature. Do we really need all this fully disclosed at the board meeting?" asked Brandon.

"Brandon, it will not be necessary for you to explain; I will do this myself," answered Elizabeth. Jonathan did not resist.

Elizabeth recollected the sordid tale that had brought them to this present position. Looking at her daughter, she proclaimed, "Christiana, I am so sorry. It was never my intent to hurt you. The document Brandon just mentioned was prepared when Barrington first needed my working capital for survival and later for expansion. Your father clearly accepted my intentions, stipulations and mandates in the delivering of the funds. As outlined, he had no objections to my controlling interest in the business."

Jonathan threw down the document and anticipating his objections, Elizabeth charged forward. "It was changed when I learned the truth about Christian. I never fathomed this situation but I will not allow you and Christian to redirect the Barrington succession plan and rob Christiana of that which is legally and legitimately hers. "

No one moved nor spoke a word as the drama unfolded. "Ladies and gentlemen, Christian Luke is the son of Danielle Reynard, the Swiss pianist, and my husband, Jonathan Robert Barrington. This is very difficult and I beg the board's indulgence as I reveal a very personal and private accounting of our lives. Christiana was born in 1965, and when she was about twelve months old, I wished to have another child. Jonathan and I tried unsuccessfully for some time. Visits to several specialists reaffirmed we could have additional children. However, without discussion, Jonathan informed me after the fact he had determined to have a vasectomy since he no longer desired more children. The vasectomy was performed in New York on September 5, 1966, and it is my understanding Christian Luke was born one year later. Am I correct, Christian?"

"Yes, Mrs. Barrington, I was born in 1967," acknowledged Christian.

Elizabeth continued. "Jonathan informed me of this revelation with a copy of the medical invoice, which was never submitted for reimbursement through our insurance carrier. When I received a call from our business manager questioning the reason the claims had not been submitted, I became curious, and suspicious. Per my request, she did submit for reimbursement, only to be informed by the insurance company they had no record of said physician at that address in Manhattan. The invoice was fictitious, the procedure never done and the doctor did not exist. The amendment Jonathan holds in his hand was never signed by me due to the facts just presented."

Both Elizabeth and Jonathan glanced at Brandon, who nodded in affirmation.

"Elizabeth, you've known *this* all these years?" Jonathan asked, clearly troubled.

With regret in her voice, Elizabeth said, "Yes, Jonathan, I have. I determined never to divulge this secret as long as you never hurt *our* daughter emotionally or financially. Unless you wish me to exercise my voting control, I request you announce Christiana as your successor and discuss the timeframe for her to assume the Chairmanship and CEO responsibilities of BHI."

Cornered, Jonathan shot back, "And if I won't? Elizabeth, you wouldn't dare."

"Jonathan, I would and I have. Either have Christian dismissed or fired or I will bring criminal charges against him for fraud, embezzlement, and forgery. And I *will* prosecute!" she exclaimed.

"This is crazy. Are you insane, Elizabeth?" Jonathan squirmed in his seat.

"No, Jonathan, she is perfectly sane," stated Grant.

"Here are the forgeries of Christiana's signatures on checks made payable to Christian Luke Reynard. The checks total more than three million dollars."

Christiana, now fully engaged, addressed her mother with, "May I see the checks?" She diligently looked over each item and after deliberation, she responded, "These are not my signatures. I added a small trademark to help protect against this sort of forgery."

"What are you talking about, Christiana?" asked Jonathan.

Elizabeth answered before Christiana could respond to her father. "Christiana set up this mechanism years ago as a means of protection in the event of an unforeseen transaction or tragedy such as a kidnapping or health incapacitation, which could make Barrington vulnerable."

"Father," Christiana added humbly, "it was for your own protection that I did not reveal this information. But now it seems I must."

She took a blank piece of paper and wrote her signature in the manner she signed on behalf of Barrington Holdings International.

Christiana L. Barrington ~

Then she presented both a check with Christian's signature and the paper with her signature to her father.

Jonathan placed the returned bank check with Christian's handwriting on top of Christiana's signature and scrutinized both for similarities.

Christiana L. Barrington

Christiana L. Barrington ~

"I don't understand. They look identical to me!" Jonathan appeared puzzled.

Christiana walked behind her father's chair and pointed out the small ~ at the side of her name.

"I change the location of the symbol ~ and make it small enough to appear like an eyelash or mark on the paper. It had been totally indistinguishable until now," she stated reluctantly.

"You can't be serious, Christiana," grumbled Jonathan. Grant strode to the front of the room, placing several legal documents and checks for further evidence in front of Jonathan. The symbol ~ was evident on each item to substantiate Christiana's claim.

"I see," sighed Jonathan. "It appears I am without argument or defense in this matter."

"That is correct, Father," announced Christiana.

Now Elizabeth added with consternation, "You have seen the proof and heard the truth from Christiana; understand I am prepared to use all legal recourse necessary if you oppose my action."

Jonathan cleared his throat, preparing to speak but Elizabeth whipped around with, "Jonathan, if you oppose me, you can anticipate your removal as Chairman and CEO. I will step in and assume your roles and work with Christiana." Elizabeth snapped, "This is an ultimatum. You have no choice, Jonathan. You maintain your position as long as Christiana is immediately promoted to Co-CEO. In addition, Christian must leave this meeting and, effective immediately, his employment at BHI is terminated. I have taken the necessary steps to remove him from the office in London and he is not to reenter the building. On another matter, Grant will resume his position as General Manager of European Operations." Elizabeth remained calm yet determined and did not waver during her speech and painful personal revelations.

Grant now motioned for security personnel to enter the room to remove Christian. He docilely left the board meeting. Jonathan nodded in humble disbelief.

"Before I end this meeting, since this has all been duly recorded, we must take the vote on succession," proclaimed Elizabeth.

Simultaneous questions, comments and conversations erupted from the board members. There was a consensus to hear from Christiana. "Before the Board votes we need to understand if Christiana agrees with this," registered several directors.

In a dramatic shift in command and position, Christiana looked to her mother instead of her father. Christiana drew strength and power from her mother's penetrating gaze. "This has been as much a shock and surprise to me as it has been to most of you assembled here today." With her voice breaking, "Before commencing with the business at hand, I would like to express my profound sorrow for the pain and anguish my mother has suffered all these years. She deserves none of this disgrace and heartache."

Christiana continued, "The clues, both subtle and blatant, have been around Barrington for many years. Maybe I was just naïve or simply chose to ignore the obvious. I didn't want to understand some of the inconsistencies that were present and capable of rocking my structure and prescribed Barrington existence. Or at least, what I thought was my structure, and ultimate legacy."

Christiana looked over to Jonathan as she spoke. "Father, you taught me well. 'Failure is not an option. Barringtons never fail. Barringtons think only of success.' *I will not fail, Father.* I will succeed with or without you!" Christiana proclaimed and her words met with resounding applause. "I want to assure the directors that with total resolve and dedication, I shall lead Barrington Holdings International, to the best of my abilities in the most prudent and responsible manner. I shall assume the role as Co-CEO with Jonathan in the succession timeframe as set forth earlier in this meeting," concluded Christiana.

A stiff smile found its way to Jonathan's face, as he sat quietly between Christiana and Elizabeth.

When Christiana finished speaking, Elizabeth added a few additional comments, attending to procedural items. In conclusion, she stated, "I believe we are now ready to vote on the following items, which I shall recap. We need motions for the removal of Christian's nomination as Chairman and CEO of Barrington Holdings International and his employment termination from BHI effective immediately. After completion of the vote on these actions, we need a motion made to have Christiana nominated as Co-CEO of BHI under the provisions and timeframes previously discussed." Then she said, "Jonathan, I turn the meeting back over to you."

Jonathan resumed his post as Chairman and proceeded with the vote. Motions were posed and carried. Grant took the opportunity to add the motion calling for the nomination of Christiana Lynn Barrington. "I so move that the board elect Christiana Lynn Barrington as Co-CEO of BHI. She shall hold this position for a period of one to two years and at such time a successful transition of control shall be complete with the retirement of Jonathan Robert Barrington. At that juncture, Christiana Lynn Barrington will become Chairman and Chief Executive Officer of Barrington Holdings International."

"May I have a second to the motion?" asked Jonathan.

"I second it," announced Max.

"All those in favor say aye." The vote was approved.

Jonathan refrained from voting on either motion.

Elizabeth went to the back of the room, waiting to take her leave from the meeting. Jonathan shot Elizabeth a glance. He asked sarcastically, "Elizabeth, has this been done to your satisfaction?"

"Yes, Jonathan," she said. Grasping the handle on the door, she turned briefly to her husband, who had not yet resumed speaking, sending a penetrating reminder with, "Jonathan, you were right about one thing. A Barrington will always control the company."

With a wink to Christiana, she walked out and closed the door.